# Henry James

**Henry James OM** (15 April 1843 – 28 February 1916) was an American-British author regarded as a key transitional figure between literary realism and literary modernism, and is considered by many to be among the greatest novelists in the English language. He was the son of Henry James Sr. and the brother of renowned philosopher and psychologist William James and diarist Alice James.

He is best known for a number of novels dealing with the social and marital interplay between émigré Americans, English people, and continental Europeans. Examples of such novels include The Portrait of a Lady, The Ambassadors, and The Wings of the Dove. His later works were increasingly experimental. In describing the internal states of mind and social dynamics of his characters, James often made use of a style in which ambiguous or contradictory motives and impressions were overlaid or juxtaposed in the discussion of a character's psyche.(Source: Wikipedia)

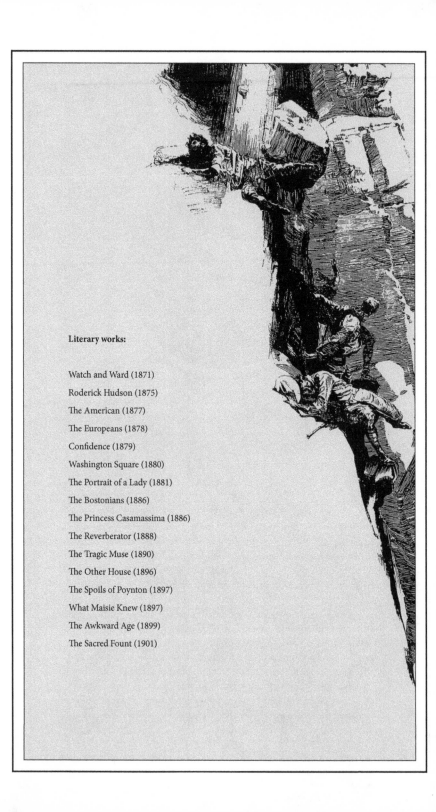

**Literary works:**

Watch and Ward (1871)

Roderick Hudson (1875)

The American (1877)

The Europeans (1878)

Confidence (1879)

Washington Square (1880)

The Portrait of a Lady (1881)

The Bostonians (1886)

The Princess Casamassima (1886)

The Reverberator (1888)

The Tragic Muse (1890)

The Other House (1896)

The Spoils of Poynton (1897)

What Maisie Knew (1897)

The Awkward Age (1899)

The Sacred Fount (1901)

THE
WORKS
OF
HENRY JAMES

VOL. 15 (OF 24)

THE DIARY OF A MAN OF FIFTY
THE EUROPEANS
THE FIGURE IN THE CARPET

An Imprint of Moon Classics LLC

A Wholly Owned Subsidiary of Queenior LLC

A Melodragon Company

Copyright © 2020

First Printing: 2020

ISBN 978-1-6627-1648-5 (Paperback)

ISBN 978-1-6627-1649-2 (Hardcover)

Published by Moon Classics

www.moonclassics.com

# Contents

# THE
# WORKS
## OF
# HENRY JAMES
## VOL. 15 (OF 24)

# THE DIARY OF A MAN OF FIFTY

# THE DIARY OF A MAN OF FIFTY

Florence, *April 5th*, 1874.—They told me I should find Italy greatly changed; and in seven-and-twenty years there is room for changes. But to me everything is so perfectly the same that I seem to be living my youth over again; all the forgotten impressions of that enchanting time come back to me. At the moment they were powerful enough; but they afterwards faded away. What in the world became of them? Whatever becomes of such things, in the long intervals of consciousness? Where do they hide themselves away? in what unvisited cupboards and crannies of our being do they preserve themselves? They are like the lines of a letter written in sympathetic ink; hold the letter to the fire for a while and the grateful warmth brings out the invisible words. It is the warmth of this yellow sun of Florence that has been restoring the text of my own young romance; the thing has been lying before me today as a clear, fresh page. There have been moments during the last ten years when I have fell so portentously old, so fagged and finished, that I should have taken as a very bad joke any intimation that this present sense of juvenility was still in store for me. It won't last, at any rate; so I had better make the best of it. But I confess it surprises me. I have led too serious a life; but that perhaps, after all, preserves one's youth. At all events, I have travelled too far, I have worked too hard, I have lived in brutal climates and associated with tiresome people. When a man has reached his fifty-second year without being, materially, the worse for wear—when he has fair health, a fair fortune, a tidy conscience and a complete exemption from embarrassing relatives—I suppose he is bound, in delicacy, to write himself happy. But I confess I shirk this obligation. I have not been miserable; I won't go so far as to say that—or at least as to write it. But happiness—positive happiness—would have been something different. I don't know that it would have been better, by all measurements—that it would have left me better off at the present time. But it certainly would have made this difference—that I should not have been reduced, in pursuit of pleasant images, to disinter a buried episode of more than a quarter of a century ago. I should have found entertainment more—what shall I call it?—more contemporaneous. I should have had a wife and children, and I should not be in the way of making, as the French say, infidelities to the present. Of course it's a great gain to have had an escape, not to have committed an act of thumping folly; and I suppose that, whatever serious step one might have taken at twenty-five, after a struggle, and with a violent effort, and however one's conduct might appear to be justified by events, there would always remain a certain element of regret; a certain sense of loss lurking in the sense of gain; a tendency to wonder, rather wishfully, what *might* have been. What might have been, in this case, would, without doubt, have been very sad, and what has been has been very cheerful and comfortable; but there are nevertheless two or three questions I might ask myself. Why, for instance, have I never married—why have I never been able to care for any woman as I cared for that one? Ah, why are the mountains blue and why is the sunshine warm? Happiness mitigated by impertinent conjectures—that's about my ticket.

6th.—I knew it wouldn't last; it's already passing away. But I have spent a delightful day; I have been strolling all over the place. Everything reminds me of something else, and yet of itself at the same time; my imagination makes a great circuit and comes back to the starting-point. There is that well-remembered odour of spring in the air, and the flowers, as they used to be, are gathered into great sheaves and stacks, all along the rugged base of the Strozzi Palace. I wandered for an hour in the Boboli Gardens; we went there several times together. I remember all those days individually; they seem to me as yesterday. I found the corner where she always chose to sit—the bench of sun-warmed marble, in front of the screen of ilex, with that exuberant statue of Pomona just beside it. The place is exactly the same, except that poor Pomona has lost one of her tapering fingers. I sat there for half an hour, and it was strange how near to me she seemed. The place was perfectly empty—that is, it was filled with *her.* I closed my eyes and listened; I could almost hear the rustle of her dress on the gravel. Why do we make such an ado about death? What is it, after all, but a sort of refinement of life? She died ten years ago, and yet, as I sat there in the sunny stillness, she was a palpable, audible presence. I went afterwards into the gallery of the palace, and wandered for an hour from room to room. The same great pictures hung in the same places, and the same dark frescoes arched above them. Twice, of old, I went there with her; she had a great understanding of art. She understood all sorts of things. Before the Madonna of the Chair I stood a long time. The face is not a particle like hers, and yet it reminded me of her. But everything does that. We stood and looked at it together once for half an hour; I remember perfectly what she said.

8th.—Yesterday I felt blue—blue and bored; and when I got up this morning I had half a mind to leave Florence. But I went out into the street, beside the Arno, and looked up and down—looked at the yellow river and the violet hills, and then decided to remain—or rather, I decided nothing. I simply stood gazing at the beauty of Florence, and before I had gazed my fill I was in good-humour again, and it was too late to start for Rome. I strolled along the quay, where something presently happened that rewarded me for staying. I stopped in front of a little jeweller's shop, where a great many objects in mosaic were exposed in the window; I stood there for some minutes—I don't know why, for I have no taste for mosaic. In a moment a little girl came and stood beside me—a little girl with a frowsy Italian head, carrying a basket. I turned away, but, as I turned, my eyes happened to fall on her basket. It was covered with a napkin, and on the napkin was pinned a piece of paper, inscribed with an address. This address caught my glance—there was a name on it I knew. It was very legibly written—evidently by a scribe who had made up in zeal what was lacking in skill. *Contessa Salvi-Scarabelli, Via Ghibellina*—so ran the superscription; I looked at it for some moments; it caused me a sudden emotion. Presently the little girl, becoming aware of my attention, glanced up at me, wondering, with a pair of timid brown eyes.

"Are you carrying your basket to the Countess Salvi?" I asked.

The child stared at me. "To the Countess Scarabelli."

"Do you know the Countess?"

"Know her?" murmured the child, with an air of small dismay.

"I mean, have you seen her?"

"Yes, I have seen her." And then, in a moment, with a sudden soft smile—"*E bella!*" said the little girl. She was beautiful herself as she said it.

15

"Precisely; and is she fair or dark?"

The child kept gazing at me. "*Bionda—bionda*," she answered, looking about into the golden sunshine for a comparison.

"And is she young?"

"She is not young—like me. But she is not old like—like—"

"Like me, eh? And is she married?"

The little girl began to look wise. "I have never seen the Signor Conte."

"And she lives in Via Ghibellina?"

"*Sicuro.* In a beautiful palace."

I had one more question to ask, and I pointed it with certain copper coins. "Tell me a little—is she good?"

The child inspected a moment the contents of her little brown fist. "It's you who are good," she answered.

"Ah, but the Countess?" I repeated.

My informant lowered her big brown eyes, with an air of conscientious meditation that was inexpressibly quaint. "To me she appears so," she said at last, looking up.

"Ah, then, she must be so," I said, "because, for your age, you are very intelligent." And having delivered myself of this compliment I walked away and left the little girl counting her *soldi*.

I walked back to the hotel, wondering how I could learn something about the Contessa Salvi-Scarabelli. In the doorway I found the innkeeper, and near him stood a young man whom I immediately perceived to be a compatriot, and with whom, apparently, he had been in conversation.

"I wonder whether you can give me a piece of information," I said to the landlord. "Do you know anything about the Count Salvi-Scarabelli?"

The landlord looked down at his boots, then slowly raised his shoulders, with a melancholy smile. "I have many regrets, dear sir—"

16

"You don't know the name?"

"I know the name, assuredly. But I don't know the gentleman."

I saw that my question had attracted the attention of the young Englishman, who looked at me with a good deal of earnestness. He was apparently satisfied with what he saw, for he presently decided to speak.

"The Count Scarabelli is dead," he said, very gravely.

I looked at him a moment; he was a pleasing young fellow. "And his widow lives," I observed, "in Via Ghibellina?"

"I daresay that is the name of the street." He was a handsome young Englishman, but he was also an awkward one; he wondered who I was and what I wanted, and he did me the honour to perceive that, as regards these points, my appearance was reassuring. But he hesitated, very properly, to talk with a perfect stranger about a lady whom he knew, and he had not the art to conceal his hesitation. I instantly felt it to be singular that though he regarded me as a perfect stranger, I had not the same feeling about him. Whether it was that I had seen him before, or simply that I was struck with his agreeable young face—at any rate, I felt myself, as they say here, in sympathy with him. If I have seen him before I don't remember the occasion, and neither, apparently, does he; I suppose it's only a part of the feeling I have had the last three days about everything. It was this feeling that made me suddenly act as if I had known him a long time.

"Do you know the Countess Salvi?" I asked.

He looked at me a little, and then, without resenting the freedom of my question—"The Countess Scarabelli, you mean," he said.

"Yes," I answered; "she's the daughter."

"The daughter is a little girl."

"She must be grown up now. She must be—let me see—close upon thirty."

My young Englishman began to smile. "Of whom are you speaking?"

17

"I was speaking of the daughter," I said, understanding his smile. "But I was thinking of the mother."

"Of the mother?"

"Of a person I knew twenty-seven years ago—the most charming woman I have ever known. She was the Countess Salvi—she lived in a wonderful old house in Via Ghibellina."

"A wonderful old house!" my young Englishman repeated.

"She had a little girl," I went on; "and the little girl was very fair, like her mother; and the mother and daughter had the same name—Bianca." I stopped and looked at my companion, and he blushed a little. "And Bianca Salvi," I continued, "was the most charming woman in the world." He blushed a little more, and I laid my hand on his shoulder. "Do you know why I tell you this? Because you remind me of what I was when I knew her— when I loved her." My poor young Englishman gazed at me with a sort of embarrassed and fascinated stare, and still I went on. "I say that's the reason I told you this—but you'll think it a strange reason. You remind me of my younger self. You needn't resent that—I was a charming young fellow. The Countess Salvi thought so. Her daughter thinks the same of you."

Instantly, instinctively, he raised his hand to my arm. "Truly?"

"Ah, you are wonderfully like me!" I said, laughing. "That was just my state of mind. I wanted tremendously to please her." He dropped his hand and looked away, smiling, but with an air of ingenuous confusion which quickened my interest in him. "You don't know what to make of me," I pursued. "You don't know why a stranger should suddenly address you in this way and pretend to read your thoughts. Doubtless you think me a little cracked. Perhaps I am eccentric; but it's not so bad as that. I have lived about the world a great deal, following my profession, which is that of a soldier. I have been in India, in Africa, in Canada, and I have lived a good deal alone. That inclines people, I think, to sudden bursts of confidence. A week ago I came into Italy, where I spent six months when I was your age. I came straight to Florence—I was eager to see it again, on account of associations.

They have been crowding upon me ever so thickly. I have taken the liberty of giving you a hint of them." The young man inclined himself a little, in silence, as if he had been struck with a sudden respect. He stood and looked away for a moment at the river and the mountains. "It's very beautiful," I said.

"Oh, it's enchanting," he murmured.

"That's the way I used to talk. But that's nothing to you."

He glanced at me again. "On the contrary, I like to hear."

"Well, then, let us take a walk. If you too are staying at this inn, we are fellow-travellers. We will walk down the Arno to the Cascine. There are several things I should like to ask of you."

My young Englishman assented with an air of almost filial confidence, and we strolled for an hour beside the river and through the shady alleys of that lovely wilderness. We had a great deal of talk: it's not only myself, it's my whole situation over again.

"Are you very fond of Italy?" I asked.

He hesitated a moment. "One can't express that."

"Just so; I couldn't express it. I used to try—I used to write verses. On the subject of Italy I was very ridiculous."

"So am I ridiculous," said my companion.

"No, my dear boy," I answered, "we are not ridiculous; we are two very reasonable, superior people."

"The first time one comes—as I have done—it's a revelation."

"Oh, I remember well; one never forgets it. It's an introduction to beauty."

"And it must be a great pleasure," said my young friend, "to come back."

"Yes, fortunately the beauty is always here. What form of it," I asked, "do you prefer?"

19

My companion looked a little mystified; and at last he said, "I am very fond of the pictures."

"So was I. And among the pictures, which do you like best?"

"Oh, a great many."

"So did I; but I had certain favourites."

Again the young man hesitated a little, and then he confessed that the group of painters he preferred, on the whole, to all others, was that of the early Florentines.

I was so struck with this that I stopped short. "That was exactly my taste!" And then I passed my hand into his arm and we went our way again.

We sat down on an old stone bench in the Cascine, and a solemn blank-eyed Hermes, with wrinkles accentuated by the dust of ages, stood above us and listened to our talk.

"The Countess Salvi died ten years ago," I said.

My companion admitted that he had heard her daughter say so.

"After I knew her she married again," I added. "The Count Salvi died before I knew her—a couple of years after their marriage."

"Yes, I have heard that."

"And what else have you heard?"

My companion stared at me; he had evidently heard nothing.

"She was a very interesting woman—there are a great many things to be said about her. Later, perhaps, I will tell you. Has the daughter the same charm?"

"You forget," said my young man, smiling, "that I have never seen the mother."

"Very true. I keep confounding. But the daughter—how long have you known her?"

"Only since I have been here. A very short time."

"A week?"

For a moment he said nothing. "A month."

"That's just the answer I should have made. A week, a month—it was all the same to me."

"I think it is more than a month," said the young man.

"It's probably six. How did you make her acquaintance?"

"By a letter—an introduction given me by a friend in England."

"The analogy is complete," I said. "But the friend who gave me my letter to Madame de Salvi died many years ago. He, too, admired her greatly. I don't know why it never came into my mind that her daughter might be living in Florence. Somehow I took for granted it was all over. I never thought of the little girl; I never heard what had become of her. I walked past the palace yesterday and saw that it was occupied; but I took for granted it had changed hands."

"The Countess Scarabelli," said my friend, "brought it to her husband as her marriage-portion."

"I hope he appreciated it! There is a fountain in the court, and there is a charming old garden beyond it. The Countess's sitting-room looks into that garden. The staircase is of white marble, and there is a medallion by Luca della Robbia set into the wall at the place where it makes a bend. Before you come into the drawing-room you stand a moment in a great vaulted place hung round with faded tapestry, paved with bare tiles, and furnished only with three chairs. In the drawing-room, above the fireplace, is a superb Andrea del Sarto. The furniture is covered with pale sea-green."

My companion listened to all this.

"The Andrea del Sarto is there; it's magnificent. But the furniture is in pale red."

"Ah, they have changed it, then—in twenty-seven years."

21

"And there's a portrait of Madame de Salvi," continued my friend.

I was silent a moment. "I should like to see that."

He too was silent. Then he asked, "Why don't you go and see it? If you knew the mother so well, why don't you call upon the daughter?"

"From what you tell me I am afraid."

"What have I told you to make you afraid?"

I looked a little at his ingenuous countenance. "The mother was a very dangerous woman."

The young Englishman began to blush again. "The daughter is not," he said.

"Are you very sure?"

He didn't say he was sure, but he presently inquired in what way the Countess Salvi had been dangerous.

"You must not ask me that," I answered "for after all, I desire to remember only what was good in her." And as we walked back I begged him to render me the service of mentioning my name to his friend, and of saying that I had known her mother well, and that I asked permission to come and see her.

9th.—I have seen that poor boy half a dozen times again, and a most amiable young fellow he is. He continues to represent to me, in the most extraordinary manner, my own young identity; the correspondence is perfect at all points, save that he is a better boy than I. He is evidently acutely interested in his Countess, and leads quite the same life with her that I led with Madame de Salvi. He goes to see her every evening and stays half the night; these Florentines keep the most extraordinary hours. I remember, towards 3 A.M., Madame de Salvi used to turn me out.—"Come, come," she would say, "it's time to go. If you were to stay later people might talk." I don't know at what time he comes home, but I suppose his evening seems as short as mine did. Today he brought me a message from his Contessa—a very gracious little speech. She remembered often to have heard her mother speak of me—she called me her English friend. All her mother's friends were dear to her, and she begged I would do her the honour to come and see her. She is always at home of an evening. Poor young Stanmer (he is of the Devonshire Stanmers—a great property) reported this speech verbatim, and of course it can't in the least signify to him that a poor grizzled, battered soldier, old enough to be his father, should come to call upon his *inammorata*. But I remember how it used to matter to me when other men came; that's a point of difference. However, it's only because I'm so old. At twenty-five I shouldn't have been afraid of myself at fifty-two. Camerino was thirty-four—and then the others! She was always at home in the evening, and they all used to come. They were old Florentine names. But she used to let me stay after them all; she thought an old English name as good. What a transcendent coquette! . . . But *basta così* as she used to say. I meant to go tonight to Casa Salvi, but I couldn't bring myself to the point. I don't know what I'm afraid of; I used to be in a hurry enough to go there once. I suppose I am afraid of the very look of the place—of the old rooms, the old walls. I shall go tomorrow night. I am afraid of the very echoes.

10th.—She has the most extraordinary resemblance to her mother. When I went in I was tremendously startled; I stood starting at her. I have just come home; it is past midnight; I have been all the evening at Casa Salvi. It is very warm—my window is open—I can look out on the river gliding past in the starlight. So, of old, when I came home, I used to stand and look out. There are the same cypresses on the opposite hills.

Poor young Stanmer was there, and three or four other admirers; they all got up when I came in. I think I had been talked about, and there was some curiosity. But why should I have been talked about? They were all youngish men—none of them of my time. She is a wonderful likeness of her mother; I couldn't get over it. Beautiful like her mother, and yet with the same faults in her face; but with her mother's perfect head and brow and sympathetic, almost pitying, eyes. Her face has just that peculiarity of her mother's, which, of all human countenances that I have ever known, was the one that passed most quickly and completely from the expression of gaiety to that of repose. Repose in her face always suggested sadness; and while you were watching it with a kind of awe, and wondering of what tragic secret it was the token, it kindled, on the instant, into a radiant Italian smile. The Countess Scarabelli's smiles tonight, however, were almost uninterrupted. She greeted me—divinely, as her mother used to do; and young Stanmer sat in the corner of the sofa—as I used to do—and watched her while she talked. She is thin and very fair, and was dressed in light, vaporous black that completes the resemblance. The house, the rooms, are almost absolutely the same; there may be changes of detail, but they don't modify the general effect. There are the same precious pictures on the walls of the salon—the same great dusky fresco in the concave ceiling. The daughter is not rich, I suppose, any more than the mother. The furniture is worn and faded, and I was admitted by a solitary servant, who carried a twinkling taper before me up the great dark marble staircase.

"I have often heard of you," said the Countess, as I sat down near her; "my mother often spoke of you."

"Often?" I answered. "I am surprised at that."

"Why are you surprised? Were you not good friends?"

"Yes, for a certain time—very good friends. But I was sure she had forgotten me."

"She never forgot," said the Countess, looking at me intently and smiling. "She was not like that."

"She was not like most other women in any way," I declared.

"Ah, she was charming," cried the Countess, rattling open her fan. "I have always been very curious to see you. I have received an impression of you."

"A good one, I hope."

She looked at me, laughing, and not answering this: it was just her mother's trick.

"'My Englishman,' she used to call you—'*il mio Inglese*.'"

"I hope she spoke of me kindly," I insisted.

The Countess, still laughing, gave a little shrug balancing her hand to and fro. "So-so; I always supposed you had had a quarrel. You don't mind my being frank like this—eh?"

"I delight in it; it reminds me of your mother."

"Every one tells me that. But I am not clever like her. You will see for yourself."

"That speech," I said, "completes the resemblance. She was always pretending she was not clever, and in reality—"

"In reality she was an angel, eh? To escape from dangerous comparisons I will admit, then, that I am clever. That will make a difference. But let us talk of you. You are very—how shall I say it?—very eccentric."

"Is that what your mother told you?"

"To tell the truth, she spoke of you as a great original. But aren't all Englishmen eccentric? All except that one!" and the Countess pointed to poor Stanmer, in his corner of the sofa.

"Oh, I know just what he is," I said.

"He's as quiet as a lamb—he's like all the world," cried the Countess.

"Like all the world—yes. He is in love with you."

She looked at me with sudden gravity. "I don't object to your saying that for all the world—but I do for him."

"Well," I went on, "he is peculiar in this: he is rather afraid of you."

Instantly she began to smile; she turned her face toward Stanmer. He had seen that we were talking about him; he coloured and got up—then came toward us.

"I like men who are afraid of nothing," said our hostess.

"I know what you want," I said to Stanmer. "You want to know what the Signora Contessa says about you."

25

Stanmer looked straight into her face, very gravely. "I don't care a straw what she says."

"You are almost a match for the Signora Contessa," I answered. "She declares she doesn't care a pin's head what you think."

"I recognise the Countess's style!" Stanmer exclaimed, turning away.

"One would think," said the Countess, "that you were trying to make a quarrel between us."

I watched him move away to another part of the great saloon; he stood in front of the Andrea del Sarto, looking up at it. But he was not seeing it; he was listening to what we might say. I often stood there in just that way. "He can't quarrel with you, any more than I could have quarrelled with your mother."

"Ah, but you did. Something painful passed between you."

"Yes, it was painful, but it was not a quarrel. I went away one day and never saw her again. That was all."

The Countess looked at me gravely. "What do you call it when a man does that?"

"It depends upon the case."

"Sometimes," said the Countess in French, "it's a *lâcheté*."

"Yes, and sometimes it's an act of wisdom."

"And sometimes," rejoined the Countess, "it's a mistake."

I shook my head. "For me it was no mistake."

She began to laugh again. "Caro Signore, you're a great original. What had my poor mother done to you?"

I looked at our young Englishman, who still had his back turned to us and was staring up at the picture. "I will tell you some other time," I said.

"I shall certainly remind you; I am very curious to know." Then she opened and shut her fan two or three times, still looking at me. What eyes they have! "Tell me a little," she went on, "if I may ask without indiscretion. Are you married?"

"No, Signora Contessa."

"Isn't that at least a mistake?"

"Do I look very unhappy?"

She dropped her head a little to one side. "For an Englishman—no!"

"Ah," said I, laughing, "you are quite as clever as your mother."

"And they tell me that you are a great soldier," she continued; "you have lived in India. It was very kind of you, so far away, to have remembered our poor dear Italy."

"One always remembers Italy; the distance makes no difference. I remembered it well the day I heard of your mother's death!"

"Ah, that was a sorrow!" said the Countess. "There's not a day that I don't weep for her. But *che vuole*? She's a saint its paradise."

"*Sicuro*," I answered; and I looked some time at the ground. "But tell me about yourself, dear lady," I asked at last, raising my eyes. "You have also had the sorrow of losing your husband."

"I am a poor widow, as you see. *Che vuole*? My husband died after three years of marriage."

I waited for her to remark that the late Count Scarabelli was also a saint in paradise, but I waited in vain.

"That was like your distinguished father," I said.

"Yes, he too died young. I can't be said to have known him; I was but of the age of my own little girl. But I weep for him all the more."

Again I was silent for a moment.

"It was in India too," I said presently, "that I heard of your mother's second marriage."

27

The Countess raised her eyebrows.

"In India, then, one hears of everything! Did that news please you?"

"Well, since you ask me—no."

"I understand that," said the Countess, looking at her open fan. "I shall not marry again like that."

"That's what your mother said to me," I ventured to observe.

She was not offended, but she rose from her seat and stood looking at me a moment. Then—"You should not have gone away!" she exclaimed. I stayed for another hour; it is a very pleasant house.

Two or three of the men who were sitting there seemed very civil and intelligent; one of them was a major of engineers, who offered me a profusion of information upon the new organisation of the Italian army. While he talked, however, I was observing our hostess, who was talking with the others; very little, I noticed, with her young Inglese. She is altogether charming— full of frankness and freedom, of that inimitable *disinvoltura* which in an Englishwoman would be vulgar, and which in her is simply the perfection of apparent spontaneity. But for all her spontaneity she's as subtle as a needle-point, and knows tremendously well what she is about. If she is not a consummate coquette . . . What had she in her head when she said that I should not have gone away?—Poor little Stanmer didn't go away. I left him there at midnight.

12th.—I found him today sitting in the church of Santa Croce, into which I wandered to escape from the heat of the sun.

In the nave it was cool and dim; he was staring at the blaze of candles on the great altar, and thinking, I am sure, of his incomparable Countess. I sat down beside him, and after a while, as if to avoid the appearance of eagerness, he asked me how I had enjoyed my visit to Casa Salvi, and what I thought of the *padrona*.

"I think half a dozen things," I said, "but I can only tell you one now. She's an enchantress. You shall hear the rest when we have left the church."

"An enchantress?" repeated Stanmer, looking at me askance.

He is a very simple youth, but who am I to blame him?

"A charmer," I said "a fascinatress!"

He turned away, staring at the altar candles.

"An artist—an actress," I went on, rather brutally.

He gave me another glance.

"I think you are telling me all," he said.

"No, no, there is more." And we sat a long time in silence.

At last he proposed that we should go out; and we passed in the street, where the shadows had begun to stretch themselves.

"I don't know what you mean by her being an actress," he said, as we turned homeward.

"I suppose not. Neither should I have known, if any one had said that to me."

"You are thinking about the mother," said Stanmer. "Why are you always bringing *her* in?"

"My dear boy, the analogy is so great it forces itself upon me."

He stopped and stood looking at me with his modest, perplexed young face. I thought he was going to exclaim—"The analogy be hanged!"—but he said after a moment—

"Well, what does it prove?"

"I can't say it proves anything; but it suggests a great many things."

"Be so good as to mention a few," he said, as we walked on.

"You are not sure of her yourself," I began.

"Never mind that—go on with your analogy."

"That's a part of it. You *are* very much in love with her."

"That's a part of it too, I suppose?"

"Yes, as I have told you before. You are in love with her, and yet you can't make her out; that's just where I was with regard to Madame de Salvi."

"And she too was an enchantress, an actress, an artist, and all the rest of it?"

"She was the most perfect coquette I ever knew, and the most dangerous, because the most finished."

"What you mean, then, is that her daughter is a finished coquette?"

"I rather think so."

Stanmer walked along for some moments in silence.

"Seeing that you suppose me to be a—a great admirer of the Countess," he said at last, "I am rather surprised at the freedom with which you speak of her."

I confessed that I was surprised at it myself. "But it's on account of the interest I take in you."

"I am immensely obliged to you!" said the poor boy.

"Ah, of course you don't like it. That is, you like my interest—I don't see how you can help liking that; but you don't like my freedom. That's natural enough; but, my dear young friend, I want only to help you. If a man had said to me—so many years ago—what I am saying to you, I should certainly also, at first, have thought him a great brute. But after a little, I should have been grateful—I should have felt that he was helping me."

"You seem to have been very well able to help yourself," said Stanmer. "You tell me you made your escape."

"Yes, but it was at the cost of infinite perplexity—of what I may call keen suffering. I should like to save you all that."

30

"I can only repeat—it is really very kind of you."

"Don't repeat it too often, or I shall begin to think you don't mean it."

"Well," said Stanmer, "I think this, at any rate—that you take an extraordinary responsibility in trying to put a man out of conceit of a woman who, as he believes, may make him very happy."

I grasped his arm, and we stopped, going on with our talk like a couple of Florentines.

"Do you wish to marry her?"

He looked away, without meeting my eyes. "It's a great responsibility," he repeated.

"Before Heaven," I said, "I would have married the mother! You are exactly in my situation."

"Don't you think you rather overdo the analogy?" asked poor Stanmer.

"A little more, a little less—it doesn't matter. I believe you are in my shoes. But of course if you prefer it, I will beg a thousand pardons and leave them to carry you where they will."

He had been looking away, but now he slowly turned his face and met my eyes. "You have gone too far to retreat; what is it you know about her?"

"About this one—nothing. But about the other—"

"I care nothing about the other!"

"My dear fellow," I said, "they are mother and daughter—they are as like as two of Andrea's Madonnas."

"If they resemble each other, then, you were simply mistaken in the mother."

I took his arm and we walked on again; there seemed no adequate reply to such a charge. "Your state of mind brings back my own so completely," I said presently. "You admire her—you adore her, and yet, secretly, you mistrust her. You are enchanted with her personal charm, her grace, her wit, her everything; and yet in your private heart you are afraid of her."

"Afraid of her?"

"Your mistrust keeps rising to the surface; you can't rid yourself of the suspicion that at the bottom of all things she is hard and cruel, and you would be immensely relieved if some one should persuade you that your suspicion is right."

Stanmer made no direct reply to this; but before we reached the hotel he said—"What did you ever know about the mother?"

"It's a terrible story," I answered.

He looked at me askance. "What did she do?"

"Come to my rooms this evening and I will tell you."

He declared he would, but he never came. Exactly the way I should have acted!

14th.—I went again, last evening, to Casa Salvi, where I found the same little circle, with the addition of a couple of ladies. Stanmer was there, trying hard to talk to one of them, but making, I am sure, a very poor business of it. The Countess—well, the Countess was admirable. She greeted me like a friend of ten years, toward whom familiarity should not have engendered a want of ceremony; she made me sit near her, and she asked me a dozen questions about my health and my occupations.

"I live in the past," I said. "I go into the galleries, into the old palaces and the churches. Today I spent an hour in Michael Angelo's chapel at San Loreozo."

"Ah yes, that's the past," said the Countess. "Those things are very old."

"Twenty-seven years old," I answered.

"Twenty-seven? *Altro*!"

"I mean my own past," I said. "I went to a great many of those places with your mother."

32

"Ah, the pictures are beautiful," murmured the Countess, glancing at Stanmer.

"Have you lately looked at any of them?" I asked. "Have you gone to the galleries with *him*?"

She hesitated a moment, smiling. "It seems to me that your question is a little impertinent. But I think you are like that."

"A little impertinent? Never. As I say, your mother did me the honour, more than once, to accompany me to the Uffizzi."

"My mother must have been very kind to you."

"So it seemed to me at the time."

"At the time only?"

"Well, if you prefer, so it seems to me now."

"Eh," said the Countess, "she made sacrifices."

"To what, cara Signora? She was perfectly free. Your lamented father was dead—and she had not yet contracted her second marriage."

"If she was intending to marry again, it was all the more reason she should have been careful."

I looked at her a moment; she met my eyes gravely, over the top of her fan. "Are *you* very careful?" I said.

She dropped her fan with a certain violence. "Ah, yes, you are impertinent!"

"Ah no," I said. "Remember that I am old enough to be your father; that I knew you when you were three years old. I may surely ask such questions. But you are right; one must do your mother justice. She was certainly thinking of her second marriage."

"You have not forgiven her that!" said the Countess, very gravely.

"Have you?" I asked, more lightly.

"I don't judge my mother. That is a mortal sin. My stepfather was very kind to me."

"I remember him," I said; "I saw him a great many times—your mother already received him."

My hostess sat with lowered eyes, saying nothing; but she presently looked up.

"She was very unhappy with my father."

"That I can easily believe. And your stepfather—is he still living?"

"He died—before my mother."

"Did he fight any more duels?"

"He was killed in a duel," said the Countess, discreetly.

It seems almost monstrous, especially as I can give no reason for it—but this announcement, instead of shocking me, caused me to feel a strange exhilaration. Most assuredly, after all these years, I bear the poor man no resentment. Of course I controlled my manner, and simply remarked to the Countess that as his fault had been so was his punishment. I think, however, that the feeling of which I speak was at the bottom of my saying to her that I hoped that, unlike her mother's, her own brief married life had been happy.

"If it was not," she said, "I have forgotten it now."—I wonder if the late Count Scarabelli was also killed in a duel, and if his adversary . . . Is it on the books that his adversary, as well, shall perish by the pistol? Which of those gentlemen is he, I wonder? Is it reserved for poor little Stanmer to put a bullet into him? No; poor little Stanmer, I trust, will do as I did. And yet, unfortunately for him, that woman is consummately plausible. She was wonderfully nice last evening; she was really irresistible. Such frankness and freedom, and yet something so soft and womanly; such graceful gaiety, so much of the brightness, without any of the stiffness, of good breeding, and over it all something so picturesquely simple and southern. She is a perfect Italian. But she comes honestly by it. After the talk I have just jotted down she changed her place, and the conversation for half an hour was general.

Stanmer indeed said very little; partly, I suppose, because he is shy of talking a foreign tongue. Was I like that—was I so constantly silent? I suspect I was when I was perplexed, and Heaven knows that very often my perplexity was extreme. Before I went away I had a few more words *tête-à-tête* with the Countess.

"I hope you are not leaving Florence yet," she said; "you will stay a while longer?"

I answered that I came only for a week, and that my week was over.

"I stay on from day to day, I am so much interested."

"Eh, it's the beautiful moment. I'm glad our city pleases you!"

"Florence pleases me—and I take a paternal interest to our young friend," I added, glancing at Stanmer. "I have become very fond of him."

"*Bel tipo inglese*," said my hostess. "And he is very intelligent; he has a beautiful mind."

She stood there resting her smile and her clear, expressive eyes upon me.

"I don't like to praise him too much," I rejoined, "lest I should appear to praise myself; he reminds me so much of what I was at his age. If your beautiful mother were to come to life for an hour she would see the resemblance."

She gave me a little amused stare.

"And yet you don't look at all like him!"

"Ah, you didn't know me when I was twenty-five. I was very handsome! And, moreover, it isn't that, it's the mental resemblance. I was ingenuous, candid, trusting, like him."

"Trusting? I remember my mother once telling me that you were the most suspicious and jealous of men!"

"I fell into a suspicious mood, but I was, fundamentally, not in the least addicted to thinking evil. I couldn't easily imagine any harm of any one."

"And so you mean that Mr. Stanmer is in a suspicious mood?"

"Well, I mean that his situation is the same as mine."

The Countess gave me one of her serious looks. "Come," she said, "what was it—this famous situation of yours? I have heard you mention it before."

"Your mother might have told you, since she occasionally did me the honour to speak of me."

"All my mother ever told me was that you were—a sad puzzle to her."

At this, of course, I laughed out—I laugh still as I write it.

"Well, then, that was my situation—I was a sad puzzle to a very clever woman."

"And you mean, therefore, that I am a puzzle to poor Mr. Stanmer?"

"He is racking his brains to make you out. Remember it was you who said he was intelligent."

She looked round at him, and as fortune would have it, his appearance at that moment quite confirmed my assertion. He was lounging back in his chair with an air of indolence rather too marked for a drawing-room, and staring at the ceiling with the expression of a man who has just been asked a conundrum. Madame Scarabelli seemed struck with his attitude.

"Don't you see," I said, "he can't read the riddle?"

"You yourself," she answered, "said he was incapable of thinking evil. I should be sorry to have him think any evil of *me*."

And she looked straight at me—seriously, appealingly—with her beautiful candid brow.

I inclined myself, smiling, in a manner which might have meant—"How could that be possible?"

"I have a great esteem for him," she went on; "I want him to think well of me. If I am a puzzle to him, do me a little service. Explain me to him."

"Explain you, dear lady?"

"You are older and wiser than he. Make him understand me."

She looked deep into my eyes for a moment, and then she turned away.

26th.—I have written nothing for a good many days, but meanwhile I have been half a dozen times to Casa Salvi. I have seen a good deal also of my young friend—had a good many walks and talks with him. I have proposed to him to come with me to Venice for a fortnight, but he won't listen to the idea of leaving Florence. He is very happy in spite of his doubts, and I confess that in the perception of his happiness I have lived over again my own. This is so much the case that when, the other day, he at last made up his mind to ask me to tell him the wrong that Madame de Salvi had done me, I rather checked his curiosity. I told him that if he was bent upon knowing I would satisfy him, but that it seemed a pity, just now, to indulge in painful imagery.

"But I thought you wanted so much to put me out of conceit of our friend."

"I admit I am inconsistent, but there are various reasons for it. In the first place—it's obvious—I am open to the charge of playing a double game. I profess an admiration for the Countess Scarabelli, for I accept her hospitality, and at the same time I attempt to poison your mind; isn't that the proper expression? I can't exactly make up my mind to that, though my admiration for the Countess and my desire to prevent you from taking a foolish step are equally sincere. And then, in the second place, you seem to me, on the whole, so happy! One hesitates to destroy an illusion, no matter how pernicious, that is so delightful while it lasts. These are the rare moments of life. To be young and ardent, in the midst of an Italian spring, and to believe in the moral perfection of a beautiful woman—what an admirable situation! Float with the current; I'll stand on the brink and watch you."

"Your real reason is that you feel you have no case against the poor lady," said Stanmer. "You admire her as much as I do."

"I just admitted that I admired her. I never said she was a vulgar flirt; her mother was an absolutely scientific one. Heaven knows I admired that!

It's a nice point, however, how much one is bound in honour not to warn a young friend against a dangerous woman because one also has relations of civility with the lady."

"In such a case," said Stanmer, "I would break off my relations."

I looked at him, and I think I laughed.

"Are you jealous of me, by chance?"

He shook his head emphatically.

"Not in the least; I like to see you there, because your conduct contradicts your words."

"I have always said that the Countess is fascinating."

"Otherwise," said Stanmer, "in the case you speak of I would give the lady notice."

"Give her notice?"

"Mention to her that you regard her with suspicion, and that you propose to do your best to rescue a simple-minded youth from her wiles. That would be more loyal." And he began to laugh again.

It is not the first time he has laughed at me; but I have never minded it, because I have always understood it.

"Is that what you recommend me to say to the Countess?" I asked.

"Recommend you!" he exclaimed, laughing again; "I recommend nothing. I may be the victim to be rescued, but I am at least not a partner to the conspiracy. Besides," he added in a moment, "the Countess knows your state of mind."

"Has she told you so?"

Stanmer hesitated.

"She has begged me to listen to everything you may say against her. She declares that she has a good conscience."

38

"Ah," said I, "she's an accomplished woman!"

And it is indeed very clever of her to take that tone. Stanmer afterwards assured me explicitly that he has never given her a hint of the liberties I have taken in conversation with—what shall I call it?—with her moral nature; she has guessed them for herself. She must hate me intensely, and yet her manner has always been so charming to me! She is truly an accomplished woman!

May 4th.—I have stayed away from Casa Salvi for a week, but I have lingered on in Florence, under a mixture of impulses. I have had it on my conscience not to go near the Countess again—and yet from the moment she is aware of the way I feel about her, it is open war. There need be no scruples on either side. She is as free to use every possible art to entangle poor Stanmer more closely as I am to clip her fine-spun meshes. Under the circumstances, however, we naturally shouldn't meet very cordially. But as regards her meshes, why, after all, should I clip them? It would really be very interesting to see Stanmer swallowed up. I should like to see how he would agree with her after she had devoured him—(to what vulgar imagery, by the way, does curiosity reduce a man!) Let him finish the story in his own way, as I finished it in mine. It is the same story; but why, a quarter of a century later, should it have the same *dénoûment*? Let him make his own *dénoûment*.

5th.—Hang it, however, I don't want the poor boy to be miserable.

6th.—Ah, but did my *dénoûment* then prove such a happy one?

7th.—He came to my room late last night; he was much excited.

"What was it she did to you?" he asked.

I answered him first with another question. "Have you quarrelled with the Countess?"

But he only repeated his own. "What was it she did to you?"

"Sit down and I'll tell you." And he sat there beside the candle, staring at me. "There was a man always there—Count Camerino."

"The man she married?"

39

"The man she married. I was very much in love with her, and yet I didn't trust her. I was sure that she lied; I believed that she could be cruel. Nevertheless, at moments, she had a charm which made it pure pedantry to be conscious of her faults; and while these moments lasted I would have done anything for her. Unfortunately they didn't last long. But you know what I mean; am I not describing the Scarabelli?"

"The Countess Scarabelli never lied!" cried Stanmer.

"That's just what I would have said to any one who should have made the insinuation! But I suppose you are not asking me the question you put to me just now from dispassionate curiosity."

"A man may want to know!" said the innocent fellow.

I couldn't help laughing out. "This, at any rate, is my story. Camerino was always there; he was a sort of fixture in the house. If I had moments of dislike for the divine Bianca, I had no moments of liking for him. And yet he was a very agreeable fellow, very civil, very intelligent, not in the least disposed to make a quarrel with me. The trouble, of course, was simply that I was jealous of him. I don't know, however, on what ground I could have quarrelled with him, for I had no definite rights. I can't say what I expected—I can't say what, as the matter stood, I was prepared to do. With my name and my prospects, I might perfectly have offered her my hand. I am not sure that she would have accepted it—I am by no means clear that she wanted that. But she wanted, wanted keenly, to attach me to her; she wanted to have me about. I should have been capable of giving up everything—England, my career, my family—simply to devote myself to her, to live near her and see her every day."

"Why didn't you do it, then?" asked Stanmer.

"Why don't you?"

"To be a proper rejoinder to my question," he said, rather neatly, "yours should be asked twenty-five years hence."

"It remains perfectly true that at a given moment I was capable of doing as I say. That was what she wanted—a rich, susceptible, credulous, convenient young Englishman established near her *en permanence.* And yet," I added, "I must do her complete justice. I honestly believe she was fond of me." At this Stanmer got up and walked to the window; he stood looking out a moment, and then he turned round. "You know she was older than I," I went on. "Madame Scarabelli is older than you. One day in the garden, her mother asked me in an angry tone why I disliked Camerino; for I had been at no pains to conceal my feeling about him, and something had just happened to bring it out. 'I dislike him,' I said, 'because you like him so much.' 'I assure you I don't like him,' she answered. 'He has all the appearance of being your lover,' I retorted. It was a brutal speech, certainly, but any other man in my place would have made it. She took it very strangely; she turned pale, but she was not indignant. 'How can he be my lover after what he has done?' she asked. 'What has he done?' She hesitated a good while, then she said: 'He killed my husband.' 'Good heavens!' I cried, 'and you receive him!' Do you know what she said? She said, '*Che voule?*'"

"Is that all?" asked Stanmer.

"No; she went on to say that Camerino had killed Count Salvi in a duel, and she admitted that her husband's jealousy had been the occasion of it. The Count, it appeared, was a monster of jealousy—he had led her a dreadful life. He himself, meanwhile, had been anything but irreproachable; he had done a mortal injury to a man of whom he pretended to be a friend, and this affair had become notorious. The gentleman in question had demanded satisfaction for his outraged honour; but for some reason or other (the Countess, to do her justice, did not tell me that her husband was a coward), he had not as yet obtained it. The duel with Camerino had come on first; in an access of jealous fury the Count had struck Camerino in the face; and this outrage, I know not how justly, was deemed expiable before the other. By an extraordinary arrangement (the Italians have certainly no sense of fair play) the other man was allowed to be Camerino's second. The duel was fought with swords, and the Count received a wound of which, though at first it was not expected to be fatal, he died on the following day. The matter was hushed up as much as possible for the sake of the Countess's good name, and so successfully that it was presently observed that, among the public, the other gentleman had the credit of having put his blade through M. de Salvi. This gentleman took a fancy not to contradict the impression, and it was allowed to subsist. So long as he consented, it was of course in Camerino's interest not to contradict it, as it left him much more free to keep up his intimacy with the Countess."

Stanmer had listened to all this with extreme attention. "Why didn't *she* contradict it?"

I shrugged my shoulders. "I am bound to believe it was for the same reason. I was horrified, at any rate, by the whole story. I was extremely shocked at the Countess's want of dignity in continuing to see the man by whose hand her husband had fallen."

"The husband had been a great brute, and it was not known," said Stanmer.

"Its not being known made no difference. And as for Salvi having been a brute, that is but a way of saying that his wife, and the man whom his wife subsequently married, didn't like him."

Stanmer hooked extremely meditative; his eyes were fixed on mine. "Yes, that marriage is hard to get over. It was not becoming."

"Ah," said I, "what a long breath I drew when I heard of it! I remember the place and the hour. It was at a hill-station in India, seven years after I had left Florence. The post brought me some English papers, and in one of them was a letter from Italy, with a lot of so-called 'fashionable intelligence.' There, among various scandals in high life, and other delectable items, I read that the Countess Bianca Salvi, famous for some years as the presiding genius of the most agreeable seen in Florence, was about to bestow her hand upon Count Camerino, a distinguished Bolognese. Ah, my dear boy, it was a tremendous escape! I had been ready to marry the woman who was capable of that! But my instinct had warned me, and I had trusted my instinct."

"'Instinct's everything,' as Falstaff says!" And Stanmer began to laugh. "Did you tell Madame de Salvi that your instinct was against her?"

"No; I told her that she frightened me, shocked me, horrified me."

"That's about the same thing. And what did she say?"

"She asked me what I would have? I called her friendship with Camerino a scandal, and she answered that her husband had been a brute. Besides, no one knew it; therefore it was no scandal. Just *your* argument! I retorted that this was odious reasoning, and that she had no moral sense. We had a passionate argument, and I declared I would never see her again. In the heat of my displeasure I left Florence, and I kept my vow. I never saw her again."

"You couldn't have been much in love with her," said Stanmer.

"I was not—three months after."

"If you had been you would have come back—three days after."

"So doubtless it seems to you. All I can say is that it was the great effort of my life. Being a military man, I have had on various occasions to face time enemy. But it was not then I needed my resolution; it was when I left Florence in a post-chaise."

Stanmer turned about the room two or three times, and then he said: "I don't understand! I don't understand why she should have told you that Camerino had killed her husband. It could only damage her."

"She was afraid it would damage her more that I should think he was her lover. She wished to say the thing that would most effectually persuade me that he was not her lover—that he could never be. And then she wished to get the credit of being very frank."

"Good heavens, how you must have analysed her!" cried my companion, staring.

"There is nothing so analytic as disillusionment. But there it is. She married Camerino."

"Yes, I don't lime that," said Stanmer. He was silent a while, and then he added—"Perhaps she wouldn't have done so if you had remained."

He has a little innocent way! "Very likely she would have dispensed with the ceremony," I answered, drily.

"Upon my word," he said, "you *have* analysed her!"

"You ought to be grateful to me. I have done for you what you seem unable to do for yourself."

"I don't see any Camerino in my case," he said.

"Perhaps among those gentlemen I can find one for you."

"Thank you," he cried; "I'll take care of that myself!" And he went away—satisfied, I hope.

10th.—He's an obstinate little wretch; it irritates me to see him sticking to it. Perhaps he is looking for his Camerino. I shall leave him, at any rate, to his fate; it is growing insupportably hot.

11th.—I went this evening to bid farewell to the Scarabelli. There was no one there; she was alone in her great dusky drawing-room, which was lighted only by a couple of candles, with the immense windows open over the garden. She was dressed in white; she was deucedly pretty. She asked me, of course, why I had been so long without coming.

"I think you say that only for form," I answered. "I imagine you know."

"*Chè*! what have I done?"

"Nothing at all. You are too wise for that."

She looked at me a while. "I think you are a little crazy."

"Ah no, I am only too sane. I have too much reason rather than too little."

"You have, at any rate, what we call a fixed idea."

"There is no harm in that so long as it's a good one."

"But yours is abominable!" she exclaimed, with a laugh.

"Of course you can't like me or my ideas. All things considered, you have treated me with wonderful kindness, and I thank you and kiss your hands. I leave Florence tomorrow."

"I won't say I'm sorry!" she said, laughing again. "But I am very glad to have seen you. I always wondered about you. You are a curiosity."

"Yes, you must find me so. A man who can resist your charms! The fact is, I can't. This evening you are enchanting; and it is the first time I have been alone with you."

She gave no heed to this; she turned away. But in a moment she came back, and stood looking at me, and her beautiful solemn eyes seemed to shine in the dimness of the room.

"How *could* you treat my mother so?" she asked.

"Treat her so?"

"How could you desert the most charming woman in the world?"

"It was not a case of desertion; and if it had been it seems to me she was consoled."

At this moment there was the sound of a step in the ante-chamber, and I saw that the Countess perceived it to be Stanmer's.

"That wouldn't have happened," she murmured. "My poor mother needed a protector."

Stanmer came in, interrupting our talk, and looking at me, I thought, with a little air of bravado. He must think me indeed a tiresome, meddlesome bore; and upon my word, turning it all over, I wonder at his docility. After all, he's five-and-twenty—and yet I *must* add, it *does* irritate me—the way he sticks! He was followed in a moment by two or three of the regular Italians, and I made my visit short.

"Good-bye, Countess," I said; and she gave me her hand in silence. "Do you need a protector?" I added, softly.

She looked at me from head to foot, and then, almost angrily—"Yes, Signore."

But, to deprecate her anger, I kept her hand an instant, and then bent my venerable head and kissed it. I think I appeased her.

45

BOLOGNA, 14th.—I left Florence on the 11th, and have been here these three days. Delightful old Italian town—but it lacks the charm of my Florentine secret.

I wrote that last entry five days ago, late at night, after coming back from Casa Salsi. I afterwards fell asleep in my chair; the night was half over when I woke up. Instead of going to bed, I stood a long time at the window, looking out at the river. It was a warm, still night, and the first faint streaks of sunrise were in the sky. Presently I heard a slow footstep beneath my window, and looking down, made out by the aid of a street lamp that Stanmer was but just coming home. I called to him to come to my rooms, and, after an interval, he made his appearance.

"I want to bid you good-bye," I said; "I shall depart in the morning. Don't go to the trouble of saying you are sorry. Of course you are not; I must have bullied you immensely."

He made no attempt to say he was sorry, but he said he was very glad to have made my acquaintance.

"Your conversation," he said, with his little innocent air, "has been very suggestive."

"Have you found Camerino?" I asked, smiling.

"I have given up the search."

"Well," I said, "some day when you find that you have made a great mistake, remember I told you so."

He looked for a minute as if he were trying to anticipate that day by the exercise of his reason.

"Has it ever occurred to you that *you* may have made a great mistake?"

"Oh yes; everything occurs to one sooner or later."

That's what I said to him; but I didn't say that the question, pointed by his candid young countenance, had, for the moment, a greater force than it had ever had before.

And then he asked me whether, as things had turned out, I myself had been so especially happy.

PARIS, *December* 17th.—A note from young Stanmer, whom I saw in Florence—a remarkable little note, dated Rome, and worth transcribing.

"My dear General—I have it at heart to tell you that I was married a week ago to the Countess Salvi-Scarabelli. You talked me into a great muddle; but a month after that it was all very clear. Things that involve a risk are like the Christian faith; they must be seen from the inside.—Yours ever, E. S.

"P. S.—A fig for analogies unless you can find an analogy for my happiness!"

His happiness makes him very clever. I hope it will last—I mean his cleverness, not his happiness.

LONDON, *April* 19th, 1877.—Last night, at Lady H---'s, I met Edmund Stanmer, who married Bianca Salvi's daughter. I heard the other day that they had come to England. A handsome young fellow, with a fresh contented face. He reminded me of Florence, which I didn't pretend to forget; but it was rather awkward, for I remember I used to disparage that woman to him. I had a complete theory about her. But he didn't seem at all stiff; on the contrary, he appeared to enjoy our encounter. I asked him if his wife were there. I had to do that.

"Oh yes, she's in one of the other rooms. Come and make her acquaintance; I want you to know her."

"You forget that I do know her."

"Oh no, you don't; you never did." And he gave a little significant laugh.

I didn't feel like facing the *ci-devant* Scarabelli at that moment; so I said that I was leaving the house, but that I would do myself the honour of calling upon his wife. We talked for a minute of something else, and then, suddenly breaking off and looking at me, he laid his hand on my arm. I must do him the justice to say that he looks felicitous.

"Depend upon it you were wrong!" he said.

"My dear young friend," I answered, "imagine the alacrity with which I concede it."

Something else again was spoken of, but in an instant he repeated his movement.

"Depend upon it you were wrong."

"I am sure the Countess has forgiven me," I said, "and in that case you ought to bear no grudge. As I have had the honour to say, I will call upon her immediately."

"I was not alluding to my wife," he answered. "I was thinking of your own story."

"My own story?"

"So many years ago. Was it not rather a mistake?"

I looked at him a moment; he's positively rosy.

"That's not a question to solve in a London crush."

And I turned away.

22d.—I haven't yet called on the *ci-devant*; I am afraid of finding her at home. And that boy's words have been thrumming in my ears—"Depend upon it you were wrong. Wasn't it rather a mistake?" *Was* I wrong—*was* it a mistake? Was I too cautious—too suspicious—too logical? Was it really a protector she needed—a man who might have helped her? Would it have been for his benefit to believe in her, and was her fault only that I had forsaken her? Was the poor woman very unhappy? God forgive me, how the questions come crowding in! If I marred her happiness, I certainly didn't make my own. And I might have made it—eh? That's a charming discovery for a man of my age!

# THE EUROPEANS

# CHAPTER I

A narrow grave-yard in the heart of a bustling, indifferent city, seen from the windows of a gloomy-looking inn, is at no time an object of enlivening suggestion; and the spectacle is not at its best when the mouldy tombstones and funereal umbrage have received the ineffectual refreshment of a dull, moist snow-fall. If, while the air is thickened by this frosty drizzle, the calendar should happen to indicate that the blessed vernal season is already six weeks old, it will be admitted that no depressing influence is absent from the scene. This fact was keenly felt on a certain 12th of May, upwards of thirty years since, by a lady who stood looking out of one of the windows of the best hotel in the ancient city of Boston. She had stood there for half an hour—stood there, that is, at intervals; for from time to time she turned back into the room and measured its length with a restless step. In the chimney-place was a red-hot fire which emitted a small blue flame; and in front of the fire, at a table, sat a young man who was busily plying a pencil. He had a number of sheets of paper cut into small equal squares, and he was apparently covering them with pictorial designs—strange-looking figures. He worked rapidly and attentively, sometimes threw back his head and held out his drawing at arm's-length, and kept up a soft, gay-sounding humming and whistling. The lady brushed past him in her walk; her much-trimmed skirts were voluminous. She never dropped her eyes upon his work; she only turned them, occasionally, as she passed, to a mirror suspended above the toilet-table on the other side of the room. Here she paused a moment, gave a pinch to her waist with her two hands, or raised these members—they were very plump and pretty—to the multifold braids of her hair, with a movement half caressing, half corrective. An attentive observer might have fancied that during these periods of desultory self-inspection her face forgot its melancholy; but as soon as she neared the window again it began to proclaim that she was a very ill-pleased woman. And indeed, in what met her eyes there was little to be pleased with. The window-panes were battered by the sleet; the head-stones in the grave-yard beneath seemed to be holding themselves askance to keep it out of their faces. A tall iron railing protected them from the street, and on the other side of the railing an assemblage of Bostonians were trampling about in the liquid snow. Many of them were looking up and down; they appeared to be waiting for something. From time to time a strange vehicle drew near to the place where they stood,—such a vehicle as the lady at the window, in spite of a considerable acquaintance with human inventions, had never seen before: a huge, low omnibus, painted in brilliant colors, and decorated apparently with jangling bells, attached to a species of groove in the pavement, through which it was dragged, with a great deal of rumbling, bouncing and scratching, by a couple of remarkably small horses. When it reached a certain point the people in front of the grave-yard, of whom much the greater number were women, carrying satchels and parcels, projected themselves upon it in a compact body—a movement suggesting the scramble for places in a life-boat at sea—and were engulfed in its large interior. Then the life-boat—or the life-car, as the lady at the window of the hotel vaguely designated it—went bumping and jingling away upon its invisible wheels, with the helmsman (the man at the wheel) guiding its course incongruously from the prow. This phenomenon was repeated every three minutes, and the supply of eagerly-moving women in cloaks, bearing reticules and bundles, renewed itself in the most liberal manner. On the other side of the grave-yard was a row of small red brick houses, showing a series of homely, domestic-looking backs; at the end opposite the hotel a tall wooden church-spire, painted white, rose high into the vagueness of the snow-flakes. The lady at the window looked at it for some time; for reasons of her own she thought it the ugliest thing she had ever seen. She hated it, she despised it; it threw her into a state of irritation that was quite out of proportion to any sensible motive. She had never known herself to care so much about church-spires.

She was not pretty; but even when it expressed perplexed irritation her face was most interesting and agreeable. Neither was she in her first youth; yet, though slender, with a great deal of extremely well-fashioned roundness of contour—a suggestion both of maturity and flexibility—she carried her three and thirty years as a light-wristed Hebe might have carried a brimming wine-cup. Her complexion was fatigued, as the French say; her mouth was large, her lips too full, her teeth uneven, her chin rather commonly modeled; she had a thick nose, and when she smiled—she was constantly smiling—the lines beside it rose too high, toward her eyes. But these eyes were charming: gray in color, brilliant, quickly glancing, gently resting, full of intelligence. Her forehead was very low—it was her only handsome feature; and she had a great abundance of crisp dark hair, finely frizzled, which was always braided in a manner that suggested some Southern or Eastern, some remotely foreign, woman. She had a large collection of ear-rings, and wore them in alternation; and they seemed to give a point to her Oriental or exotic aspect. A compliment had once been paid her, which, being repeated to her, gave her greater pleasure than anything she had ever heard. "A pretty woman?" someone had said. "Why, her features are very bad." "I don't know about her features," a very discerning observer had answered; "but she carries her head like a pretty woman." You may imagine whether, after this, she carried her head less becomingly.

She turned away from the window at last, pressing her hands to her eyes. "It's too horrible!" she exclaimed. "I shall go back—I shall go back!" And she flung herself into a chair before the fire.

"Wait a little, dear child," said the young man softly, sketching away at his little scraps of paper.

The lady put out her foot; it was very small, and there was an immense rosette on her slipper. She fixed her eyes for a while on this ornament, and then she looked at the glowing bed of anthracite coal in the grate. "Did you ever see anything so hideous as that fire?" she demanded. "Did you ever see anything so—so *affreux* as—as everything?" She spoke English with perfect purity; but she brought out this French epithet in a manner that indicated that she was accustomed to using French epithets.

"I think the fire is very pretty," said the young man, glancing at it a moment. "Those little blue tongues, dancing on top of the crimson embers, are extremely picturesque. They are like a fire in an alchemist's laboratory."

"You are too good-natured, my dear," his companion declared.

55

The young man held out one of his drawings, with his head on one side. His tongue was gently moving along his under-lip. "Good-natured—yes. Too good-natured—no."

"You are irritating," said the lady, looking at her slipper.

He began to retouch his sketch. "I think you mean simply that you are irritated."

"Ah, for that, yes!" said his companion, with a little bitter laugh. "It's the darkest day of my life—and you know what that means."

"Wait till tomorrow," rejoined the young man.

"Yes, we have made a great mistake. If there is any doubt about it today, there certainly will be none tomorrow. *Ce sera clair, au moins!*"

The young man was silent a few moments, driving his pencil. Then at last, "There are no such things as mistakes," he affirmed.

"Very true—for those who are not clever enough to perceive them. Not to recognize one's mistakes—that would be happiness in life," the lady went on, still looking at her pretty foot.

"My dearest sister," said the young man, always intent upon his drawing, "it's the first time you have told me I am not clever."

"Well, by your own theory I can't call it a mistake," answered his sister, pertinently enough.

The young man gave a clear, fresh laugh. "You, at least, are clever enough, dearest sister," he said.

"I was not so when I proposed this."

"Was it you who proposed it?" asked her brother.

She turned her head and gave him a little stare. "Do you desire the credit of it?"

"If you like, I will take the blame," he said, looking up with a smile.

"Yes," she rejoined in a moment, "you make no difference in these things. You have no sense of property."

The young man gave his joyous laugh again. "If that means I have no property, you are right!"

"Don't joke about your poverty," said his sister. "That is quite as vulgar as to boast about it."

"My poverty! I have just finished a drawing that will bring me fifty francs!"

"*Voyons,*" said the lady, putting out her hand.

He added a touch or two, and then gave her his sketch. She looked at it, but she went on with her idea of a moment before. "If a woman were to ask you to marry her you would say, 'Certainly, my dear, with pleasure!' And you would marry her and be ridiculously happy. Then at the end of three months you would say to her, 'You know that blissful day when I begged you to be mine!'"

The young man had risen from the table, stretching his arms a little; he walked to the window. "That is a description of a charming nature," he said.

"Oh, yes, you have a charming nature; I regard that as our capital. If I had not been convinced of that I should never have taken the risk of bringing you to this dreadful country."

"This comical country, this delightful country!" exclaimed the young man, and he broke into the most animated laughter.

"Is it those women scrambling into the omnibus?" asked his companion. "What do you suppose is the attraction?"

"I suppose there is a very good-looking man inside," said the young man.

"In each of them? They come along in hundreds, and the men in this country don't seem at all handsome. As for the women—I have never seen so many at once since I left the convent."

"The women are very pretty," her brother declared, "and the whole affair is very amusing. I must make a sketch of it." And he came back to the table quickly, and picked up his utensils—a small sketching-board, a sheet of paper, and three or four crayons. He took his place at the window with these things, and stood there glancing out, plying his pencil with an air of easy skill. While he worked he wore a brilliant smile. Brilliant is indeed the word at this moment for his strongly-lighted face. He was eight and twenty years old; he had a short, slight, well-made figure. Though he bore a noticeable resemblance to his sister, he was a better favored person: fair-haired, clear-faced, witty-looking, with a delicate finish of feature and an expression at once urbane and not at all serious, a warm blue eye, an eyebrow finely drawn and excessively arched—an eyebrow which, if ladies wrote sonnets to those of their lovers, might have been made the subject of such a piece of verse—and a light moustache that flourished upwards as if blown that way by the breath of a constant smile. There was something in his physiognomy at once benevolent and picturesque. But, as I have hinted, it was not at all serious. The young man's face was, in this respect, singular; it was not at all serious, and yet it inspired the liveliest confidence.

"Be sure you put in plenty of snow," said his sister. "*Bonté divine*, what a climate!"

"I shall leave the sketch all white, and I shall put in the little figures in black," the young man answered, laughing. "And I shall call it—what is that line in Keats?—Mid-May's Eldest Child!"

"I don't remember," said the lady, "that mamma ever told me it was like this."

"Mamma never told you anything disagreeable. And it's not like this—every day. You will see that tomorrow we shall have a splendid day."

"*Qu'en savez-vous?* Tomorrow I shall go away."

"Where shall you go?"

"Anywhere away from here. Back to Silberstadt. I shall write to the Reigning Prince."

The young man turned a little and looked at her, with his crayon poised. "My dear Eugenia," he murmured, "were you so happy at sea?"

Eugenia got up; she still held in her hand the drawing her brother had given her. It was a bold, expressive sketch of a group of miserable people on the deck of a steamer, clinging together and clutching at each other, while the vessel lurched downward, at a terrific angle, into the hollow of a wave. It was extremely clever, and full of a sort of tragi-comical power. Eugenia dropped her eyes upon it and made a sad grimace. "How can you draw such odious scenes?" she asked. "I should like to throw it into the fire!" And she tossed the paper away. Her brother watched, quietly, to see where it went. It fluttered down to the floor, where he let it lie. She came toward the window, pinching in her waist. "Why don't you reproach me—abuse me?" she asked. "I think I should feel better then. Why don't you tell me that you hate me for bringing you here?"

"Because you would not believe it. I adore you, dear sister! I am delighted to be here, and I am charmed with the prospect."

"I don't know what had taken possession of me. I had lost my head," Eugenia went on.

The young man, on his side, went on plying his pencil. "It is evidently a most curious and interesting country. Here we are, and I mean to enjoy it."

His companion turned away with an impatient step, but presently came back. "High spirits are doubtless an excellent thing," she said; "but you give one too much of them, and I can't see that they have done you any good."

The young man stared, with lifted eyebrows, smiling; he tapped his handsome nose with his pencil. "They have made me happy!"

"That was the least they could do; they have made you nothing else. You have gone through life thanking fortune for such very small favors that she has never put herself to any trouble for you."

"She must have put herself to a little, I think, to present me with so admirable a sister."

"Be serious, Felix. You forget that I am your elder."

"With a sister, then, so elderly!" rejoined Felix, laughing. "I hoped we had left seriousness in Europe."

"I fancy you will find it here. Remember that you are nearly thirty years old, and that you are nothing but an obscure Bohemian—a penniless correspondent of an illustrated newspaper."

"Obscure as much as you please, but not so much of a Bohemian as you think. And not at all penniless! I have a hundred pounds in my pocket. I have an engagement to make fifty sketches, and I mean to paint the portraits of all our cousins, and of all *their* cousins, at a hundred dollars a head."

"You are not ambitious," said Eugenia.

"You are, dear Baroness," the young man replied.

The Baroness was silent a moment, looking out at the sleet-darkened grave-yard and the bumping horse-cars. "Yes, I am ambitious," she said at last. "And my ambition has brought me to this dreadful place!" She glanced about her—the room had a certain vulgar nudity; the bed and the window were curtainless—and she gave a little passionate sigh. "Poor old ambition!" she exclaimed. Then she flung herself down upon a sofa which stood near against the wall, and covered her face with her hands.

Her brother went on with his drawing, rapidly and skillfully; after some moments he sat down beside her and showed her his sketch. "Now, don't you think that's pretty good for an obscure Bohemian?" he asked. "I have knocked off another fifty francs."

Eugenia glanced at the little picture as he laid it on her lap. "Yes, it is very clever," she said. And in a moment she added, "Do you suppose our cousins do that?"

"Do what?"

"Get into those things, and look like that."

Felix meditated awhile. "I really can't say. It will be interesting to discover."

"Oh, the rich people can't!" said the Baroness.

"Are you very sure they are rich?" asked Felix, lightly.

His sister slowly turned in her place, looking at him. "Heavenly powers!" she murmured. "You have a way of bringing out things!"

"It will certainly be much pleasanter if they are rich," Felix declared.

"Do you suppose if I had not known they were rich I would ever have come?"

The young man met his sister's somewhat peremptory eye with his bright, contented glance. "Yes, it certainly will be pleasanter," he repeated.

"That is all I expect of them," said the Baroness. "I don't count upon their being clever or friendly—at first—or elegant or interesting. But I assure you I insist upon their being rich."

Felix leaned his head upon the back of the sofa and looked awhile at the oblong patch of sky to which the window served as frame. The snow was ceasing; it seemed to him that the sky had begun to brighten. "I count upon their being rich," he said at last, "and powerful, and clever, and friendly, and elegant, and interesting, and generally delightful! *Tu vas voir.*" And he bent forward and kissed his sister. "Look there!" he went on. "As a portent, even while I speak, the sky is turning the color of gold; the day is going to be splendid."

And indeed, within five minutes the weather had changed. The sun broke out through the snow-clouds and jumped into the Baroness's room. "*Bonté divine,*" exclaimed this lady, "what a climate!"

"We will go out and see the world," said Felix.

And after a while they went out. The air had grown warm as well as brilliant; the sunshine had dried the pavements. They walked about the streets at hazard, looking at the people and the houses, the shops and the vehicles, the blazing blue sky and the muddy crossings, the hurrying men and the slow-strolling maidens, the fresh red bricks and the bright green trees, the extraordinary mixture of smartness and shabbiness. From one hour to another the day had grown vernal; even in the bustling streets there was an odor of earth and blossom. Felix was immensely entertained. He had called it a comical country, and he went about laughing at everything he saw. You would have said that American civilization expressed itself to his sense in a tissue of capital jokes. The jokes were certainly excellent, and the young man's merriment was joyous and genial. He possessed what is called the pictorial sense; and this first glimpse of democratic manners stirred the same sort of attention that he would have given to the movements of a lively young person with a bright complexion. Such attention would have been demonstrative and complimentary; and in the present case Felix might have passed for an undispirited young exile revisiting the haunts of his childhood. He kept looking at the violent blue of the sky, at the scintillating air, at the scattered and multiplied patches of color.

"*Comme c'est bariolé*, eh?" he said to his sister in that foreign tongue which they both appeared to feel a mysterious prompting occasionally to use.

"Yes, it is *bariolé* indeed," the Baroness answered. "I don't like the coloring; it hurts my eyes."

"It shows how extremes meet," the young man rejoined. "Instead of coming to the West we seem to have gone to the East. The way the sky touches the house-tops is just like Cairo; and the red and blue sign-boards patched over the face of everything remind one of Mahometan decorations."

"The young women are not Mahometan," said his companion. "They can't be said to hide their faces. I never saw anything so bold."

"Thank Heaven they don't hide their faces!" cried Felix. "Their faces are uncommonly pretty."

"Yes, their faces are often very pretty," said the Baroness, who was a very clever woman. She was too clever a woman not to be capable of a great deal of just and fine observation. She clung more closely than usual to her brother's arm; she was not exhilarated, as he was; she said very little, but she noted a great many things and made her reflections. She was a little excited; she felt that she had indeed come to a strange country, to make her fortune. Superficially, she was conscious of a good deal of irritation and displeasure; the Baroness was a very delicate and fastidious person. Of old, more than once, she had gone, for entertainment's sake and in brilliant company, to a fair in a provincial town. It seemed to her now that she was at an enormous fair—that the entertainment and the *désagréments* were very much the same. She found herself alternately smiling and shrinking; the show was very curious, but it was probable, from moment to moment, that one would be jostled. The Baroness had never seen so many people walking about before; she had never been so mixed up with people she did not know. But little by little she felt that this fair was a more serious undertaking. She went with her brother into a large public garden, which seemed very pretty, but where she was surprised at seeing no carriages. The afternoon was drawing to a close; the coarse, vivid grass and the slender tree-boles were gilded by the level sunbeams—gilded as with gold that was fresh from the mine. It was the hour at which ladies should come out for an airing and roll past a hedge of pedestrians, holding their parasols askance. Here, however, Eugenia observed no indications of this custom, the absence of which was more anomalous as there was a charming avenue of remarkably graceful, arching elms in the most convenient contiguity to a large, cheerful street, in which, evidently, among the more prosperous members of the *bourgeoisie*, a great deal of pedestrianism went forward. Our friends passed out into this well lighted promenade, and Felix noticed a great many more pretty girls and called his sister's attention to them. This latter measure, however, was superfluous; for the Baroness had inspected, narrowly, these charming young ladies.

"I feel an intimate conviction that our cousins are like that," said Felix.

The Baroness hoped so, but this is not what she said. "They are very pretty," she said, "but they are mere little girls. Where are the women—the women of thirty?"

"Of thirty-three, do you mean?" her brother was going to ask; for he understood often both what she said and what she did not say. But he only exclaimed upon the beauty of the sunset, while the Baroness, who had come to seek her fortune, reflected that it would certainly be well for her if the persons against whom she might need to measure herself should all be mere little girls. The sunset was superb; they stopped to look at it; Felix declared that he had never seen such a gorgeous mixture of colors. The Baroness also thought it splendid; and she was perhaps the more easily pleased from the fact that while she stood there she was conscious of much admiring observation on the part of various nice-looking people who passed that way, and to whom a distinguished, strikingly-dressed woman with a foreign air, exclaiming upon the beauties of nature on a Boston street corner in the French tongue, could not be an object of indifference. Eugenia's spirits rose. She surrendered herself to a certain tranquil gaiety. If she had come to seek her fortune, it seemed to her that her fortune would be easy to find. There was a promise of it in the gorgeous purity of the western sky; there was an intimation in the mild, unimpertinent gaze of the passers of a certain natural facility in things.

"You will not go back to Silberstadt, eh?" asked Felix.

"Not tomorrow," said the Baroness.

"Nor write to the Reigning Prince?"

"I shall write to him that they evidently know nothing about him over here."

"He will not believe you," said the young man. "I advise you to let him alone."

Felix himself continued to be in high good humor. Brought up among ancient customs and in picturesque cities, he yet found plenty of local color in the little Puritan metropolis. That evening, after dinner, he told his sister that he should go forth early on the morrow to look up their cousins.

"You are very impatient," said Eugenia.

"What can be more natural," he asked, "after seeing all those pretty girls today? If one's cousins are of that pattern, the sooner one knows them the better."

"Perhaps they are not," said Eugenia. "We ought to have brought some letters—to some other people."

"The other people would not be our kinsfolk."

"Possibly they would be none the worse for that," the Baroness replied.

Her brother looked at her with his eyebrows lifted. "That was not what you said when you first proposed to me that we should come out here and fraternize with our relatives. You said that it was the prompting of natural affection; and when I suggested some reasons against it you declared that the *voix du sang* should go before everything."

"You remember all that?" asked the Baroness.

"Vividly! I was greatly moved by it."

She was walking up and down the room, as she had done in the morning; she stopped in her walk and looked at her brother. She apparently was going to say something, but she checked herself and resumed her walk. Then, in a few moments, she said something different, which had the effect of an explanation of the suppression of her earlier thought. "You will never be anything but a child, dear brother."

"One would suppose that you, madam," answered Felix, laughing, "were a thousand years old."

"I am—sometimes," said the Baroness.

"I will go, then, and announce to our cousins the arrival of a personage so extraordinary. They will immediately come and pay you their respects."

Eugenia paced the length of the room again, and then she stopped before her brother, laying her hand upon his arm. "They are not to come and see me," she said. "You are not to allow that. That is not the way I shall meet them first." And in answer to his interrogative glance she went on. "You will go and examine, and report. You will come back and tell me who they are and what they are; their number, gender, their respective ages—all about them. Be sure you observe everything; be ready to describe to me the locality, the accessories—how shall I say it?—the *mise en scène*. Then, at my own time, at my own hour, under circumstances of my own choosing, I will go to them. I will present myself—I will appear before them!" said the Baroness, this time phrasing her idea with a certain frankness.

"And what message am I to take to them?" asked Felix, who had a lively faith in the justness of his sister's arrangements.

She looked at him a moment—at his expression of agreeable veracity; and, with that justness that he admired, she replied, "Say what you please. Tell my story in the way that seems to you most—natural." And she bent her forehead for him to kiss.

# CHAPTER II

The next day was splendid, as Felix had prophesied; if the winter had suddenly leaped into spring, the spring had for the moment as quickly leaped into summer. This was an observation made by a young girl who came out of a large square house in the country, and strolled about in the spacious garden which separated it from a muddy road. The flowering shrubs and the neatly-disposed plants were basking in the abundant light and warmth; the transparent shade of the great elms—they were magnificent trees—seemed to thicken by the hour; and the intensely habitual stillness offered a submissive medium to the sound of a distant church-bell. The young girl listened to the church-bell; but she was not dressed for church. She was bare-headed; she wore a white muslin waist, with an embroidered border, and the skirt of her dress was of colored muslin. She was a young lady of some two or three and twenty years of age, and though a young person of her sex walking bareheaded in a garden, of a Sunday morning in spring-time, can, in the nature of things, never be a displeasing object, you would not have pronounced this innocent Sabbath-breaker especially pretty. She was tall and pale, thin and a little awkward; her hair was fair and perfectly straight; her eyes were dark, and they had the singularity of seeming at once dull and restless—differing herein, as you see, fatally from the ideal "fine eyes," which we always imagine to be both brilliant and tranquil. The doors and windows of the large square house were all wide open, to admit the purifying sunshine, which lay in generous patches upon the floor of a wide, high, covered piazza adjusted to two sides of the mansion—a piazza on which several straw-bottomed rocking-chairs and half a dozen of those small cylindrical stools in green and blue porcelain, which suggest an affiliation between the residents and the Eastern trade, were symmetrically disposed. It was an ancient house—ancient in the sense of being eighty years old; it was built of wood, painted a clean, clear, faded gray, and adorned along the front, at intervals, with flat wooden pilasters, painted white. These pilasters appeared to support a kind of classic pediment, which was decorated in the middle by a large triple window in a boldly carved frame, and in each of its smaller angles by a glazed circular aperture. A large white door, furnished with a highly-polished brass knocker, presented itself to the rural-looking road, with which it was connected by a spacious pathway, paved with worn and cracked, but very clean, bricks. Behind it there were meadows and orchards, a barn and a pond; and facing it, a short distance along the road, on the opposite side, stood a smaller house, painted white, with external shutters painted green, a little garden on one hand and an orchard on the other. All this was shining in the morning air, through which the simple details of the picture addressed themselves to the eye as distinctly as the items of a "sum" in addition.

A second young lady presently came out of the house, across the piazza, descended into the garden and approached the young girl of whom I have spoken. This second young lady was also thin and pale; but she was older than the other; she was shorter; she had dark, smooth hair. Her eyes, unlike the other's, were quick and bright; but they were not at all restless. She wore a straw bonnet with white ribbons, and a long, red, India scarf, which, on the front of her dress, reached to her feet. In her hand she carried a little key.

"Gertrude," she said, "are you very sure you had better not go to church?"

Gertrude looked at her a moment, plucked a small sprig from a lilac-bush, smelled it and threw it away. "I am not very sure of anything!" she answered.

The other young lady looked straight past her, at the distant pond, which lay shining between the long banks of fir trees. Then she said in a very soft voice, "This is the key of the dining-room closet. I think you had better have it, if anyone should want anything."

"Who is there to want anything?" Gertrude demanded. "I shall be all alone in the house."

"Someone may come," said her companion.

"Do you mean Mr. Brand?"

"Yes, Gertrude. He may like a piece of cake."

"I don't like men that are always eating cake!" Gertrude declared, giving a pull at the lilac-bush.

Her companion glanced at her, and then looked down on the ground. "I think father expected you would come to church," she said. "What shall I say to him?"

"Say I have a bad headache."

"Would that be true?" asked the elder lady, looking straight at the pond again.

"No, Charlotte," said the younger one simply.

Charlotte transferred her quiet eyes to her companion's face. "I am afraid you are feeling restless."

"I am feeling as I always feel," Gertrude replied, in the same tone.

Charlotte turned away; but she stood there a moment. Presently she looked down at the front of her dress. "Doesn't it seem to you, somehow, as if my scarf were too long?" she asked.

Gertrude walked half round her, looking at the scarf. "I don't think you wear it right," she said.

"How should I wear it, dear?"

"I don't know; differently from that. You should draw it differently over your shoulders, round your elbows; you should look differently behind."

"How should I look?" Charlotte inquired.

"I don't think I can tell you," said Gertrude, plucking out the scarf a little behind. "I could do it myself, but I don't think I can explain it."

Charlotte, by a movement of her elbows, corrected the laxity that had come from her companion's touch. "Well, some day you must do it for me. It doesn't matter now. Indeed, I don't think it matters," she added, "how one looks behind."

"I should say it mattered more," said Gertrude. "Then you don't know who may be observing you. You are not on your guard. You can't try to look pretty."

Charlotte received this declaration with extreme gravity. "I don't think one should ever try to look pretty," she rejoined, earnestly.

Her companion was silent. Then she said, "Well, perhaps it's not of much use."

Charlotte looked at her a little, and then kissed her. "I hope you will be better when we come back."

"My dear sister, I am very well!" said Gertrude.

Charlotte went down the large brick walk to the garden gate; her companion strolled slowly toward the house. At the gate Charlotte met a young man, who was coming in—a tall, fair young man, wearing a high hat and a pair of thread gloves. He was handsome, but rather too stout. He had a pleasant smile. "Oh, Mr. Brand!" exclaimed the young lady.

"I came to see whether your sister was not going to church," said the young man.

"She says she is not going; but I am very glad you have come. I think if you were to talk to her a little".... And Charlotte lowered her voice. "It seems as if she were restless."

Mr. Brand smiled down on the young lady from his great height. "I shall be very glad to talk to her. For that I should be willing to absent myself from almost any occasion of worship, however attractive."

"Well, I suppose you know," said Charlotte, softly, as if positive acceptance of this proposition might be dangerous. "But I am afraid I shall be late."

"I hope you will have a pleasant sermon," said the young man.

"Oh, Mr. Gilman is always pleasant," Charlotte answered. And she went on her way.

Mr. Brand went into the garden, where Gertrude, hearing the gate close behind him, turned and looked at him. For a moment she watched him coming; then she turned away. But almost immediately she corrected this movement, and stood still, facing him. He took off his hat and wiped his forehead as he approached. Then he put on his hat again and held out his hand. His hat being removed, you would have perceived that his forehead was very large and smooth, and his hair abundant but rather colorless. His nose was too large, and his mouth and eyes were too small; but for all this he was, as I have said, a young man of striking appearance. The expression of his little clean-colored blue eyes was irresistibly gentle and serious; he looked, as the phrase is, as good as gold. The young girl, standing in the garden path, glanced, as he came up, at his thread gloves.

"I hoped you were going to church," he said. "I wanted to walk with you."

"I am very much obliged to you," Gertrude answered. "I am not going to church."

She had shaken hands with him; he held her hand a moment. "Have you any special reason for not going?"

"Yes, Mr. Brand," said the young girl.

"May I ask what it is?"

She looked at him smiling; and in her smile, as I have intimated, there was a certain dullness. But mingled with this dullness was something sweet and suggestive. "Because the sky is so blue!" she said.

He looked at the sky, which was magnificent, and then said, smiling too, "I have heard of young ladies staying at home for bad weather, but never for good. Your sister, whom I met at the gate, tells me you are depressed," he added.

"Depressed? I am never depressed."

"Oh, surely, sometimes," replied Mr. Brand, as if he thought this a regrettable account of one's self.

"I am never depressed," Gertrude repeated. "But I am sometimes wicked. When I am wicked I am in high spirits. I was wicked just now to my sister."

"What did you do to her?"

"I said things that puzzled her—on purpose."

"Why did you do that, Miss Gertrude?" asked the young man.

She began to smile again. "Because the sky is so blue!"

"You say things that puzzle *me*," Mr. Brand declared.

"I always know when I do it," proceeded Gertrude. "But people puzzle me more, I think. And they don't seem to know!"

"This is very interesting," Mr. Brand observed, smiling.

"You told me to tell you about my—my struggles," the young girl went on.

"Let us talk about them. I have so many things to say."

Gertrude turned away a moment; and then, turning back, "You had better go to church," she said.

"You know," the young man urged, "that I have always one thing to say."

Gertrude looked at him a moment. "Please don't say it now!"

"We are all alone," he continued, taking off his hat; "all alone in this beautiful Sunday stillness."

Gertrude looked around her, at the breaking buds, the shining distance, the blue sky to which she had referred as a pretext for her irregularities. "That's the reason," she said, "why I don't want you to speak. Do me a favor; go to church."

"May I speak when I come back?" asked Mr. Brand.

"If you are still disposed," she answered.

"I don't know whether you are wicked," he said, "but you are certainly puzzling."

She had turned away; she raised her hands to her ears. He looked at her a moment, and then he slowly walked to church.

She wandered for a while about the garden, vaguely and without purpose. The church-bell had stopped ringing; the stillness was complete. This young lady relished highly, on occasions, the sense of being alone—the absence of the whole family and the emptiness of the house. Today, apparently, the servants had also gone to church; there was never a figure at the open windows; behind the house there was no stout negress in a red turban, lowering the bucket into the great shingle-hooded well. And the front door of the big, unguarded home stood open, with the trustfulness of the golden age; or what is more to the purpose, with that of New England's silvery prime. Gertrude slowly passed through it, and went from one of the empty rooms to the other—large, clear-colored rooms, with white wainscots, ornamented with thin-legged mahogany furniture, and, on the walls, with old-fashioned engravings, chiefly of scriptural subjects, hung very high. This agreeable sense of solitude, of having the house to herself, of which I have spoken, always excited Gertrude's imagination; she could not have told you why, and neither can her humble historian. It always seemed to her that she must do something particular—that she must honor the occasion; and while she roamed about, wondering what she could do, the occasion usually came to an end. Today she wondered more than ever. At last she took down a book; there was no library in the house, but there were books in all the rooms. None of them were forbidden books, and Gertrude had not stopped at home for the sake of a chance to climb to the inaccessible shelves. She possessed herself of a very obvious volume—one of the series of the *Arabian Nights*—and she brought it out into the portico and sat down with it in her lap. There, for a quarter of an hour, she read the history of the loves of the Prince Camaralzaman and the Princess Badoura. At last, looking up, she beheld, as it seemed to her, the Prince Camaralzaman standing before her. A beautiful young man was making her a very low bow—a magnificent bow, such as she had never seen before. He appeared to have dropped from the clouds; he was wonderfully handsome; he smiled—smiled as if he were smiling on purpose. Extreme surprise, for a moment, kept Gertrude sitting still; then she rose, without even keeping her finger in her book. The young man, with his hat in his hand, still looked at her, smiling and smiling. It was very strange.

"Will you kindly tell me," said the mysterious visitor, at last, "whether I have the honor of speaking to Miss Wentworth?"

"My name is Gertrude Wentworth," murmured the young woman.

"Then—then—I have the honor—the pleasure—of being your cousin."

The young man had so much the character of an apparition that this announcement seemed to complete his unreality. "What cousin? Who are you?" said Gertrude.

He stepped back a few paces and looked up at the house; then glanced round him at the garden and the distant view. After this he burst out laughing. "I see it must seem to you very strange," he said. There was, after all, something substantial in his laughter. Gertrude looked at him from head to foot. Yes, he was remarkably handsome; but his smile was almost a grimace. "It is very still," he went on, coming nearer again. And as she only looked at him, for reply, he added, "Are you all alone?"

"Everyone has gone to church," said Gertrude.

"I was afraid of that!" the young man exclaimed. "But I hope you are not afraid of me."

"You ought to tell me who you are," Gertrude answered.

"I am afraid of you!" said the young man. "I had a different plan. I expected the servant would take in my card, and that you would put your heads together, before admitting me, and make out my identity."

Gertrude had been wondering with a quick intensity which brought its result; and the result seemed an answer—a wondrous, delightful answer—to her vague wish that something would befall her. "I know—I know," she said. "You come from Europe."

"We came two days ago. You have heard of us, then—you believe in us?"

"We have known, vaguely," said Gertrude, "that we had relations in France."

"And have you ever wanted to see us?" asked the young man.

Gertrude was silent a moment. "I have wanted to see you."

"I am glad, then, it is you I have found. We wanted to see you, so we came."

"On purpose?" asked Gertrude.

The young man looked round him, smiling still. "Well, yes; on purpose. Does that sound as if we should bore you?" he added. "I don't think we shall—I really don't think we shall. We are rather fond of wandering, too; and we were glad of a pretext."

"And you have just arrived?"

"In Boston, two days ago. At the inn I asked for Mr. Wentworth. He must be your father. They found out for me where he lived; they seemed often to have heard of him. I determined to come, without ceremony. So, this lovely morning, they set my face in the right direction, and told me to walk straight before me, out of town. I came on foot because I wanted to see the country. I walked and walked, and here I am! It's a good many miles."

"It is seven miles and a half," said Gertrude, softly. Now that this handsome young man was proving himself a reality she found herself vaguely trembling; she was deeply excited. She had never in her life spoken to a foreigner, and she had often thought it would be delightful to do so. Here was one who had suddenly been engendered by the Sabbath stillness for her private use; and such a brilliant, polite, smiling one! She found time and means to compose herself, however: to remind herself that she must exercise a sort of official hospitality. "We are very—very glad to see you," she said. "Won't you come into the house?" And she moved toward the open door.

"You are not afraid of me, then?" asked the young man again, with his light laugh.

She wondered a moment, and then, "We are not afraid—here," she said.

*"Ah, comme vous devez avoir raison!"* cried the young man, looking all round him, appreciatively. It was the first time that Gertrude had heard so many words of French spoken. They gave her something of a sensation. Her companion followed her, watching, with a certain excitement of his own, this tall, interesting-looking girl, dressed in her clear, crisp muslin. He paused in the hall, where there was a broad white staircase with a white balustrade. "What a pleasant house!" he said. "It's lighter inside than it is out."

"It's pleasanter here," said Gertrude, and she led the way into the parlor,—a high, clean, rather empty-looking room. Here they stood looking at each other,—the young man smiling more than ever; Gertrude, very serious, trying to smile.

"I don't believe you know my name," he said. "I am called Felix Young. Your father is my uncle. My mother was his half sister, and older than he."

"Yes," said Gertrude, "and she turned Roman Catholic and married in Europe."

"I see you know," said the young man. "She married and she died. Your father's family didn't like her husband. They called him a foreigner; but he was not. My poor father was born in Sicily, but his parents were American."

"In Sicily?" Gertrude murmured.

"It is true," said Felix Young, "that they had spent their lives in Europe. But they were very patriotic. And so are we."

"And you are Sicilian," said Gertrude.

"Sicilian, no! Let's see. I was born at a little place—a dear little place—in France. My sister was born at Vienna."

"So you are French," said Gertrude.

"Heaven forbid!" cried the young man. Gertrude's eyes were fixed upon him almost insistently. He began to laugh again. "I can easily be French, if that will please you."

"You are a foreigner of some sort," said Gertrude.

"Of some sort—yes; I suppose so. But who can say of what sort? I don't think we have ever had occasion to settle the question. You know there are people like that. About their country, their religion, their profession, they can't tell."

Gertrude stood there gazing; she had not asked him to sit down. She had never heard of people like that; she wanted to hear. "Where do you live?" she asked.

"They can't tell that, either!" said Felix. "I am afraid you will think they are little better than vagabonds. I have lived anywhere—everywhere. I really think I have lived in every city in Europe." Gertrude gave a little long soft exhalation. It made the young man smile at her again; and his smile made her blush a little. To take refuge from blushing she asked him if, after his long walk, he was not hungry or thirsty. Her hand was in her pocket; she was fumbling with the little key that her sister had given her. "Ah, my dear young lady," he said, clasping his hands a little, "if you could give me, in charity, a glass of wine!"

Gertrude gave a smile and a little nod, and went quickly out of the room. Presently she came back with a very large decanter in one hand and a plate in the other, on which was placed a big, round cake with a frosted top. Gertrude, in taking the cake from the closet, had had a moment of acute consciousness that it composed the refection of which her sister had thought that Mr. Brand would like to partake. Her kinsman from across the seas was looking at the pale, high-hung engravings. When she came in he turned and smiled at her, as if they had been old friends meeting after a separation. "You wait upon me yourself?" he asked. "I am served like the gods!" She had waited upon a great many people, but none of them had ever told her that. The observation added a certain lightness to the step with which she went to a little table where there were some curious red glasses—glasses covered with little gold sprigs, which Charlotte used to dust every morning with her own hands. Gertrude thought the glasses very handsome, and it was a pleasure to her to know that the wine was good; it was her father's famous madeira. Felix Young thought it excellent; he wondered why he had been told that there was no wine in America. She cut him an immense triangle out of the cake, and again she thought of Mr. Brand. Felix sat there, with his glass in one hand and his huge morsel of cake in the other—eating, drinking, smiling, talking. "I am very hungry," he said. "I am not at all tired; I am never tired. But I am very hungry."

"You must stay to dinner," said Gertrude. "At two o'clock. They will all have come back from church; you will see the others."

"Who are the others?" asked the young man. "Describe them all."

"You will see for yourself. It is you that must tell me; now, about your sister."

"My sister is the Baroness Münster," said Felix.

On hearing that his sister was a Baroness, Gertrude got up and walked about slowly, in front of him. She was silent a moment. She was thinking of it. "Why didn't she come, too?" she asked.

"She did come; she is in Boston, at the hotel."

"We will go and see her," said Gertrude, looking at him.

"She begs you will not!" the young man replied. "She sends you her love; she sent me to announce her. She will come and pay her respects to your father."

Gertrude felt herself trembling again. A Baroness Münster, who sent a brilliant young man to "announce" her; who was coming, as the Queen of Sheba came to Solomon, to pay her "respects" to quiet Mr. Wentworth—such a personage presented herself to Gertrude's vision with a most effective unexpectedness. For a moment she hardly knew what to say. "When will she come?" she asked at last.

"As soon as you will allow her—tomorrow. She is very impatient," answered Felix, who wished to be agreeable.

"Tomorrow, yes," said Gertrude. She wished to ask more about her; but she hardly knew what could be predicated of a Baroness Münster. "Is she—is she—married?"

Felix had finished his cake and wine; he got up, fixing upon the young girl his bright, expressive eyes. "She is married to a German prince—Prince Adolf, of Silberstadt-Schreckenstein. He is not the reigning prince; he is a younger brother."

Gertrude gazed at her informant; her lips were slightly parted. "Is she a—a *Princess*?" she asked at last.

"Oh, no," said the young man; "her position is rather a singular one. It's a morganatic marriage."

"Morganatic?" These were new names and new words to poor Gertrude.

"That's what they call a marriage, you know, contracted between a scion of a ruling house and—and a common mortal. They made Eugenia a Baroness, poor woman; but that was all they could do. Now they want to dissolve the marriage. Prince Adolf, between ourselves, is a ninny; but his brother, who is a clever man, has plans for him. Eugenia, naturally enough, makes difficulties; not, however, that I think she cares much—she's a very clever woman; I'm sure you'll like her—but she wants to bother them. Just now everything is *en l'air*."

The cheerful, off-hand tone in which her visitor related this darkly romantic tale seemed to Gertrude very strange; but it seemed also to convey a certain flattery to herself, a recognition of her wisdom and dignity. She felt a dozen impressions stirring within her, and presently the one that was uppermost found words. "They want to dissolve her marriage?" she asked.

"So it appears."

"And against her will?"

"Against her right."

"She must be very unhappy!" said Gertrude.

Her visitor looked at her, smiling; he raised his hand to the back of his head and held it there a moment. "So she says," he answered. "That's her story. She told me to tell it you."

"Tell me more," said Gertrude.

"No, I will leave that to her; she does it better."

Gertrude gave her little excited sigh again. "Well, if she is unhappy," she said, "I am glad she has come to us."

She had been so interested that she failed to notice the sound of a footstep in the portico; and yet it was a footstep that she always recognized. She heard it in the hall, and then she looked out of the window. They were all coming back from church—her father, her sister and brother, and their cousins, who always came to dinner on Sunday. Mr. Brand had come in first; he was in advance of the others, because, apparently, he was still disposed to say what she had not wished him to say an hour before. He came into the parlor, looking for Gertrude. He had two little books in his hand. On seeing Gertrude's companion he slowly stopped, looking at him.

"Is this a cousin?" asked Felix.

Then Gertrude saw that she must introduce him; but her ears, and, by sympathy, her lips, were full of all that he had been telling her. "This is the Prince," she said, "the Prince of Silberstadt-Schreckenstein!"

Felix burst out laughing, and Mr. Brand stood staring, while the others, who had passed into the house, appeared behind him in the open doorway.

# CHAPTER III

That evening at dinner Felix Young gave his sister, the Baroness Münster, an account of his impressions. She saw that he had come back in the highest possible spirits; but this fact, to her own mind, was not a reason for rejoicing. She had but a limited confidence in her brother's judgment; his capacity for taking rose-colored views was such as to vulgarize one of the prettiest of tints. Still, she supposed he could be trusted to give her the mere facts; and she invited him with some eagerness to communicate them. "I suppose, at least, they didn't turn you out from the door;" she said. "You have been away some ten hours."

"Turn me from the door!" Felix exclaimed. "They took me to their hearts; they killed the fatted calf."

"I know what you want to say: they are a collection of angels."

"Exactly," said Felix. "They are a collection of angels—simply."

"*C'est bien vague*," remarked the Baroness. "What are they like?"

"Like nothing you ever saw."

"I am sure I am much obliged; but that is hardly more definite. Seriously, they were glad to see you?"

"Enchanted. It has been the proudest day of my life. Never, never have I been so lionized! I assure you, I was cock of the walk. My dear sister," said the young man, "*nous n'avons qu'à nous tenir*, we shall be great swells!"

Madame Münster looked at him, and her eye exhibited a slight responsive spark. She touched her lips to a glass of wine, and then she said, "Describe them. Give me a picture."

Felix drained his own glass. "Well, it's in the country, among the meadows and woods; a wild sort of place, and yet not far from here. Only, such a road, my dear! Imagine one of the Alpine glaciers reproduced in mud.

But you will not spend much time on it, for they want you to come and stay, once for all."

"Ah," said the Baroness, "they want me to come and stay, once for all? *Bon.*"

"It's intensely rural, tremendously natural; and all overhung with this strange white light, this far-away blue sky. There's a big wooden house—a kind of three-story bungalow; it looks like a magnified Nuremberg toy. There was a gentleman there that made a speech to me about it and called it a 'venerable mansion;' but it looks as if it had been built last night."

"Is it handsome—is it elegant?" asked the Baroness.

Felix looked at her a moment, smiling. "It's very clean! No splendors, no gilding, no troops of servants; rather straight-backed chairs. But you might eat off the floors, and you can sit down on the stairs."

"That must be a privilege. And the inhabitants are straight-backed too, of course."

"My dear sister," said Felix, "the inhabitants are charming."

"In what style?"

"In a style of their own. How shall I describe it? It's primitive; it's patriarchal; it's the *ton* of the golden age."

"And have they nothing golden but their *ton*? Are there no symptoms of wealth?"

"I should say there was wealth without symptoms. A plain, homely way of life: nothing for show, and very little for—what shall I call it?—for the senses; but a great *aisance*, and a lot of money, out of sight, that comes forward very quietly for subscriptions to institutions, for repairing tenements, for paying doctor's bills; perhaps even for portioning daughters."

"And the daughters?" Madame Münster demanded. "How many are there?"

"There are two, Charlotte and Gertrude."

"Are they pretty?"

"One of them," said Felix.

"Which is that?"

The young man was silent, looking at his sister. "Charlotte," he said at last.

She looked at him in return. "I see. You are in love with Gertrude. They must be Puritans to their finger-tips; anything but gay!"

"No, they are not gay," Felix admitted. "They are sober; they are even severe. They are of a pensive cast; they take things hard. I think there is something the matter with them; they have some melancholy memory or some depressing expectation. It's not the epicurean temperament. My uncle, Mr. Wentworth, is a tremendously high-toned old fellow; he looks as if he were undergoing martyrdom, not by fire, but by freezing. But we shall cheer them up; we shall do them good. They will take a good deal of stirring up; but they are wonderfully kind and gentle. And they are appreciative. They think one clever; they think one remarkable!"

"That is very fine, so far as it goes," said the Baroness. "But are we to be shut up to these three people, Mr. Wentworth and the two young women—what did you say their names were—Deborah and Hephzibah?"

"Oh, no; there is another little girl, a cousin of theirs, a very pretty creature; a thorough little American. And then there is the son of the house."

"Good!" said the Baroness. "We are coming to the gentlemen. What of the son of the house?"

"I am afraid he gets tipsy."

"He, then, has the epicurean temperament! How old is he?"

"He is a boy of twenty; a pretty young fellow, but I am afraid he has vulgar tastes. And then there is Mr. Brand—a very tall young man, a sort of lay-priest. They seem to think a good deal of him, but I don't exactly make him out."

"And is there nothing," asked the Baroness, "between these extremes—this mysterious ecclesiastic and that intemperate youth?"

"Oh, yes, there is Mr. Acton. I think," said the young man, with a nod at his sister, "that you will like Mr. Acton."

"Remember that I am very fastidious," said the Baroness. "Has he very good manners?"

"He will have them with you. He is a man of the world; he has been to China."

Madame Münster gave a little laugh. "A man of the Chinese world! He must be very interesting."

"I have an idea that he brought home a fortune," said Felix.

"That is always interesting. Is he young, good-looking, clever?"

"He is less than forty; he has a baldish head; he says witty things. I rather think," added the young man, "that he will admire the Baroness Münster."

"It is very possible," said this lady. Her brother never knew how she would take things; but shortly afterwards she declared that he had made a very pretty description and that on the morrow she would go and see for herself.

They mounted, accordingly, into a great barouche—a vehicle as to which the Baroness found nothing to criticise but the price that was asked for it and the fact that the coachman wore a straw hat. (At Silberstadt Madame Münster had had liveries of yellow and crimson.) They drove into the country, and the Baroness, leaning far back and swaying her lace-fringed parasol, looked to right and to left and surveyed the way-side objects. After a while she pronounced them *affreux*. Her brother remarked that it was apparently a country in which the foreground was inferior to the *plans reculés*; and the Baroness rejoined that the landscape seemed to be all foreground. Felix had fixed with his new friends the hour at which he should bring his sister; it was four o'clock in the afternoon. The large, clean-faced house wore, to his eyes, as the barouche drove up to it, a very friendly aspect; the high, slender elms made lengthening shadows in front of it. The Baroness descended; her American kinsfolk were stationed in the portico. Felix waved his hat to them, and a tall, lean gentleman, with a high forehead and a clean shaven face, came forward toward the garden gate. Charlotte Wentworth walked at his side. Gertrude came behind, more slowly. Both of these young ladies wore rustling silk dresses. Felix ushered his sister into the gate. "Be very gracious," he said to her. But he saw the admonition was superfluous. Eugenia was prepared to be gracious as only Eugenia could be. Felix knew no keener pleasure than to be able to admire his sister unrestrictedly; for if the opportunity was frequent, it was not inveterate. When she desired to please she was to him, as to everyone else, the most charming woman in the world. Then he forgot that she was ever anything else; that she was sometimes hard and perverse; that he was occasionally afraid of her. Now, as she took his arm to pass into the garden, he felt that she desired, that she proposed, to please, and this situation made him very happy. Eugenia would please.

The tall gentleman came to meet her, looking very rigid and grave. But it was a rigidity that had no illiberal meaning. Mr. Wentworth's manner was pregnant, on the contrary, with a sense of grand responsibility, of the solemnity of the occasion, of its being difficult to show sufficient deference to a lady at once so distinguished and so unhappy. Felix had observed on the day before his characteristic pallor; and now he perceived that there was something almost cadaverous in his uncle's high-featured white face. But so clever were this young man's quick sympathies and perceptions that he already learned that in these semi-mortuary manifestations there was no cause for alarm. His light imagination had gained a glimpse of Mr. Wentworth's spiritual mechanism, and taught him that, the old man being infinitely conscientious, the special operation of conscience within him announced itself by several of the indications of physical faintness.

The Baroness took her uncle's hand, and stood looking at him with her ugly face and her beautiful smile. "Have I done right to come?" she asked.

"Very right, very right," said Mr. Wentworth, solemnly. He had arranged in his mind a little speech; but now it quite faded away. He felt almost frightened. He had never been looked at in just that way—with just that fixed, intense smile—by any woman; and it perplexed and weighed upon him, now, that the woman who was smiling so and who had instantly given him a vivid sense of her possessing other unprecedented attributes, was his own niece, the child of his own father's daughter. The idea that his niece should be a German Baroness, married "morganatically" to a Prince, had already given him much to think about. Was it right, was it just, was it acceptable? He always slept badly, and the night before he had lain awake much more even than usual, asking himself these questions. The strange word "morganatic" was constantly in his ears; it reminded him of a certain Mrs. Morgan whom he had once known and who had been a bold, unpleasant woman. He had a feeling that it was his duty, so long as the Baroness looked at him, smiling in that way, to meet her glance with his own scrupulously adjusted, consciously frigid organs of vision; but on this occasion he failed to perform his duty to the last. He looked away toward his daughters. "We are very glad to see you," he had said. "Allow me to introduce my daughters—Miss Charlotte Wentworth, Miss Gertrude Wentworth."

The Baroness thought she had never seen people less demonstrative. But Charlotte kissed her and took her hand, looking at her sweetly and solemnly. Gertrude seemed to her almost funereal, though Gertrude might have found a source of gaiety in the fact that Felix, with his magnificent smile, had been talking to her; he had greeted her as a very old friend. When she kissed the Baroness she had tears in her eyes. Madame Münster took each of these young women by the hand, and looked at them all over. Charlotte thought her very strange-looking and singularly dressed; she could not have said whether it was well or ill. She was glad, at any rate, that they had put on their silk gowns—especially Gertrude. "My cousins are very pretty," said the Baroness, turning her eyes from one to the other. "Your daughters are very handsome, sir."

Charlotte blushed quickly; she had never yet heard her personal appearance alluded to in a loud, expressive voice. Gertrude looked away—not at Felix; she was extremely pleased. It was not the compliment that pleased her; she did not believe it; she thought herself very plain. She could hardly have told you the source of her satisfaction; it came from something in the way the Baroness spoke, and it was not diminished—it was rather deepened, oddly enough—by the young girl's disbelief. Mr. Wentworth was silent; and then he asked, formally, "Won't you come into the house?"

"These are not all; you have some other children," said the Baroness.

"I have a son," Mr. Wentworth answered.

"And why doesn't he come to meet me?" Eugenia cried. "I am afraid he is not so charming as his sisters."

"I don't know; I will see about it," the old man declared.

"He is rather afraid of ladies," Charlotte said, softly.

"He is very handsome," said Gertrude, as loud as she could.

"We will go in and find him. We will draw him out of his *cachette*." And the Baroness took Mr. Wentworth's arm, who was not aware that he had offered it to her, and who, as they walked toward the house, wondered whether he ought to have offered it and whether it was proper for her to take it if it had not been offered. "I want to know you well," said the Baroness, interrupting these meditations, "and I want you to know me."

"It seems natural that we should know each other," Mr. Wentworth rejoined. "We are near relatives."

"Ah, there comes a moment in life when one reverts, irresistibly, to one's natural ties—to one's natural affections. You must have found that!" said Eugenia.

Mr. Wentworth had been told the day before by Felix that Eugenia was very clever, very brilliant, and the information had held him in some suspense. This was the cleverness, he supposed; the brilliancy was beginning. "Yes, the natural affections are very strong," he murmured.

"In some people," the Baroness declared. "Not in all." Charlotte was walking beside her; she took hold of her hand again, smiling always. "And you, *cousine*, where did you get that enchanting complexion?" she went on; "such lilies and roses?" The roses in poor Charlotte's countenance began speedily to predominate over the lilies, and she quickened her step and reached the portico. "This is the country of complexions," the Baroness continued, addressing herself to Mr. Wentworth. "I am convinced they are more delicate. There are very good ones in England—in Holland; but they are very apt to be coarse. There is too much red."

"I think you will find," said Mr. Wentworth, "that this country is superior in many respects to those you mention. I have been to England and Holland."

"Ah, you have been to Europe?" cried the Baroness. "Why didn't you come and see me? But it's better, after all, this way," she said. They were entering the house; she paused and looked round her. "I see you have arranged your house—your beautiful house—in the—in the Dutch taste!"

"The house is very old," remarked Mr. Wentworth. "General Washington once spent a week here."

"Oh, I have heard of Washington," cried the Baroness. "My father used to tell me of him."

Mr. Wentworth was silent a moment, and then, "I found he was very well known in Europe," he said.

Felix had lingered in the garden with Gertrude; he was standing before her and smiling, as he had done the day before. What had happened the day before seemed to her a kind of dream. He had been there and he had changed everything; the others had seen him, they had talked with him; but that he should come again, that he should be part of the future, part of her small, familiar, much-meditating life—this needed, afresh, the evidence of her senses. The evidence had come to her senses now; and her senses seemed to rejoice in it. "What do you think of Eugenia?" Felix asked. "Isn't she charming?"

"She is very brilliant," said Gertrude. "But I can't tell yet. She seems to me like a singer singing an air. You can't tell till the song is done."

"Ah, the song will never be done!" exclaimed the young man, laughing. "Don't you think her handsome?"

Gertrude had been disappointed in the beauty of the Baroness Münster; she had expected her, for mysterious reasons, to resemble a very pretty portrait of the Empress Josephine, of which there hung an engraving in one of the parlors, and which the younger Miss Wentworth had always greatly admired. But the Baroness was not at all like that—not at all. Though different, however, she was very wonderful, and Gertrude felt herself most suggestively corrected. It was strange, nevertheless, that Felix should speak in that positive way about his sister's beauty. "I think I *shall* think her handsome," Gertrude said. "It must be very interesting to know her. I don't feel as if I ever could."

"Ah, you will know her well; you will become great friends," Felix declared, as if this were the easiest thing in the world.

"She is very graceful," said Gertrude, looking after the Baroness, suspended to her father's arm. It was a pleasure to her to say that anyone was graceful.

Felix had been looking about him. "And your little cousin, of yesterday," he said, "who was so wonderfully pretty—what has become of her?"

"She is in the parlor," Gertrude answered. "Yes, she is very pretty." She felt as if it were her duty to take him straight into the house, to where he might be near her cousin. But after hesitating a moment she lingered still. "I didn't believe you would come back," she said.

"Not come back!" cried Felix, laughing. "You didn't know, then, the impression made upon this susceptible heart of mine."

She wondered whether he meant the impression her cousin Lizzie had made. "Well," she said, "I didn't think we should ever see you again."

"And pray what did you think would become of me?"

"I don't know. I thought you would melt away."

"That's a compliment to my solidity! I melt very often," said Felix, "but there is always something left of me."

"I came and waited for you by the door, because the others did," Gertrude went on. "But if you had never appeared I should not have been surprised."

"I hope," declared Felix, looking at her, "that you would have been disappointed."

She looked at him a little, and shook her head. "No—no!"

*"Ah, par exemple!"* cried the young man. "You deserve that I should never leave you."

Going into the parlor they found Mr. Wentworth performing introductions. A young man was standing before the Baroness, blushing a good deal, laughing a little, and shifting his weight from one foot to the other—a slim, mild-faced young man, with neatly-arranged features, like those of Mr. Wentworth. Two other gentlemen, behind him, had risen from their seats, and a little apart, near one of the windows, stood a remarkably pretty young girl. The young girl was knitting a stocking; but, while her fingers quickly moved, she looked with wide, brilliant eyes at the Baroness.

"And what is your son's name?" said Eugenia, smiling at the young man.

"My name is Clifford Wentworth, ma'am," he said in a tremulous voice.

"Why didn't you come out to meet me, Mr. Clifford Wentworth?" the Baroness demanded, with her beautiful smile.

"I didn't think you would want me," said the young man, slowly sidling about.

"One always wants a *beau cousin*,—if one has one! But if you are very nice to me in future I won't remember it against you." And Madame Münster transferred her smile to the other persons present. It rested first upon the candid countenance and long-skirted figure of Mr. Brand, whose eyes were intently fixed upon Mr. Wentworth, as if to beg him not to prolong an anomalous situation. Mr. Wentworth pronounced his name. Eugenia gave him a very charming glance, and then looked at the other gentleman.

This latter personage was a man of rather less than the usual stature and the usual weight, with a quick, observant, agreeable dark eye, a small quantity of thin dark hair, and a small moustache. He had been standing with his hands in his pockets; and when Eugenia looked at him he took them out. But he did not, like Mr. Brand, look evasively and urgently at their host. He met Eugenia's eyes; he appeared to appreciate the privilege of meeting them. Madame Münster instantly felt that he was, intrinsically, the most important person present. She was not unconscious that this impression was in some degree manifested in the little sympathetic nod with which she acknowledged Mr. Wentworth's announcement, "My cousin, Mr. Acton!"

"Your cousin—not mine?" said the Baroness.

"It only depends upon you," Mr. Acton declared, laughing.

The Baroness looked at him a moment, and noticed that he had very white teeth. "Let it depend upon your behavior," she said. "I think I had better wait. I have cousins enough. Unless I can also claim relationship," she added, "with that charming young lady," and she pointed to the young girl at the window.

"That's my sister," said Mr. Acton. And Gertrude Wentworth put her arm round the young girl and led her forward. It was not, apparently, that she needed much leading. She came toward the Baroness with a light, quick step, and with perfect self-possession, rolling her stocking round its needles. She had dark blue eyes and dark brown hair; she was wonderfully pretty.

Eugenia kissed her, as she had kissed the other young women, and then held her off a little, looking at her. "Now this is quite another *type*," she said; she pronounced the word in the French manner. "This is a different outline, my uncle, a different character, from that of your own daughters. This, Felix," she went on, "is very much more what we have always thought of as the American type."

The young girl, during this exposition, was smiling askance at everyone in turn, and at Felix out of turn. "I find only one type here!" cried Felix, laughing. "The type adorable!"

91

This sally was received in perfect silence, but Felix, who learned all things quickly, had already learned that the silences frequently observed among his new acquaintances were not necessarily restrictive or resentful. It was, as one might say, the silence of expectation, of modesty. They were all standing round his sister, as if they were expecting her to acquit herself of the exhibition of some peculiar faculty, some brilliant talent. Their attitude seemed to imply that she was a kind of conversational mountebank, attired, intellectually, in gauze and spangles. This attitude gave a certain ironical force to Madame Münster's next words. "Now this is your circle," she said to her uncle. "This is your *salon*. These are your regular *habitués*, eh? I am so glad to see you all together."

"Oh," said Mr. Wentworth, "they are always dropping in and out. You must do the same."

"Father," interposed Charlotte Wentworth, "they must do something more." And she turned her sweet, serious face, that seemed at once timid and placid, upon their interesting visitor. "What is your name?" she asked.

"Eugenia-Camilla-Dolores," said the Baroness, smiling. "But you needn't say all that."

"I will say Eugenia, if you will let me. You must come and stay with us."

The Baroness laid her hand upon Charlotte's arm very tenderly; but she reserved herself. She was wondering whether it would be possible to "stay" with these people. "It would be very charming—very charming," she said; and her eyes wandered over the company, over the room. She wished to gain time before committing herself. Her glance fell upon young Mr. Brand, who stood there, with his arms folded and his hand on his chin, looking at her. "The gentleman, I suppose, is a sort of ecclesiastic," she said to Mr. Wentworth, lowering her voice a little.

"He is a minister," answered Mr. Wentworth.

"A Protestant?" asked Eugenia.

"I am a Unitarian, madam," replied Mr. Brand, impressively.

"Ah, I see," said Eugenia. "Something new." She had never heard of this form of worship.

Mr. Acton began to laugh, and Gertrude looked anxiously at Mr. Brand.

"You have come very far," said Mr. Wentworth.

"Very far—very far," the Baroness replied, with a graceful shake of her head—a shake that might have meant many different things.

"That's a reason why you ought to settle down with us," said Mr. Wentworth, with that dryness of utterance which, as Eugenia was too intelligent not to feel, took nothing from the delicacy of his meaning.

She looked at him, and for an instant, in his cold, still face, she seemed to see a far-away likeness to the vaguely remembered image of her mother. Eugenia was a woman of sudden emotions, and now, unexpectedly, she felt one rising in her heart. She kept looking round the circle; she knew that there was admiration in all the eyes that were fixed upon her. She smiled at them all.

"I came to look—to try—to ask," she said. "It seems to me I have done well. I am very tired; I want to rest." There were tears in her eyes. The luminous interior, the gentle, tranquil people, the simple, serious life—the sense of these things pressed upon her with an overmastering force, and she felt herself yielding to one of the most genuine emotions she had ever known. "I should like to stay here," she said. "Pray take me in."

Though she was smiling, there were tears in her voice as well as in her eyes. "My dear niece," said Mr. Wentworth, softly. And Charlotte put out her arms and drew the Baroness toward her; while Robert Acton turned away, with his hands stealing into his pockets.

# CHAPTER IV

A few days after the Baroness Münster had presented herself to her American kinsfolk she came, with her brother, and took up her abode in that small white house adjacent to Mr. Wentworth's own dwelling of which mention has already been made. It was on going with his daughters to return her visit that Mr. Wentworth placed this comfortable cottage at her service; the offer being the result of a domestic colloquy, diffused through the ensuing twenty-four hours, in the course of which the two foreign visitors were discussed and analyzed with a great deal of earnestness and subtlety. The discussion went forward, as I say, in the family circle; but that circle on the evening following Madame Münster's return to town, as on many other occasions, included Robert Acton and his pretty sister. If you had been present, it would probably not have seemed to you that the advent of these brilliant strangers was treated as an exhilarating occurrence, a pleasure the more in this tranquil household, a prospective source of entertainment. This was not Mr. Wentworth's way of treating any human occurrence. The sudden irruption into the well-ordered consciousness of the Wentworths of an element not allowed for in its scheme of usual obligations required a readjustment of that sense of responsibility which constituted its principal furniture. To consider an event, crudely and baldly, in the light of the pleasure it might bring them was an intellectual exercise with which Felix Young's American cousins were almost wholly unacquainted, and which they scarcely supposed to be largely pursued in any section of human society. The arrival of Felix and his sister was a satisfaction, but it was a singularly joyless and inelastic satisfaction. It was an extension of duty, of the exercise of the more recondite virtues; but neither Mr. Wentworth, nor Charlotte, nor Mr. Brand, who, among these excellent people, was a great promoter of reflection and aspiration, frankly adverted to it as an extension of enjoyment. This function was ultimately assumed by Gertrude Wentworth, who was a peculiar girl, but the full compass of whose peculiarities had not been exhibited before they very ingeniously found their pretext in the presence of these possibly too agreeable foreigners. Gertrude, however, had to struggle with a great accumulation of obstructions, both of the subjective, as the metaphysicians say, and of the objective, order; and indeed it is no small part of the purpose of this little history to set forth her struggle. What seemed paramount in this abrupt enlargement of Mr. Wentworth's sympathies and those of his daughters was an extension of the field of possible mistakes; and the doctrine, as it may almost be called, of the oppressive gravity of mistakes was one of the most cherished traditions of the Wentworth family.

"I don't believe she wants to come and stay in this house," said Gertrude; Madame Münster, from this time forward, receiving no other designation than the personal pronoun. Charlotte and Gertrude acquired considerable facility in addressing her, directly, as "Eugenia;" but in speaking of her to each other they rarely called her anything but "she."

"Doesn't she think it good enough for her?" cried little Lizzie Acton, who was always asking unpractical questions that required, in strictness, no answer, and to which indeed she expected no other answer than such as she herself invariably furnished in a small, innocently-satirical laugh.

"She certainly expressed a willingness to come," said Mr. Wentworth.

"That was only politeness," Gertrude rejoined.

"Yes, she is very polite—very polite," said Mr. Wentworth.

"She is too polite," his son declared, in a softly growling tone which was habitual to him, but which was an indication of nothing worse than a vaguely humorous intention. "It is very embarrassing."

"That is more than can be said of you, sir," said Lizzie Acton, with her little laugh.

"Well, I don't mean to encourage her," Clifford went on.

"I'm sure I don't care if you do!" cried Lizzie.

"She will not think of you, Clifford," said Gertrude, gravely.

"I hope not!" Clifford exclaimed.

"She will think of Robert," Gertrude continued, in the same tone.

Robert Acton began to blush; but there was no occasion for it, for everyone was looking at Gertrude—everyone, at least, save Lizzie, who, with her pretty head on one side, contemplated her brother.

"Why do you attribute motives, Gertrude?" asked Mr. Wentworth.

"I don't attribute motives, father," said Gertrude. "I only say she will think of Robert; and she will!"

"Gertrude judges by herself!" Acton exclaimed, laughing. "Don't you, Gertrude? Of course the Baroness will think of me. She will think of me from morning till night."

"She will be very comfortable here," said Charlotte, with something of a housewife's pride. "She can have the large northeast room. And the French bedstead," Charlotte added, with a constant sense of the lady's foreignness.

"She will not like it," said Gertrude; "not even if you pin little tidies all over the chairs."

"Why not, dear?" asked Charlotte, perceiving a touch of irony here, but not resenting it.

Gertrude had left her chair; she was walking about the room; her stiff silk dress, which she had put on in honor of the Baroness, made a sound upon the carpet. "I don't know," she replied. "She will want something more—more private."

"If she wants to be private she can stay in her room," Lizzie Acton remarked.

Gertrude paused in her walk, looking at her. "That would not be pleasant," she answered. "She wants privacy and pleasure together."

Robert Acton began to laugh again. "My dear cousin, what a picture!"

Charlotte had fixed her serious eyes upon her sister; she wondered whence she had suddenly derived these strange notions. Mr. Wentworth also observed his younger daughter.

"I don't know what her manner of life may have been," he said; "but she certainly never can have enjoyed a more refined and salubrious home."

Gertrude stood there looking at them all. "She is the wife of a Prince," she said.

"We are all princes here," said Mr. Wentworth; "and I don't know of any palace in this neighborhood that is to let."

"Cousin William," Robert Acton interposed, "do you want to do something handsome? Make them a present, for three months, of the little house over the way."

"You are very generous with other people's things!" cried his sister.

"Robert is very generous with his own things," Mr. Wentworth observed dispassionately, and looking, in cold meditation, at his kinsman.

"Gertrude," Lizzie went on, "I had an idea you were so fond of your new cousin."

"Which new cousin?" asked Gertrude.

"I don't mean the Baroness!" the young girl rejoined, with her laugh. "I thought you expected to see so much of him."

"Of Felix? I hope to see a great deal of him," said Gertrude, simply.

"Then why do you want to keep him out of the house?"

Gertrude looked at Lizzie Acton, and then looked away.

"Should you want me to live in the house with you, Lizzie?" asked Clifford.

"I hope you never will. I hate you!" Such was this young lady's reply.

"Father," said Gertrude, stopping before Mr. Wentworth and smiling, with a smile the sweeter, as her smile always was, for its rarity; "do let them live in the little house over the way. It will be lovely!"

Robert Acton had been watching her. "Gertrude is right," he said. "Gertrude is the cleverest girl in the world. If I might take the liberty, I should strongly recommend their living there."

"There is nothing there so pretty as the northeast room," Charlotte urged.

"She will make it pretty. Leave her alone!" Acton exclaimed.

Gertrude, at his compliment, had blushed and looked at him: it was as if someone less familiar had complimented her. "I am sure she will make it pretty. It will be very interesting. It will be a place to go to. It will be a foreign house."

"Are we very sure that we need a foreign house?" Mr. Wentworth inquired. "Do you think it desirable to establish a foreign house—in this quiet place?"

"You speak," said Acton, laughing, "as if it were a question of the poor Baroness opening a wine-shop or a gaming-table."

"It would be too lovely!" Gertrude declared again, laying her hand on the back of her father's chair.

"That she should open a gaming-table?" Charlotte asked, with great gravity.

Gertrude looked at her a moment, and then, "Yes, Charlotte," she said, simply.

"Gertrude is growing pert," Clifford Wentworth observed, with his humorous young growl. "That comes of associating with foreigners."

Mr. Wentworth looked up at his daughter, who was standing beside him; he drew her gently forward. "You must be careful," he said. "You must keep watch. Indeed, we must all be careful. This is a great change; we are to be exposed to peculiar influences. I don't say they are bad. I don't judge them in advance. But they may perhaps make it necessary that we should exercise a great deal of wisdom and self-control. It will be a different tone."

Gertrude was silent a moment, in deference to her father's speech; then she spoke in a manner that was not in the least an answer to it. "I want to see how they will live. I am sure they will have different hours. She will do all kinds of little things differently. When we go over there it will be like going to Europe. She will have a boudoir. She will invite us to dinner—very late. She will breakfast in her room."

Charlotte gazed at her sister again. Gertrude's imagination seemed to her to be fairly running riot. She had always known that Gertrude had a great deal of imagination—she had been very proud of it. But at the same time she had always felt that it was a dangerous and irresponsible faculty; and now, to her sense, for the moment, it seemed to threaten to make her sister a strange person who should come in suddenly, as from a journey, talking of the peculiar and possibly unpleasant things she had observed. Charlotte's imagination took no journeys whatever; she kept it, as it were, in her pocket, with the other furniture of this receptacle—a thimble, a little box of peppermint, and a morsel of court-plaster. "I don't believe she would have any dinner—or any breakfast," said Miss Wentworth. "I don't believe she knows how to do anything herself. I should have to get her ever so many servants, and she wouldn't like them."

"She has a maid," said Gertrude; "a French maid. She mentioned her."

"I wonder if the maid has a little fluted cap and red slippers," said Lizzie Acton. "There was a French maid in that play that Robert took me to see. She had pink stockings; she was very wicked."

"She was a *soubrette*," Gertrude announced, who had never seen a play in her life. "They call that a soubrette. It will be a great chance to learn French." Charlotte gave a little soft, helpless groan. She had a vision of a wicked, theatrical person, clad in pink stockings and red shoes, and speaking, with confounding volubility, an incomprehensible tongue, flitting through the sacred penetralia of that large, clean house. "That is one reason in favor of their coming here," Gertrude went on. "But we can make Eugenia speak French to us, and Felix. I mean to begin—the next time."

Mr. Wentworth had kept her standing near him, and he gave her his earnest, thin, unresponsive glance again. "I want you to make me a promise, Gertrude," he said.

"What is it?" she asked, smiling.

"Not to get excited. Not to allow these—these occurrences to be an occasion for excitement."

She looked down at him a moment, and then she shook her head. "I don't think I can promise that, father. I am excited already."

Mr. Wentworth was silent a while; they all were silent, as if in recognition of something audacious and portentous.

"I think they had better go to the other house," said Charlotte, quietly.

"I shall keep them in the other house," Mr. Wentworth subjoined, more pregnantly.

Gertrude turned away; then she looked across at Robert Acton. Her cousin Robert was a great friend of hers; she often looked at him this way instead of saying things. Her glance on this occasion, however, struck him as a substitute for a larger volume of diffident utterance than usual, inviting him to observe, among other things, the inefficiency of her father's design—if design it was—for diminishing, in the interest of quiet nerves, their occasions of contact with their foreign relatives. But Acton immediately complimented Mr. Wentworth upon his liberality. "That's a very nice thing to do," he said, "giving them the little house. You will have treated them handsomely, and, whatever happens, you will be glad of it." Mr. Wentworth was liberal, and he knew he was liberal. It gave him pleasure to know it, to feel it, to see it recorded; and this pleasure is the only palpable form of self-indulgence with which the narrator of these incidents will be able to charge him.

"A three days' visit at most, over there, is all I should have found possible," Madame Münster remarked to her brother, after they had taken possession of the little white house. "It would have been too *intime*—decidedly too *intime*. Breakfast, dinner, and tea *en famille*—it would have been the end of the world if I could have reached the third day." And she made the same observation to her maid Augustine, an intelligent person, who enjoyed a liberal share of her confidence. Felix declared that he would willingly spend his life in the bosom of the Wentworth family; that they were the kindest, simplest, most amiable people in the world, and that he had taken a prodigious fancy to them all. The Baroness quite agreed with him that they were simple and kind; they were thoroughly nice people, and she liked them extremely. The girls were perfect ladies; it was impossible to be more of a lady than Charlotte Wentworth, in spite of her little village air. "But as for thinking them the best company in the world," said the Baroness, "that is another thing; and as for wishing to live *porte à porte* with them, I should as soon think of wishing myself back in the convent again, to wear a bombazine apron and sleep in a dormitory." And yet the Baroness was in high good humor; she had been very much pleased. With her lively perception and her refined imagination, she was capable of enjoying anything that was characteristic, anything that was good of its kind. The Wentworth household seemed to her very perfect in its kind—wonderfully peaceful and unspotted; pervaded by a sort of dove-colored freshness that had all the quietude and benevolence of what she deemed to be Quakerism, and yet seemed to be founded upon a degree of material abundance for which, in certain matters of detail, one might have looked in vain at the frugal little court of Silberstadt-Schreckenstein. She perceived immediately that her American relatives thought and talked very little about money; and this of itself made an impression upon Eugenia's imagination. She perceived at the same time that if Charlotte or Gertrude should ask their father for a very considerable sum he would at once place it in their hands; and this made a still greater impression. The greatest impression of all, perhaps, was made by another rapid induction. The Baroness had an immediate conviction that Robert Acton would put his hand into his pocket every day in the week if that rattle-pated little sister of his should bid him. The men in this country, said the Baroness, are evidently very obliging. Her declaration that she was looking for rest and retirement had been by no means wholly untrue; nothing that the Baroness said was wholly untrue. It is but fair to add, perhaps, that nothing that she said was wholly true. She wrote to a friend in Germany that it was a return to nature; it was like drinking new milk, and she was very fond of new milk. She said to herself, of course, that it would be a little dull; but there can be no better proof of her good spirits than the fact that she thought she should not mind its being a little dull. It seemed to her, when from the piazza of her eleemosynary cottage she looked out over the soundless fields, the stony pastures, the clear-faced ponds, the rugged little orchards, that she had never been in the midst of so peculiarly intense a stillness; it was almost a delicate sensual pleasure. It was all very good, very innocent and safe, and out of it something good must come. Augustine, indeed, who had an unbounded faith in her mistress's wisdom and far-sightedness, was a great deal perplexed and depressed. She was always ready to take her cue when she understood it; but she liked to understand it, and on this occasion comprehension failed. What, indeed, was the Baroness doing *dans cette galère*? what fish did she expect to land out of these very stagnant waters? The game was evidently a deep one. Augustine could trust her; but the sense of walking in the dark betrayed itself in the physiognomy of this spare, sober, sallow, middle-aged person, who had nothing in common with Gertrude Wentworth's conception of a soubrette, by the most ironical scowl that had ever rested upon the unpretending tokens of the peace and plenty of the Wentworths. Fortunately, Augustine could quench skepticism in action. She quite agreed with her mistress—or rather she quite out-stripped her mistress—in thinking that the little white house was pitifully bare. *"Il faudra,"* said Augustine, *"lui faire un peu de toilette."* And she began to hang up *portières* in the doorways; to place wax candles, procured after some research, in unexpected situations; to dispose anomalous draperies over the arms of sofas and the backs of chairs. The Baroness had brought with her to the New World a copious provision of the element of costume; and the two Miss Wentworths, when they came over to see her, were somewhat bewildered by the obtrusive distribution of her wardrobe. There were India shawls suspended, curtain-wise, in the parlor door, and curious fabrics, corresponding to Gertrude's metaphysical vision of an opera-cloak, tumbled about in the sitting-places. There were pink silk blinds in the windows, by which the room was strangely bedimmed; and along the chimney-piece was disposed a remarkable band of velvet, covered with coarse, dirty-looking lace. "I have been making myself a little comfortable," said the Baroness, much to the confusion of Charlotte, who had been on the point of proposing to come and help her put her superfluous draperies away. But what Charlotte mistook for an almost culpably delayed subsidence Gertrude very presently perceived to be the most ingenious, the most interesting, the most romantic intention. "What is life, indeed, without curtains?" she secretly asked herself; and she appeared to herself to have been leading hitherto an existence singularly garish and totally devoid of festoons.

Felix was not a young man who troubled himself greatly about anything—least of all about the conditions of enjoyment. His faculty of enjoyment was so large, so unconsciously eager, that it may be said of it that it had a permanent advance upon embarrassment and sorrow. His sentient faculty was intrinsically joyous, and novelty and change were in themselves a delight to him. As they had come to him with a great deal of frequency, his life had been more agreeable than appeared. Never was a nature more perfectly fortunate. It was not a restless, apprehensive, ambitious spirit, running a race with the tyranny of fate, but a temper so unsuspicious as to put Adversity off her guard, dodging and evading her with the easy, natural motion of a wind-shifted flower. Felix extracted entertainment from all things, and all his faculties—his imagination, his intelligence, his affections, his senses—had a hand in the game. It seemed to him that Eugenia and he had been very well treated; there was something absolutely touching in that combination of paternal liberality and social considerateness which marked Mr. Wentworth's deportment. It was most uncommonly kind of him, for instance, to have given them a house. Felix was positively amused at having a house of his own; for the little white cottage among the apple trees—the chalet, as Madame Münster always called it—was much more sensibly his own than any domiciliary *quatrième*, looking upon a court, with the rent overdue. Felix had spent a good deal of his life in looking into courts, with a perhaps slightly tattered pair of elbows resting upon the ledge of a high-perched window, and the thin smoke of a cigarette rising into an atmosphere in which street-cries died away and the vibration of chimes from ancient belfries became sensible. He had never known anything so infinitely rural as these New England fields; and he took a great fancy to all their pastoral roughnesses. He had never had a greater sense of luxurious security; and at the risk of making him seem a rather sordid adventurer I must declare that he found an irresistible charm in the fact that he might dine every day at his uncle's. The charm was irresistible, however, because his fancy flung a rosy light over this homely privilege. He appreciated highly the fare that was set before him. There was a kind of fresh-looking abundance about it which made him think that people must have lived so in the mythological era, when they spread their tables upon the grass, replenished them from cornucopias, and had no particular need of kitchen stoves. But the great thing that Felix enjoyed was having found a family—sitting in the midst of gentle, generous people whom he might call by their first names. He had never known anything more charming than the attention they paid to what he said. It was like a large sheet of clean, fine-grained drawing-paper, all ready to be washed over with effective splashes of water-color. He had never had any cousins, and he had never before found himself in contact so unrestricted with young unmarried ladies. He was extremely fond of the society of ladies, and it was new to him that it might be enjoyed in just this manner. At first he hardly knew what to make of his state of mind. It seemed to him that he was in love, indiscriminately, with three girls at once. He saw that Lizzie Acton was more brilliantly pretty than Charlotte and Gertrude; but this was scarcely a superiority. His pleasure came from something they had in common—a part of which was, indeed, that physical delicacy which seemed to make it proper that they should always dress in thin materials and clear colors. But they were delicate in other ways, and it was most agreeable to him to feel that these latter delicacies were appreciable by contact, as it were. He had known, fortunately, many virtuous gentlewomen, but it now appeared to him that in his relations with them (especially when they were unmarried) he had been looking at pictures under glass. He perceived at present what a nuisance the glass had been—how it perverted and interfered, how it caught the reflection of other objects and kept you walking from side to side. He had no need to ask himself whether Charlotte and Gertrude, and Lizzie Acton, were in the right light; they were always in the right light. He liked everything about them: he was, for instance, not at all above liking the fact that they had very slender feet and high insteps. He liked their pretty noses; he liked their surprised eyes and their hesitating, not at all positive way of speaking; he liked so much knowing that he was perfectly at liberty to be alone for hours, anywhere, with either of them; that preference for one to the other, as a companion of solitude, remained a minor affair. Charlotte Wentworth's sweetly severe features were as agreeable as Lizzie Acton's wonderfully expressive blue eyes; and Gertrude's air of being always ready to walk about and listen was as charming as anything else, especially as she walked very gracefully. After a while Felix began to distinguish; but even then he would often wish, suddenly, that they were not all so sad. Even Lizzie Acton, in spite of her fine little chatter and laughter, appeared sad. Even Clifford Wentworth, who had extreme youth in his favor, and kept a buggy with enormous wheels and a little sorrel mare with the prettiest legs in the world—even this fortunate lad was apt to have an averted, uncomfortable glance, and to edge away from you at times, in the manner of a person with a bad conscience. The only person in the circle with no sense of oppression of any kind was, to Felix's perception, Robert Acton.

It might perhaps have been feared that after the completion of those graceful domiciliary embellishments which have been mentioned Madame Münster would have found herself confronted with alarming possibilities of *ennui*. But as yet she had not taken the alarm. The Baroness was a restless soul, and she projected her restlessness, as it may be said, into any situation that lay before her. Up to a certain point her restlessness might be counted upon to entertain her. She was always expecting something to happen, and, until it was disappointed, expectancy itself was a delicate pleasure. What the Baroness expected just now it would take some ingenuity to set forth; it is enough that while she looked about her she found something to occupy her imagination. She assured herself that she was enchanted with her new relatives; she professed to herself that, like her brother, she felt it a sacred satisfaction to have found a family. It is certain that she enjoyed to the utmost the gentleness of her kinsfolk's deference. She had, first and last, received a great deal of admiration, and her experience of well-turned compliments was very considerable; but she knew that she had never been so real a power, never counted for so much, as now when, for the first time, the standard of comparison of her little circle was a prey to vagueness. The sense, indeed, that the good people about her had, as regards her remarkable self, no standard of comparison at all gave her a feeling of almost illimitable power. It was true, as she said to herself, that if for this reason they would be able to discover nothing against her, so they would perhaps neglect to perceive some of her superior points; but she always wound up her reflections by declaring that she would take care of that.

Charlotte and Gertrude were in some perplexity between their desire to show all proper attention to Madame Münster and their fear of being importunate. The little house in the orchard had hitherto been occupied during the summer months by intimate friends of the family, or by poor relations who found in Mr. Wentworth a landlord attentive to repairs and oblivious of quarter-day. Under these circumstances the open door of the small house and that of the large one, facing each other across their homely gardens, levied no tax upon hourly visits. But the Misses Wentworth received an impression that Eugenia was no friend to the primitive custom of "dropping in;" she evidently had no idea of living without a door-keeper. "One goes into your house as into an inn—except that there are no servants rushing forward," she said to Charlotte. And she added that that was very charming. Gertrude explained to her sister that she meant just the reverse; she didn't like it at all. Charlotte inquired why she should tell an untruth, and Gertrude answered that there was probably some very good reason for it which they should discover when they knew her better. "There can surely be no good reason for telling an untruth," said Charlotte. "I hope she does not think so."

They had of course desired, from the first, to do everything in the way of helping her to arrange herself. It had seemed to Charlotte that there would be a great many things to talk about; but the Baroness was apparently inclined to talk about nothing.

"Write her a note, asking her leave to come and see her. I think that is what she will like," said Gertrude.

"Why should I give her the trouble of answering me?" Charlotte asked. "She will have to write a note and send it over."

"I don't think she will take any trouble," said Gertrude, profoundly.

"What then will she do?"

"That is what I am curious to see," said Gertrude, leaving her sister with an impression that her curiosity was morbid.

They went to see the Baroness without preliminary correspondence; and in the little salon which she had already created, with its becoming light and its festoons, they found Robert Acton.

Eugenia was intensely gracious, but she accused them of neglecting her cruelly. "You see Mr. Acton has had to take pity upon me," she said. "My brother goes off sketching, for hours; I can never depend upon him. So I was to send Mr. Acton to beg you to come and give me the benefit of your wisdom."

Gertrude looked at her sister. She wanted to say, "*That* is what she would have done." Charlotte said that they hoped the Baroness would always come and dine with them; it would give them so much pleasure; and, in that case, she would spare herself the trouble of having a cook.

"Ah, but I must have a cook!" cried the Baroness. "An old negress in a yellow turban. I have set my heart upon that. I want to look out of my window and see her sitting there on the grass, against the background of those crooked, dusky little apple trees, pulling the husks off a lapful of Indian corn. That will be local color, you know. There isn't much of it here—you don't mind my saying that, do you?—so one must make the most of what one can get. I shall be most happy to dine with you whenever you will let me; but I want to be able to ask you sometimes. And I want to be able to ask Mr. Acton," added the Baroness.

"You must come and ask me at home," said Acton. "You must come and see me; you must dine with me first. I want to show you my place; I want to introduce you to my mother." He called again upon Madame Münster, two days later. He was constantly at the other house; he used to walk across the fields from his own place, and he appeared to have fewer scruples than his cousins with regard to dropping in. On this occasion he found that Mr. Brand had come to pay his respects to the charming stranger; but after Acton's arrival the young theologian said nothing. He sat in his chair with his two hands clasped, fixing upon his hostess a grave, fascinated stare. The Baroness talked to Robert Acton, but, as she talked, she turned and smiled at Mr. Brand, who never took his eyes off her. The two men walked away together; they were going to Mr. Wentworth's. Mr. Brand still said nothing; but after they had passed into Mr. Wentworth's garden he stopped and looked back for some time at the little white house. Then, looking at his companion, with his head bent a little to one side and his eyes somewhat contracted, "Now I suppose that's what is called conversation," he said; "real conversation."

"It's what I call a very clever woman," said Acton, laughing.

"It is most interesting," Mr. Brand continued. "I only wish she would speak French; it would seem more in keeping. It must be quite the style that we have heard about, that we have read about—the style of conversation of Madame de Staël, of Madame Récamier."

Acton also looked at Madame Münster's residence among its hollyhocks and apple trees. "What I should like to know," he said, smiling, "is just what has brought Madame Récamier to live in that place!"

# CHAPTER V

Mr. Wentworth, with his cane and his gloves in his hand, went every afternoon to call upon his niece. A couple of hours later she came over to the great house to tea. She had let the proposal that she should regularly dine there fall to the ground; she was in the enjoyment of whatever satisfaction was to be derived from the spectacle of an old negress in a crimson turban shelling peas under the apple trees. Charlotte, who had provided the ancient negress, thought it must be a strange household, Eugenia having told her that Augustine managed everything, the ancient negress included—Augustine who was naturally devoid of all acquaintance with the expurgatory English tongue. By far the most immoral sentiment which I shall have occasion to attribute to Charlotte Wentworth was a certain emotion of disappointment at finding that, in spite of these irregular conditions, the domestic arrangements at the small house were apparently not—from Eugenia's peculiar point of view—strikingly offensive. The Baroness found it amusing to go to tea; she dressed as if for dinner. The tea-table offered an anomalous and picturesque repast; and on leaving it they all sat and talked in the large piazza, or wandered about the garden in the starlight, with their ears full of those sounds of strange insects which, though they are supposed to be, all over the world, a part of the magic of summer nights, seemed to the Baroness to have beneath these western skies an incomparable resonance.

Mr. Wentworth, though, as I say, he went punctiliously to call upon her, was not able to feel that he was getting used to his niece. It taxed his imagination to believe that she was really his half-sister's child. His sister was a figure of his early years; she had been only twenty when she went abroad, never to return, making in foreign parts a willful and undesirable marriage. His aunt, Mrs. Whiteside, who had taken her to Europe for the benefit of the tour, gave, on her return, so lamentable an account of Mr. Adolphus Young, to whom the headstrong girl had united her destiny, that it operated as a chill upon family feeling—especially in the case of the half-brothers. Catherine had done nothing subsequently to propitiate her family; she had not even written to them in a way that indicated a lucid appreciation of their suspended sympathy; so that it had become a tradition in Boston circles that the highest charity, as regards this young lady, was to think it well to forget her, and to abstain from conjecture as to the extent to which her aberrations were reproduced in her descendants. Over these young people—a vague report of their existence had come to his ears—Mr. Wentworth had not, in the course of years, allowed his imagination to hover. It had plenty of occupation nearer home, and though he had many cares upon his conscience the idea that he had been an unnatural uncle was, very properly, never among the number. Now that his nephew and niece had come before him, he perceived that they were the fruit of influences and circumstances very different from those under which his own familiar progeny had reached a vaguely-qualified maturity. He felt no provocation to say that these influences had been exerted for evil; but he was sometimes afraid that he should not be able to like his distinguished, delicate, lady-like niece. He was paralyzed and bewildered by her foreignness. She spoke, somehow, a different language. There was something strange in her words. He had a feeling that another man, in his place, would accommodate himself to her tone; would ask her questions and joke with her, reply to those pleasantries of her own which sometimes seemed startling as addressed to an uncle. But Mr. Wentworth could not do these things. He could not even bring himself to attempt to measure her position in the world. She was the wife of a foreign nobleman who desired to repudiate her. This had a singular sound, but the old man felt himself destitute of the materials for a judgment. It seemed to him that he ought to find them in his own experience, as a man of the world and an almost public character; but they were not there, and he was ashamed to confess to himself—much more to reveal to Eugenia by interrogations possibly too innocent—the unfurnished condition of this repository.

It appeared to him that he could get much nearer, as he would have said, to his nephew; though he was not sure that Felix was altogether safe. He was so bright and handsome and talkative that it was impossible not to think well of him; and yet it seemed as if there were something almost impudent, almost vicious—or as if there ought to be—in a young man being at once so joyous and so positive. It was to be observed that while Felix was not at all a serious young man there was somehow more of him—he had more weight and volume and resonance—than a number of young men who were distinctly serious. While Mr. Wentworth meditated upon this anomaly his nephew was admiring him unrestrictedly. He thought him a most delicate, generous, high-toned old gentleman, with a very handsome head, of the ascetic type, which he promised himself the profit of sketching. Felix was far from having made a secret of the fact that he wielded the paint-brush, and it was not his own fault if it failed to be generally understood that he was prepared to execute the most striking likenesses on the most reasonable terms. "He is an artist—my cousin is an artist," said Gertrude; and she offered this information to everyone who would receive it. She offered it to herself, as it were, by way of admonition and reminder; she repeated to herself at odd moments, in lonely places, that Felix was invested with this sacred character. Gertrude had never seen an artist before; she had only read about such people. They seemed to her a romantic and mysterious class, whose life was made up of those agreeable accidents that never happened to other persons. And it merely quickened her meditations on this point that Felix should declare, as he repeatedly did, that he was really not an artist. "I have never gone into the thing seriously," he said. "I have never studied; I have had no training. I do a little of everything, and nothing well. I am only an amateur."

It pleased Gertrude even more to think that he was an amateur than to think that he was an artist; the former word, to her fancy, had an even subtler connotation. She knew, however, that it was a word to use more soberly. Mr. Wentworth used it freely; for though he had not been exactly familiar with it, he found it convenient as a help toward classifying Felix, who, as a young man extremely clever and active and apparently respectable and yet not engaged in any recognized business, was an importunate anomaly. Of course the Baroness and her brother—she was always spoken of first—were a welcome topic of conversation between Mr. Wentworth and his daughters and their occasional visitors.

"And the young man, your nephew, what is his profession?" asked an old gentleman—Mr. Broderip, of Salem—who had been Mr. Wentworth's classmate at Harvard College in the year 1809, and who came into his office in Devonshire Street. (Mr. Wentworth, in his later years, used to go but three times a week to his office, where he had a large amount of highly confidential trust-business to transact.)

"Well, he's an amateur," said Felix's uncle, with folded hands, and with a certain satisfaction in being able to say it. And Mr. Broderip had gone back to Salem with a feeling that this was probably a "European" expression for a broker or a grain exporter.

"I should like to do your head, sir," said Felix to his uncle one evening, before them all—Mr. Brand and Robert Acton being also present. "I think I should make a very fine thing of it. It's an interesting head; it's very mediaeval."

Mr. Wentworth looked grave; he felt awkwardly, as if all the company had come in and found him standing before the looking-glass. "The Lord made it," he said. "I don't think it is for man to make it over again."

"Certainly the Lord made it," replied Felix, laughing, "and he made it very well. But life has been touching up the work. It is a very interesting type of head. It's delightfully wasted and emaciated. The complexion is wonderfully bleached." And Felix looked round at the circle, as if to call their attention to these interesting points. Mr. Wentworth grew visibly paler. "I should like to do you as an old prelate, an old cardinal, or the prior of an order."

"A prelate, a cardinal?" murmured Mr. Wentworth. "Do you refer to the Roman Catholic priesthood?"

"I mean an old ecclesiastic who should have led a very pure, abstinent life. Now I take it that has been the case with you, sir; one sees it in your face," Felix proceeded. "You have been very—a very moderate. Don't you think one always sees that in a man's face?"

"You see more in a man's face than I should think of looking for," said Mr. Wentworth coldly.

The Baroness rattled her fan, and gave her brilliant laugh. "It is a risk to look so close!" she exclaimed. "My uncle has some peccadilloes on his conscience." Mr. Wentworth looked at her, painfully at a loss; and in so far as the signs of a pure and abstinent life were visible in his face they were then probably peculiarly manifest. "You are a *beau vieillard*, dear uncle," said Madame Münster, smiling with her foreign eyes.

"I think you are paying me a compliment," said the old man.

"Surely, I am not the first woman that ever did so!" cried the Baroness.

"I think you are," said Mr. Wentworth gravely. And turning to Felix he added, in the same tone, "Please don't take my likeness. My children have my daguerreotype. That is quite satisfactory."

"I won't promise," said Felix, "not to work your head into something!"

Mr. Wentworth looked at him and then at all the others; then he got up and slowly walked away.

"Felix," said Gertrude, in the silence that followed, "I wish you would paint my portrait."

Charlotte wondered whether Gertrude was right in wishing this; and she looked at Mr. Brand as the most legitimate way of ascertaining. Whatever Gertrude did or said, Charlotte always looked at Mr. Brand. It was a standing pretext for looking at Mr. Brand—always, as Charlotte thought, in the interest of Gertrude's welfare. It is true that she felt a tremulous interest in Gertrude being right; for Charlotte, in her small, still way, was an heroic sister.

"We should be glad to have your portrait, Miss Gertrude," said Mr. Brand.

"I should be delighted to paint so charming a model," Felix declared.

"Do you think you are so lovely, my dear?" asked Lizzie Acton, with her little inoffensive pertness, biting off a knot in her knitting.

"It is not because I think I am beautiful," said Gertrude, looking all round. "I don't think I am beautiful, at all." She spoke with a sort of conscious deliberateness; and it seemed very strange to Charlotte to hear her discussing this question so publicly. "It is because I think it would be amusing to sit and be painted. I have always thought that."

"I am sorry you have not had better things to think about, my daughter," said Mr. Wentworth.

"You are very beautiful, cousin Gertrude," Felix declared.

"That's a compliment," said Gertrude. "I put all the compliments I receive into a little money-jug that has a slit in the side. I shake them up and down, and they rattle. There are not many yet—only two or three."

"No, it's not a compliment," Felix rejoined. "See; I am careful not to give it the form of a compliment. I didn't think you were beautiful at first. But you have come to seem so little by little."

"Take care, now, your jug doesn't burst!" exclaimed Lizzie.

"I think sitting for one's portrait is only one of the various forms of idleness," said Mr. Wentworth. "Their name is legion."

"My dear sir," cried Felix, "you can't be said to be idle when you are making a man work so!"

"One might be painted while one is asleep," suggested Mr. Brand, as a contribution to the discussion.

"Ah, do paint me while I am asleep," said Gertrude to Felix, smiling. And she closed her eyes a little. It had by this time become a matter of almost exciting anxiety to Charlotte what Gertrude would say or would do next.

She began to sit for her portrait on the following day—in the open air, on the north side of the piazza. "I wish you would tell me what you think of us—how we seem to you," she said to Felix, as he sat before his easel.

"You seem to me the best people in the world," said Felix.

"You say that," Gertrude resumed, "because it saves you the trouble of saying anything else."

The young man glanced at her over the top of his canvas. "What else should I say? It would certainly be a great deal of trouble to say anything different."

114

"Well," said Gertrude, "you have seen people before that you have liked, have you not?"

"Indeed I have, thank Heaven!"

"And they have been very different from us," Gertrude went on.

"That only proves," said Felix, "that there are a thousand different ways of being good company."

"Do you think us good company?" asked Gertrude.

"Company for a king!"

Gertrude was silent a moment; and then, "There must be a thousand different ways of being dreary," she said; "and sometimes I think we make use of them all."

Felix stood up quickly, holding up his hand. "If you could only keep that look on your face for half an hour—while I catch it!" he said. "It is uncommonly handsome."

"To look handsome for half an hour—that is a great deal to ask of me," she answered.

"It would be the portrait of a young woman who has taken some vow, some pledge, that she repents of," said Felix, "and who is thinking it over at leisure."

"I have taken no vow, no pledge," said Gertrude, very gravely; "I have nothing to repent of."

"My dear cousin, that was only a figure of speech. I am very sure that no one in your excellent family has anything to repent of."

"And yet we are always repenting!" Gertrude exclaimed. "That is what I mean by our being dreary. You know it perfectly well; you only pretend that you don't."

Felix gave a quick laugh. "The half hour is going on, and yet you are handsomer than ever. One must be careful what one says, you see."

"To me," said Gertrude, "you can say anything."

Felix looked at her, as an artist might, and painted for some time in silence.

"Yes, you seem to me different from your father and sister—from most of the people you have lived with," he observed.

"To say that one's self," Gertrude went on, "is like saying—by implication, at least—that one is better. I am not better; I am much worse. But they say themselves that I am different. It makes them unhappy."

"Since you accuse me of concealing my real impressions, I may admit that I think the tendency—among you generally—is to be made unhappy too easily."

"I wish you would tell that to my father," said Gertrude.

"It might make him more unhappy!" Felix exclaimed, laughing.

"It certainly would. I don't believe you have seen people like that."

"Ah, my dear cousin, how do you know what I have seen?" Felix demanded. "How can I tell you?"

"You might tell me a great many things, if you only would. You have seen people like yourself—people who are bright and gay and fond of amusement. We are not fond of amusement."

"Yes," said Felix, "I confess that rather strikes me. You don't seem to me to get all the pleasure out of life that you might. You don't seem to me to enjoy..... Do you mind my saying this?" he asked, pausing.

"Please go on," said the girl, earnestly.

"You seem to me very well placed for enjoying. You have money and liberty and what is called in Europe a 'position.' But you take a painful view of life, as one may say."

"One ought to think it bright and charming and delightful, eh?" asked Gertrude.

116

"I should say so—if one can. It is true it all depends upon that," Felix added.

"You know there is a great deal of misery in the world," said his model.

"I have seen a little of it," the young man rejoined. "But it was all over there—beyond the sea. I don't see any here. This is a paradise."

Gertrude said nothing; she sat looking at the dahlias and the currant-bushes in the garden, while Felix went on with his work. "To 'enjoy,'" she began at last, "to take life—not painfully, must one do something wrong?"

Felix gave his long, light laugh again. "Seriously, I think not. And for this reason, among others: you strike me as very capable of enjoying, if the chance were given you, and yet at the same time as incapable of wrong-doing."

"I am sure," said Gertrude, "that you are very wrong in telling a person that she is incapable of that. We are never nearer to evil than when we believe that."

"You are handsomer than ever," observed Felix, irrelevantly.

Gertrude had got used to hearing him say this. There was not so much excitement in it as at first. "What ought one to do?" she continued. "To give parties, to go to the theatre, to read novels, to keep late hours?"

"I don't think it's what one does or one doesn't do that promotes enjoyment," her companion answered. "It is the general way of looking at life."

"They look at it as a discipline—that's what they do here. I have often been told that."

"Well, that's very good. But there is another way," added Felix, smiling: "to look at it as an opportunity."

"An opportunity—yes," said Gertrude. "One would get more pleasure that way."

"I don't attempt to say anything better for it than that it has been my own way—and that is not saying much!" Felix had laid down his palette and brushes; he was leaning back, with his arms folded, to judge the effect of his work. "And you know," he said, "I am a very petty personage."

"You have a great deal of talent," said Gertrude.

"No—no," the young man rejoined, in a tone of cheerful impartiality, "I have not a great deal of talent. It is nothing at all remarkable. I assure you I should know if it were. I shall always be obscure. The world will never hear of me." Gertrude looked at him with a strange feeling. She was thinking of the great world which he knew and which she did not, and how full of brilliant talents it must be, since it could afford to make light of his abilities. "You needn't in general attach much importance to anything I tell you," he pursued; "but you may believe me when I say this,—that I am little better than a good-natured feather-head."

"A feather-head?" she repeated.

"I am a species of Bohemian."

"A Bohemian?" Gertrude had never heard this term before, save as a geographical denomination; and she quite failed to understand the figurative meaning which her companion appeared to attach to it. But it gave her pleasure.

Felix had pushed back his chair and risen to his feet; he slowly came toward her, smiling. "I am a sort of adventurer," he said, looking down at her.

She got up, meeting his smile. "An adventurer?" she repeated. "I should like to hear your adventures."

For an instant she believed that he was going to take her hand; but he dropped his own hands suddenly into the pockets of his painting-jacket. "There is no reason why you shouldn't," he said. "I have been an adventurer, but my adventures have been very innocent. They have all been happy ones; I don't think there are any I shouldn't tell. They were very pleasant and very pretty; I should like to go over them in memory. Sit down again, and I will begin," he added in a moment, with his naturally persuasive smile.

118

Gertrude sat down again on that day, and she sat down on several other days. Felix, while he plied his brush, told her a great many stories, and she listened with charmed avidity. Her eyes rested upon his lips; she was very serious; sometimes, from her air of wondering gravity, he thought she was displeased. But Felix never believed for more than a single moment in any displeasure of his own producing. This would have been fatuity if the optimism it expressed had not been much more a hope than a prejudice. It is beside the matter to say that he had a good conscience; for the best conscience is a sort of self-reproach, and this young man's brilliantly healthy nature spent itself in objective good intentions which were ignorant of any test save exactness in hitting their mark. He told Gertrude how he had walked over France and Italy with a painter's knapsack on his back, paying his way often by knocking off a flattering portrait of his host or hostess. He told her how he had played the violin in a little band of musicians—not of high celebrity—who traveled through foreign lands giving provincial concerts. He told her also how he had been a momentary ornament of a troupe of strolling actors, engaged in the arduous task of interpreting Shakespeare to French and German, Polish and Hungarian audiences.

While this periodical recital was going on, Gertrude lived in a fantastic world; she seemed to herself to be reading a romance that came out in daily numbers. She had known nothing so delightful since the perusal of *Nicholas Nickleby*. One afternoon she went to see her cousin, Mrs. Acton, Robert's mother, who was a great invalid, never leaving the house. She came back alone, on foot, across the fields—this being a short way which they often used. Felix had gone to Boston with her father, who desired to take the young man to call upon some of his friends, old gentlemen who remembered his mother—remembered her, but said nothing about her—and several of whom, with the gentle ladies their wives, had driven out from town to pay their respects at the little house among the apple trees, in vehicles which reminded the Baroness, who received her visitors with discriminating civility, of the large, light, rattling barouche in which she herself had made her journey to this neighborhood. The afternoon was waning; in the western sky the great picture of a New England sunset, painted in crimson and silver, was suspended from the zenith; and the stony pastures, as Gertrude traversed them, thinking intently to herself, were covered with a light, clear glow. At the open gate of one of the fields she saw from the distance a man's figure; he stood there as if he were waiting for her, and as she came nearer she recognized Mr. Brand. She had a feeling as of not having seen him for some time; she could not have said for how long, for it yet seemed to her that he had been very lately at the house.

"May I walk back with you?" he asked. And when she had said that he might if he wanted, he observed that he had seen her and recognized her half a mile away.

"You must have very good eyes," said Gertrude.

"Yes, I have very good eyes, Miss Gertrude," said Mr. Brand. She perceived that he meant something; but for a long time past Mr. Brand had constantly meant something, and she had almost got used to it. She felt, however, that what he meant had now a renewed power to disturb her, to perplex and agitate her. He walked beside her in silence for a moment, and then he added, "I have had no trouble in seeing that you are beginning to avoid me. But perhaps," he went on, "one needn't have had very good eyes to see that."

"I have not avoided you," said Gertrude, without looking at him.

"I think you have been unconscious that you were avoiding me," Mr. Brand replied. "You have not even known that I was there."

"Well, you are here now, Mr. Brand!" said Gertrude, with a little laugh. "I know that very well."

He made no rejoinder. He simply walked beside her slowly, as they were obliged to walk over the soft grass. Presently they came to another gate, which was closed. Mr. Brand laid his hand upon it, but he made no movement to open it; he stood and looked at his companion. "You are very much interested—very much absorbed," he said.

Gertrude glanced at him; she saw that he was pale and that he looked excited. She had never seen Mr. Brand excited before, and she felt that the spectacle, if fully carried out, would be impressive, almost painful. "Absorbed in what?" she asked. Then she looked away at the illuminated sky. She felt guilty and uncomfortable, and yet she was vexed with herself for feeling so. But Mr. Brand, as he stood there looking at her with his small, kind, persistent eyes, represented an immense body of half-obliterated obligations, that were rising again into a certain distinctness.

"You have new interests, new occupations," he went on. "I don't know that I can say that you have new duties. We have always old ones, Gertrude," he added.

"Please open the gate, Mr. Brand," she said; and she felt as if, in saying so, she were cowardly and petulant. But he opened the gate, and allowed her to pass; then he closed it behind himself. Before she had time to turn away he put out his hand and held her an instant by the wrist.

"I want to say something to you," he said.

"I know what you want to say," she answered. And she was on the point of adding, "And I know just how you will say it;" but these words she kept back.

"I love you, Gertrude," he said. "I love you very much; I love you more than ever."

He said the words just as she had known he would; she had heard them before. They had no charm for her; she had said to herself before that it was very strange. It was supposed to be delightful for a woman to listen to such words; but these seemed to her flat and mechanical. "I wish you would forget that," she declared.

"How can I—why should I?" he asked.

"I have made you no promise—given you no pledge," she said, looking at him, with her voice trembling a little.

"You have let me feel that I have an influence over you. You have opened your mind to me."

121

"I never opened my mind to you, Mr. Brand!" Gertrude cried, with some vehemence.

"Then you were not so frank as I thought—as we all thought."

"I don't see what anyone else had to do with it!" cried the girl.

"I mean your father and your sister. You know it makes them happy to think you will listen to me."

She gave a little laugh. "It doesn't make them happy," she said. "Nothing makes them happy. No one is happy here."

"I think your cousin is very happy—Mr. Young," rejoined Mr. Brand, in a soft, almost timid tone.

"So much the better for him!" And Gertrude gave her little laugh again.

The young man looked at her a moment. "You are very much changed," he said.

"I am glad to hear it," Gertrude declared.

"I am not. I have known you a long time, and I have loved you as you were."

"I am much obliged to you," said Gertrude. "I must be going home."

He on his side, gave a little laugh.

"You certainly do avoid me—you see!"

"Avoid me, then," said the girl.

He looked at her again; and then, very gently, "No I will not avoid you," he replied; "but I will leave you, for the present, to yourself. I think you will remember—after a while—some of the things you have forgotten. I think you will come back to me; I have great faith in that."

This time his voice was very touching; there was a strong, reproachful force in what he said, and Gertrude could answer nothing. He turned away and stood there, leaning his elbows on the gate and looking at the beautiful sunset. Gertrude left him and took her way home again; but when she reached the middle of the next field she suddenly burst into tears. Her tears seemed to her to have been a long time gathering, and for some moments it was a kind of glee to shed them. But they presently passed away. There was something a little hard about Gertrude; and she never wept again.

# CHAPTER VI

Going of an afternoon to call upon his niece, Mr. Wentworth more than once found Robert Acton sitting in her little drawing-room. This was in no degree, to Mr. Wentworth, a perturbing fact, for he had no sense of competing with his young kinsman for Eugenia's good graces. Madame Münster's uncle had the highest opinion of Robert Acton, who, indeed, in the family at large, was the object of a great deal of undemonstrative appreciation. They were all proud of him, in so far as the charge of being proud may be brought against people who were, habitually, distinctly guiltless of the misdemeanor known as "taking credit." They never boasted of Robert Acton, nor indulged in vainglorious reference to him; they never quoted the clever things he had said, nor mentioned the generous things he had done. But a sort of frigidly-tender faith in his unlimited goodness was a part of their personal sense of right; and there can, perhaps, be no better proof of the high esteem in which he was held than the fact that no explicit judgment was ever passed upon his actions. He was no more praised than he was blamed; but he was tacitly felt to be an ornament to his circle. He was the man of the world of the family. He had been to China and brought home a collection of curiosities; he had made a fortune—or rather he had quintupled a fortune already considerable; he was distinguished by that combination of celibacy, "property," and good humor which appeals to even the most subdued imaginations; and it was taken for granted that he would presently place these advantages at the disposal of some well-regulated young woman of his own "set." Mr. Wentworth was not a man to admit to himself that—his paternal duties apart—he liked any individual much better than all other individuals; but he thought Robert Acton extremely judicious; and this was perhaps as near an approach as he was capable of to the eagerness of preference, which his temperament repudiated as it would have disengaged itself from something slightly unchaste. Acton was, in fact, very judicious—and something more beside; and indeed it must be claimed for Mr. Wentworth that in the more illicit parts of his preference there hovered the vague adumbration of a belief that his cousin's final merit was a certain enviable capacity for whistling, rather gallantly, at the sanctions of mere judgment—for showing a larger courage, a finer quality of pluck, than common occasion demanded. Mr. Wentworth would never have risked the intimation that Acton was made, in the smallest degree, of the stuff of a hero; but this is small blame to him, for Robert would certainly never have risked it himself. Acton certainly exercised great discretion in all things—beginning with his estimate of himself. He knew that he was by no means so much of a man of the world as he was supposed to be in local circles; but it must be added that he knew also that his natural shrewdness had a reach of which he had never quite given local circles the measure. He was addicted to taking the humorous view of things, and he had discovered that even in the narrowest circles such a disposition may find frequent opportunities. Such opportunities had formed for some time—that is, since his return from China, a year and a half before—the most active element in this gentleman's life, which had just now a rather indolent air. He was perfectly willing to get married. He was very fond of books, and he had a handsome library; that is, his books were much more numerous than Mr. Wentworth's. He was also very fond of pictures; but it must be confessed, in the fierce light of contemporary criticism, that his walls were adorned with several rather abortive masterpieces. He had got his learning—and there was more of it than commonly appeared—at Harvard College; and he took a pleasure in old associations, which made it a part of his daily contentment to live so near this institution that he often passed it in driving to Boston. He was extremely interested in the Baroness Münster.

She was very frank with him; or at least she intended to be. "I am sure you find it very strange that I should have settled down in this out-of-the-way part of the world!" she said to him three or four weeks after she had installed herself. "I am certain you are wondering about my motives. They are very pure." The Baroness by this time was an old inhabitant; the best society in Boston had called upon her, and Clifford Wentworth had taken her several times to drive in his buggy.

Robert Acton was seated near her, playing with a fan; there were always several fans lying about her drawing-room, with long ribbons of different colors attached to them, and Acton was always playing with one. "No, I don't find it at all strange," he said slowly, smiling. "That a clever woman should turn up in Boston, or its suburbs—that does not require so much explanation. Boston is a very nice place."

"If you wish to make me contradict you," said the Baroness, "*vous vous y prenez mal*. In certain moods there is nothing I am not capable of agreeing to. Boston is a paradise, and we are in the suburbs of Paradise."

"Just now I am not at all in the suburbs; I am in the place itself," rejoined Acton, who was lounging a little in his chair. He was, however, not always lounging; and when he was he was not quite so relaxed as he pretended. To a certain extent, he sought refuge from shyness in this appearance of relaxation; and like many persons in the same circumstances he somewhat exaggerated the appearance. Beyond this, the air of being much at his ease was a cover for vigilant observation. He was more than interested in this clever woman, who, whatever he might say, was clever not at all after the Boston fashion; she plunged him into a kind of excitement, held him in vague suspense. He was obliged to admit to himself that he had never yet seen a woman just like this—not even in China. He was ashamed, for inscrutable reasons, of the vivacity of his emotion, and he carried it off, superficially, by taking, still superficially, the humorous view of Madame Münster. It was not at all true that he thought it very natural of her to have made this pious pilgrimage. It might have been said of him in advance that he was too good a Bostonian to regard in the light of an eccentricity the desire of even the remotest alien to visit the New England metropolis. This was an impulse for which, surely, no apology was needed; and Madame Münster was the fortunate possessor of several New England cousins. In fact, however, Madame Münster struck him as out of keeping with her little circle; she was at the best a very agreeable, a gracefully mystifying anomaly. He knew very well that it would not do to address these reflections too crudely to Mr. Wentworth; he would never have remarked to the old gentleman that he wondered what the Baroness was up to. And indeed he had no great desire to share his vague mistrust with anyone. There was a personal pleasure in it; the greatest pleasure he had known at least since he had come from China. He would keep the Baroness, for better or worse, to himself; he had a feeling that he deserved to enjoy a monopoly of her, for he was certainly the person who had most adequately gauged her capacity for social intercourse. Before long it became apparent to him that the Baroness was disposed to lay no tax upon such a monopoly.

One day (he was sitting there again and playing with a fan) she asked him to apologize, should the occasion present itself, to certain people in Boston for her not having returned their calls. "There are half a dozen places," she said; "a formidable list. Charlotte Wentworth has written it out for me, in a terrifically distinct hand. There is no ambiguity on the subject; I know perfectly where I must go. Mr. Wentworth informs me that the carriage is always at my disposal, and Charlotte offers to go with me, in a pair of tight gloves and a very stiff petticoat. And yet for three days I have been putting it off. They must think me horribly vicious."

"You ask me to apologize," said Acton, "but you don't tell me what excuse I can offer."

"That is more," the Baroness declared, "than I am held to. It would be like my asking you to buy me a bouquet and giving you the money. I have no reason except that—somehow—it's too violent an effort. It is not inspiring. Wouldn't that serve as an excuse, in Boston? I am told they are very sincere; they don't tell fibs. And then Felix ought to go with me, and he is never in readiness. I don't see him. He is always roaming about the fields and sketching old barns, or taking ten-mile walks, or painting someone's portrait, or rowing on the pond, or flirting with Gertrude Wentworth."

"I should think it would amuse you to go and see a few people," said Acton. "You are having a very quiet time of it here. It's a dull life for you."

"Ah, the quiet,—the quiet!" the Baroness exclaimed. "That's what I like. It's rest. That's what I came here for. Amusement? I have had amusement. And as for seeing people—I have already seen a great many in my life. If it didn't sound ungracious I should say that I wish very humbly your people here would leave me alone!"

Acton looked at her a moment, and she looked at him. She was a woman who took being looked at remarkably well. "So you have come here for rest?" he asked.

"So I may say. I came for many of those reasons that are no reasons—don't you know?—and yet that are really the best: to come away, to change, to break with everything. When once one comes away one must arrive somewhere, and I asked myself why I shouldn't arrive here."

"You certainly had time on the way!" said Acton, laughing.

Madame Münster looked at him again; and then, smiling: "And I have certainly had time, since I got here, to ask myself why I came. However, I never ask myself idle questions. Here I am, and it seems to me you ought only to thank me."

"When you go away you will see the difficulties I shall put in your path."

"You mean to put difficulties in my path?" she asked, rearranging the rosebud in her corsage.

"The greatest of all—that of having been so agreeable——"

"That I shall be unable to depart? Don't be too sure. I have left some very agreeable people over there."

"Ah," said Acton, "but it was to come here, where I am!"

"I didn't know of your existence. Excuse me for saying anything so rude; but, honestly speaking, I did not. No," the Baroness pursued, "it was precisely not to see you—such people as you—that I came."

"Such people as me?" cried Acton.

"I had a sort of longing to come into those natural relations which I knew I should find here. Over there I had only, as I may say, artificial relations. Don't you see the difference?"

"The difference tells against me," said Acton. "I suppose I am an artificial relation."

"Conventional," declared the Baroness; "very conventional."

"Well, there is one way in which the relation of a lady and a gentleman may always become natural," said Acton.

"You mean by their becoming lovers? That may be natural or not. And at any rate," rejoined Eugenia, *"nous n'en sommes pas là!"*

They were not, as yet; but a little later, when she began to go with him to drive, it might almost have seemed that they were. He came for her several times, alone, in his high "wagon," drawn by a pair of charming light-limbed horses. It was different, her having gone with Clifford Wentworth, who was her cousin, and so much younger. It was not to be imagined that she should have a flirtation with Clifford, who was a mere shame-faced boy, and whom a large section of Boston society supposed to be "engaged" to Lizzie Acton. Not, indeed, that it was to be conceived that the Baroness was a possible party to any flirtation whatever; for she was undoubtedly a married lady. It was generally known that her matrimonial condition was of the "morganatic" order; but in its natural aversion to suppose that this meant anything less than absolute wedlock, the conscience of the community took refuge in the belief that it implied something even more.

Acton wished her to think highly of American scenery, and he drove her to great distances, picking out the prettiest roads and the largest points of view. If we are good when we are contented, Eugenia's virtues should now certainly have been uppermost; for she found a charm in the rapid movement through a wild country, and in a companion who from time to time made the vehicle dip, with a motion like a swallow's flight, over roads of primitive construction, and who, as she felt, would do a great many things that she might ask him. Sometimes, for a couple of hours together, there were almost no houses; there were nothing but woods and rivers and lakes and horizons adorned with bright-looking mountains. It seemed to the Baroness very wild, as I have said, and lovely; but the impression added something to that sense of the enlargement of opportunity which had been born of her arrival in the New World.

One day—it was late in the afternoon—Acton pulled up his horses on the crest of a hill which commanded a beautiful prospect. He let them stand a long time to rest, while he sat there and talked with Madame Münster. The prospect was beautiful in spite of there being nothing human within sight. There was a wilderness of woods, and the gleam of a distant river, and a glimpse of half the hill-tops in Massachusetts. The road had a wide, grassy margin, on the further side of which there flowed a deep, clear brook; there were wild flowers in the grass, and beside the brook lay the trunk of a fallen tree. Acton waited a while; at last a rustic wayfarer came trudging along the road. Acton asked him to hold the horses—a service he consented to render, as a friendly turn to a fellow-citizen. Then he invited the Baroness to descend, and the two wandered away, across the grass, and sat down on the log beside the brook.

"I imagine it doesn't remind you of Silberstadt," said Acton. It was the first time that he had mentioned Silberstadt to her, for particular reasons. He knew she had a husband there, and this was disagreeable to him; and, furthermore, it had been repeated to him that this husband wished to put her away—a state of affairs to which even indirect reference was to be deprecated. It was true, nevertheless, that the Baroness herself had often alluded to Silberstadt; and Acton had often wondered why her husband wished to get rid of her. It was a curious position for a lady—this being known as a repudiated wife; and it is worthy of observation that the Baroness carried it off with exceeding grace and dignity. She had made it felt, from the first, that there were two sides to the question, and that her own side, when she should choose to present it, would be replete with touching interest.

"It does not remind me of the town, of course," she said, "of the sculptured gables and the Gothic churches, of the wonderful Schloss, with its moat and its clustering towers. But it has a little look of some other parts of the principality. One might fancy one's self among those grand old German forests, those legendary mountains; the sort of country one sees from the windows at Schreckenstein."

"What is Schreckenstein?" asked Acton.

130

"It is a great castle,—the summer residence of the Reigning Prince."

"Have you ever lived there?"

"I have stayed there," said the Baroness. Acton was silent; he looked a while at the uncastled landscape before him. "It is the first time you have ever asked me about Silberstadt," she said. "I should think you would want to know about my marriage; it must seem to you very strange."

Acton looked at her a moment. "Now you wouldn't like me to say that!"

"You Americans have such odd ways!" the Baroness declared. "You never ask anything outright; there seem to be so many things you can't talk about."

"We Americans are very polite," said Acton, whose national consciousness had been complicated by a residence in foreign lands, and who yet disliked to hear Americans abused. "We don't like to tread upon people's toes," he said. "But I should like very much to hear about your marriage. Now tell me how it came about."

"The Prince fell in love with me," replied the Baroness simply. "He pressed his suit very hard. At first he didn't wish me to marry him; on the contrary. But on that basis I refused to listen to him. So he offered me marriage—in so far as he might. I was young, and I confess I was rather flattered. But if it were to be done again now, I certainly should not accept him."

"How long ago was this?" asked Acton.

"Oh—several years," said Eugenia. "You should never ask a woman for dates."

"Why, I should think that when a woman was relating history " Acton answered. "And now he wants to break it off?"

"They want him to make a political marriage. It is his brother's idea. His brother is very clever."

"They must be a precious pair!" cried Robert Acton.

The Baroness gave a little philosophic shrug. "*Que voulez-vous?* They are princes. They think they are treating me very well. Silberstadt is a perfectly despotic little state, and the Reigning Prince may annul the marriage by a stroke of his pen. But he has promised me, nevertheless, not to do so without my formal consent."

"And this you have refused?"

"Hitherto. It is an indignity, and I have wished at least to make it difficult for them. But I have a little document in my writing-desk which I have only to sign and send back to the Prince."

"Then it will be all over?"

The Baroness lifted her hand, and dropped it again. "Of course I shall keep my title; at least, I shall be at liberty to keep it if I choose. And I suppose I shall keep it. One must have a name. And I shall keep my pension. It is very small—it is wretchedly small; but it is what I live on."

"And you have only to sign that paper?" Acton asked.

The Baroness looked at him a moment. "Do you urge it?"

He got up slowly, and stood with his hands in his pockets. "What do you gain by not doing it?"

"I am supposed to gain this advantage—that if I delay, or temporize, the Prince may come back to me, may make a stand against his brother. He is very fond of me, and his brother has pushed him only little by little."

"If he were to come back to you," said Acton, "would you—would you take him back?"

The Baroness met his eyes; she colored just a little. Then she rose. "I should have the satisfaction of saying, 'Now it is my turn. I break with your Serene Highness!'"

They began to walk toward the carriage. "Well," said Robert Acton, "it's a curious story! How did you make his acquaintance?"

"I was staying with an old lady—an old Countess—in Dresden. She had been a friend of my father's. My father was dead; I was very much alone. My brother was wandering about the world in a theatrical troupe."

"Your brother ought to have stayed with you," Acton observed, "and kept you from putting your trust in princes."

The Baroness was silent a moment, and then, "He did what he could," she said. "He sent me money. The old Countess encouraged the Prince; she was even pressing. It seems to me," Madame Münster added, gently, "that—under the circumstances—I behaved very well."

Acton glanced at her, and made the observation—he had made it before—that a woman looks the prettier for having unfolded her wrongs or her sufferings. "Well," he reflected, audibly, "I should like to see you send his Serene Highness—somewhere!"

Madame Münster stooped and plucked a daisy from the grass. "And not sign my renunciation?"

"Well, I don't know—I don't know," said Acton.

"In one case I should have my revenge; in another case I should have my liberty."

Acton gave a little laugh as he helped her into the carriage. "At any rate," he said, "take good care of that paper."

A couple of days afterward he asked her to come and see his house. The visit had already been proposed, but it had been put off in consequence of his mother's illness. She was a constant invalid, and she had passed these recent years, very patiently, in a great flowered arm-chair at her bedroom window. Lately, for some days, she had been unable to see anyone; but now she was better, and she sent the Baroness a very civil message. Acton had wished their visitor to come to dinner; but Madame Münster preferred to begin with a simple call. She had reflected that if she should go to dinner Mr. Wentworth and his daughters would also be asked, and it had seemed to her that the peculiar character of the occasion would be best preserved in a *tête-à-tête* with her host. Why the occasion should have a peculiar character she explained to no one. As far as anyone could see, it was simply very pleasant. Acton came for her and drove her to his door, an operation which was rapidly performed. His house the Baroness mentally pronounced a very good one; more articulately, she declared that it was enchanting. It was large and square and painted brown; it stood in a well-kept shrubbery, and was approached, from the gate, by a short drive. It was, moreover, a much more modern dwelling than Mr. Wentworth's, and was more redundantly upholstered and expensively ornamented. The Baroness perceived that her entertainer had analyzed material comfort to a sufficiently fine point. And then he possessed the most delightful *chinoiseries*—trophies of his sojourn in the Celestial Empire: pagodas of ebony and cabinets of ivory; sculptured monsters, grinning and leering on chimney-pieces, in front of beautifully figured hand-screens; porcelain dinner-sets, gleaming behind the glass doors of mahogany buffets; large screens, in corners, covered with tense silk and embroidered with mandarins and dragons. These things were scattered all over the house, and they gave Eugenia a pretext for a complete domiciliary visit. She liked it, she enjoyed it; she thought it a very nice place. It had a mixture of the homely and the liberal, and though it was almost a museum, the large, little-used rooms were as fresh and clean as a well-kept dairy. Lizzie Acton told her that she dusted all the pagodas and other curiosities every day with her own hands; and the Baroness answered that she was evidently a household fairy. Lizzie had not at all the look of a young lady who dusted things; she wore such pretty dresses and had such delicate fingers that it was difficult to imagine her immersed in sordid cares. She came to meet Madame Münster on her arrival, but she said nothing, or almost nothing, and the Baroness again reflected—she had had occasion to do so before—that American girls had no manners. She disliked this little American girl, and she was quite prepared to learn that she had failed to commend herself to Miss Acton. Lizzie struck her as positive and explicit almost to pertness; and the idea of her combining the apparent incongruities of a taste for housework and the wearing of fresh, Parisian-looking dresses suggested the possession of a dangerous energy. It was a source of irritation to the Baroness that in this country it should seem to matter whether a little girl were a trifle less or a trifle more of a nonentity;

for Eugenia had hitherto been conscious of no moral pressure as regards the appreciation of diminutive virgins. It was perhaps an indication of Lizzie's pertness that she very soon retired and left the Baroness on her brother's hands. Acton talked a great deal about his *chinoiseries*; he knew a good deal about porcelain and bric-à-brac. The Baroness, in her progress through the house, made, as it were, a great many stations. She sat down everywhere, confessed to being a little tired, and asked about the various objects with a curious mixture of alertness and inattention. If there had been anyone to say it to she would have declared that she was positively in love with her host; but she could hardly make this declaration—even in the strictest confidence—to Acton himself. It gave her, nevertheless, a pleasure that had some of the charm of unwontedness to feel, with that admirable keenness with which she was capable of feeling things, that he had a disposition without any edges; that even his humorous irony always expanded toward the point. One's impression of his honesty was almost like carrying a bunch of flowers; the perfume was most agreeable, but they were occasionally an inconvenience. One could trust him, at any rate, round all the corners of the world; and, withal, he was not absolutely simple, which would have been excess; he was only relatively simple, which was quite enough for the Baroness.

Lizzie reappeared to say that her mother would now be happy to receive Madame Münster; and the Baroness followed her to Mrs. Acton's apartment. Eugenia reflected, as she went, that it was not the affectation of impertinence that made her dislike this young lady, for on that ground she could easily have beaten her. It was not an aspiration on the girl's part to rivalry, but a kind of laughing, childishly-mocking indifference to the results of comparison. Mrs. Acton was an emaciated, sweet-faced woman of five and fifty, sitting with pillows behind her, and looking out on a clump of hemlocks. She was very modest, very timid, and very ill; she made Eugenia feel grateful that she herself was not like that—neither so ill, nor, possibly, so modest. On a chair, beside her, lay a volume of Emerson's Essays. It was a great occasion for poor Mrs. Acton, in her helpless condition, to be confronted with a clever foreign lady, who had more manner than any lady—any dozen ladies—that she had ever seen.

"I have heard a great deal about you," she said, softly, to the Baroness.

"From your son, eh?" Eugenia asked. "He has talked to me immensely of you. Oh, he talks of you as you would like," the Baroness declared; "as such a son *must* talk of such a mother!"

Mrs. Acton sat gazing; this was part of Madame Münster's "manner." But Robert Acton was gazing too, in vivid consciousness that he had barely mentioned his mother to their brilliant guest. He never talked of this still maternal presence,—a presence refined to such delicacy that it had almost resolved itself, with him, simply into the subjective emotion of gratitude. And Acton rarely talked of his emotions. The Baroness turned her smile toward him, and she instantly felt that she had been observed to be fibbing. She had struck a false note. But who were these people to whom such fibbing was not pleasing? If they were annoyed, the Baroness was equally so; and after the exchange of a few civil inquiries and low-voiced responses she took leave of Mrs. Acton. She begged Robert not to come home with her; she would get into the carriage alone; she preferred that. This was imperious, and she thought he looked disappointed. While she stood before the door with him—the carriage was turning in the gravel-walk—this thought restored her serenity.

When she had given him her hand in farewell she looked at him a moment. "I have almost decided to dispatch that paper," she said.

He knew that she alluded to the document that she had called her renunciation; and he assisted her into the carriage without saying anything. But just before the vehicle began to move he said, "Well, when you have in fact dispatched it, I hope you will let me know!"

# CHAPTER VII

Felix Young finished Gertrude's portrait, and he afterwards transferred to canvas the features of many members of that circle of which it may be said that he had become for the time the pivot and the centre. I am afraid it must be confessed that he was a decidedly flattering painter, and that he imparted to his models a romantic grace which seemed easily and cheaply acquired by the payment of a hundred dollars to a young man who made "sitting" so entertaining. For Felix was paid for his pictures, making, as he did, no secret of the fact that in guiding his steps to the Western world affectionate curiosity had gone hand in hand with a desire to better his condition. He took his uncle's portrait quite as if Mr. Wentworth had never averted himself from the experiment; and as he compassed his end only by the exercise of gentle violence, it is but fair to add that he allowed the old man to give him nothing but his time. He passed his arm into Mr. Wentworth's one summer morning—very few arms indeed had ever passed into Mr. Wentworth's—and led him across the garden and along the road into the studio which he had extemporized in the little house among the apple trees. The grave gentleman felt himself more and more fascinated by his clever nephew, whose fresh, demonstrative youth seemed a compendium of experiences so strangely numerous. It appeared to him that Felix must know a great deal; he would like to learn what he thought about some of those things as regards which his own conversation had always been formal, but his knowledge vague. Felix had a confident, gayly trenchant way of judging human actions which Mr. Wentworth grew little by little to envy; it seemed like criticism made easy. Forming an opinion—say on a person's conduct—was, with Mr. Wentworth, a good deal like fumbling in a lock with a key chosen at hazard. He seemed to himself to go about the world with a big bunch of these ineffectual instruments at his girdle. His nephew, on the other hand, with a single turn of the wrist, opened any door as adroitly as a horse-thief. He felt obliged to keep up the convention that an uncle is always wiser than a nephew, even if he could keep it up no otherwise than by listening in serious silence to Felix's quick, light, constant discourse.

But there came a day when he lapsed from consistency and almost asked his nephew's advice.

"Have you ever entertained the idea of settling in the United States?" he asked one morning, while Felix brilliantly plied his brush.

"My dear uncle," said Felix, "excuse me if your question makes me smile a little. To begin with, I have never entertained an idea. Ideas often entertain *me*; but I am afraid I have never seriously made a plan. I know what you are going to say; or rather, I know what you think, for I don't think you will say it—that this is very frivolous and loose-minded on my part. So it is; but I am made like that; I take things as they come, and somehow there is always some new thing to follow the last. In the second place, I should never propose to *settle*. I can't settle, my dear uncle; I'm not a settler. I know that is what strangers are supposed to do here; they always settle. But I haven't—to answer your question—entertained that idea."

"You intend to return to Europe and resume your irregular manner of life?" Mr. Wentworth inquired.

"I can't say I intend. But it's very likely I shall go back to Europe. After all, I am a European. I feel that, you know. It will depend a good deal upon my sister. She's even more of a European than I; here, you know, she's a picture out of her setting. And as for 'resuming,' dear uncle, I really have never given up my irregular manner of life. What, for me, could be more irregular than this?"

"Than what?" asked Mr. Wentworth, with his pale gravity.

"Well, than everything! Living in the midst of you, this way; this charming, quiet, serious family life; fraternizing with Charlotte and Gertrude; calling upon twenty young ladies and going out to walk with them; sitting with you in the evening on the piazza and listening to the crickets, and going to bed at ten o'clock."

"Your description is very animated," said Mr. Wentworth; "but I see nothing improper in what you describe."

"Neither do I, dear uncle. It is extremely delightful; I shouldn't like it if it were improper. I assure you I don't like improper things; though I dare say you think I do," Felix went on, painting away.

"I have never accused you of that."

"Pray don't," said Felix, "because, you see, at bottom I am a terrible Philistine."

"A Philistine?" repeated Mr. Wentworth.

"I mean, as one may say, a plain, God-fearing man." Mr. Wentworth looked at him reservedly, like a mystified sage, and Felix continued, "I trust I shall enjoy a venerable and venerated old age. I mean to live long. I can hardly call that a plan, perhaps; but it's a keen desire—a rosy vision. I shall be a lively, perhaps even a frivolous old man!"

"It is natural," said his uncle, sententiously, "that one should desire to prolong an agreeable life. We have perhaps a selfish indisposition to bring our pleasure to a close. But I presume," he added, "that you expect to marry."

"That too, dear uncle, is a hope, a desire, a vision," said Felix. It occurred to him for an instant that this was possibly a preface to the offer of the hand of one of Mr. Wentworth's admirable daughters. But in the name of decent modesty and a proper sense of the hard realities of this world, Felix banished the thought. His uncle was the incarnation of benevolence, certainly; but from that to accepting—much more postulating—the idea of a union between a young lady with a dowry presumptively brilliant and a penniless artist with no prospect of fame, there was a very long way. Felix had lately become conscious of a luxurious preference for the society—if possible unshared with others—of Gertrude Wentworth; but he had relegated this young lady, for the moment, to the coldly brilliant category of unattainable possessions. She was not the first woman for whom he had entertained an unpractical admiration. He had been in love with duchesses and countesses, and he had made, once or twice, a perilously near approach to cynicism in declaring that the disinterestedness of women had been overrated. On the whole, he had tempered audacity with modesty; and it is but fair to him now to say explicitly that he would have been incapable of taking advantage of his present large allowance of familiarity to make love to the younger of his handsome cousins. Felix had grown up among traditions in the light of which such a proceeding looked like a grievous breach of hospitality. I have said that he was always happy, and it may be counted among the present sources of his happiness that he had as regards this matter of his relations with Gertrude a deliciously good conscience. His own deportment seemed to him suffused with the beauty of virtue—a form of beauty that he admired with the same vivacity with which he admired all other forms.

"I think that if you marry," said Mr. Wentworth presently, "it will conduce to your happiness."

"*Sicurissimo!*" Felix exclaimed; and then, arresting his brush, he looked at his uncle with a smile. "There is something I feel tempted to say to you. May I risk it?"

Mr. Wentworth drew himself up a little. "I am very safe; I don't repeat things." But he hoped Felix would not risk too much.

Felix was laughing at his answer.

"It's odd to hear you telling me how to be happy. I don't think you know yourself, dear uncle. Now, does that sound brutal?"

The old man was silent a moment, and then, with a dry dignity that suddenly touched his nephew: "We may sometimes point out a road we are unable to follow."

"Ah, don't tell me you have had any sorrows," Felix rejoined. "I didn't suppose it, and I didn't mean to allude to them. I simply meant that you all don't amuse yourselves."

"Amuse ourselves? We are not children."

"Precisely not! You have reached the proper age. I was saying that the other day to Gertrude," Felix added. "I hope it was not indiscreet."

"If it was," said Mr. Wentworth, with a keener irony than Felix would have thought him capable of, "it was but your way of amusing yourself. I am afraid you have never had a trouble."

"Oh, yes, I have!" Felix declared, with some spirit; "before I knew better. But you don't catch me at it again."

Mr. Wentworth maintained for a while a silence more expressive than a deep-drawn sigh. "You have no children," he said at last.

"Don't tell me," Felix exclaimed, "that your charming young people are a source of grief to you!"

"I don't speak of Charlotte." And then, after a pause, Mr. Wentworth continued, "I don't speak of Gertrude. But I feel considerable anxiety about Clifford. I will tell you another time."

The next time he gave Felix a sitting his nephew reminded him that he had taken him into his confidence. "How is Clifford today?" Felix asked. "He has always seemed to me a young man of remarkable discretion. Indeed, he is only too discreet; he seems on his guard against me—as if he thought me rather light company. The other day he told his sister—Gertrude repeated it to me—that I was always laughing at him. If I laugh it is simply from the impulse to try and inspire him with confidence. That is the only way I have."

"Clifford's situation is no laughing matter," said Mr. Wentworth. "It is very peculiar, as I suppose you have guessed."

"Ah, you mean his love affair with his cousin?"

Mr. Wentworth stared, blushing a little. "I mean his absence from college. He has been suspended. We have decided not to speak of it unless we are asked."

"Suspended?" Felix repeated.

"He has been requested by the Harvard authorities to absent himself for six months. Meanwhile he is studying with Mr. Brand. We think Mr. Brand will help him; at least we hope so."

"What befell him at college?" Felix asked. "He was too fond of pleasure? Mr. Brand certainly will not teach him any of those secrets!"

"He was too fond of something of which he should not have been fond. I suppose it is considered a pleasure."

Felix gave his light laugh. "My dear uncle, is there any doubt about its being a pleasure? *C'est de son âge*, as they say in France."

"I should have said rather it was a vice of later life—of disappointed old age."

Felix glanced at his uncle, with his lifted eyebrows, and then, "Of what are you speaking?" he demanded, smiling.

"Of the situation in which Clifford was found."

"Ah, he was found—he was caught?"

"Necessarily, he was caught. He couldn't walk; he staggered."

"Oh," said Felix, "he drinks! I rather suspected that, from something I observed the first day I came here. I quite agree with you that it is a low taste. It's not a vice for a gentleman. He ought to give it up."

"We hope for a good deal from Mr. Brand's influence," Mr. Wentworth went on. "He has talked to him from the first. And he never touches anything himself."

"I will talk to him—I will talk to him!" Felix declared, gayly.

"What will you say to him?" asked his uncle, with some apprehension.

Felix for some moments answered nothing. "Do you mean to marry him to his cousin?" he asked at last.

"Marry him?" echoed Mr. Wentworth. "I shouldn't think his cousin would want to marry him."

"You have no understanding, then, with Mrs. Acton?"

Mr. Wentworth stared, almost blankly. "I have never discussed such subjects with her."

"I should think it might be time," said Felix. "Lizzie Acton is admirably pretty, and if Clifford is dangerous...."

"They are not engaged," said Mr. Wentworth. "I have no reason to suppose they are engaged."

"*Par exemple!*" cried Felix. "A clandestine engagement? Trust me, Clifford, as I say, is a charming boy. He is incapable of that. Lizzie Acton, then, would not be jealous of another woman."

"I certainly hope not," said the old man, with a vague sense of jealousy being an even lower vice than a love of liquor.

"The best thing for Clifford, then," Felix propounded, "is to become interested in some clever, charming woman." And he paused in his painting, and, with his elbows on his knees, looked with bright communicativeness at his uncle. "You see, I believe greatly in the influence of women. Living with women helps to make a man a gentleman. It is very true Clifford has his sisters, who are so charming. But there should be a different sentiment in play from the fraternal, you know. He has Lizzie Acton; but she, perhaps, is rather immature."

"I suspect Lizzie has talked to him, reasoned with him," said Mr. Wentworth.

"On the impropriety of getting tipsy—on the beauty of temperance? That is dreary work for a pretty young girl. No," Felix continued; "Clifford ought to frequent some agreeable woman, who, without ever mentioning such unsavory subjects, would give him a sense of its being very ridiculous to be fuddled. If he could fall in love with her a little, so much the better. The thing would operate as a cure."

"Well, now, what lady should you suggest?" asked Mr. Wentworth.

"There is a clever woman under your hand. My sister."

143

"Your sister—under my hand?" Mr. Wentworth repeated.

"Say a word to Clifford. Tell him to be bold. He is well disposed already; he has invited her two or three times to drive. But I don't think he comes to see her. Give him a hint to come—to come often. He will sit there of an afternoon, and they will talk. It will do him good."

Mr. Wentworth meditated. "You think she will exercise a helpful influence?"

"She will exercise a civilizing—I may call it a sobering—influence. A charming, clever, witty woman always does—especially if she is a little of a coquette. My dear uncle, the society of such women has been half my education. If Clifford is suspended, as you say, from college, let Eugenia be his preceptress."

Mr. Wentworth continued thoughtful. "You think Eugenia is a coquette?" he asked.

"What pretty woman is not?" Felix demanded in turn. But this, for Mr. Wentworth, could at the best have been no answer, for he did not think his niece pretty. "With Clifford," the young man pursued, "Eugenia will simply be enough of a coquette to be a little ironical. That's what he needs. So you recommend him to be nice with her, you know. The suggestion will come best from you."

"Do I understand," asked the old man, "that I am to suggest to my son to make a—a profession of—of affection to Madame Münster?"

"Yes, yes—a profession!" cried Felix sympathetically.

"But, as I understand it, Madame Münster is a married woman."

"Ah," said Felix, smiling, "of course she can't marry him. But she will do what she can."

Mr. Wentworth sat for some time with his eyes on the floor; at last he got up. "I don't think," he said, "that I can undertake to recommend my son any such course." And without meeting Felix's surprised glance he broke off his sitting, which was not resumed for a fortnight.

Felix was very fond of the little lake which occupied so many of Mr. Wentworth's numerous acres, and of a remarkable pine grove which lay upon the further side of it, planted upon a steep embankment and haunted by the summer breeze. The murmur of the air in the far off tree-tops had a strange distinctness; it was almost articulate. One afternoon the young man came out of his painting-room and passed the open door of Eugenia's little salon. Within, in the cool dimness, he saw his sister, dressed in white, buried in her arm-chair, and holding to her face an immense bouquet. Opposite to her sat Clifford Wentworth, twirling his hat. He had evidently just presented the bouquet to the Baroness, whose fine eyes, as she glanced at him over the big roses and geraniums, wore a conversational smile. Felix, standing on the threshold of the cottage, hesitated for a moment as to whether he should retrace his steps and enter the parlor. Then he went his way and passed into Mr. Wentworth's garden. That civilizing process to which he had suggested that Clifford should be subjected appeared to have come on of itself. Felix was very sure, at least, that Mr. Wentworth had not adopted his ingenious device for stimulating the young man's aesthetic consciousness. "Doubtless he supposes," he said to himself, after the conversation that has been narrated, "that I desire, out of fraternal benevolence, to procure for Eugenia the amusement of a flirtation—or, as he probably calls it, an intrigue—with the too susceptible Clifford. It must be admitted—and I have noticed it before—that nothing exceeds the license occasionally taken by the imagination of very rigid people." Felix, on his own side, had of course said nothing to Clifford; but he had observed to Eugenia that Mr. Wentworth was much mortified at his son's low tastes. "We ought to do something to help them, after all their kindness to us," he had added. "Encourage Clifford to come and see you, and inspire him with a taste for conversation. That will supplant the other, which only comes from his puerility, from his not taking his position in the world—that of a rich young man of ancient stock—seriously enough. Make him a little more serious. Even if he makes love to you it is no great matter."

"I am to offer myself as a superior form of intoxication—a substitute for a brandy bottle, eh?" asked the Baroness. "Truly, in this country one comes to strange uses."

But she had not positively declined to undertake Clifford's higher education, and Felix, who had not thought of the matter again, being haunted with visions of more personal profit, now reflected that the work of redemption had fairly begun. The idea in prospect had seemed of the happiest, but in operation it made him a trifle uneasy. "What if Eugenia— what if Eugenia"—he asked himself softly; the question dying away in his sense of Eugenia's undetermined capacity. But before Felix had time either to accept or to reject its admonition, even in this vague form, he saw Robert Acton turn out of Mr. Wentworth's enclosure, by a distant gate, and come toward the cottage in the orchard. Acton had evidently walked from his own house along a shady by-way and was intending to pay a visit to Madame Münster. Felix watched him a moment; then he turned away. Acton could be left to play the part of Providence and interrupt—if interruption were needed—Clifford's entanglement with Eugenia.

Felix passed through the garden toward the house and toward a postern gate which opened upon a path leading across the fields, beside a little wood, to the lake. He stopped and looked up at the house; his eyes rested more particularly upon a certain open window, on the shady side. Presently Gertrude appeared there, looking out into the summer light. He took off his hat to her and bade her good-day; he remarked that he was going to row across the pond, and begged that she would do him the honor to accompany him. She looked at him a moment; then, without saying anything, she turned away. But she soon reappeared below in one of those quaint and charming Leghorn hats, tied with white satin bows, that were worn at that period; she also carried a green parasol. She went with him to the edge of the lake, where a couple of boats were always moored; they got into one of them, and Felix, with gentle strokes, propelled it to the opposite shore. The day was the perfection of summer weather; the little lake was the color of sunshine; the plash of the oars was the only sound, and they found themselves listening to it. They disembarked, and, by a winding path, ascended the pine-crested mound which overlooked the water, whose white expanse glittered between the trees. The place was delightfully cool, and had the added charm that—in the softly sounding pine boughs—you seemed to hear the coolness as well as feel it. Felix and Gertrude sat down on the rust-colored carpet of pine-needles and talked of many things. Felix spoke at last, in the course of talk, of his going away; it was the first time he had alluded to it.

"You are going away?" said Gertrude, looking at him.

"Some day—when the leaves begin to fall. You know I can't stay forever."

Gertrude transferred her eyes to the outer prospect, and then, after a pause, she said, "I shall never see you again."

"Why not?" asked Felix. "We shall probably both survive my departure."

But Gertrude only repeated, "I shall never see you again. I shall never hear of you," she went on. "I shall know nothing about you. I knew nothing about you before, and it will be the same again."

"I knew nothing about you then, unfortunately," said Felix. "But now I shall write to you."

"Don't write to me. I shall not answer you," Gertrude declared.

"I should of course burn your letters," said Felix.

Gertrude looked at him again. "Burn my letters? You sometimes say strange things."

"They are not strange in themselves," the young man answered. "They are only strange as said to you. You will come to Europe."

"With whom shall I come?" She asked this question simply; she was very much in earnest. Felix was interested in her earnestness; for some moments he hesitated. "You can't tell me that," she pursued. "You can't say that I shall go with my father and my sister; you don't believe that."

"I shall keep your letters," said Felix, presently, for all answer.

"I never write. I don't know how to write." Gertrude, for some time, said nothing more; and her companion, as he looked at her, wished it had not been "disloyal" to make love to the daughter of an old gentleman who had offered one hospitality. The afternoon waned; the shadows stretched themselves; and the light grew deeper in the western sky. Two persons appeared on the opposite side of the lake, coming from the house and crossing the meadow. "It is Charlotte and Mr. Brand," said Gertrude. "They are coming over here." But Charlotte and Mr. Brand only came down to the edge of the water, and stood there, looking across; they made no motion to enter the boat that Felix had left at the mooring-place. Felix waved his hat to them; it was too far to call. They made no visible response, and they presently turned away and walked along the shore.

"Mr. Brand is not demonstrative," said Felix. "He is never demonstrative to me. He sits silent, with his chin in his hand, looking at me. Sometimes he looks away. Your father tells me he is so eloquent; and I should like to hear him talk. He looks like such a noble young man. But with me he will never talk. And yet I am so fond of listening to brilliant imagery!"

"He is very eloquent," said Gertrude; "but he has no brilliant imagery. I have heard him talk a great deal. I knew that when they saw us they would not come over here."

"Ah, he is making *la cour*, as they say, to your sister? They desire to be alone?"

"No," said Gertrude, gravely, "they have no such reason as that for being alone."

"But why doesn't he make *la cour* to Charlotte?" Felix inquired. "She is so pretty, so gentle, so good."

Gertrude glanced at him, and then she looked at the distantly-seen couple they were discussing. Mr. Brand and Charlotte were walking side by side. They might have been a pair of lovers, and yet they might not. "They think I should not be here," said Gertrude.

"With me? I thought you didn't have those ideas."

"You don't understand. There are a great many things you don't understand."

"I understand my stupidity. But why, then, do not Charlotte and Mr. Brand, who, as an elder sister and a clergyman, are free to walk about together, come over and make me wiser by breaking up the unlawful interview into which I have lured you?"

"That is the last thing they would do," said Gertrude.

Felix stared at her a moment, with his lifted eyebrows. *"Je n'y comprends rien!"* he exclaimed; then his eyes followed for a while the retreating figures of this critical pair. "You may say what you please," he declared; "it is evident to me that your sister is not indifferent to her clever companion. It is agreeable to her to be walking there with him. I can see that from here." And in the excitement of observation Felix rose to his feet.

Gertrude rose also, but she made no attempt to emulate her companion's discovery; she looked rather in another direction. Felix's words had struck her; but a certain delicacy checked her. "She is certainly not indifferent to Mr. Brand; she has the highest opinion of him."

"One can see it—one can see it," said Felix, in a tone of amused contemplation, with his head on one side. Gertrude turned her back to the opposite shore; it was disagreeable to her to look, but she hoped Felix would say something more. "Ah, they have wandered away into the wood," he added.

Gertrude turned round again. "She is *not* in love with him," she said; it seemed her duty to say that.

"Then he is in love with her; or if he is not, he ought to be. She is such a perfect little woman of her kind. She reminds me of a pair of old-fashioned silver sugar-tongs; you know I am very fond of sugar. And she is very nice with Mr. Brand; I have noticed that; very gentle and gracious."

Gertrude reflected a moment. Then she took a great resolution. "She wants him to marry me," she said. "So of course she is nice."

Felix's eyebrows rose higher than ever. "To marry you! Ah, ah, this is interesting. And you think one must be very nice with a man to induce him to do that?"

Gertrude had turned a little pale, but she went on, "Mr. Brand wants it himself."

Felix folded his arms and stood looking at her. "I see—I see," he said quickly. "Why did you never tell me this before?"

"It is disagreeable to me to speak of it even now. I wished simply to explain to you about Charlotte."

"You don't wish to marry Mr. Brand, then?"

"No," said Gertrude, gravely.

"And does your father wish it?"

"Very much."

"And you don't like him—you have refused him?"

"I don't wish to marry him."

"Your father and sister think you ought to, eh?"

"It is a long story," said Gertrude. "They think there are good reasons. I can't explain it. They think I have obligations, and that I have encouraged him."

Felix smiled at her, as if she had been telling him an amusing story about someone else. "I can't tell you how this interests me," he said. "Now you don't recognize these reasons—these obligations?"

"I am not sure; it is not easy." And she picked up her parasol and turned away, as if to descend the slope.

"Tell me this," Felix went on, going with her: "are you likely to give in—to let them persuade you?"

Gertrude looked at him with the serious face that she had constantly worn, in opposition to his almost eager smile. "I shall never marry Mr. Brand," she said.

"I see!" Felix rejoined. And they slowly descended the hill together, saying nothing till they reached the margin of the pond. "It is your own affair," he then resumed; "but do you know, I am not altogether glad? If it were settled that you were to marry Mr. Brand I should take a certain comfort in the arrangement. I should feel more free. I have no right to make love to you myself, eh?" And he paused, lightly pressing his argument upon her.

"None whatever," replied Gertrude quickly—too quickly.

"Your father would never hear of it; I haven't a penny. Mr. Brand, of course, has property of his own, eh?"

"I believe he has some property; but that has nothing to do with it."

"With you, of course not; but with your father and sister it must have. So, as I say, if this were settled, I should feel more at liberty."

"More at liberty?" Gertrude repeated. "Please unfasten the boat."

Felix untwisted the rope and stood holding it. "I should be able to say things to you that I can't give myself the pleasure of saying now," he went on. "I could tell you how much I admire you, without seeming to pretend to that which I have no right to pretend to. I should make violent love to you," he added, laughing, "if I thought you were so placed as not to be offended by it."

"You mean if I were engaged to another man? That is strange reasoning!" Gertrude exclaimed.

"In that case you would not take me seriously."

"I take everyone seriously," said Gertrude. And without his help she stepped lightly into the boat.

Felix took up the oars and sent it forward. "Ah, this is what you have been thinking about? It seemed to me you had something on your mind. I wish very much," he added, "that you would tell me some of these so-called reasons—these obligations."

"They are not real reasons—good reasons," said Gertrude, looking at the pink and yellow gleams in the water.

"I can understand that! Because a handsome girl has had a spark of coquetry, that is no reason."

"If you mean me, it's not that. I have not done that."

"It is something that troubles you, at any rate," said Felix.

"Not so much as it used to," Gertrude rejoined.

He looked at her, smiling always. "That is not saying much, eh?" But she only rested her eyes, very gravely, on the lighted water. She seemed to him to be trying to hide the signs of the trouble of which she had just told him. Felix felt, at all times, much the same impulse to dissipate visible melancholy that a good housewife feels to brush away dust. There was something he wished to brush away now; suddenly he stopped rowing and poised his oars. "Why should Mr. Brand have addressed himself to you, and not to your sister?" he asked. "I am sure she would listen to him."

Gertrude, in her family, was thought capable of a good deal of levity; but her levity had never gone so far as this. It moved her greatly, however, to hear Felix say that he was sure of something; so that, raising her eyes toward him, she tried intently, for some moments, to conjure up this wonderful image of a love-affair between her own sister and her own suitor. We know that Gertrude had an imaginative mind; so that it is not impossible that this effort should have been partially successful. But she only murmured, "Ah, Felix! ah, Felix!"

"Why shouldn't they marry? Try and make them marry!" cried Felix.

"Try and make them?"

"Turn the tables on them. Then they will leave you alone. I will help you as far as I can."

Gertrude's heart began to beat; she was greatly excited; she had never had anything so interesting proposed to her before. Felix had begun to row again, and he now sent the boat home with long strokes. "I believe she *does* care for him!" said Gertrude, after they had disembarked.

"Of course she does, and we will marry them off. It will make them happy; it will make everyone happy. We shall have a wedding and I will write an epithalamium."

"It seems as if it would make *me* happy," said Gertrude.

"To get rid of Mr. Brand, eh? To recover your liberty?"

Gertrude walked on. "To see my sister married to so good a man."

Felix gave his light laugh. "You always put things on those grounds; you will never say anything for yourself. You are all so afraid, here, of being selfish. I don't think you know how," he went on. "Let me show you! It will make me happy for myself, and for just the reverse of what I told you a while ago. After that, when I make love to you, you will have to think I mean it."

"I shall never think you mean anything," said Gertrude. "You are too fantastic."

"Ah," cried Felix, "that's a license to say everything! Gertrude, I adore you!"

# CHAPTER VIII

Charlotte and Mr. Brand had not returned when they reached the house; but the Baroness had come to tea, and Robert Acton also, who now regularly asked for a place at this generous repast or made his appearance later in the evening. Clifford Wentworth, with his juvenile growl, remarked upon it.

"You are always coming to tea nowadays, Robert," he said. "I should think you had drunk enough tea in China."

"Since when is Mr. Acton more frequent?" asked the Baroness.

"Since you came," said Clifford. "It seems as if you were a kind of attraction."

"I suppose I am a curiosity," said the Baroness. "Give me time and I will make you a salon."

"It would fall to pieces after you go!" exclaimed Acton.

"Don't talk about her going, in that familiar way," Clifford said. "It makes me feel gloomy."

Mr. Wentworth glanced at his son, and taking note of these words, wondered if Felix had been teaching him, according to the programme he had sketched out, to make love to the wife of a German prince.

Charlotte came in late with Mr. Brand; but Gertrude, to whom, at least, Felix had taught something, looked in vain, in her face, for the traces of a guilty passion. Mr. Brand sat down by Gertrude, and she presently asked him why they had not crossed the pond to join Felix and herself.

"It is cruel of you to ask me that," he answered, very softly. He had a large morsel of cake before him; but he fingered it without eating it. "I sometimes think you are growing cruel," he added.

Gertrude said nothing; she was afraid to speak. There was a kind of rage in her heart; she felt as if she could easily persuade herself that she was

Henry James

persecuted. She said to herself that it was quite right that she should not allow him to make her believe she was wrong. She thought of what Felix had said to her; she wished indeed Mr. Brand would marry Charlotte. She looked away from him and spoke no more. Mr. Brand ended by eating his cake, while Felix sat opposite, describing to Mr. Wentworth the students' duels at Heidelberg. After tea they all dispersed themselves, as usual, upon the piazza and in the garden; and Mr. Brand drew near to Gertrude again.

"I didn't come to you this afternoon because you were not alone," he began; "because you were with a newer friend."

"Felix? He is an old friend by this time."

Mr. Brand looked at the ground for some moments. "I thought I was prepared to hear you speak in that way," he resumed. "But I find it very painful."

"I don't see what else I can say," said Gertrude.

Mr. Brand walked beside her for a while in silence; Gertrude wished he would go away. "He is certainly very accomplished. But I think I ought to advise you."

"To advise me?"

"I think I know your nature."

"I think you don't," said Gertrude, with a soft laugh.

"You make yourself out worse than you are—to please him," Mr. Brand said, gently.

"Worse—to please him? What do you mean?" asked Gertrude, stopping.

Mr. Brand stopped also, and with the same soft straight-forwardness, "He doesn't care for the things you care for—the great questions of life."

Gertrude, with her eyes on his, shook her head. "I don't care for the great questions of life. They are much beyond me."

"There was a time when you didn't say that," said Mr. Brand.

155

"Oh," rejoined Gertrude, "I think you made me talk a great deal of nonsense. And it depends," she added, "upon what you call the great questions of life. There are some things I care for."

"Are they the things you talk about with your cousin?"

"You should not say things to me against my cousin, Mr. Brand," said Gertrude. "That is dishonorable."

He listened to this respectfully; then he answered, with a little vibration of the voice, "I should be very sorry to do anything dishonorable. But I don't see why it is dishonorable to say that your cousin is frivolous."

"Go and say it to himself!"

"I think he would admit it," said Mr. Brand. "That is the tone he would take. He would not be ashamed of it."

"Then I am not ashamed of it!" Gertrude declared. "That is probably what I like him for. I am frivolous myself."

"You are trying, as I said just now, to lower yourself."

"I am trying for once to be natural!" cried Gertrude passionately. "I have been pretending, all my life; I have been dishonest; it is you that have made me so!" Mr. Brand stood gazing at her, and she went on, "Why shouldn't I be frivolous, if I want? One has a right to be frivolous, if it's one's nature. No, I don't care for the great questions. I care for pleasure—for amusement. Perhaps I am fond of wicked things; it is very possible!"

Mr. Brand remained staring; he was even a little pale, as if he had been frightened. "I don't think you know what you are saying!" he exclaimed.

"Perhaps not. Perhaps I am talking nonsense. But it is only with you that I talk nonsense. I never do so with my cousin."

"I will speak to you again, when you are less excited," said Mr. Brand.

"I am always excited when you speak to me. I must tell you that—even if it prevents you altogether, in future. Your speaking to me irritates me. With my cousin it is very different. That seems quiet and natural."

He looked at her, and then he looked away, with a kind of helpless distress, at the dusky garden and the faint summer stars. After which, suddenly turning back, "Gertrude, Gertrude!" he softly groaned. "Am I really losing you?"

She was touched—she was pained; but it had already occurred to her that she might do something better than say so. It would not have alleviated her companion's distress to perceive, just then, whence she had sympathetically borrowed this ingenuity. "I am not sorry for you," Gertrude said; "for in paying so much attention to me you are following a shadow—you are wasting something precious. There is something else you might have that you don't look at—something better than I am. That is a reality!" And then, with intention, she looked at him and tried to smile a little. He thought this smile of hers very strange; but she turned away and left him.

She wandered about alone in the garden wondering what Mr. Brand would make of her words, which it had been a singular pleasure for her to utter. Shortly after, passing in front of the house, she saw at a distance two persons standing near the garden gate. It was Mr. Brand going away and bidding good-night to Charlotte, who had walked down with him from the house. Gertrude saw that the parting was prolonged. Then she turned her back upon it. She had not gone very far, however, when she heard her sister slowly following her. She neither turned round nor waited for her; she knew what Charlotte was going to say. Charlotte, who at last overtook her, in fact presently began; she had passed her arm into Gertrude's.

"Will you listen to me, dear, if I say something very particular?"

"I know what you are going to say," said Gertrude. "Mr. Brand feels very badly."

"Oh, Gertrude, how can you treat him so?" Charlotte demanded. And as her sister made no answer she added, "After all he has done for you!"

"What has he done for me?"

"I wonder you can ask, Gertrude. He has helped you so. You told me so yourself, a great many times. You told me that he helped you to struggle with your—your peculiarities. You told me that he had taught you how to govern your temper."

For a moment Gertrude said nothing. Then, "Was my temper very bad?" she asked.

"I am not accusing you, Gertrude," said Charlotte.

"What are you doing, then?" her sister demanded, with a short laugh.

"I am pleading for Mr. Brand—reminding you of all you owe him."

"I have given it all back," said Gertrude, still with her little laugh. "He can take back the virtue he imparted! I want to be wicked again."

Her sister made her stop in the path, and fixed upon her, in the darkness, a sweet, reproachful gaze. "If you talk this way I shall almost believe it. Think of all we owe Mr. Brand. Think of how he has always expected something of you. Think how much he has been to us. Think of his beautiful influence upon Clifford."

"He is very good," said Gertrude, looking at her sister. "I know he is very good. But he shouldn't speak against Felix."

"Felix is good," Charlotte answered, softly but promptly. "Felix is very wonderful. Only he is so different. Mr. Brand is much nearer to us. I should never think of going to Felix with a trouble—with a question. Mr. Brand is much more to us, Gertrude."

"He is very—very good," Gertrude repeated. "He is more to you; yes, much more. Charlotte," she added suddenly, "you are in love with him!"

"Oh, Gertrude!" cried poor Charlotte; and her sister saw her blushing in the darkness.

Gertrude put her arm round her. "I wish he would marry you!" she went on.

Charlotte shook herself free. "You must not say such things!" she exclaimed, beneath her breath.

"You like him more than you say, and he likes you more than he knows."

"This is very cruel of you!" Charlotte Wentworth murmured.

But if it was cruel Gertrude continued pitiless. "Not if it's true," she answered. "I wish he would marry you."

"Please don't say that."

"I mean to tell him so!" said Gertrude.

"Oh, Gertrude, Gertrude!" her sister almost moaned.

"Yes, if he speaks to me again about myself. I will say, 'Why don't you marry Charlotte? She's a thousand times better than I.'"

"You *are* wicked; you *are* changed!" cried her sister.

"If you don't like it you can prevent it," said Gertrude. "You can prevent it by keeping him from speaking to me!" And with this she walked away, very conscious of what she had done; measuring it and finding a certain joy and a quickened sense of freedom in it.

Mr. Wentworth was rather wide of the mark in suspecting that Clifford had begun to pay unscrupulous compliments to his brilliant cousin; for the young man had really more scruples than he received credit for in his family. He had a certain transparent shamefacedness which was in itself a proof that he was not at his ease in dissipation. His collegiate peccadilloes had aroused a domestic murmur as disagreeable to the young man as the creaking of his boots would have been to a house-breaker. Only, as the house-breaker would have simplified matters by removing his *chaussures*, it had seemed to Clifford that the shortest cut to comfortable relations with people—relations which should make him cease to think that when they spoke to him they meant something improving—was to renounce all ambition toward a nefarious development. And, in fact, Clifford's ambition took the most commendable form. He thought of himself in the future as the well-known and much-liked Mr. Wentworth, of Boston, who should, in the natural course of prosperity, have married his pretty cousin, Lizzie Acton; should live in a wide-fronted house, in view of the Common; and should drive, behind a light wagon, over the damp autumn roads, a pair of beautifully matched sorrel horses. Clifford's vision of the coming years was very simple; its most definite features were this element of familiar matrimony and the duplication of his resources for trotting. He had not yet asked his cousin to marry him; but he meant to do so as soon as he had taken his degree. Lizzie was serenely conscious of his intention, and she had made up her mind that he would improve. Her brother, who was very fond of this light, quick, competent little Lizzie, saw on his side no reason to interpose. It seemed to him a graceful social law that Clifford and his sister should become engaged; he himself was not engaged, but everyone else, fortunately, was not such a fool as he. He was fond of Clifford, as well, and had his own way—of which it must be confessed he was a little ashamed—of looking at those aberrations which had led to the young man's compulsory retirement from the neighboring seat of learning. Acton had seen the world, as he said to himself; he had been to China and had knocked about among men. He had learned the essential difference between a nice young fellow and a mean young fellow, and was satisfied that there was no harm in Clifford. He believed—although it must be added that he had not quite the courage to declare it—in the doctrine of wild oats, and thought it a useful preventive of superfluous fears. If Mr. Wentworth and Charlotte and Mr. Brand would only apply it in Clifford's case, they would be happier; and Acton thought it a pity they should not be happier. They took the boy's misdemeanors too much to heart; they talked to him too solemnly; they frightened and bewildered him. Of course there was the great standard of morality, which forbade that a man should get tipsy, play at billiards for money, or cultivate his sensual consciousness; but what fear was there that poor Clifford was going to run a tilt at any great standard? It had, however, never occurred to Acton to dedicate the Baroness Münster to the redemption of a refractory collegian. The instrument, here, would have seemed to him quite too complex for the operation. Felix, on the other hand, had spoken in obedience to the belief that the more charming a woman is the more numerous, literally, are her definite social uses.

Eugenia herself, as we know, had plenty of leisure to enumerate her uses. As I have had the honor of intimating, she had come four thousand miles to seek her fortune; and it is not to be supposed that after this great effort she could neglect any apparent aid to advancement. It is my misfortune that in attempting to describe in a short compass the deportment of this remarkable woman I am obliged to express things rather brutally. I feel this to be the case, for instance, when I say that she had primarily detected such an aid to advancement in the person of Robert Acton, but that she had afterwards remembered that a prudent archer has always a second bowstring. Eugenia was a woman of finely-mingled motive, and her intentions were never sensibly gross. She had a sort of aesthetic ideal for Clifford which seemed to her a disinterested reason for taking him in hand. It was very well for a fresh-colored young gentleman to be ingenuous; but Clifford, really, was crude. With such a pretty face he ought to have prettier manners. She would teach him that, with a beautiful name, the expectation of a large property, and, as they said in Europe, a social position, an only son should know how to carry himself.

Once Clifford had begun to come and see her by himself and for himself, he came very often. He hardly knew why he should come; he saw her almost every evening at his father's house; he had nothing particular to say to her. She was not a young girl, and fellows of his age called only upon young girls. He exaggerated her age; she seemed to him an old woman; it was happy that the Baroness, with all her intelligence, was incapable of guessing this. But gradually it struck Clifford that visiting old women might be, if not a natural, at least, as they say of some articles of diet, an acquired taste. The Baroness was certainly a very amusing old woman; she talked to him as no lady—and indeed no gentleman—had ever talked to him before.

"You should go to Europe and make the tour," she said to him one afternoon. "Of course, on leaving college you will go."

"I don't want to go," Clifford declared. "I know some fellows who have been to Europe. They say you can have better fun here."

"That depends. It depends upon your idea of fun. Your friends probably were not introduced."

"Introduced?" Clifford demanded.

161

"They had no opportunity of going into society; they formed no *relations*." This was one of a certain number of words that the Baroness often pronounced in the French manner.

"They went to a ball, in Paris; I know that," said Clifford.

"Ah, there are balls and balls; especially in Paris. No, you must go, you know; it is not a thing from which you can dispense yourself. You need it."

"Oh, I'm very well," said Clifford. "I'm not sick."

"I don't mean for your health, my poor child. I mean for your manners."

"I haven't got any manners!" growled Clifford.

"Precisely. You don't mind my assenting to that, eh?" asked the Baroness with a smile. "You must go to Europe and get a few. You can get them better there. It is a pity you might not have come while I was living in—in Germany. I would have introduced you; I had a charming little circle. You would perhaps have been rather young; but the younger one begins, I think, the better. Now, at any rate, you have no time to lose, and when I return you must immediately come to me."

All this, to Clifford's apprehension, was a great mixture—his beginning young, Eugenia's return to Europe, his being introduced to her charming little circle. What was he to begin, and what was her little circle? His ideas about her marriage had a good deal of vagueness; but they were in so far definite as that he felt it to be a matter not to be freely mentioned. He sat and looked all round the room; he supposed she was alluding in some way to her marriage.

"Oh, I don't want to go to Germany," he said; it seemed to him the most convenient thing to say.

She looked at him a while, smiling with her lips, but not with her eyes.

"You have scruples?" she asked.

"Scruples?" said Clifford.

"You young people, here, are very singular; one doesn't know where to expect you. When you are not extremely improper you are so terribly proper. I dare say you think that, owing to my irregular marriage, I live with loose people. You were never more mistaken. I have been all the more particular."

"Oh, no," said Clifford, honestly distressed. "I never thought such a thing as that."

"Are you very sure? I am convinced that your father does, and your sisters. They say to each other that here I am on my good behavior, but that over there—married by the left hand—I associate with light women."

"Oh, no," cried Clifford, energetically, "they don't say such things as that to each other!"

"If they think them they had better say them," the Baroness rejoined. "Then they can be contradicted. Please contradict that whenever you hear it, and don't be afraid of coming to see me on account of the company I keep. I have the honor of knowing more distinguished men, my poor child, than you are likely to see in a life-time. I see very few women; but those are women of rank. So, my dear young Puritan, you needn't be afraid. I am not in the least one of those who think that the society of women who have lost their place in the *vrai monde* is necessary to form a young man. I have never taken that tone. I have kept my place myself, and I think we are a much better school than the others. Trust me, Clifford, and I will prove that to you," the Baroness continued, while she made the agreeable reflection that she could not, at least, be accused of perverting her young kinsman. "So if you ever fall among thieves don't go about saying I sent you to them."

Clifford thought it so comical that he should know—in spite of her figurative language—what she meant, and that she should mean what he knew, that he could hardly help laughing a little, although he tried hard. "Oh, no! oh, no!" he murmured.

"Laugh out, laugh out, if I amuse you!" cried the Baroness. "I am here for that!" And Clifford thought her a very amusing person indeed. "But remember," she said on this occasion, "that you are coming—next year—to pay me a visit over there."

About a week afterwards she said to him, point-blank, "Are you seriously making love to your little cousin?"

"Seriously making love"—these words, on Madame Münster's lips, had to Clifford's sense a portentous and embarrassing sound; he hesitated about assenting, lest he should commit himself to more than he understood. "Well, I shouldn't say it if I was!" he exclaimed.

"Why wouldn't you say it?" the Baroness demanded. "Those things ought to be known."

"I don't care whether it is known or not," Clifford rejoined. "But I don't want people looking at me."

"A young man of your importance ought to learn to bear observation— to carry himself as if he were quite indifferent to it. I won't say, exactly, unconscious," the Baroness explained. "No, he must seem to know he is observed, and to think it natural he should be; but he must appear perfectly used to it. Now you haven't that, Clifford; you haven't that at all. You must have that, you know. Don't tell me you are not a young man of importance," Eugenia added. "Don't say anything so flat as that."

"Oh, no, you don't catch me saying that!" cried Clifford.

"Yes, you must come to Germany," Madame Münster continued. "I will show you how people can be talked about, and yet not seem to know it. You will be talked about, of course, with me; it will be said you are my lover. I will show you how little one may mind that—how little I shall mind it."

Clifford sat staring, blushing and laughing. "I shall mind it a good deal!" he declared.

"Ah, not too much, you know; that would be uncivil. But I give you leave to mind it a little; especially if you have a passion for Miss Acton. *Voyons*; as regards that, you either have or you have not. It is very simple to say it."

"I don't see why you want to know," said Clifford.

"You ought to want me to know. If one is arranging a marriage, one tells one's friends."

"Oh, I'm not arranging anything," said Clifford.

"You don't intend to marry your cousin?"

"Well, I expect I shall do as I choose!"

The Baroness leaned her head upon the back of her chair and closed her eyes, as if she were tired. Then opening them again, "Your cousin is very charming!" she said.

"She is the prettiest girl in this place," Clifford rejoined.

"'In this place' is saying little; she would be charming anywhere. I am afraid you are entangled."

"Oh, no, I'm not entangled."

"Are you engaged? At your age that is the same thing."

Clifford looked at the Baroness with some audacity. "Will you tell no one?"

"If it's as sacred as that—no."

"Well, then—we are not!" said Clifford.

"That's the great secret—that you are not, eh?" asked the Baroness, with a quick laugh. "I am very glad to hear it. You are altogether too young. A young man in your position must choose and compare; he must see the world first. Depend upon it," she added, "you should not settle that matter before you have come abroad and paid me that visit. There are several things I should like to call your attention to first."

"Well, I am rather afraid of that visit," said Clifford. "It seems to me it will be rather like going to school again."

The Baroness looked at him a moment.

"My dear child," she said, "there is no agreeable man who has not, at some moment, been to school to a clever woman—probably a little older than himself. And you must be thankful when you get your instructions gratis. With me you would get it gratis."

The next day Clifford told Lizzie Acton that the Baroness thought her the most charming girl she had ever seen.

Lizzie shook her head. "No, she doesn't!" she said.

"Do you think everything she says," asked Clifford, "is to be taken the opposite way?"

"I think that is!" said Lizzie.

Clifford was going to remark that in this case the Baroness must desire greatly to bring about a marriage between Mr. Clifford Wentworth and Miss Elizabeth Acton; but he resolved, on the whole, to suppress this observation.

# CHAPTER IX

It seemed to Robert Acton, after Eugenia had come to his house, that something had passed between them which made them a good deal more intimate. It was hard to say exactly what, except her telling him that she had taken her resolution with regard to the Prince Adolf; for Madame Münster's visit had made no difference in their relations. He came to see her very often; but he had come to see her very often before. It was agreeable to him to find himself in her little drawing-room; but this was not a new discovery. There was a change, however, in this sense: that if the Baroness had been a great deal in Acton's thoughts before, she was now never out of them. From the first she had been personally fascinating; but the fascination now had become intellectual as well. He was constantly pondering her words and motions; they were as interesting as the factors in an algebraic problem. This is saying a good deal; for Acton was extremely fond of mathematics. He asked himself whether it could be that he was in love with her, and then hoped he was not; hoped it not so much for his own sake as for that of the amatory passion itself. If this was love, love had been overrated. Love was a poetic impulse, and his own state of feeling with regard to the Baroness was largely characterized by that eminently prosaic sentiment—curiosity. It was true, as Acton with his quietly cogitative habit observed to himself, that curiosity, pushed to a given point, might become a romantic passion; and he certainly thought enough about this charming woman to make him restless and even a little melancholy. It puzzled and vexed him at times to feel that he was not more ardent. He was not in the least bent upon remaining a bachelor. In his younger years he had been—or he had tried to be—of the opinion that it would be a good deal "jollier" not to marry, and he had flattered himself that his single condition was something of a citadel. It was a citadel, at all events, of which he had long since leveled the outworks. He had removed the guns from the ramparts; he had lowered the draw-bridge across the moat. The draw-bridge had swayed lightly under Madame Münster's step; why should he not cause it to be raised again, so that she might be kept prisoner? He had an idea that she would become—in time at least, and on learning the conveniences of the place for making a lady comfortable—a tolerably patient captive. But the draw-bridge was never raised, and Acton's brilliant visitor was as free to depart as she had been to come. It was part of his curiosity to know why the deuce so susceptible a man was *not* in love with so charming a woman. If her various graces were, as I have said, the factors in an algebraic problem, the answer to this question was the indispensable unknown quantity. The pursuit of the unknown quantity was extremely absorbing; for the present it taxed all Acton's faculties.

Toward the middle of August he was obliged to leave home for some days; an old friend, with whom he had been associated in China, had begged him to come to Newport, where he lay extremely ill. His friend got better, and at the end of a week Acton was released. I use the word "released" advisedly; for in spite of his attachment to his Chinese comrade he had been but a half-hearted visitor. He felt as if he had been called away from the theatre during the progress of a remarkably interesting drama. The curtain was up all this time, and he was losing the fourth act; that fourth act which would have been so essential to a just appreciation of the fifth. In other words, he was thinking about the Baroness, who, seen at this distance, seemed a truly brilliant figure. He saw at Newport a great many pretty women, who certainly were figures as brilliant as beautiful light dresses could make them; but though they talked a great deal—and the Baroness's strong point was perhaps also her conversation—Madame Münster appeared to lose nothing by the comparison. He wished she had come to Newport too. Would it not be possible to make up, as they said, a party for visiting the famous watering-place and invite Eugenia to join it? It was true that the complete satisfaction would be to spend a fortnight at Newport with Eugenia alone. It would be a great pleasure to see her, in society, carry everything before her, as he was sure she would do. When Acton caught himself thinking these thoughts he began to walk up and down, with his hands in his pockets, frowning a little and looking at the floor. What did it prove—for it certainly proved something— this lively disposition to be "off" somewhere with Madame Münster, away from all the rest of them? Such a vision, certainly, seemed a refined implication of matrimony, after the Baroness should have formally got rid of her informal husband. At any rate, Acton, with his characteristic discretion, forbore to give expression to whatever else it might imply, and the narrator of these incidents is not obliged to be more definite.

He returned home rapidly, and, arriving in the afternoon, lost as little time as possible in joining the familiar circle at Mr. Wentworth's. On reaching the house, however, he found the piazzas empty. The doors and windows were open, and their emptiness was made clear by the shafts of lamp-light from the parlors. Entering the house, he found Mr. Wentworth sitting alone in one of these apartments, engaged in the perusal of the *North American Review*. After they had exchanged greetings and his cousin had made discreet inquiry about his journey, Acton asked what had become of Mr. Wentworth's companions.

"They are scattered about, amusing themselves as usual," said the old man. "I saw Charlotte, a short time since, seated, with Mr. Brand, upon the piazza. They were conversing with their customary animation. I suppose they have joined her sister, who, for the hundredth time, was doing the honors of the garden to her foreign cousin."

"I suppose you mean Felix," said Acton. And on Mr. Wentworth's assenting, he said, "And the others?"

"Your sister has not come this evening. You must have seen her at home," said Mr. Wentworth.

"Yes. I proposed to her to come. She declined."

"Lizzie, I suppose, was expecting a visitor," said the old man, with a kind of solemn slyness.

"If she was expecting Clifford, he had not turned up."

Mr. Wentworth, at this intelligence, closed the *North American Review* and remarked that he had understood Clifford to say that he was going to see his cousin. Privately, he reflected that if Lizzie Acton had had no news of his son, Clifford must have gone to Boston for the evening: an unnatural course of a summer night, especially when accompanied with disingenuous representations.

"You must remember that he has two cousins," said Acton, laughing. And then, coming to the point, "If Lizzie is not here," he added, "neither apparently is the Baroness."

Mr. Wentworth stared a moment, and remembered that queer proposition of Felix's. For a moment he did not know whether it was not to be wished that Clifford, after all, might have gone to Boston. "The Baroness has not honored us tonight," he said. "She has not come over for three days."

"Is she ill?" Acton asked.

"No; I have been to see her."

"What is the matter with her?"

"Well," said Mr. Wentworth, "I infer she has tired of us."

Acton pretended to sit down, but he was restless; he found it impossible to talk with Mr. Wentworth. At the end of ten minutes he took up his hat and said that he thought he would "go off." It was very late; it was ten o'clock.

His quiet-faced kinsman looked at him a moment. "Are you going home?" he asked.

Acton hesitated, and then answered that he had proposed to go over and take a look at the Baroness.

"Well, you are honest, at least," said Mr. Wentworth, sadly.

"So are you, if you come to that!" cried Acton, laughing. "Why shouldn't I be honest?"

The old man opened the *North American* again, and read a few lines. "If we have ever had any virtue among us, we had better keep hold of it now," he said. He was not quoting.

"We have a Baroness among us," said Acton. "That's what we must keep hold of!" He was too impatient to see Madame Münster again to wonder what Mr. Wentworth was talking about. Nevertheless, after he had passed out of the house and traversed the garden and the little piece of road that separated him from Eugenia's provisional residence, he stopped a moment outside. He stood in her little garden; the long window of her parlor was open, and he could see the white curtains, with the lamp-light shining through them, swaying softly to and fro in the warm night wind. There was a sort of excitement in the idea of seeing Madame Münster again; he became aware that his heart was beating rather faster than usual. It was this that made him stop, with a half-amused surprise. But in a moment he went along the piazza, and, approaching the open window, tapped upon its lintel with his stick. He could see the Baroness within; she was standing in the middle of the room. She came to the window and pulled aside the curtain; then she stood looking at him a moment. She was not smiling; she seemed serious.

*"Mais entrez donc!"* she said at last. Acton passed in across the window-sill; he wondered, for an instant, what was the matter with her. But the next moment she had begun to smile and had put out her hand. "Better late than never," she said. "It is very kind of you to come at this hour."

"I have just returned from my journey," said Acton.

"Ah, very kind, very kind," she repeated, looking about her where to sit.

"I went first to the other house," Acton continued. "I expected to find you there."

She had sunk into her usual chair; but she got up again, and began to move about the room. Acton had laid down his hat and stick; he was looking at her, conscious that there was in fact a great charm in seeing her again. "I don't know whether I ought to tell you to sit down," she said. "It is too late to begin a visit."

"It's too early to end one," Acton declared; "and we needn't mind the beginning."

She looked at him again, and, after a moment, dropped once more into her low chair, while he took a place near her. "We are in the middle, then?" she asked. "Was that where we were when you went away? No, I haven't been to the other house."

"Not yesterday, nor the day before, eh?"

"I don't know how many days it is."

"You are tired of it," said Acton.

She leaned back in her chair; her arms were folded. "That is a terrible accusation, but I have not the courage to defend myself."

"I am not attacking you," said Acton. "I expected something of this kind."

"It's a proof of extreme intelligence. I hope you enjoyed your journey."

"Not at all," Acton declared. "I would much rather have been here with you."

"Now you *are* attacking me," said the Baroness. "You are contrasting my inconstancy with your own fidelity."

"I confess I never get tired of people I like."

"Ah, you are not a poor wicked foreign woman, with irritable nerves and a sophisticated mind!"

"Something has happened to you since I went away," said Acton, changing his place.

"Your going away—that is what has happened to me."

"Do you mean to say that you have missed me?" he asked.

"If I had meant to say it, it would not be worth your making a note of. I am very dishonest and my compliments are worthless."

Acton was silent for some moments. "You have broken down," he said at last.

Madame Münster left her chair, and began to move about.

"Only for a moment. I shall pull myself together again."

"You had better not take it too hard. If you are bored, you needn't be afraid to say so—to me at least."

"You shouldn't say such things as that," the Baroness answered. "You should encourage me."

"I admire your patience; that is encouraging."

"You shouldn't even say that. When you talk of my patience you are disloyal to your own people. Patience implies suffering; and what have I had to suffer?"

"Oh, not hunger, not unkindness, certainly," said Acton, laughing. "Nevertheless, we all admire your patience."

"You all detest me!" cried the Baroness, with a sudden vehemence, turning her back toward him.

"You make it hard," said Acton, getting up, "for a man to say something tender to you." This evening there was something particularly striking and touching about her; an unwonted softness and a look of suppressed emotion. He felt himself suddenly appreciating the fact that she had behaved very well. She had come to this quiet corner of the world under the weight of a cruel indignity, and she had been so gracefully, modestly thankful for the rest she found there. She had joined that simple circle over the way; she had mingled in its plain, provincial talk; she had shared its meagre and savorless pleasures. She had set herself a task, and she had rigidly performed it. She had conformed to the angular conditions of New England life, and she had had the tact and pluck to carry it off as if she liked them. Acton felt a more downright need than he had ever felt before to tell her that he admired her and that she struck him as a very superior woman. All along, hitherto, he had been on his guard with her; he had been cautious, observant, suspicious. But now a certain light tumult in his blood seemed to tell him that a finer degree of confidence in this charming woman would be its own reward. "We don't detest you," he went on. "I don't know what you mean. At any rate, I speak for myself; I don't know anything about the others. Very likely, you detest them for the dull life they make you lead. Really, it would give me a sort of pleasure to hear you say so."

Eugenia had been looking at the door on the other side of the room; now she slowly turned her eyes toward Robert Acton. "What can be the motive," she asked, "of a man like you—an honest man, a *galant homme*—in saying so base a thing as that?"

"Does it sound very base?" asked Acton, candidly. "I suppose it does, and I thank you for telling me so. Of course, I don't mean it literally."

The Baroness stood looking at him. "How do you mean it?" she asked.

This question was difficult to answer, and Acton, feeling the least bit foolish, walked to the open window and looked out. He stood there, thinking a moment, and then he turned back. "You know that document that you were to send to Germany," he said. "You called it your 'renunciation.' Did you ever send it?"

Madame Münster's eyes expanded; she looked very grave. "What a singular answer to my question!"

"Oh, it isn't an answer," said Acton. "I have wished to ask you, many times. I thought it probable you would tell me yourself. The question, on my part, seems abrupt now; but it would be abrupt at any time."

The Baroness was silent a moment; and then, "I think I have told you too much!" she said.

This declaration appeared to Acton to have a certain force; he had indeed a sense of asking more of her than he offered her. He returned to the window, and watched, for a moment, a little star that twinkled through the lattice of the piazza. There were at any rate offers enough he could make; perhaps he had hitherto not been sufficiently explicit in doing so. "I wish you would ask something of me," he presently said. "Is there nothing I can do for you? If you can't stand this dull life any more, let me amuse you!"

The Baroness had sunk once more into a chair, and she had taken up a fan which she held, with both hands, to her mouth. Over the top of the fan her eyes were fixed on him. "You are very strange tonight," she said, with a little laugh.

"I will do anything in the world," he rejoined, standing in front of her. "Shouldn't you like to travel about and see something of the country? Won't you go to Niagara? You ought to see Niagara, you know."

"With you, do you mean?"

"I should be delighted to take you."

"You alone?"

Acton looked at her, smiling, and yet with a serious air. "Well, yes; we might go alone," he said.

"If you were not what you are," she answered, "I should feel insulted."

"How do you mean—what I am?"

"If you were one of the gentlemen I have been used to all my life. If you were not a queer Bostonian."

"If the gentlemen you have been used to have taught you to expect insults," said Acton, "I am glad I am what I am. You had much better come to Niagara."

"If you wish to 'amuse' me," the Baroness declared, "you need go to no further expense. You amuse me very effectually."

He sat down opposite to her; she still held her fan up to her face, with her eyes only showing above it. There was a moment's silence, and then he said, returning to his former question, "Have you sent that document to Germany?"

Again there was a moment's silence. The expressive eyes of Madame Münster seemed, however, half to break it.

"I will tell you—at Niagara!" she said.

She had hardly spoken when the door at the further end of the room opened—the door upon which, some minutes previous, Eugenia had fixed her gaze. Clifford Wentworth stood there, blushing and looking rather awkward. The Baroness rose, quickly, and Acton, more slowly, did the same. Clifford gave him no greeting; he was looking at Eugenia.

"Ah, you were here?" exclaimed Acton.

"He was in Felix's studio," said Madame Münster. "He wanted to see his sketches."

Clifford looked at Robert Acton, but said nothing; he only fanned himself with his hat. "You chose a bad moment," said Acton; "you hadn't much light."

"I hadn't any!" said Clifford, laughing.

"Your candle went out?" Eugenia asked. "You should have come back here and lighted it again."

Clifford looked at her a moment. "So I have—come back. But I have left the candle!"

Eugenia turned away. "You are very stupid, my poor boy. You had better go home."

"Well," said Clifford, "good-night!"

"Haven't you a word to throw to a man when he has safely returned from a dangerous journey?" Acton asked.

"How do you do?" said Clifford. "I thought—I thought you were——" and he paused, looking at the Baroness again.

"You thought I was at Newport, eh? So I was—this morning."

"Good-night, clever child!" said Madame Münster, over her shoulder.

Clifford stared at her—not at all like a clever child; and then, with one of his little facetious growls, took his departure.

"What is the matter with him?" asked Acton, when he was gone. "He seemed rather in a muddle."

Eugenia, who was near the window, glanced out, listening a moment. "The matter—the matter"—she answered. "But you don't say such things here."

"If you mean that he had been drinking a little, you can say that."

"He doesn't drink any more. I have cured him. And in return—he's in love with me."

It was Acton's turn to stare. He instantly thought of his sister; but he said nothing about her. He began to laugh. "I don't wonder at his passion! But I wonder at his forsaking your society for that of your brother's paint-brushes."

Eugenia was silent a little. "He had not been in the studio. I invented that at the moment."

"Invented it? For what purpose?"

"He has an idea of being romantic. He has adopted the habit of coming to see me at midnight—passing only through the orchard and through Felix's painting-room, which has a door opening that way. It seems to amuse him," added Eugenia, with a little laugh.

Acton felt more surprise than he confessed to, for this was a new view of Clifford, whose irregularities had hitherto been quite without the romantic element. He tried to laugh again, but he felt rather too serious, and after a moment's hesitation his seriousness explained itself. "I hope you don't encourage him," he said. "He must not be inconstant to poor Lizzie."

"To your sister?"

"You know they are decidedly intimate," said Acton.

"Ah," cried Eugenia, smiling, "has she—has she——"

"I don't know," Acton interrupted, "what she has. But I always supposed that Clifford had a desire to make himself agreeable to her."

"Ah, *par exemple!*" the Baroness went on. "The little monster! The next time he becomes sentimental I will him tell that he ought to be ashamed of himself."

Acton was silent a moment. "You had better say nothing about it."

"I had told him as much already, on general grounds," said the Baroness. "But in this country, you know, the relations of young people are so extraordinary that one is quite at sea. They are not engaged when you would quite say they ought to be. Take Charlotte Wentworth, for instance, and that young ecclesiastic. If I were her father I should insist upon his marrying her; but it appears to be thought there is no urgency. On the other hand, you suddenly learn that a boy of twenty and a little girl who is still with her governess—your sister has no governess? Well, then, who is never away from her mamma—a young couple, in short, between whom you have noticed nothing beyond an exchange of the childish pleasantries characteristic of their age, are on the point of setting up as man and wife." The Baroness spoke with a certain exaggerated volubility which was in contrast with the languid grace that had characterized her manner before Clifford made his appearance. It seemed to Acton that there was a spark of irritation in her eye—a note of irony (as when she spoke of Lizzie being never away from her mother) in her voice. If Madame Münster was irritated, Robert Acton was vaguely mystified; she began to move about the room again, and he looked at her without saying anything. Presently she took out her watch, and, glancing at it, declared that it was three o'clock in the morning and that he must go.

"I have not been here an hour," he said, "and they are still sitting up at the other house. You can see the lights. Your brother has not come in."

"Oh, at the other house," cried Eugenia, "they are terrible people! I don't know what they may do over there. I am a quiet little humdrum woman; I have rigid rules and I keep them. One of them is not to have visitors in the small hours—especially clever men like you. So good-night!"

Decidedly, the Baroness was incisive; and though Acton bade her good-night and departed, he was still a good deal mystified.

The next day Clifford Wentworth came to see Lizzie, and Acton, who was at home and saw him pass through the garden, took note of the circumstance. He had a natural desire to make it tally with Madame Münster's account of Clifford's disaffection; but his ingenuity, finding itself unequal to the task, resolved at last to ask help of the young man's candor. He waited till he saw him going away, and then he went out and overtook him in the grounds.

"I wish very much you would answer me a question," Acton said. "What were you doing, last night, at Madame Münster's?"

Clifford began to laugh and to blush, by no means like a young man with a romantic secret. "What did she tell you?" he asked.

"That is exactly what I don't want to say."

"Well, I want to tell you the same," said Clifford; "and unless I know it perhaps I can't."

They had stopped in a garden path; Acton looked hard at his rosy young kinsman. "She said she couldn't fancy what had got into you; you appeared to have taken a violent dislike to her."

Clifford stared, looking a little alarmed. "Oh, come," he growled, "you don't mean that!"

"And that when—for common civility's sake—you came occasionally to the house you left her alone and spent your time in Felix's studio, under pretext of looking at his sketches."

"Oh, come!" growled Clifford, again.

"Did you ever know me to tell an untruth?"

"Yes, lots of them!" said Clifford, seeing an opening, out of the discussion, for his sarcastic powers. "Well," he presently added, "I thought you were my father."

"You knew someone was there?"

"We heard you coming in."

Acton meditated. "You had been with the Baroness, then?"

"I was in the parlor. We heard your step outside. I thought it was my father."

"And on that," asked Acton, "you ran away?"

"She told me to go—to go out by the studio."

Acton meditated more intensely; if there had been a chair at hand he would have sat down. "Why should she wish you not to meet your father?"

"Well," said Clifford, "father doesn't like to see me there."

Acton looked askance at his companion and forbore to make any comment upon this assertion. "Has he said so," he asked, "to the Baroness?"

"Well, I hope not," said Clifford. "He hasn't said so—in so many words—to me. But I know it worries him; and I want to stop worrying him. The Baroness knows it, and she wants me to stop, too."

"To stop coming to see her?"

"I don't know about that; but to stop worrying father. Eugenia knows everything," Clifford added, with an air of knowingness of his own.

"Ah," said Acton, interrogatively, "Eugenia knows everything?"

"She knew it was not father coming in."

"Then why did you go?"

Clifford blushed and laughed afresh. "Well, I was afraid it was. And besides, she told me to go, at any rate."

"Did she think it was I?" Acton asked.

"She didn't say so."

Again Robert Acton reflected. "But you didn't go," he presently said; "you came back."

"I couldn't get out of the studio," Clifford rejoined. "The door was locked, and Felix has nailed some planks across the lower half of the confounded windows to make the light come in from above. So they were no use. I waited there a good while, and then, suddenly, I felt ashamed. I didn't want to be hiding away from my own father. I couldn't stand it any longer. I bolted out, and when I found it was you I was a little flurried. But Eugenia carried it off, didn't she?" Clifford added, in the tone of a young humorist whose perception had not been permanently clouded by the sense of his own discomfort.

"Beautifully!" said Acton. "Especially," he continued, "when one remembers that you were very imprudent and that she must have been a good deal annoyed."

"Oh," cried Clifford, with the indifference of a young man who feels that however he may have failed of felicity in behavior he is extremely just in his impressions, "Eugenia doesn't care for anything!"

Acton hesitated a moment. "Thank you for telling me this," he said at last. And then, laying his hand on Clifford's shoulder, he added, "Tell me one thing more: are you by chance a little in love with the Baroness?"

"No, sir!" said Clifford, almost shaking off his hand.

# CHAPTER X

The first sunday that followed Robert Acton's return from Newport witnessed a change in the brilliant weather that had long prevailed. The rain began to fall and the day was cold and dreary. Mr. Wentworth and his daughters put on overshoes and went to church, and Felix Young, without overshoes, went also, holding an umbrella over Gertrude. It is to be feared that, in the whole observance, this was the privilege he most highly valued. The Baroness remained at home; she was in neither a cheerful nor a devotional mood. She had, however, never been, during her residence in the United States, what is called a regular attendant at divine service; and on this particular Sunday morning of which I began with speaking she stood at the window of her little drawing-room, watching the long arm of a rose tree that was attached to her piazza, but a portion of which had disengaged itself, sway to and fro, shake and gesticulate, against the dusky drizzle of the sky. Every now and then, in a gust of wind, the rose tree scattered a shower of water-drops against the window-pane; it appeared to have a kind of human movement—a menacing, warning intention. The room was very cold; Madame Münster put on a shawl and walked about. Then she determined to have some fire; and summoning her ancient negress, the contrast of whose polished ebony and whose crimson turban had been at first a source of satisfaction to her, she made arrangements for the production of a crackling flame. This old woman's name was Azarina. The Baroness had begun by thinking that there would be a savory wildness in her talk, and, for amusement, she had encouraged her to chatter. But Azarina was dry and prim; her conversation was anything but African; she reminded Eugenia of the tiresome old ladies she met in society. She knew, however, how to make a fire; so that after she had laid the logs, Eugenia, who was terribly bored, found a quarter of an hour's entertainment in sitting and watching them blaze and sputter. She had thought it very likely Robert Acton would come and see her; she had not met him since that infelicitous evening. But the morning waned without his coming; several times she thought she heard his step on the piazza; but it was only a window-shutter shaking in a rain-gust. The Baroness, since the beginning of that episode in her career of which a slight sketch has been attempted in these pages, had had many moments of irritation. But today her irritation had a peculiar keenness; it appeared to feed upon itself. It urged her to do something; but it suggested no particularly profitable line of action. If she could have done something at the moment, on the spot, she would have stepped upon a European steamer and turned her back, with a kind of rapture, upon that profoundly mortifying failure, her visit to her American relations. It is not exactly apparent why she should have termed this enterprise a failure, inasmuch as she had been treated with the highest distinction for which allowance had been made in American institutions. Her irritation came, at bottom, from the sense, which, always present, had suddenly grown acute, that the social soil on this big, vague continent was somehow not adapted for growing those plants whose fragrance she especially inclined to inhale and by which she liked to see herself surrounded—a species of vegetation for which she carried a collection of seedlings, as we may say, in her pocket. She found her chief happiness in the sense of exerting a certain power and making a certain impression; and now she felt the annoyance of a rather wearied swimmer who, on nearing shore, to land, finds a smooth straight wall of rock when he had counted upon a clean firm beach. Her power, in the American air, seemed to have lost its prehensile attributes; the smooth wall of rock was insurmountable. *"Surely je n'en suis pas là,"* she said to herself, "that I let it make me uncomfortable that a Mr. Robert Acton shouldn't honor me with a visit!" Yet she was vexed that he had not come; and she was vexed at her vexation.

Her brother, at least, came in, stamping in the hall and shaking the wet from his coat. In a moment he entered the room, with a glow in his cheek and half-a-dozen rain-drops glistening on his moustache. "Ah, you have a fire," he said.

*"Les beaux jours sont passés,"* replied the Baroness.

"Never, never! They have only begun," Felix declared, planting himself before the hearth. He turned his back to the fire, placed his hands behind him, extended his legs and looked away through the window with an expression of face which seemed to denote the perception of rose-color even in the tints of a wet Sunday.

His sister, from her chair, looked up at him, watching him; and what she saw in his face was not grateful to her present mood. She was puzzled by many things, but her brother's disposition was a frequent source of wonder to her. I say frequent and not constant, for there were long periods during which she gave her attention to other problems. Sometimes she had said to herself that his happy temper, his eternal gaiety, was an affectation, a *pose*; but she was vaguely conscious that during the present summer he had been a highly successful comedian. They had never yet had an explanation; she had not known the need of one. Felix was presumably following the bent of his disinterested genius, and she felt that she had no advice to give him that he would understand. With this, there was always a certain element of comfort about Felix—the assurance that he would not interfere. He was very delicate, this pure-minded Felix; in effect, he was her brother, and Madame Münster felt that there was a great propriety, every way, in that. It is true that Felix was delicate; he was not fond of explanations with his sister; this was one of the very few things in the world about which he was uncomfortable. But now he was not thinking of anything uncomfortable.

"Dear brother," said Eugenia at last, "do stop making *les yeux doux* at the rain."

"With pleasure. I will make them at you!" answered Felix.

"How much longer," asked Eugenia, in a moment, "do you propose to remain in this lovely spot?"

Felix stared. "Do you want to go away—already?"

"'Already' is delicious. I am not so happy as you."

Felix dropped into a chair, looking at the fire. "The fact is I *am* happy," he said in his light, clear tone.

"And do you propose to spend your life in making love to Gertrude Wentworth?"

"Yes!" said Felix, smiling sidewise at his sister.

The Baroness returned his glance, much more gravely; and then, "Do you like her?" she asked.

"Don't you?" Felix demanded.

The Baroness was silent a moment. "I will answer you in the words of the gentleman who was asked if he liked music: *'Je ne la crains pas!'*"

"She admires you immensely," said Felix.

"I don't care for that. Other women should not admire one."

"They should dislike you?"

Again Madame Münster hesitated. "They should hate me! It's a measure of the time I have been losing here that they don't."

"No time is lost in which one has been happy!" said Felix, with a bright sententiousness which may well have been a little irritating.

"And in which," rejoined his sister, with a harsher laugh, "one has secured the affections of a young lady with a fortune!"

Felix explained, very candidly and seriously. "I have secured Gertrude's affection, but I am by no means sure that I have secured her fortune. That may come—or it may not."

"Ah, well, it *may!* That's the great point."

"It depends upon her father. He doesn't smile upon our union. You know he wants her to marry Mr. Brand."

"I know nothing about it!" cried the Baroness. "Please to put on a log." Felix complied with her request and sat watching the quickening of the flame. Presently his sister added, "And you propose to elope with mademoiselle?"

"By no means. I don't wish to do anything that's disagreeable to Mr. Wentworth. He has been far too kind to us."

"But you must choose between pleasing yourself and pleasing him."

"I want to please everyone!" exclaimed Felix, joyously. "I have a good conscience. I made up my mind at the outset that it was not my place to make love to Gertrude."

"So, to simplify matters, she made love to you!"

Felix looked at his sister with sudden gravity. "You say you are not afraid of her," he said. "But perhaps you ought to be—a little. She's a very clever person."

"I begin to see it!" cried the Baroness. Her brother, making no rejoinder, leaned back in his chair, and there was a long silence. At last, with an altered accent, Madame Münster put another question. "You expect, at any rate, to marry?"

"I shall be greatly disappointed if we don't."

"A disappointment or two will do you good!" the Baroness declared. "And, afterwards, do you mean to turn American?"

"It seems to me I am a very good American already. But we shall go to Europe. Gertrude wants extremely to see the world."

"Ah, like me, when I came here!" said the Baroness, with a little laugh.

"No, not like you," Felix rejoined, looking at his sister with a certain gentle seriousness. While he looked at her she rose from her chair, and he also got up. "Gertrude is not at all like you," he went on; "but in her own way she is almost as clever." He paused a moment; his soul was full of an agreeable feeling and of a lively disposition to express it. His sister, to his spiritual vision, was always like the lunar disk when only a part of it is lighted. The shadow on this bright surface seemed to him to expand and to contract; but whatever its proportions, he always appreciated the moonlight. He looked at the Baroness, and then he kissed her. "I am very much in love with Gertrude," he said. Eugenia turned away and walked about the room, and Felix continued. "She is very interesting, and very different from what she seems. She has never had a chance. She is very brilliant. We will go to Europe and amuse ourselves."

The Baroness had gone to the window, where she stood looking out. The day was drearier than ever; the rain was doggedly falling. "Yes, to amuse yourselves," she said at last, "you had decidedly better go to Europe!" Then she turned round, looking at her brother. A chair stood near her; she leaned her hands upon the back of it. "Don't you think it is very good of me," she asked, "to come all this way with you simply to see you properly married—if properly it is?"

"Oh, it will be properly!" cried Felix, with light eagerness.

The Baroness gave a little laugh. "You are thinking only of yourself, and you don't answer my question. While you are amusing yourself—with the brilliant Gertrude—what shall I be doing?"

*"Vous serez de la partie!"* cried Felix.

"Thank you: I should spoil it." The Baroness dropped her eyes for some moments. "Do you propose, however, to leave me here?" she inquired.

Felix smiled at her. "My dearest sister, where you are concerned I never propose. I execute your commands."

"I believe," said Eugenia, slowly, "that you are the most heartless person living. Don't you see that I am in trouble?"

"I saw that you were not cheerful, and I gave you some good news."

"Well, let me give you some news," said the Baroness. "You probably will not have discovered it for yourself. Robert Acton wants to marry me."

"No, I had not discovered that. But I quite understand it. Why does it make you unhappy?"

"Because I can't decide."

"Accept him, accept him!" cried Felix, joyously. "He is the best fellow in the world."

"He is immensely in love with me," said the Baroness.

"And he has a large fortune. Permit me in turn to remind you of that."

"Oh, I am perfectly aware of it," said Eugenia. "That's a great item in his favor. I am terribly candid." And she left her place and came nearer her brother, looking at him hard. He was turning over several things; she was wondering in what manner he really understood her.

There were several ways of understanding her: there was what she said, and there was what she meant, and there was something, between the two, that was neither. It is probable that, in the last analysis, what she meant was that Felix should spare her the necessity of stating the case more exactly and should hold himself commissioned to assist her by all honorable means to marry the best fellow in the world. But in all this it was never discovered what Felix understood.

"Once you have your liberty, what are your objections?" he asked.

"Well, I don't particularly like him."

"Oh, try a little."

"I am trying now," said Eugenia. "I should succeed better if he didn't live here. I could never live here."

"Make him go to Europe," Felix suggested.

"Ah, there you speak of happiness based upon violent effort," the Baroness rejoined. "That is not what I am looking for. He would never live in Europe."

"He would live anywhere, with you!" said Felix, gallantly.

His sister looked at him still, with a ray of penetration in her charming eyes; then she turned away again. "You see, at all events," she presently went on, "that if it had been said of me that I had come over here to seek my fortune it would have to be added that I have found it!"

"Don't leave it lying!" urged Felix, with smiling solemnity.

"I am much obliged to you for your interest," his sister declared, after a moment. "But promise me one thing: *pas de zèle!* If Mr. Acton should ask you to plead his cause, excuse yourself."

"I shall certainly have the excuse," said Felix, "that I have a cause of my own to plead."

"If he should talk of me—favorably," Eugenia continued, "warn him against dangerous illusions. I detest importunities; I want to decide at my leisure, with my eyes open."

"I shall be discreet," said Felix, "except to you. To you I will say, Accept him outright."

She had advanced to the open doorway, and she stood looking at him. "I will go and dress and think of it," she said; and he heard her moving slowly to her apartments.

Late in the afternoon the rain stopped, and just afterwards there was a great flaming, flickering, trickling sunset. Felix sat in his painting-room and did some work; but at last, as the light, which had not been brilliant, began to fade, he laid down his brushes and came out to the little piazza of the cottage. Here he walked up and down for some time, looking at the splendid blaze of the western sky and saying, as he had often said before, that this was certainly the country of sunsets. There was something in these glorious deeps of fire that quickened his imagination; he always found images and promises in the western sky. He thought of a good many things—of roaming about the world with Gertrude Wentworth; he seemed to see their possible adventures, in a glowing frieze, between the cloud-bars; then of what Eugenia had just been telling him. He wished very much that Madame Münster would make a comfortable and honorable marriage. Presently, as the sunset expanded and deepened, the fancy took him of making a note of so magnificent a piece of coloring. He returned to his studio and fetched out a small panel, with his palette and brushes, and, placing the panel against a window-sill, he began to daub with great gusto. While he was so occupied he saw Mr. Brand, in the distance, slowly come down from Mr. Wentworth's house, nursing a large folded umbrella. He walked with a joyless, meditative tread, and his eyes were bent upon the ground. Felix poised his brush for a moment, watching him; then, by a sudden impulse, as he drew nearer, advanced to the garden-gate and signaled to him—the palette and bunch of brushes contributing to this effect.

Mr. Brand stopped and started; then he appeared to decide to accept Felix's invitation. He came out of Mr. Wentworth's gate and passed along the road; after which he entered the little garden of the cottage. Felix had gone back to his sunset; but he made his visitor welcome while he rapidly brushed it in.

"I wanted so much to speak to you that I thought I would call you," he said, in the friendliest tone. "All the more that you have been to see me so little. You have come to see my sister; I know that. But you haven't come to see me—the celebrated artist. Artists are very sensitive, you know; they notice those things." And Felix turned round, smiling, with a brush in his mouth.

Mr. Brand stood there with a certain blank, candid majesty, pulling together the large flaps of his umbrella. "Why should I come to see you?" he asked. "I know nothing of Art."

"It would sound very conceited, I suppose," said Felix, "if I were to say that it would be a good little chance for you to learn something. You would ask me why you should learn; and I should have no answer to that. I suppose a minister has no need for Art, eh?"

"He has need for good temper, sir," said Mr. Brand, with decision.

Felix jumped up, with his palette on his thumb and a movement of the liveliest deprecation. "That's because I keep you standing there while I splash my red paint! I beg a thousand pardons! You see what bad manners Art gives a man; and how right you are to let it alone. I didn't mean you should stand, either. The piazza, as you see, is ornamented with rustic chairs; though indeed I ought to warn you that they have nails in the wrong places. I was just making a note of that sunset. I never saw such a blaze of different reds. It looks as if the Celestial City were in flames, eh? If that were really the case I suppose it would be the business of you theologians to put out the fire. Fancy me—an ungodly artist—quietly sitting down to paint it!"

Mr. Brand had always credited Felix Young with a certain impudence, but it appeared to him that on this occasion his impudence was so great as to make a special explanation—or even an apology—necessary. And the impression, it must be added, was sufficiently natural. Felix had at all times a brilliant assurance of manner which was simply the vehicle of his good spirits and his good will; but at present he had a special design, and as he would have admitted that the design was audacious, so he was conscious of having summoned all the arts of conversation to his aid. But he was so far from desiring to offend his visitor that he was rapidly asking himself what personal compliment he could pay the young clergyman that would gratify him most. If he could think of it, he was prepared to pay it down. "Have you been preaching one of your beautiful sermons today?" he suddenly asked, laying down his palette. This was not what Felix had been trying to think of, but it was a tolerable stop-gap.

Mr. Brand frowned—as much as a man can frown who has very fair, soft eyebrows, and, beneath them, very gentle, tranquil eyes. "No, I have not preached any sermon today. Did you bring me over here for the purpose of making that inquiry?"

Felix saw that he was irritated, and he regretted it immensely; but he had no fear of not being, in the end, agreeable to Mr. Brand. He looked at him, smiling and laying his hand on his arm. "No, no, not for that—not for that. I wanted to ask you something; I wanted to tell you something. I am sure it will interest you very much. Only—as it is something rather private—we had better come into my little studio. I have a western window; we can still see the sunset. *Andiamo!*" And he gave a little pat to his companion's arm.

He led the way in; Mr. Brand stiffly and softly followed. The twilight had thickened in the little studio; but the wall opposite the western window was covered with a deep pink flush. There were a great many sketches and half-finished canvasses suspended in this rosy glow, and the corners of the room were vague and dusky. Felix begged Mr. Brand to sit down; then glancing round him, "By Jove, how pretty it looks!" he cried. But Mr. Brand would not sit down; he went and leaned against the window; he wondered what Felix wanted of him. In the shadow, on the darker parts of the wall, he saw the gleam of three or four pictures that looked fantastic and surprising. They seemed to represent naked figures. Felix stood there, with his head a little bent and his eyes fixed upon his visitor, smiling intensely, pulling his moustache. Mr. Brand felt vaguely uneasy. "It is very delicate—what I want to say," Felix began. "But I have been thinking of it for some time."

"Please to say it as quickly as possible," said Mr. Brand.

"It's because you are a clergyman, you know," Felix went on. "I don't think I should venture to say it to a common man."

Mr. Brand was silent a moment. "If it is a question of yielding to a weakness, of resenting an injury, I am afraid I am a very common man."

"My dearest friend," cried Felix, "this is not an injury; it's a benefit—a great service! You will like it extremely. Only it's so delicate!" And, in the dim light, he continued to smile intensely. "You know I take a great interest in my cousins—in Charlotte and Gertrude Wentworth. That's very evident from my having traveled some five thousand miles to see them." Mr. Brand said nothing and Felix proceeded. "Coming into their society as a perfect stranger I received of course a great many new impressions, and my impressions had a great freshness, a great keenness. Do you know what I mean?"

"I am not sure that I do; but I should like you to continue."

"I think my impressions have always a good deal of freshness," said Mr. Brand's entertainer; "but on this occasion it was perhaps particularly natural that—coming in, as I say, from outside—I should be struck with things that passed unnoticed among yourselves. And then I had my sister to help me; and she is simply the most observant woman in the world."

"I am not surprised," said Mr. Brand, "that in our little circle two intelligent persons should have found food for observation. I am sure that, of late, I have found it myself!"

"Ah, but I shall surprise you yet!" cried Felix, laughing. "Both my sister and I took a great fancy to my cousin Charlotte."

"Your cousin Charlotte?" repeated Mr. Brand.

"We fell in love with her from the first!"

"You fell in love with Charlotte?" Mr. Brand murmured.

192

"*Dame!*" exclaimed Felix, "she's a very charming person; and Eugenia was especially smitten." Mr. Brand stood staring, and he pursued, "Affection, you know, opens one's eyes, and we noticed something. Charlotte is not happy! Charlotte is in love." And Felix, drawing nearer, laid his hand again upon his companion's arm.

There was something akin to an acknowledgment of fascination in the way Mr. Brand looked at him; but the young clergyman retained as yet quite enough self-possession to be able to say, with a good deal of solemnity, "She is not in love with you."

Felix gave a light laugh, and rejoined with the alacrity of a maritime adventurer who feels a puff of wind in his sail. "Ah, no; if she were in love with me I should know it! I am not so blind as you."

"As I?"

"My dear sir, you are stone blind. Poor Charlotte is dead in love with *you!*"

Mr. Brand said nothing for a moment; he breathed a little heavily. "Is that what you wanted to say to me?" he asked.

"I have wanted to say it these three weeks. Because of late she has been worse. I told you," added Felix, "it was very delicate."

"Well, sir"—Mr. Brand began; "well, sir——"

"I was sure you didn't know it," Felix continued. "But don't you see—as soon as I mention it—how everything is explained?" Mr. Brand answered nothing; he looked for a chair and softly sat down. Felix could see that he was blushing; he had looked straight at his host hitherto, but now he looked away. The foremost effect of what he had heard had been a sort of irritation of his modesty. "Of course," said Felix, "I suggest nothing; it would be very presumptuous in me to advise you. But I think there is no doubt about the fact."

Mr. Brand looked hard at the floor for some moments; he was oppressed with a mixture of sensations. Felix, standing there, was very sure that one of them was profound surprise. The innocent young man had been completely unsuspicious of poor Charlotte's hidden flame. This gave Felix great hope; he was sure that Mr. Brand would be flattered. Felix thought him very transparent, and indeed he was so; he could neither simulate nor dissimulate. "I scarcely know what to make of this," he said at last, without looking up; and Felix was struck with the fact that he offered no protest or contradiction. Evidently Felix had kindled a train of memories—a retrospective illumination. It was making, to Mr. Brand's astonished eyes, a very pretty blaze; his second emotion had been a gratification of vanity.

"Thank me for telling you," Felix rejoined. "It's a good thing to know."

"I am not sure of that," said Mr. Brand.

"Ah, don't let her languish!" Felix murmured, lightly and softly.

"You *do* advise me, then?" And Mr. Brand looked up.

"I congratulate you!" said Felix, smiling. He had thought at first his visitor was simply appealing; but he saw he was a little ironical.

"It is in your interest; you have interfered with me," the young clergyman went on.

Felix still stood and smiled. The little room had grown darker, and the crimson glow had faded; but Mr. Brand could see the brilliant expression of his face. "I won't pretend not to know what you mean," said Felix at last. "But I have not really interfered with you. Of what you had to lose—with another person—you have lost nothing. And think what you have gained!"

"It seems to me I am the proper judge, on each side," Mr. Brand declared. He got up, holding the brim of his hat against his mouth and staring at Felix through the dusk.

"You have lost an illusion!" said Felix.

"What do you call an illusion?"

"The belief that you really know—that you have ever really known—Gertrude Wentworth. Depend upon that," pursued Felix. "I don't know her yet; but I have no illusions; I don't pretend to."

Mr. Brand kept gazing, over his hat. "She has always been a lucid, limpid nature," he said, solemnly.

"She has always been a dormant nature. She was waiting for a touchstone. But now she is beginning to awaken."

"Don't praise her to me!" said Mr. Brand, with a little quaver in his voice. "If you have the advantage of me that is not generous."

"My dear sir, I am melting with generosity!" exclaimed Felix. "And I am not praising my cousin. I am simply attempting a scientific definition of her. She doesn't care for abstractions. Now I think the contrary is what you have always fancied—is the basis on which you have been building. She is extremely preoccupied with the concrete. I care for the concrete, too. But Gertrude is stronger than I; she whirls me along!"

Mr. Brand looked for a moment into the crown of his hat. "It's a most interesting nature."

"So it is," said Felix. "But it pulls—it pulls—like a runaway horse. Now I like the feeling of a runaway horse; and if I am thrown out of the vehicle it is no great matter. But if *you* should be thrown, Mr. Brand"—and Felix paused a moment—"another person also would suffer from the accident."

"What other person?"

"Charlotte Wentworth!"

Mr. Brand looked at Felix for a moment sidewise, mistrustfully; then his eyes slowly wandered over the ceiling. Felix was sure he was secretly struck with the romance of the situation. "I think this is none of our business," the young minister murmured.

"None of mine, perhaps; but surely yours!"

Mr. Brand lingered still, looking at the ceiling; there was evidently something he wanted to say. "What do you mean by Miss Gertrude being strong?" he asked abruptly.

"Well," said Felix meditatively, "I mean that she has had a great deal of self-possession. She was waiting—for years; even when she seemed, perhaps, to be living in the present. She knew how to wait; she had a purpose. That's what I mean by her being strong."

"But what do you mean by her purpose?"

"Well—the purpose to see the world!"

Mr. Brand eyed his strange informant askance again; but he said nothing. At last he turned away, as if to take leave. He seemed bewildered, however; for instead of going to the door he moved toward the opposite corner of the room. Felix stood and watched him for a moment—almost groping about in the dusk; then he led him to the door, with a tender, almost fraternal movement. "Is that all you have to say?" asked Mr. Brand.

"Yes, it's all—but it will bear a good deal of thinking of."

Felix went with him to the garden-gate, and watched him slowly walk away into the thickening twilight with a relaxed rigidity that tried to rectify itself. "He is offended, excited, bewildered, perplexed—and enchanted!" Felix said to himself. "That's a capital mixture."

# CHAPTER XI

Since that visit paid by the Baroness Münster to Mrs. Acton, of which some account was given at an earlier stage of this narrative, the intercourse between these two ladies had been neither frequent nor intimate. It was not that Mrs. Acton had failed to appreciate Madame Münster's charms; on the contrary, her perception of the graces of manner and conversation of her brilliant visitor had been only too acute. Mrs. Acton was, as they said in Boston, very "intense," and her impressions were apt to be too many for her. The state of her health required the restriction of emotion; and this is why, receiving, as she sat in her eternal arm-chair, very few visitors, even of the soberest local type, she had been obliged to limit the number of her interviews with a lady whose costume and manner recalled to her imagination—Mrs. Acton's imagination was a marvel—all that she had ever read of the most stirring historical periods. But she had sent the Baroness a great many quaintly-worded messages and a great many nosegays from her garden and baskets of beautiful fruit. Felix had eaten the fruit, and the Baroness had arranged the flowers and returned the baskets and the messages. On the day that followed that rainy Sunday of which mention has been made, Eugenia determined to go and pay the beneficent invalid a *"visite d'adieux"*; so it was that, to herself, she qualified her enterprise. It may be noted that neither on the Sunday evening nor on the Monday morning had she received that expected visit from Robert Acton. To his own consciousness, evidently he was "keeping away;" and as the Baroness, on her side, was keeping away from her uncle's, whither, for several days, Felix had been the unembarrassed bearer of apologies and regrets for absence, chance had not taken the cards from the hands of design. Mr. Wentworth and his daughters had respected Eugenia's seclusion; certain intervals of mysterious retirement appeared to them, vaguely, a natural part of the graceful, rhythmic movement of so remarkable a life. Gertrude especially held these periods in honor; she wondered what Madame Münster did at such times, but she would not have permitted herself to inquire too curiously.

The long rain had freshened the air, and twelve hours' brilliant sunshine had dried the roads; so that the Baroness, in the late afternoon, proposing to walk to Mrs. Acton's, exposed herself to no great discomfort. As with her charming undulating step she moved along the clean, grassy margin of the road, beneath the thickly-hanging boughs of the orchards, through the quiet of the hour and place and the rich maturity of the summer, she was even conscious of a sort of luxurious melancholy. The Baroness had the amiable weakness of attaching herself to places—even when she had begun with a little aversion; and now, with the prospect of departure, she felt tenderly toward this well-wooded corner of the Western world, where the sunsets were so beautiful and one's ambitions were so pure. Mrs. Acton was able to receive her; but on entering this lady's large, freshly-scented room the Baroness saw that she was looking very ill. She was wonderfully white and transparent, and, in her flowered arm-chair, she made no attempt to move. But she flushed a little—like a young girl, the Baroness thought—and she rested her clear, smiling eyes upon those of her visitor. Her voice was low and monotonous, like a voice that had never expressed any human passions.

"I have come to bid you good-bye," said Eugenia. "I shall soon be going away."

"When are you going away?"

"Very soon—any day."

"I am very sorry," said Mrs. Acton. "I hoped you would stay—always."

"Always?" Eugenia demanded.

"Well, I mean a long time," said Mrs. Acton, in her sweet, feeble tone. "They tell me you are so comfortable—that you have got such a beautiful little house."

Eugenia stared—that is, she smiled; she thought of her poor little chalet and she wondered whether her hostess were jesting. "Yes, my house is exquisite," she said; "though not to be compared to yours."

"And my son is so fond of going to see you," Mrs. Acton added. "I am afraid my son will miss you."

"Ah, dear madam," said Eugenia, with a little laugh, "I can't stay in America for your son!"

"Don't you like America?"

The Baroness looked at the front of her dress. "If I liked it—that would not be staying for your son!"

Mrs. Acton gazed at her with her grave, tender eyes, as if she had not quite understood. The Baroness at last found something irritating in the sweet, soft stare of her hostess; and if one were not bound to be merciful to great invalids she would almost have taken the liberty of pronouncing her, mentally, a fool. "I am afraid, then, I shall never see you again," said Mrs. Acton. "You know I am dying."

"Ah, dear madam," murmured Eugenia.

"I want to leave my children cheerful and happy. My daughter will probably marry her cousin."

"Two such interesting young people," said the Baroness, vaguely. She was not thinking of Clifford Wentworth.

"I feel so tranquil about my end," Mrs. Acton went on. "It is coming so easily, so surely." And she paused, with her mild gaze always on Eugenia's.

The Baroness hated to be reminded of death; but even in its imminence, so far as Mrs. Acton was concerned, she preserved her good manners. "Ah, madam, you are too charming an invalid," she rejoined.

But the delicacy of this rejoinder was apparently lost upon her hostess, who went on in her low, reasonable voice. "I want to leave my children bright and comfortable. You seem to me all so happy here—just as you are. So I wish you could stay. It would be so pleasant for Robert."

Eugenia wondered what she meant by its being pleasant for Robert; but she felt that she would never know what such a woman as that meant. She got up; she was afraid Mrs. Acton would tell her again that she was dying. "Good-bye, dear madam," she said. "I must remember that your strength is precious."

Mrs. Acton took her hand and held it a moment. "Well, you *have* been happy here, haven't you? And you like us all, don't you? I wish you would stay," she added, "in your beautiful little house."

She had told Eugenia that her waiting-woman would be in the hall, to show her downstairs; but the large landing outside her door was empty, and Eugenia stood there looking about. She felt irritated; the dying lady had not *"la main heureuse."* She passed slowly downstairs, still looking about. The broad staircase made a great bend, and in the angle was a high window, looking westward, with a deep bench, covered with a row of flowering plants in curious old pots of blue china-ware. The yellow afternoon light came in through the flowers and flickered a little on the white wainscots. Eugenia paused a moment; the house was perfectly still, save for the ticking, somewhere, of a great clock. The lower hall stretched away at the foot of the stairs, half covered over with a large Oriental rug. Eugenia lingered a little, noticing a great many things. *"Comme c'est bien!"* she said to herself; such a large, solid, irreproachable basis of existence the place seemed to her to indicate. And then she reflected that Mrs. Acton was soon to withdraw from it. The reflection accompanied her the rest of the way downstairs, where she paused again, making more observations. The hall was extremely broad, and on either side of the front door was a wide, deeply-set window, which threw the shadows of everything back into the house. There were high-backed chairs along the wall and big Eastern vases upon tables, and, on either side, a large cabinet with a glass front and little curiosities within, dimly gleaming. The doors were open—into the darkened parlor, the library, the dining-room. All these rooms seemed empty. Eugenia passed along, and stopped a moment on the threshold of each. *"Comme c'est bien!"* she murmured again; she had thought of just such a house as this when she decided to come to America. She opened the front door for herself—her light tread had summoned none of the servants—and on the threshold she gave a last look. Outside, she was still in the humor for curious contemplation; so instead of going directly down the little drive, to the gate, she wandered away towards the garden, which lay to the right of the house. She had not gone many yards over the grass before she paused quickly; she perceived a gentleman stretched upon the level verdure, beneath a tree. He had not heard her coming, and he lay motionless, flat on his back, with his hands clasped under his head, staring up at the sky; so that the Baroness was able to reflect, at her leisure, upon the question of his identity. It was that of a person who had lately been much in her thoughts; but her first impulse, nevertheless, was to turn away; the last thing she desired was to have the air of coming in quest of Robert Acton. The gentleman on the grass, however, gave her no time to decide; he could not long remain unconscious of so agreeable a presence. He rolled back his eyes, stared, gave an exclamation, and then jumped up. He stood an instant, looking at her.

"Excuse my ridiculous position," he said.

"I have just now no sense of the ridiculous. But, in case you have, don't imagine I came to see you."

"Take care," rejoined Acton, "how you put it into my head! I was thinking of you."

"The occupation of extreme leisure!" said the Baroness. "To think of a woman when you are in that position is no compliment."

"I didn't say I was thinking well!" Acton affirmed, smiling.

She looked at him, and then she turned away.

"Though I didn't come to see you," she said, "remember at least that I am within your gates."

"I am delighted—I am honored! Won't you come into the house?"

"I have just come out of it. I have been calling upon your mother. I have been bidding her farewell."

"Farewell?" Acton demanded.

"I am going away," said the Baroness. And she turned away again, as if to illustrate her meaning.

"When are you going?" asked Acton, standing a moment in his place. But the Baroness made no answer, and he followed her.

"I came this way to look at your garden," she said, walking back to the gate, over the grass. "But I must go."

"Let me at least go with you." He went with her, and they said nothing till they reached the gate. It was open, and they looked down the road which was darkened over with long bosky shadows. "Must you go straight home?" Acton asked.

But she made no answer. She said, after a moment, "Why have you not been to see me?" He said nothing, and then she went on, "Why don't you answer me?"

"I am trying to invent an answer," Acton confessed.

"Have you none ready?"

"None that I can tell you," he said. "But let me walk with you now."

"You may do as you like."

She moved slowly along the road, and Acton went with her. Presently he said, "If I had done as I liked I would have come to see you several times."

"Is that invented?" asked Eugenia.

"No, that is natural. I stayed away because——"

"Ah, here comes the reason, then!"

"Because I wanted to think about you."

"Because you wanted to lie down!" said the Baroness. "I have seen you lie down—almost—in my drawing-room."

Acton stopped in the road, with a movement which seemed to beg her to linger a little. She paused, and he looked at her awhile; he thought her very charming. "You are jesting," he said; "but if you are really going away it is very serious."

"If I stay," and she gave a little laugh, "it is more serious still!"

"When shall you go?"

"As soon as possible."

"And why?"

"Why should I stay?"

"Because we all admire you so."

"That is not a reason. I am admired also in Europe." And she began to walk homeward again.

"What could I say to keep you?" asked Acton. He wanted to keep her, and it was a fact that he had been thinking of her for a week. He was in love with her now; he was conscious of that, or he thought he was; and the only question with him was whether he could trust her.

"What you can say to keep me?" she repeated. "As I want very much to go it is not in my interest to tell you. Besides, I can't imagine."

He went on with her in silence; he was much more affected by what she had told him than appeared. Ever since that evening of his return from Newport her image had had a terrible power to trouble him. What Clifford Wentworth had told him—that had affected him, too, in an adverse sense; but it had not liberated him from the discomfort of a charm of which his intelligence was impatient. "She is not honest, she is not honest," he kept murmuring to himself. That is what he had been saying to the summer sky, ten minutes before. Unfortunately, he was unable to say it finally, definitively; and now that he was near her it seemed to matter wonderfully little. "She is a woman who will lie," he had said to himself. Now, as he went along, he reminded himself of this observation; but it failed to frighten him as it had done before. He almost wished he could make her lie and then convict her of it, so that he might see how he should like that. He kept thinking of this as he walked by her side, while she moved forward with her light, graceful dignity. He had sat with her before; he had driven with her; but he had never walked with her.

"By Jove, how *comme il faut* she is!" he said, as he observed her sidewise. When they reached the cottage in the orchard she passed into the gate without asking him to follow; but she turned round, as he stood there, to bid him good-night.

"I asked you a question the other night which you never answered," he said. "Have you sent off that document—liberating yourself?"

She hesitated for a single moment—very naturally. Then, "Yes," she said, simply.

He turned away; he wondered whether that would do for his lie. But he saw her again that evening, for the Baroness reappeared at her uncle's. He had little talk with her, however; two gentlemen had driven out from Boston, in a buggy, to call upon Mr. Wentworth and his daughters, and Madame Münster was an object of absorbing interest to both of the visitors. One of them, indeed, said nothing to her; he only sat and watched with intense gravity, and leaned forward solemnly, presenting his ear (a very large one), as if he were deaf, whenever she dropped an observation. He had evidently been impressed with the idea of her misfortunes and reverses: he never smiled. His companion adopted a lighter, easier style; sat as near as possible to Madame Münster; attempted to draw her out, and proposed every few moments a new topic of conversation. Eugenia was less vividly responsive than usual and had less to say than, from her brilliant reputation, her interlocutor expected, upon the relative merits of European and American institutions; but she was inaccessible to Robert Acton, who roamed about the piazza with his hands in his pockets, listening for the grating sound of the buggy from Boston, as it should be brought round to the side-door. But he listened in vain, and at last he lost patience. His sister came to him and begged him to take her home, and he presently went off with her. Eugenia observed him leaving the house with Lizzie; in her present mood the fact seemed a contribution to her irritated conviction that he had several precious qualities. "Even that *mal-élevée* little girl," she reflected, "makes him do what she wishes."

She had been sitting just within one of the long windows that opened upon the piazza; but very soon after Acton had gone away she got up abruptly, just when the talkative gentleman from Boston was asking her what she thought of the "moral tone" of that city. On the piazza she encountered Clifford Wentworth, coming round from the other side of the house. She stopped him; she told him she wished to speak to him.

"Why didn't you go home with your cousin?" she asked.

Clifford stared. "Why, Robert has taken her," he said.

"Exactly so. But you don't usually leave that to him."

"Oh," said Clifford, "I want to see those fellows start off. They don't know how to drive."

"It is not, then, that you have quarreled with your cousin?"

Clifford reflected a moment, and then with a simplicity which had, for the Baroness, a singularly baffling quality, "Oh, no; we have made up!" he said.

She looked at him for some moments; but Clifford had begun to be afraid of the Baroness's looks, and he endeavored, now, to shift himself out of their range. "Why do you never come to see me any more?" she asked. "Have I displeased you?"

"Displeased me? Well, I guess not!" said Clifford, with a laugh.

"Why haven't you come, then?"

"Well, because I am afraid of getting shut up in that back room."

Eugenia kept looking at him. "I should think you would like that."

"Like it!" cried Clifford.

"I should, if I were a young man calling upon a charming woman."

"A charming woman isn't much use to me when I am shut up in that back room!"

205

"I am afraid I am not of much use to you anywhere!" said Madame Münster. "And yet you know how I have offered to be."

"Well," observed Clifford, by way of response, "there comes the buggy."

"Never mind the buggy. Do you know I am going away?"

"Do you mean now?"

"I mean in a few days. I leave this place."

"You are going back to Europe?"

"To Europe, where you are to come and see me."

"Oh, yes, I'll come out there," said Clifford.

"But before that," Eugenia declared, "you must come and see me here."

"Well, I shall keep clear of that back room!" rejoined her simple young kinsman.

The Baroness was silent a moment. "Yes, you must come frankly—boldly. That will be very much better. I see that now."

"I see it!" said Clifford. And then, in an instant, "What's the matter with that buggy?" His practiced ear had apparently detected an unnatural creak in the wheels of the light vehicle which had been brought to the portico, and he hurried away to investigate so grave an anomaly.

The Baroness walked homeward, alone, in the starlight, asking herself a question. Was she to have gained nothing—was she to have gained nothing?

Gertrude Wentworth had held a silent place in the little circle gathered about the two gentlemen from Boston. She was not interested in the visitors; she was watching Madame Münster, as she constantly watched her. She knew that Eugenia also was not interested—that she was bored; and Gertrude was absorbed in study of the problem how, in spite of her indifference and her absent attention, she managed to have such a charming manner. That was the manner Gertrude would have liked to have; she determined to cultivate it, and she wished that—to give her the charm—she might in future very often be bored. While she was engaged in these researches, Felix Young was looking for Charlotte, to whom he had something to say. For some time, now, he had had something to say to Charlotte, and this evening his sense of the propriety of holding some special conversation with her had reached the motive-point—resolved itself into acute and delightful desire. He wandered through the empty rooms on the large ground-floor of the house, and found her at last in a small apartment denominated, for reasons not immediately apparent, Mr. Wentworth's "office:" an extremely neat and well-dusted room, with an array of law-books, in time-darkened sheep-skin, on one of the walls; a large map of the United States on the other, flanked on either side by an old steel engraving of one of Raphael's Madonnas; and on the third several glass cases containing specimens of butterflies and beetles. Charlotte was sitting by a lamp, embroidering a slipper. Felix did not ask for whom the slipper was destined; he saw it was very large.

He moved a chair toward her and sat down, smiling as usual, but, at first, not speaking. She watched him, with her needle poised, and with a certain shy, fluttered look which she always wore when he approached her. There was something in Felix's manner that quickened her modesty, her self-consciousness; if absolute choice had been given her she would have preferred never to find herself alone with him; and in fact, though she thought him a most brilliant, distinguished, and well-meaning person, she had exercised a much larger amount of tremulous tact than he had ever suspected, to circumvent the accident of *tête-à-tête*. Poor Charlotte could have given no account of the matter that would not have seemed unjust both to herself and to her foreign kinsman; she could only have said—or rather, she would never have said it—that she did not like so much gentleman's society at once. She was not reassured, accordingly, when he began, emphasizing his words with a kind of admiring radiance, "My dear cousin, I am enchanted at finding you alone."

"I am very often alone," Charlotte observed. Then she quickly added, "I don't mean I am lonely!"

"So clever a woman as you is never lonely," said Felix. "You have company in your beautiful work." And he glanced at the big slipper.

"I like to work," declared Charlotte, simply.

"So do I!" said her companion. "And I like to idle too. But it is not to idle that I have come in search of you. I want to tell you something very particular."

"Well," murmured Charlotte; "of course, if you must———"

"My dear cousin," said Felix, "it's nothing that a young lady may not listen to. At least I suppose it isn't. But *voyons*; you shall judge. I am terribly in love."

"Well, Felix," began Miss Wentworth, gravely. But her very gravity appeared to check the development of her phrase.

"I am in love with your sister; but in love, Charlotte—in love!" the young man pursued. Charlotte had laid her work in her lap; her hands were tightly folded on top of it; she was staring at the carpet. "In short, I'm in love, dear lady," said Felix. "Now I want you to help me."

"To help you?" asked Charlotte, with a tremor.

"I don't mean with Gertrude; she and I have a perfect understanding; and oh, how well she understands one! I mean with your father and with the world in general, including Mr. Brand."

"Poor Mr. Brand!" said Charlotte, slowly, but with a simplicity which made it evident to Felix that the young minister had not repeated to Miss Wentworth the talk that had lately occurred between them.

"Ah, now, don't say 'poor' Mr. Brand! I don't pity Mr. Brand at all. But I pity your father a little, and I don't want to displease him. Therefore, you see, I want you to plead for me. You don't think me very shabby, eh?"

"Shabby?" exclaimed Charlotte softly, for whom Felix represented the most polished and iridescent qualities of mankind.

"I don't mean in my appearance," rejoined Felix, laughing; for Charlotte was looking at his boots. "I mean in my conduct. You don't think it's an abuse of hospitality?"

"To—to care for Gertrude?" asked Charlotte.

"To have really expressed one's self. Because I *have* expressed myself, Charlotte; I must tell you the whole truth—I have! Of course I want to marry her—and here is the difficulty. I held off as long as I could; but she is such a terribly fascinating person! She's a strange creature, Charlotte; I don't believe you really know her." Charlotte took up her tapestry again, and again she laid it down. "I know your father has had higher views," Felix continued; "and I think you have shared them. You have wanted to marry her to Mr. Brand."

"Oh, no," said Charlotte, very earnestly. "Mr. Brand has always admired her. But we did not want anything of that kind."

Felix stared. "Surely, marriage was what you proposed."

"Yes; but we didn't wish to force her."

"*A la bonne heure!* That's very unsafe you know. With these arranged marriages there is often the deuce to pay."

"Oh, Felix," said Charlotte, "we didn't want to 'arrange.'"

"I am delighted to hear that. Because in such cases—even when the woman is a thoroughly good creature—she can't help looking for a compensation. A charming fellow comes along—and *voilà!*" Charlotte sat mutely staring at the floor, and Felix presently added, "Do go on with your slipper, I like to see you work."

Charlotte took up her variegated canvas, and began to draw vague blue stitches in a big round rose. "If Gertrude is so—so strange," she said, "why do you want to marry her?"

"Ah, that's it, dear Charlotte! I like strange women; I always have liked them. Ask Eugenia! And Gertrude is wonderful; she says the most beautiful things!"

Charlotte looked at him, almost for the first time, as if her meaning required to be severely pointed. "You have a great influence over her."

"Yes—and no!" said Felix. "I had at first, I think; but now it is six of one and half-a-dozen of the other; it is reciprocal. She affects me strongly—for she *is* so strong. I don't believe you know her; it's a beautiful nature."

"Oh, yes, Felix; I have always thought Gertrude's nature beautiful."

"Well, if you think so now," cried the young man, "wait and see! She's a folded flower. Let me pluck her from the parent tree and you will see her expand. I'm sure you will enjoy it."

"I don't understand you," murmured Charlotte. "I *can't*, Felix."

"Well, you can understand this—that I beg you to say a good word for me to your father. He regards me, I naturally believe, as a very light fellow, a Bohemian, an irregular character. Tell him I am not all this; if I ever was, I have forgotten it. I am fond of pleasure—yes; but of innocent pleasure. Pain is all one; but in pleasure, you know, there are tremendous distinctions. Say to him that Gertrude is a folded flower and that I am a serious man!"

Charlotte got up from her chair slowly rolling up her work. "We know you are very kind to everyone, Felix," she said. "But we are extremely sorry for Mr. Brand."

"Of course you are—you especially! Because," added Felix hastily, "you are a woman. But I don't pity him. It ought to be enough for any man that you take an interest in him."

"It is not enough for Mr. Brand," said Charlotte, simply. And she stood there a moment, as if waiting conscientiously for anything more that Felix might have to say.

"Mr. Brand is not so keen about his marriage as he was," he presently said. "He is afraid of your sister. He begins to think she is wicked."

Charlotte looked at him now with beautiful, appealing eyes—eyes into which he saw the tears rising. "Oh, Felix, Felix," she cried, "what have you done to her?"

"I think she was asleep; I have waked her up!"

But Charlotte, apparently, was really crying, she walked straight out of the room. And Felix, standing there and meditating, had the apparent brutality to take satisfaction in her tears.

Late that night Gertrude, silent and serious, came to him in the garden; it was a kind of appointment. Gertrude seemed to like appointments. She plucked a handful of heliotrope and stuck it into the front of her dress, but she said nothing. They walked together along one of the paths, and Felix looked at the great, square, hospitable house, massing itself vaguely in the starlight, with all its windows darkened.

"I have a little of a bad conscience," he said. "I oughtn't to meet you this way till I have got your father's consent."

Gertrude looked at him for some time. "I don't understand you."

"You very often say that," he said. "Considering how little we understand each other, it is a wonder how well we get on!"

"We have done nothing but meet since you came here—but meet alone. The first time I ever saw you we were alone," Gertrude went on. "What is the difference now? Is it because it is at night?"

"The difference, Gertrude," said Felix, stopping in the path, "the difference is that I love you more—more than before!" And then they stood there, talking, in the warm stillness and in front of the closed dark house. "I have been talking to Charlotte—been trying to bespeak her interest with your father. She has a kind of sublime perversity; was ever a woman so bent upon cutting off her own head?"

"You are too careful," said Gertrude; "you are too diplomatic."

"Well," cried the young man, "I didn't come here to make anyone unhappy!"

Gertrude looked round her awhile in the odorous darkness. "I will do anything you please," she said.

"For instance?" asked Felix, smiling.

"I will go away. I will do anything you please."

Felix looked at her in solemn admiration. "Yes, we will go away," he said. "But we will make peace first."

Gertrude looked about her again, and then she broke out, passionately, "Why do they try to make one feel guilty? Why do they make it so difficult? Why can't they understand?"

"I will make them understand!" said Felix. He drew her hand into his arm, and they wandered about in the garden, talking, for an hour.

# CHAPTER XII

Felix allowed Charlotte time to plead his cause; and then, on the third day, he sought an interview with his uncle. It was in the morning; Mr. Wentworth was in his office; and, on going in, Felix found that Charlotte was at that moment in conference with her father. She had, in fact, been constantly near him since her interview with Felix; she had made up her mind that it was her duty to repeat very literally her cousin's passionate plea. She had accordingly followed Mr. Wentworth about like a shadow, in order to find him at hand when she should have mustered sufficient composure to speak. For poor Charlotte, in this matter, naturally lacked composure; especially when she meditated upon some of Felix's intimations. It was not cheerful work, at the best, to keep giving small hammer-taps to the coffin in which one had laid away, for burial, the poor little unacknowledged offspring of one's own misbehaving heart; and the occupation was not rendered more agreeable by the fact that the ghost of one's stifled dream had been summoned from the shades by the strange, bold words of a talkative young foreigner. What had Felix meant by saying that Mr. Brand was not so keen? To herself her sister's justly depressed suitor had shown no sign of faltering. Charlotte trembled all over when she allowed herself to believe for an instant now and then that, privately, Mr. Brand might have faltered; and as it seemed to give more force to Felix's words to repeat them to her father, she was waiting until she should have taught herself to be very calm. But she had now begun to tell Mr. Wentworth that she was extremely anxious. She was proceeding to develop this idea, to enumerate the objects of her anxiety, when Felix came in.

Mr. Wentworth sat there, with his legs crossed, lifting his dry, pure countenance from the Boston *Advertiser*. Felix entered smiling, as if he had something particular to say, and his uncle looked at him as if he both expected and deprecated this event. Felix vividly expressing himself had come to be a formidable figure to his uncle, who had not yet arrived at definite views as to a proper tone. For the first time in his life, as I have said, Mr. Wentworth shirked a responsibility; he earnestly desired that it might not be laid upon him to determine how his nephew's lighter propositions should be treated. He lived under an apprehension that Felix might yet beguile him into assent to doubtful inductions, and his conscience instructed him that the best form of vigilance was the avoidance of discussion. He hoped that the pleasant episode of his nephew's visit would pass away without a further lapse of consistency.

Felix looked at Charlotte with an air of understanding, and then at Mr. Wentworth, and then at Charlotte again. Mr. Wentworth bent his refined eyebrows upon his nephew and stroked down the first page of the *Advertiser*. "I ought to have brought a bouquet," said Felix, laughing. "In France they always do."

"We are not in France," observed Mr. Wentworth, gravely, while Charlotte earnestly gazed at him.

"No, luckily, we are not in France, where I am afraid I should have a harder time of it. My dear Charlotte, have you rendered me that delightful service?" And Felix bent toward her as if someone had been presenting him.

Charlotte looked at him with almost frightened eyes; and Mr. Wentworth thought this might be the beginning of a discussion. "What is the bouquet for?" he inquired, by way of turning it off.

Felix gazed at him, smiling. *"Pour la demande!"* And then, drawing up a chair, he seated himself, hat in hand, with a kind of conscious solemnity.

Presently he turned to Charlotte again. "My good Charlotte, my admirable Charlotte," he murmured, "you have not played me false—you have not sided against me?"

Charlotte got up, trembling extremely, though imperceptibly. "You must speak to my father yourself," she said. "I think you are clever enough."

But Felix, rising too, begged her to remain. "I can speak better to an audience!" he declared.

"I hope it is nothing disagreeable," said Mr. Wentworth.

"It's something delightful, for me!" And Felix, laying down his hat, clasped his hands a little between his knees. "My dear uncle," he said, "I desire, very earnestly, to marry your daughter Gertrude." Charlotte sank slowly into her chair again, and Mr. Wentworth sat staring, with a light in his face that might have been flashed back from an iceberg. He stared and stared; he said nothing. Felix fell back, with his hands still clasped. "Ah—you don't like it. I was afraid!" He blushed deeply, and Charlotte noticed it—remarking to herself that it was the first time she had ever seen him blush. She began to blush herself and to reflect that he might be much in love.

"This is very abrupt," said Mr. Wentworth, at last.

"Have you never suspected it, dear uncle?" Felix inquired. "Well, that proves how discreet I have been. Yes, I thought you wouldn't like it."

"It is very serious, Felix," said Mr. Wentworth.

"You think it's an abuse of hospitality!" exclaimed Felix, smiling again.

"Of hospitality?—an abuse?" his uncle repeated very slowly.

"That is what Felix said to me," said Charlotte, conscientiously.

"Of course you think so; don't defend yourself!" Felix pursued. "It *is* an abuse, obviously; the most I can claim is that it is perhaps a pardonable one. I simply fell head over heels in love; one can hardly help that. Though you are Gertrude's progenitor I don't believe you know how attractive she is. Dear uncle, she contains the elements of a singularly—I may say a strangely— charming woman!"

"She has always been to me an object of extreme concern," said Mr. Wentworth. "We have always desired her happiness."

"Well, here it is!" Felix declared. "I will make her happy. She believes it, too. Now hadn't you noticed that?"

"I had noticed that she was much changed," Mr. Wentworth declared, in a tone whose unexpressive, unimpassioned quality appeared to Felix to reveal a profundity of opposition. "It may be that she is only becoming what you call a charming woman."

"Gertrude, at heart, is so earnest, so true," said Charlotte, very softly, fastening her eyes upon her father.

"I delight to hear you praise her!" cried Felix.

"She has a very peculiar temperament," said Mr. Wentworth.

"Eh, even that is praise!" Felix rejoined. "I know I am not the man you might have looked for. I have no position and no fortune; I can give Gertrude no place in the world. A place in the world—that's what she ought to have; that would bring her out."

"A place to do her duty!" remarked Mr. Wentworth.

"Ah, how charmingly she does it—her duty!" Felix exclaimed, with a radiant face. "What an exquisite conception she has of it! But she comes honestly by that, dear uncle." Mr. Wentworth and Charlotte both looked at him as if they were watching a greyhound doubling. "Of course with me she will hide her light under a bushel," he continued; "I being the bushel! Now I know you like me—you have certainly proved it. But you think I am frivolous and penniless and shabby! Granted—granted—a thousand times granted. I have been a loose fish—a fiddler, a painter, an actor. But there is this to be said: In the first place, I fancy you exaggerate; you lend me qualities I haven't had. I have been a Bohemian—yes; but in Bohemia I always passed for a gentleman. I wish you could see some of my old *camarades*—they would tell you! It was the liberty I liked, but not the opportunities! My sins were all peccadilloes; I always respected my neighbor's property—my neighbor's wife. Do you see, dear uncle?" Mr. Wentworth ought to have seen; his cold blue eyes were intently fixed. "And then, *c'est fini!* It's all over. *Je me range.* I have settled down to a jog-trot. I find I can earn my living—a very fair one—by going about the world and painting bad portraits. It's not a glorious profession, but it is a perfectly respectable one. You won't deny that, eh? Going about the world, I say? I must not deny that, for that I am afraid I shall always do—in quest of agreeable sitters. When I say agreeable, I mean susceptible of delicate flattery and prompt of payment. Gertrude declares she is willing to share my wanderings and help to pose my models. She even thinks it will be charming; and that brings me to my third point. Gertrude likes me. Encourage her a little and she will tell you so."

Felix's tongue obviously moved much faster than the imagination of his auditors; his eloquence, like the rocking of a boat in a deep, smooth lake, made long eddies of silence. And he seemed to be pleading and chattering still, with his brightly eager smile, his uplifted eyebrows, his expressive mouth, after he had ceased speaking, and while, with his glance quickly turning from the father to the daughter, he sat waiting for the effect of his appeal. "It is not your want of means," said Mr. Wentworth, after a period of severe reticence.

"Now it's delightful of you to say that! Only don't say it's my want of character. Because I have a character—I assure you I have; a small one, a little slip of a thing, but still something tangible."

"Ought you not to tell Felix that it is Mr. Brand, father?" Charlotte asked, with infinite mildness.

"It is not only Mr. Brand," Mr. Wentworth solemnly declared. And he looked at his knee for a long time. "It is difficult to explain," he said. He wished, evidently, to be very just. "It rests on moral grounds, as Mr. Brand says. It is the question whether it is the best thing for Gertrude."

"What is better—what is better, dear uncle?" Felix rejoined urgently, rising in his urgency and standing before Mr. Wentworth. His uncle had been looking at his knee; but when Felix moved he transferred his gaze to the handle of the door which faced him. "It is usually a fairly good thing for a girl to marry the man she loves!" cried Felix.

While he spoke, Mr. Wentworth saw the handle of the door begin to turn; the door opened and remained slightly ajar, until Felix had delivered himself of the cheerful axiom just quoted. Then it opened altogether and Gertrude stood there. She looked excited; there was a spark in her sweet, dull eyes. She came in slowly, but with an air of resolution, and, closing the door softly, looked round at the three persons present. Felix went to her with tender gallantry, holding out his hand, and Charlotte made a place for her on the sofa. But Gertrude put her hands behind her and made no motion to sit down.

"We are talking of you!" said Felix.

217

"I know it," she answered. "That's why I came." And she fastened her eyes on her father, who returned her gaze very fixedly. In his own cold blue eyes there was a kind of pleading, reasoning light.

"It is better you should be present," said Mr. Wentworth. "We are discussing your future."

"Why discuss it?" asked Gertrude. "Leave it to me."

"That is, to me!" cried Felix.

"I leave it, in the last resort, to a greater wisdom than ours," said the old man.

Felix rubbed his forehead gently. "But *en attendant* the last resort, your father lacks confidence," he said to Gertrude.

"Haven't you confidence in Felix?" Gertrude was frowning; there was something about her that her father and Charlotte had never seen. Charlotte got up and came to her, as if to put her arm round her; but suddenly, she seemed afraid to touch her.

Mr. Wentworth, however, was not afraid. "I have had more confidence in Felix than in you," he said.

"Yes, you have never had confidence in me—never, never! I don't know why."

"Oh sister, sister!" murmured Charlotte.

"You have always needed advice," Mr. Wentworth declared. "You have had a difficult temperament."

"Why do you call it difficult? It might have been easy, if you had allowed it. You wouldn't let me be natural. I don't know what you wanted to make of me. Mr. Brand was the worst."

Charlotte at last took hold of her sister. She laid her two hands upon Gertrude's arm. "He cares so much for you," she almost whispered.

Gertrude looked at her intently an instant; then kissed her. "No, he does not," she said.

"I have never seen you so passionate," observed Mr. Wentworth, with an air of indignation mitigated by high principles.

"I am sorry if I offend you," said Gertrude.

"You offend me, but I don't think you are sorry."

"Yes, father, she is sorry," said Charlotte.

"I would even go further, dear uncle," Felix interposed. "I would question whether she really offends you. How can she offend you?"

To this Mr. Wentworth made no immediate answer. Then, in a moment, "She has not profited as we hoped."

"Profited? *Ah voilà!*" Felix exclaimed.

Gertrude was very pale; she stood looking down. "I have told Felix I would go away with him," she presently said.

"Ah, you have said some admirable things!" cried the young man.

"Go away, sister?" asked Charlotte.

"Away—away; to some strange country."

"That is to frighten you," said Felix, smiling at Charlotte.

"To—what do you call it?" asked Gertrude, turning an instant to Felix. "To Bohemia."

"Do you propose to dispense with preliminaries?" asked Mr. Wentworth, getting up.

"Dear uncle, *vous plaisantez!*" cried Felix. "It seems to me that these are preliminaries."

Gertrude turned to her father. "I *have* profited," she said. "You wanted to form my character. Well, my character is formed—for my age. I know what I want; I have chosen. I am determined to marry this gentleman."

"You had better consent, sir," said Felix very gently.

"Yes, sir, you had better consent," added a very different voice.

Charlotte gave a little jump, and the others turned to the direction from which it had come. It was the voice of Mr. Brand, who had stepped through the long window which stood open to the piazza. He stood patting his forehead with his pocket-handkerchief; he was very much flushed; his face wore a singular expression.

"Yes, sir, you had better consent," Mr. Brand repeated, coming forward. "I know what Miss Gertrude means."

"My dear friend!" murmured Felix, laying his hand caressingly on the young minister's arm.

Mr. Brand looked at him; then at Mr. Wentworth; lastly at Gertrude. He did not look at Charlotte. But Charlotte's earnest eyes were fastened to his own countenance; they were asking an immense question of it. The answer to this question could not come all at once; but some of the elements of it were there. It was one of the elements of it that Mr. Brand was very red, that he held his head very high, that he had a bright, excited eye and an air of embarrassed boldness—the air of a man who has taken a resolve, in the execution of which he apprehends the failure, not of his moral, but of his personal, resources. Charlotte thought he looked very grand; and it is incontestable that Mr. Brand felt very grand. This, in fact, was the grandest moment of his life; and it was natural that such a moment should contain opportunities of awkwardness for a large, stout, modest young man.

"Come in, sir," said Mr. Wentworth, with an angular wave of his hand. "It is very proper that you should be present."

"I know what you are talking about," Mr. Brand rejoined. "I heard what your nephew said."

"And he heard what you said!" exclaimed Felix, patting him again on the arm.

"I am not sure that I understood," said Mr. Wentworth, who had angularity in his voice as well as in his gestures.

Gertrude had been looking hard at her former suitor. She had been puzzled, like her sister; but her imagination moved more quickly than Charlotte's. "Mr. Brand asked you to let Felix take me away," she said to her father.

The young minister gave her a strange look. "It is not because I don't want to see you any more," he declared, in a tone intended as it were for publicity.

"I shouldn't think you would want to see me any more," Gertrude answered, gently.

Mr. Wentworth stood staring. "Isn't this rather a change, sir?" he inquired.

"Yes, sir." And Mr. Brand looked anywhere; only still not at Charlotte. "Yes, sir," he repeated. And he held his handkerchief a few moments to his lips.

"Where are our moral grounds?" demanded Mr. Wentworth, who had always thought Mr. Brand would be just the thing for a younger daughter with a peculiar temperament.

"It is sometimes very moral to change, you know," suggested Felix.

Charlotte had softly left her sister's side. She had edged gently toward her father, and now her hand found its way into his arm. Mr. Wentworth had folded up the *Advertiser* into a surprisingly small compass, and, holding the roll with one hand, he earnestly clasped it with the other. Mr. Brand was looking at him; and yet, though Charlotte was so near, his eyes failed to meet her own. Gertrude watched her sister.

"It is better not to speak of change," said Mr. Brand. "In one sense there is no change. There was something I desired—something I asked of you; I desire something still—I ask it of you." And he paused a moment; Mr. Wentworth looked bewildered. "I should like, in my ministerial capacity, to unite this young couple."

Gertrude, watching her sister, saw Charlotte flushing intensely, and Mr. Wentworth felt her pressing upon his arm. "Heavenly Powers!" murmured Mr. Wentworth. And it was the nearest approach to profanity he had ever made.

"That is very nice; that is very handsome!" Felix exclaimed.

"I don't understand," said Mr. Wentworth; though it was plain that everyone else did.

"That is very beautiful, Mr. Brand," said Gertrude, emulating Felix.

"I should like to marry you. It will give me great pleasure."

"As Gertrude says, it's a beautiful idea," said Felix.

Felix was smiling, but Mr. Brand was not even trying to. He himself treated his proposition very seriously. "I have thought of it, and I should like to do it," he affirmed.

Charlotte, meanwhile, was staring with expanded eyes. Her imagination, as I have said, was not so rapid as her sister's, but now it had taken several little jumps. "Father," she murmured, "consent!"

Mr. Brand heard her; he looked away. Mr. Wentworth, evidently, had no imagination at all. "I have always thought," he began, slowly, "that Gertrude's character required a special line of development."

"Father," repeated Charlotte, *"consent."*

Then, at last, Mr. Brand looked at her. Her father felt her leaning more heavily upon his folded arm than she had ever done before; and this, with a certain sweet faintness in her voice, made him wonder what was the matter. He looked down at her and saw the encounter of her gaze with the young theologian's; but even this told him nothing, and he continued to be bewildered. Nevertheless, "I consent," he said at last, "since Mr. Brand recommends it."

"I should like to perform the ceremony very soon," observed Mr. Brand, with a sort of solemn simplicity.

"Come, come, that's charming!" cried Felix, profanely.

Mr. Wentworth sank into his chair. "Doubtless, when you understand it," he said, with a certain judicial asperity.

Gertrude went to her sister and led her away, and Felix having passed his arm into Mr. Brand's and stepped out of the long window with him, the old man was left sitting there in unillumined perplexity.

Felix did no work that day. In the afternoon, with Gertrude, he got into one of the boats and floated about with idly-dipping oars. They talked a good deal of Mr. Brand—though not exclusively.

"That was a fine stroke," said Felix. "It was really heroic."

Gertrude sat musing, with her eyes upon the ripples. "That was what he wanted to be; he wanted to do something fine."

"He won't be comfortable till he has married us," said Felix. "So much the better."

"He wanted to be magnanimous; he wanted to have a fine moral pleasure. I know him so well," Gertrude went on. Felix looked at her; she spoke slowly, gazing at the clear water. "He thought of it a great deal, night and day. He thought it would be beautiful. At last he made up his mind that it was his duty, his duty to do just that—nothing less than that. He felt exalted; he felt sublime. That's how he likes to feel. It is better for him than if I had listened to him."

"It's better for me," smiled Felix. "But do you know, as regards the sacrifice, that I don't believe he admired you when this decision was taken quite so much as he had done a fortnight before?"

"He never admired me. He admires Charlotte; he pitied me. I know him so well."

"Well, then, he didn't pity you so much."

Gertrude looked at Felix a little, smiling. "You shouldn't permit yourself," she said, "to diminish the splendor of his action. He admires Charlotte," she repeated.

"That's capital!" said Felix laughingly, and dipping his oars. I cannot say exactly to which member of Gertrude's phrase he alluded; but he dipped his oars again, and they kept floating about.

Neither Felix nor his sister, on that day, was present at Mr. Wentworth's at the evening repast. The two occupants of the chalet dined together, and the young man informed his companion that his marriage was now an assured fact. Eugenia congratulated him, and replied that if he were as reasonable a husband as he had been, on the whole, a brother, his wife would have nothing to complain of.

Felix looked at her a moment, smiling. "I hope," he said, "not to be thrown back on my reason."

"It is very true," Eugenia rejoined, "that one's reason is dismally flat. It's a bed with the mattress removed."

But the brother and sister, later in the evening, crossed over to the larger house, the Baroness desiring to compliment her prospective sister-in-law. They found the usual circle upon the piazza, with the exception of Clifford Wentworth and Lizzie Acton; and as everyone stood up as usual to welcome the Baroness, Eugenia had an admiring audience for her compliment to Gertrude.

Robert Acton stood on the edge of the piazza, leaning against one of the white columns, so that he found himself next to Eugenia while she acquitted herself of a neat little discourse of congratulation.

"I shall be so glad to know you better," she said; "I have seen so much less of you than I should have liked. Naturally; now I see the reason why! You will love me a little, won't you? I think I may say I gain on being known." And terminating these observations with the softest cadence of her voice, the Baroness imprinted a sort of grand official kiss upon Gertrude's forehead.

Increased familiarity had not, to Gertrude's imagination, diminished the mysterious impressiveness of Eugenia's personality, and she felt flattered and transported by this little ceremony. Robert Acton also seemed to admire it, as he admired so many of the gracious manifestations of Madame Münster's wit.

They had the privilege of making him restless, and on this occasion he walked away, suddenly, with his hands in his pockets, and then came back and leaned against his column. Eugenia was now complimenting her uncle upon his daughter's engagement, and Mr. Wentworth was listening with his usual plain yet refined politeness. It is to be supposed that by this time his perception of the mutual relations of the young people who surrounded him had become more acute; but he still took the matter very seriously, and he was not at all exhilarated.

"Felix will make her a good husband," said Eugenia. "He will be a charming companion; he has a great quality—indestructible gaiety."

"You think that's a great quality?" asked the old man.

Eugenia meditated, with her eyes upon his. "You think one gets tired of it, eh?"

"I don't know that I am prepared to say that," said Mr. Wentworth.

"Well, we will say, then, that it is tiresome for others but delightful for one's self. A woman's husband, you know, is supposed to be her second self; so that, for Felix and Gertrude, gaiety will be a common property."

"Gertrude was always very gay," said Mr. Wentworth. He was trying to follow this argument.

Robert Acton took his hands out of his pockets and came a little nearer to the Baroness. "You say you gain by being known," he said. "One certainly gains by knowing you."

"What have *you* gained?" asked Eugenia.

"An immense amount of wisdom."

"That's a questionable advantage for a man who was already so wise!"

Acton shook his head. "No, I was a great fool before I knew you!"

"And being a fool you made my acquaintance? You are very complimentary."

"Let me keep it up," said Acton, laughing. "I hope, for our pleasure, that your brother's marriage will detain you."

"Why should I stop for my brother's marriage when I would not stop for my own?" asked the Baroness.

"Why shouldn't you stop in either case, now that, as you say, you have dissolved that mechanical tie that bound you to Europe?"

The Baroness looked at him a moment. "As I say? You look as if you doubted it."

"Ah," said Acton, returning her glance, "that is a remnant of my old folly! We have other attractions," he added. "We are to have another marriage."

But she seemed not to hear him; she was looking at him still. "My word was never doubted before," she said.

"We are to have another marriage," Acton repeated, smiling.

Then she appeared to understand. "Another marriage?" And she looked at the others. Felix was chattering to Gertrude; Charlotte, at a distance, was watching them; and Mr. Brand, in quite another quarter, was turning his back to them, and, with his hands under his coat-tails and his large head on one side, was looking at the small, tender crescent of a young moon. "It ought to be Mr. Brand and Charlotte," said Eugenia, "but it doesn't look like it."

"There," Acton answered, "you must judge just now by contraries. There is more than there looks to be. I expect that combination one of these days; but that is not what I meant."

"Well," said the Baroness, "I never guess my own lovers; so I can't guess other people's."

Acton gave a loud laugh, and he was about to add a rejoinder when Mr. Wentworth approached his niece. "You will be interested to hear," the old man said, with a momentary aspiration toward jocosity, "of another matrimonial venture in our little circle."

"I was just telling the Baroness," Acton observed.

"Mr. Acton was apparently about to announce his own engagement," said Eugenia.

Mr. Wentworth's jocosity increased. "It is not exactly that; but it is in the family. Clifford, hearing this morning that Mr. Brand had expressed a desire to tie the nuptial knot for his sister, took it into his head to arrange that, while his hand was in, our good friend should perform a like ceremony for himself and Lizzie Acton."

The Baroness threw back her head and smiled at her uncle; then turning, with an intenser radiance, to Robert Acton, "I am certainly very stupid not to have thought of that," she said. Acton looked down at his boots, as if he thought he had perhaps reached the limits of legitimate experimentation, and for a moment Eugenia said nothing more. It had been, in fact, a sharp knock, and she needed to recover herself. This was done, however, promptly enough. "Where are the young people?" she asked.

"They are spending the evening with my mother."

"Is not the thing very sudden?"

Acton looked up. "Extremely sudden. There had been a tacit understanding; but within a day or two Clifford appears to have received some mysterious impulse to precipitate the affair."

"The impulse," said the Baroness, "was the charms of your very pretty sister."

"But my sister's charms were an old story; he had always known her." Acton had begun to experiment again.

Here, however, it was evident the Baroness would not help him. "Ah, one can't say! Clifford is very young; but he is a nice boy."

"He's a likeable sort of boy, and he will be a rich man." This was Acton's last experiment. Madame Münster turned away.

She made but a short visit and Felix took her home. In her little drawing-room she went almost straight to the mirror over the chimney-piece, and, with a candle uplifted, stood looking into it. "I shall not wait for your marriage," she said to her brother. "Tomorrow my maid shall pack up."

"My dear sister," Felix exclaimed, "we are to be married immediately! Mr. Brand is too uncomfortable."

But Eugenia, turning and still holding her candle aloft, only looked about the little sitting-room at her gimcracks and curtains and cushions. "My maid shall pack up," she repeated. "*Bonté divine*, what rubbish! I feel like a strolling actress; these are my 'properties.'"

"Is the play over, Eugenia?" asked Felix.

She gave him a sharp glance. "I have spoken my part."

"With great applause!" said her brother.

"Oh, applause—applause!" she murmured. And she gathered up two or three of her dispersed draperies. She glanced at the beautiful brocade, and then, "I don't see how I can have endured it!" she said.

"Endure it a little longer. Come to my wedding."

"Thank you; that's your affair. My affairs are elsewhere."

"Where are you going?"

"To Germany—by the first ship."

"You have decided not to marry Mr. Acton?"

"I have refused him," said Eugenia.

Her brother looked at her in silence. "I am sorry," he rejoined at last. "But I was very discreet, as you asked me to be. I said nothing."

"Please continue, then, not to allude to the matter," said Eugenia.

Felix inclined himself gravely. "You shall be obeyed. But your position in Germany?" he pursued.

"Please to make no observations upon it."

"I was only going to say that I supposed it was altered."

"You are mistaken."

"But I thought you had signed——"

"I have not signed!" said the Baroness.

Felix urged her no further, and it was arranged that he should immediately assist her to embark.

Mr. Brand was indeed, it appeared, very impatient to consummate his sacrifice and deliver the nuptial benediction which would set it off so handsomely; but Eugenia's impatience to withdraw from a country in which she had not found the fortune she had come to seek was even less to be mistaken. It is true she had not made any very various exertion; but she appeared to feel justified in generalizing—in deciding that the conditions of action on this provincial continent were not favorable to really superior women. The elder world was, after all, their natural field. The unembarrassed directness with which she proceeded to apply these intelligent conclusions appeared to the little circle of spectators who have figured in our narrative but the supreme exhibition of a character to which the experience of life had imparted an inimitable pliancy. It had a distinct effect upon Robert Acton, who, for the two days preceding her departure, was a very restless and irritated mortal. She passed her last evening at her uncle's, where she had never been more charming; and in parting with Clifford Wentworth's affianced bride she drew from her own finger a curious old ring and presented it to her with the prettiest speech and kiss. Gertrude, who as an affianced bride was also indebted to her gracious bounty, admired this little incident extremely, and Robert Acton almost wondered whether it did not give him the right, as Lizzie's brother and guardian, to offer in return a handsome present to the Baroness. It would have made him extremely happy to be able to offer a handsome present to the Baroness; but he abstained from this expression of his sentiments, and they were in consequence, at the very last, by so much the less comfortable. It was almost at the very last that he saw her—late the night before she went to Boston to embark.

"For myself, I wish you might have stayed," he said. "But not for your own sake."

"I don't make so many differences," said the Baroness. "I am simply sorry to be going."

"That's a much deeper difference than mine," Acton declared; "for you mean you are simply glad!"

Felix parted with her on the deck of the ship. "We shall often meet over there," he said.

"I don't know," she answered. "Europe seems to me much larger than America."

Mr. Brand, of course, in the days that immediately followed, was not the only impatient spirit; but it may be said that of all the young spirits interested in the event none rose more eagerly to the level of the occasion. Gertrude left her father's house with Felix Young; they were imperturbably happy and they went far away. Clifford and his young wife sought their felicity in a narrower circle, and the latter's influence upon her husband was such as to justify, strikingly, that theory of the elevating effect of easy intercourse with clever women which Felix had propounded to Mr. Wentworth. Gertrude was for a good while a distant figure, but she came back when Charlotte married Mr. Brand. She was present at the wedding feast, where Felix's gaiety confessed to no change. Then she disappeared, and the echo of a gaiety of her own, mingled with that of her husband, often came back to the home of her earlier years. Mr. Wentworth at last found himself listening for it; and Robert Acton, after his mother's death, married a particularly nice young girl.

## The End

# THE FIGURE IN THE
# CARPET

# CHAPTER I

I HAD done a few things and earned a few pence—I had perhaps even had time to begin to think I was finer than was perceived by the patronising; but when I take the little measure of my course (a fidgety habit, for it's none of the longest yet) I count my real start from the evening George Corvick, breathless and worried, came in to ask me a service. He had done more things than I, and earned more pence, though there were chances for cleverness I thought he sometimes missed. I could only however that evening declare to him that he never missed one for kindness. There was almost rapture in hearing it proposed to me to prepare for *The Middle*, the organ of our lucubrations, so called from the position in the week of its day of appearance, an article for which he had made himself responsible and of which, tied up with a stout string, he laid on my table the subject. I pounced upon my opportunity—that is on the first volume of it—and paid scant attention to my friend's explanation of his appeal. What explanation could be more to the point than my obvious fitness for the task? I had written on Hugh Vereker, but never a word in *The Middle*, where my dealings were mainly with the ladies and the minor poets. This was his new novel, an advance copy, and whatever much or little it should do for his reputation I was clear on the spot as to what it should do for mine. Moreover if I always read him as soon as I could get hold of him I had a particular reason for wishing to read him now: I had accepted an invitation to Bridges for the following Sunday, and it had been mentioned in Lady Jane's note that Mr. Vereker was to be there. I was young enough for a flutter at meeting a man of his renown, and innocent enough to believe the occasion would demand the display of an acquaintance with his "last."

Corvick, who had promised a review of it, had not even had time to read it; he had gone to pieces in consequence of news requiring—as on precipitate reflexion he judged—that he should catch the night-mail to Paris. He had had a telegram from Gwendolen Erme in answer to his letter offering to fly to her aid. I knew already about Gwendolen Erme; I had never seen her, but

I had my ideas, which were mainly to the effect that Corvick would marry her if her mother would only die. That lady seemed now in a fair way to oblige him; after some dreadful mistake about a climate or a "cure" she had suddenly collapsed on the return from abroad. Her daughter, unsupported and alarmed, desiring to make a rush for home but hesitating at the risk, had accepted our friend's assistance, and it was my secret belief that at sight of him Mrs. Erme would pull round. His own belief was scarcely to be called secret; it discernibly at any rate differed from mine. He had showed me Gwendolen's photograph with the remark that she wasn't pretty but was awfully interesting; she had published at the age of nineteen a novel in three volumes, "Deep Down," about which, in *The Middle*, he had been really splendid. He appreciated my present eagerness and undertook that the periodical in question should do no less; then at the last, with his hand on the door, he said to me: "Of course you'll be all right, you know." Seeing I was a trifle vague he added: "I mean you won't be silly."

"Silly—about Vereker! Why what do I ever find him but awfully clever?"

"Well, what's that but silly? What on earth does 'awfully clever' mean? For God's sake try to get *at* him. Don't let him suffer by our arrangement. Speak of him, you know, if you can, as *I* should have spoken of him."

I wondered an instant. "You mean as far and away the biggest of the lot—that sort of thing?"

Corvick almost groaned. "Oh you know, I don't put them back to back that way; it's the infancy of art! But he gives me a pleasure so rare; the sense of"—he mused a little—"something or other."

I wondered again. "The sense, pray, of want?"

"My dear man, that's just what I want *you* to say!"

Even before he had banged the door I had begun, book in hand, to prepare myself to say it. I sat up with Vereker half the night; Corvick couldn't have done more than that. He was awfully clever—I stuck to that, but he wasn't a bit the biggest of the lot. I didn't allude to the lot, however; I flattered myself that I emerged on this occasion from the infancy of art. "It's all right," they declared vividly at the office; and when the number appeared I felt there was a basis on which I could meet the great man. It gave me confidence for a day or two—then that confidence dropped. I had fancied him reading it with relish, but if Corvick wasn't satisfied how could Vereker himself be? I reflected indeed that the heat of the admirer was sometimes grosser even than the appetite of the scribe. Corvick at all events wrote me from Paris a little ill-humouredly. Mrs. Erme was pulling round, and I hadn't at all said what Vereker gave him the sense of.

# CHAPTER II

THE effect of my visit to Bridges was to turn me out for more profundity. Hugh Vereker, as I saw him there, was of a contact so void of angles that I blushed for the poverty of imagination involved in my small precautions. If he was in spirits it wasn't because he had read my review; in fact on the Sunday morning I felt sure he hadn't read it, though *The Middle* had been out three days and bloomed, I assured myself, in the stiff garden of periodicals which gave one of the ormolu tables the air of a stand at a station. The impression he made on me personally was such that I wished him to read it, and I corrected to this end with a surreptitious hand what might be wanting in the careless conspicuity of the sheet. I'm afraid I even watched the result of my manœuvre, but up to luncheon I watched in vain.

When afterwards, in the course of our gregarious walk, I found myself for half an hour, not perhaps without another manœuvre, at the great man's side, the result of his affability was a still livelier desire that he shouldn't remain in ignorance of the peculiar justice I had done him. It wasn't that he seemed to thirst for justice; on the contrary I hadn't yet caught in his talk the faintest grunt of a grudge—a note for which my young experience had already given me an ear. Of late he had had more recognition, and it was pleasant, as we used to say in *The Middle*, to see how it drew him out. He wasn't of course popular, but I judged one of the sources of his good humour to be precisely that his success was independent of that. He had none the less become in a manner the fashion; the critics at least had put on a spurt and caught up with him. We had found out at last how clever he was, and he had had to make the best of the loss of his mystery. I was strongly tempted, as I walked beside him, to let him know how much of that unveiling was my act; and there was a moment when I probably should have done so had not one of the ladies of our party, snatching a place at his other elbow, just then appealed to him in a spirit comparatively selfish. It was very discouraging: I almost felt the liberty had been taken with myself.

I had had on my tongue's end, for my own part, a phrase or two about the right word at the right time; but later on I was glad not to have spoken, for when on our return we clustered at tea I perceived Lady Jane, who had not been out with us, brandishing *The Middle* with her longest arm. She had taken it up at her leisure; she was delighted with what she had found, and I saw that, as a mistake in a man may often be a felicity in a woman, she would practically do for me what I hadn't been able to do for myself. "Some sweet little truths that needed to be spoken," I heard her declare, thrusting the paper at rather a bewildered couple by the fireplace. She grabbed it away from them again on the reappearance of Hugh Vereker, who after our walk had been upstairs to change something. "I know you don't in general look at this kind of thing, but it's an occasion really for doing so. You *haven't* seen it? Then you must. The man has actually got *at* you, at what *I* always feel, you know." Lady Jane threw into her eyes a look evidently intended to give an idea of what she always felt; but she added that she couldn't have expressed it. The man in the paper expressed it in a striking manner. "Just see there, and there, where I've dashed it, how he brings it out." She had literally marked for him the brightest patches of my prose, and if I was a little amused Vereker himself may well have been. He showed how much he was when before us all Lady Jane wanted to read something aloud. I liked at any rate the way he defeated her purpose by jerking the paper affectionately out of her clutch. He'd take it upstairs with him and look at it on going to dress. He did this half an hour later—I saw it in his hand when he repaired to his room. That was the moment at which, thinking to give her pleasure, I mentioned to Lady Jane that I was the author of the review. I did give her pleasure, I judged, but perhaps not quite so much as I had expected. If the author was "only me" the thing didn't seem quite so remarkable. Hadn't I had the effect rather of diminishing the lustre of the article than of adding to my own? Her ladyship was subject to the most extraordinary drops. It didn't matter; the only effect I cared about was the one it would have on Vereker up there by his bedroom fire.

At dinner I watched for the signs of this impression, tried to fancy some happier light in his eyes; but to my disappointment Lady Jane gave me no chance to make sure. I had hoped she'd call triumphantly down the table, publicly demand if she hadn't been right. The party was large—there were people from outside as well, but I had never seen a table long enough to deprive Lady Jane of a triumph. I was just reflecting in truth that this interminable board would deprive *me* of one when the guest next me, dear woman—she was Miss Poyle, the vicar's sister, a robust unmodulated person—had the happy inspiration and the unusual courage to address herself across it to Vereker, who was opposite, but not directly, so that when he replied they were both leaning forward. She enquired, artless body, what he thought of Lady Jane's "panegyric," which she had read—not connecting it however with her right-hand neighbour; and while I strained my ear for his reply I heard him, to my stupefaction, call back gaily, his mouth full of bread: "Oh, it's all right—the usual twaddle!"

I had caught Vereker's glance as he spoke, but Miss Poyle's surprise was a fortunate cover for my own. "You mean he doesn't do you justice?" said the excellent woman.

Vereker laughed out, and I was happy to be able to do the same. "It's a charming article," he tossed us.

Miss Poyle thrust her chin half across the cloth. "Oh, you're so deep!" she drove home.

"As deep as the ocean! All I pretend is that the author doesn't see—" But a dish was at this point passed over his shoulder, and we had to wait while he helped himself.

"Doesn't see what?" my neighbour continued.

"Doesn't see anything."

"Dear me—how very stupid!"

"Not a bit," Vereker laughed main. "Nobody does."

The lady on his further side appealed to him, and Miss Poyle sank back to myself. "Nobody sees anything!" she cheerfully announced; to which I replied that I had often thought so too, but had somehow taken the thought for a proof on my own part of a tremendous eye. I didn't tell her the article was mine; and I observed that Lady Jane, occupied at the end of the table, had not caught Vereker's words.

I rather avoided him after dinner, for I confess he struck me as cruelly conceited, and the revelation was a pain. "The usual twaddle"—my acute little study! That one's admiration should have had a reserve or two could gall him to that point! I had thought him placid, and he was placid enough; such a surface was the hard polished glass that encased the bauble of his vanity. I was really ruffled, and the only comfort was that if nobody saw anything George Corvick was quite as much out of it as I. This comfort however was not sufficient, after the ladies had dispersed, to carry me in the proper manner—I mean in a spotted jacket and humming an air—into the smoking-room. I took my way in some dejection to bed; but in the passage I encountered Mr. Vereker, who had been up once more to change, coming out of his room. *He* was humming an air and had on a spotted jacket, and as soon as he saw me his gaiety gave a start.

"My dear young man," he exclaimed, "I'm so glad to lay hands on you! I'm afraid I most unwittingly wounded you by those words of mine at dinner to Miss Poyle. I learned but half an hour ago from Lady Jane that you're the author of the little notice in *The Middle*."

I protested that no bones were broken; but he moved with me to my own door, his hand, on my shoulder, kindly feeling for a fracture; and on hearing that I had come up to bed he asked leave to cross my threshold and just tell me in three words what his qualification of my remarks had represented. It was plain he really feared I was hurt, and the sense of his solicitude suddenly made all the difference to me. My cheap review fluttered off into space, and the best things I had said in it became flat enough beside the brilliancy of his being there. I can see him there still, on my rug, in the firelight and his spotted jacket, his fine clear face all bright with the desire to be tender to my youth. I don't know what he had at first meant to say, but I think the sight of my relief touched him, excited him, brought up words to his lips from far within. It was so these words presently conveyed to me something that, as I afterwards knew, he had never uttered to any one. I've always done justice to the generous impulse that made him speak; it was simply compunction for a snub unconsciously administered to a man of letters in a position inferior to his own, a man of letters moreover in the very act of praising him. To make the thing right he talked to me exactly as an equal and on the ground of what we both loved best. The hour, the place, the unexpectedness deepened the impression: he couldn't have done anything more intensely effective.

# CHAPTER III.

"I DON'T quite know how to explain it to you," he said, "but it was the very fact that your notice of my book had a spice of intelligence, it was just your exceptional sharpness, that produced the feeling—a very old story with me, I beg you to believe—under the momentary influence of which I used in speaking to that good lady the words you so naturally resent. I don't read the things in the newspapers unless they're thrust upon me as that one was—it's always one's best friend who does it! But I used to read them sometimes—ten years ago. I dare say they were in general rather stupider then; at any rate it always struck me they missed my little point with a perfection exactly as admirable when they patted me on the back as when they kicked me in the shins. Whenever since I've happened to have a glimpse of them they were still blazing away—still missing it, I mean, deliciously. *You* miss it, my dear fellow, with inimitable assurance; the fact of your being awfully clever and your article's being awfully nice doesn't make a hair's breadth of difference. It's quite with you rising young men," Vereker laughed, "that I feel most what a failure I am!"

I listened with keen interest; it grew keener as he talked. "*You* a failure—heavens! What then may your 'little point' happen to be?"

"Have I got to *tell* you, after all these years and labours?" There was something in the friendly reproach of this—jocosely exaggerated—that made me, as an ardent young seeker for truth, blush to the roots of my hair. I'm as much in the dark as ever, though I've grown used in a sense to my obtuseness; at that moment, however, Vereker's happy accent made me appear to myself, and probably to him, a rare dunce. I was on the point of exclaiming "Ah yes, don't tell me: for my honour, for that of the craft, don't!" when he went on in a manner that showed he had read my thought and had his own idea of the probability of our some day redeeming ourselves. "By my little point I mean—what shall I call it?—the particular thing I've written my books most *for*. Isn't there for every writer a particular thing of that sort, the thing that most makes him apply himself, the thing without the effort to achieve which he wouldn't write at all, the very passion of his passion, the part of the business in which, for him, the flame of art burns most intensely? Well, it's *that*!"

I considered a moment—that is I followed at a respectful distance, rather gasping. I was fascinated—easily, you'll say; but I wasn't going after all to be put off my guard. "Your description's certainly beautiful, but it doesn't make what you describe very distinct."

"I promise you it would be distinct if it should dawn on you at all." I saw that the charm of our topic overflowed for my companion into an emotion as lively as my own. "At any rate," he went on, "I can speak for myself: there's an idea in my work without which I wouldn't have given a straw for the whole job. It's the finest fullest intention of the lot, and the application of it has been, I think, a triumph of patience, of ingenuity. I ought to leave that to somebody else to say; but that nobody does say it is precisely what we're talking about. It stretches, this little trick of mine, from book to book, and everything else, comparatively, plays over the surface of it. The order, the form, the texture of my books will perhaps some day constitute for the initiated a complete representation of it. So it's naturally the thing for the critic to look for. It strikes me," my visitor added, smiling, "even as the thing for the critic to find."

This seemed a responsibility indeed. "You call it a little trick?"

"That's only my little modesty. It's really an exquisite scheme."

"And you hold that you've carried the scheme out?"

"The way I've carried it out is the thing in life I think a bit well of myself for."

I had a pause. "Don't you think you ought—just a trifle—to assist the critic?"

"Assist him? What else have I done with every stroke of my pen? I've shouted my intention in his great blank face!" At this, laughing out again, Vereker laid his hand on my shoulder to show the allusion wasn't to my personal appearance.

"But you talk about the initiated. There must therefore, you see, *be* initiation."

"What else in heaven's name is criticism supposed to be?" I'm afraid I coloured at this too; but I took refuge in repeating that his account of his silver lining was poor in something or other that a plain man knows things by. "That's only because you've never had a glimpse of it," he returned. "If you had had one the element in question would soon have become practically all you'd see. To me it's exactly as palpable as the marble of this chimney. Besides, the critic just *isn't* a plain man: if he were, pray, what would he be doing in his neighbour's garden? You're anything but a plain man yourself, and the very raison d'être of you all is that you're little demons of subtlety. If my great affair's a secret, that's only because it's a secret in spite of itself—the amazing event has made it one. I not only never took the smallest precaution to keep it so, but never dreamed of any such accident. If I had I shouldn't in advance have had the heart to go on. As it was, I only became aware little by little, and meanwhile I had done my work."

"And now you quite like it?" I risked.

"My work?"

"Your secret. It's the same thing."

"Your guessing that," Vereker replied, "is a proof that you're as clever as I say!" I was encouraged by this to remark that he would clearly be pained to part with it, and he confessed that it was indeed with him now the great amusement of life. "I live almost to see if it will ever be detected." He looked at me for a jesting challenge; something far within his eyes seemed to peep out. "But I needn't worry—it won't!"

"You fire me as I've never been fired," I declared; "you make me determined to do or die." Then I asked: "Is it a kind of esoteric message?"

His countenance fell at this—he put out his hand as if to bid me good-night. "Ah my dear fellow, it can't be described in cheap journalese!"

I knew of course he'd be awfully fastidious, but our talk had made me feel how much his nerves were exposed. I was unsatisfied—I kept hold of his hand. "I won't make use of the expression then," I said, "in the article in which I shall eventually announce my discovery, though I dare say I shall have hard work to do without it. But meanwhile, just to hasten that difficult birth, can't you give a fellow a clue?" I felt much more at my ease.

"My whole lucid effort gives him the clue—every page and line and letter. The thing's as concrete there as a bird in a cage, a bait on a hook, a piece of cheese in a mouse-trap. It's stuck into every volume as your foot is stuck into your shoe. It governs every line, it chooses every word, it dots every i, it places every comma."

I scratched my head. "Is it something in the style or something in the thought? An element of form or an element of feeling?"

He indulgently shook my hand again, and I felt my questions to be crude and my distinctions pitiful. "Good-night, my dear boy—don't bother about it. After all, you do like a fellow."

"And a little intelligence might spoil it?" I still detained him.

He hesitated. "Well, you've got a heart in your body. Is that an element of form or an element of feeling? What I contend that nobody has ever mentioned in my work is the organ of life."

"I see—it's some idea *about* life, some sort of philosophy. Unless it be," I added with the eagerness of a thought perhaps still happier, "some kind of game you're up to with your style, something you're after in the language. Perhaps it's a preference for the letter P!" I ventured profanely to break out. "Papa, potatoes, prunes—that sort of thing?" He was suitably indulgent: he only said I hadn't got the right letter. But his amusement was over; I could see he was bored. There was nevertheless something else I had absolutely to learn. "Should you be able, pen in hand, to state it clearly yourself—to name it, phrase it, formulate it?"

"Oh," he almost passionately sighed, "if I were only, pen in hand, one of *you* chaps!"

"That would be a great chance for you of course. But why should you despise us chaps for not doing what you can't do yourself?"

"Can't do?" He opened his eyes. "Haven't I done it in twenty volumes? I do it in my way," he continued. "Go *you* and don't do it in yours."

"Ours is so devilish difficult," I weakly observed.

"So's mine. We each choose our own. There's no compulsion. You won't come down and smoke?"

"No. I want to think this thing out."

"You'll tell me then in the morning that you've laid me bare?"

"I'll see what I can do; I'll sleep on it. But just one word more," I added. We had left the room—I walked again with him a few steps along the passage. "This extraordinary 'general intention,' as you call it—for that's the most vivid description I can induce you to make of it—is then, generally, a sort of buried treasure?"

His face lighted. "Yes, call it that, though it's perhaps not for me to do so."

"Nonsense!" I laughed. "You know you're hugely proud of it."

"Well, I didn't propose to tell you so; but it *is* the joy of my soul!"

"You mean it's a beauty so rare, so great?"

He waited a little again. "The loveliest thing in the world!" We had stopped, and on these words he left me; but at the end of the corridor, while I looked after him rather yearningly, he turned and caught sight of my puzzled face. It made him earnestly, indeed I thought quite anxiously, shake his head and wave his finger "Give it up—give it up!"

This wasn't a challenge—it was fatherly advice. If I had had one of his books at hand I'd have repeated my recent act of faith—I'd have spent half the night with him. At three o'clock in the morning, not sleeping, remembering moreover how indispensable he was to Lady Jane, I stole down to the library with a candle. There wasn't, so far as I could discover, a line of his writing in the house.

# CHAPTER IV.

RETURNING to town I feverishly collected them all; I picked out each in its order and held it up to the light. This gave me a maddening month, in the course of which several things took place. One of these, the last, I may as well immediately mention, was that I acted on Vereker's advice: I renounced my ridiculous attempt. I could really make nothing of the business; it proved a dead loss. After all I had always, as he had himself noted, liked him; and what now occurred was simply that my new intelligence and vain preoccupation damaged my liking. I not only failed to run a general intention to earth, I found myself missing the subordinate intentions I had formerly enjoyed. His books didn't even remain the charming things they had been for me; the exasperation of my search put me out of conceit of them. Instead of being a pleasure the more they became a resource the less; for from the moment I was unable to follow up the author's hint I of course felt it a point of honour not to make use professionally of my knowledge of them. I *had* no knowledge—nobody had any. It was humiliating, but I could bear it—they only annoyed me now. At last they even bored me, and I accounted for my confusion—perversely, I allow—by the idea that Vereker had made a fool of me. The buried treasure was a bad joke, the general intention a monstrous pose.

The great point of it all is, however, that I told George Corvick what had befallen me and that my information had an immense effect upon him. He had at last come back, but so, unfortunately, had Mrs. Erme, and there was as yet, I could see, no question of his nuptials. He was immensely stirred up by the anecdote I had brought from Bridges; it fell in so completely with the sense he had had from the first that there was more in Vereker than met the eye. When I remarked that the eye seemed what the printed page had been expressly invented to meet he immediately accused me of being spiteful because I had been foiled. Our commerce had always that pleasant latitude. The thing Vereker had mentioned to me was exactly the thing he, Corvick, had wanted me to speak of in my review. On my suggesting at last that with the assistance I had now given him he would doubtless be prepared to speak of it himself he admitted freely that before doing this there was more he must understand. What he would have said, had he reviewed the new book, was that there was evidently in the writer's inmost art something to *be* understood. I hadn't so much as hinted at that: no wonder the writer hadn't been flattered! I asked Corvick what he really considered he meant by his own supersubtlety, and, unmistakeably kindled, he replied: "It isn't for the vulgar—it isn't for the vulgar!" He had hold of the tail of something; he would pull hard, pull it right out. He pumped me dry on Vereker's strange confidence and, pronouncing me the luckiest of mortals, mentioned half a dozen questions he wished to goodness I had had the gumption to put. Yet on the other hand he didn't want to be told too much—it would spoil the fun of seeing what would come. The failure of *my* fun was at the moment of our meeting not complete, but I saw it ahead, and Corvick saw that I saw it. I, on my side, saw likewise that one of the first things he would do would be to rush off with my story to Gwendolen.

On the very day after my talk with him I was surprised by the receipt of a note from Hugh Vereker, to whom our encounter at Bridges had been recalled, as he mentioned, by his falling, in a magazine, on some article to which my signature was attached. "I read it with great pleasure," he wrote, "and remembered under its influence our lively conversation by your bedroom fire. The consequence of this has been that I begin to measure the temerity of my having saddled you with a knowledge that you may find something of a burden. Now that the fit's over I can't imagine how I came to be moved so much beyond my wont. I had never before mentioned, no matter in what state of expansion, the fact of my little secret, and I shall never speak of that mystery again. I was accidentally so much more explicit with you than it had ever entered into my game to be, that I find this game—I mean the pleasure of playing it—suffers considerably. In short, if you can understand it, I've rather spoiled my sport. I really don't want to give anybody what I believe you clever young men call the tip. That's of course a selfish solicitude, and I name it to you for what it may be worth to you. If you're disposed to humour me don't repeat my revelation. Think me demented—it's your right; but don't tell anybody why."

The sequel to this communication was that as early on the morrow as I dared I drove straight to Mr. Vereker's door. He occupied in those years one of the honest old houses in Kensington Square. He received me immediately, and as soon as I came in I saw I hadn't lost my power to minister to his mirth. He laughed out at sight of my face, which doubtless expressed my perturbation. I had been indiscreet—my compunction was great. "I *have* told somebody," I panted, "and I'm sure that person will by this time have told somebody else! It's a woman, into the bargain."

"The person you've told?"

"No, the other person. I'm quite sure he must have told her."

"For all the good it will do her—or do *me*! A woman will never find out."

"No, but she'll talk all over the place: she'll do just what you don't want."

Vereker thought a moment, but wasn't so disconcerted as I had feared: he felt that if the harm was done it only served him right. "It doesn't matter—don't worry."

"I'll do my best, I promise you, that your talk with me shall go no further."

"Very good; do what you can."

"In the meantime," I pursued, "George Corvick's possession of the tip may, on his part, really lead to something."

"That will be a brave day."

I told him about Corvick's cleverness, his admiration, the intensity of his interest in my anecdote; and without making too much of the divergence of our respective estimates mentioned that my friend was already of opinion that he saw much further into a certain affair than most people. He was quite as fired as I had been at Bridges. He was moreover in love with the young lady: perhaps the two together would puzzle something out.

Vereker seemed struck with this. "Do you mean they're to be married?"

"I dare say that's what it will come to."

"That may help them," he conceded, "but we must give them time!"

I spoke of my own renewed assault and confessed my difficulties; whereupon he repeated his former advice: "Give it up, give it up!" He evidently didn't think me intellectually equipped for the adventure. I stayed half an hour, and he was most good-natured, but I couldn't help pronouncing him a man of unstable moods. He had been free with me in a mood, he had repented in a mood, and now in a mood he had turned indifferent. This general levity helped me to believe that, so far as the subject of the tip went, there wasn't much in it. I contrived however to make him answer a few more questions about it, though he did so with visible impatience. For himself, beyond doubt, the thing we were all so blank about was vividly there. It was something, I guessed, in the primal plan, something like a complex figure in a Persian carpet. He highly approved of this image when I used it, and he used another himself. "It's the very string," he said, "that my pearls are strung on!" The reason of his note to me had been that he really didn't want to give us a grain of succour—our density was a thing too perfect in its way to touch. He had formed the habit of depending on it, and if the spell was to break it must break by some force of its own. He comes back to me from that last occasion—for I was never to speak to him again—as a man with some safe preserve for sport. I wondered as I walked away where he had got *his* tip.

# CHAPTER V.

WHEN I spoke to George Corvick of the caution I had received he made me feel that any doubt of his delicacy would be almost an insult. He had instantly told Gwendolen, but Gwendolen's ardent response was in itself a pledge of discretion. The question would now absorb them and would offer them a pastime too precious to be shared with the crowd. They appeared to have caught instinctively at Vereker's high idea of enjoyment. Their intellectual pride, however, was not such as to make them indifferent to any further light I might throw on the affair they had in hand. They were indeed of the "artistic temperament," and I was freshly struck with my colleague's power to excite himself over a question of art. He'd call it letters, he'd call it life, but it was all one thing. In what he said I now seemed to understand that he spoke equally for Gwendolen, to whom, as soon as Mrs. Erme was sufficiently better to allow her a little leisure, he made a point of introducing me. I remember our going together one Sunday in August to a huddled house in Chelsea, and my renewed envy of Corvick's possession of a friend who had some light to mingle with his own. He could say things to her that I could never say to him. She had indeed no sense of humour and, with her pretty way of holding her head on one side, was one of those persons whom you want, as the phrase is, to shake, but who have learnt Hungarian by themselves. She conversed perhaps in Hungarian with Corvick; she had remarkably little English for his friend. Corvick afterwards told me that I had chilled her by my apparent indisposition to oblige them with the detail of what Vereker had said to me. I allowed that I felt I had given thought enough to that indication: hadn't I even made up my mind that it was vain and would lead nowhere? The importance they attached to it was irritating and quite envenomed my doubts.

That statement looks unamiable, and what probably happened was that I felt humiliated at seeing other persons deeply beguiled by an experiment that had brought me only chagrin. I was out in the cold while, by the evening fire, under the lamp, they followed the chase for which I myself had sounded the horn. They did as I had done, only more deliberately and sociably—they went over their author from the beginning. There was no hurry, Corvick said the future was before them and the fascination could only grow; they would take him page by page, as they would take one of the classics, inhale him in slow draughts and let him sink all the way in. They would scarce have got so wound up, I think, if they hadn't been in love: poor Vereker's inner meaning gave them endless occasion to put and to keep their young heads together. None the less it represented the kind of problem for which Corvick had a special aptitude, drew out the particular pointed patience of which, had he lived, he would have given more striking and, it is to be hoped, more fruitful examples. He at least was, in Vereker's words, a little demon of subtlety. We had begun by disputing, but I soon saw that without my stirring a finger his infatuation would have its bad hours. He would bound off on false scents as I had done—he would clap his hands over new lights and see them blown out by the wind of the turned page. He was like nothing, I told him, but the maniacs who embrace some bedlamitical theory of the cryptic character of Shakespeare. To this he replied that if we had had Shakespeare's own word for his being cryptic he would at once have accepted it. The case there was altogether different—we had nothing but the word of Mr. Snooks. I returned that I was stupefied to see him attach such importance even to the word of Mr. Vereker. He wanted thereupon to know if I treated Mr. Vereker's word as a lie. I wasn't perhaps prepared, in my unhappy rebound, to go so far as that, but I insisted that till the contrary was proved I should view it as too fond an imagination. I didn't, I confess, say—I didn't at that time quite know—all I felt. Deep down, as Miss Erme would have said, I was uneasy, I was expectant. At the core of my disconcerted state—for my wonted curiosity lived in its ashes—was the sharpness of a sense that Corvick would at last probably come out somewhere. He made, in defence of his credulity, a great point of the fact that from of old, in his study of this genius, he had caught whiffs and hints of he didn't know what, faint wandering notes of a hidden music. That was just the rarity, that was the charm: it fitted so perfectly into what I reported.

If I returned on several occasions to the little house in Chelsea I dare say it was as much for news of Vereker as for news of Miss Erme's ailing parent.

The hours spent there by Corvick were present to my fancy as those of a chessplayer bent with a silent scowl, all the lamplit winter, over his board and his moves. As my imagination filled it out the picture held me fast. On the other side of the table was a ghostlier form, the faint figure of an antagonist good-humouredly but a little wearily secure—an antagonist who leaned back in his chair with his hands in his pockets and a smile on his fine clear face. Close to Corvick, behind him, was a girl who had begun to strike me as pale and wasted and even, on more familiar view, as rather handsome, and who rested on his shoulder and hung on his moves. He would take up a chessman and hold it poised a while over one of the little squares, and then would put it back in its place with a long sigh of disappointment. The young lady, at this, would slightly but uneasily shift her position and look across, very hard, very long, very strangely, at their dim participant. I had asked them at an early stage of the business if it mightn't contribute to their success to have some closer communication with him. The special circumstances would surely be held to have given me a right to introduce them. Corvick immediately replied that he had no wish to approach the altar before he had prepared the sacrifice. He quite agreed with our friend both as to the delight and as to the honour of the chase—he would bring down the animal with his own rifle. When I asked him if Miss Erme were as keen a shot he said after thinking: "No, I'm ashamed to say she wants to set a trap. She'd give anything to see him; she says she requires another tip. She's really quite morbid about it. But she must play fair—she *shan't* see him!" he emphatically added. I wondered if they hadn't even quarrelled a little on the subject—a suspicion not corrected by the way he more than once exclaimed to me: "She's quite incredibly literary, you know—quite fantastically!" I remember his saying of her that she felt in italics and thought in capitals. "Oh when I've run him to earth," he also said, "then, you know, I shall knock at his door. Rather—I beg you to believe. I'll have it from his own lips: 'Right you are, my boy; you've done it this time!' He shall crown me victor—with the critical laurel."

Meanwhile he really avoided the chances London life might have given him of meeting the distinguished novelist; a danger, however, that disappeared with Vereker's leaving England for an indefinite absence, as the newspapers announced—going to the south for motives connected with the health of his wife, which had long kept her in retirement. A year—more than a year—had elapsed since the incident at Bridges, but I had had no further sight of him. I think I was at bottom rather ashamed—I hated to remind him that, though I had irremediably missed his point, a reputation for acuteness was rapidly overtaking me. This scruple led me a dance; kept me out of Lady Jane's house, made me even decline, when in spite of my bad manners she was a second time so good as to make me a sign, an invitation to her beautiful seat. I once became aware of her under Vereker's escort at a concert, and was sure I was seen by them, but I slipped out without being caught. I felt, as on that occasion I splashed along in the rain, that I couldn't have done anything else; and yet I remember saying to myself that it was hard, was even cruel. Not only had I lost the books, but I had lost the man himself: they and their author had been alike spoiled for me. I knew too which was the loss I most regretted. I had taken to the man still more than I had ever taken to the books.

# CHAPTER VI.

SIX months after our friend had left England George Corvick, who made his living by his pen, contracted for a piece of work which imposed on him an absence of some length and a journey of some difficulty, and his undertaking of which was much of a surprise to me. His brother-in-law had become editor of a great provincial paper, and the great provincial paper, in a fine flight of fancy, had conceived the idea of sending a "special commissioner" to India. Special commissioners had begun, in the "metropolitan press," to be the fashion, and the journal in question must have felt it had passed too long for a mere country cousin. Corvick had no hand, I knew, for the big brush of the correspondent, but that was his brother-in-law's affair, and the fact that a particular task was not in his line was apt to be with himself exactly a reason for accepting it. He was prepared to out-Herod the metropolitan press; he took solemn precautions against priggishness, he exquisitely outraged taste. Nobody ever knew it—that offended principle was all his own. In addition to his expenses he was to be conveniently paid, and I found myself able to help him, for the usual fat book, to a plausible arrangement with the usual fat publisher. I naturally inferred that his obvious desire to make a little money was not unconnected with the prospect of a union with Gwendolen Erme. I was aware that her mother's opposition was largely addressed to his want of means and of lucrative abilities, but it so happened that, on my saying the last time I saw him something that bore on the question of his separation from our young lady, he brought out with an emphasis that startled me: "Ah I'm not a bit engaged to her, you know!"

"Not overtly," I answered, "because her mother doesn't like you. But I've always taken for granted a private understanding."

"Well, there *was* one. But there isn't now." That was all he said save something about Mrs. Erme's having got on her feet again in the most extraordinary way—a remark pointing, as I supposed, the moral that private understandings were of little use when the doctor didn't share them. What I took the liberty of more closely inferring was that the girl might in some way have estranged him. Well, if he had taken the turn of jealousy for instance it could scarcely be jealousy of me. In that case—over and above the absurdity of it—he wouldn't have gone away just to leave us together. For some time before his going we had indulged in no allusion to the buried treasure, and from his silence, which my reserve simply emulated, I had drawn a sharp conclusion. His courage had dropped, his ardour had gone the way of mine—this appearance at least he left me to scan. More than that he couldn't do; he couldn't face the triumph with which I might have greeted an explicit admission. He needn't have been afraid, poor dear, for I had by this time lost all need to triumph. In fact I considered I showed magnanimity in not reproaching him with his collapse, for the sense of his having thrown up the game made me feel more than ever how much I at last depended on him. If Corvick had broken down I should never know; no one would be of any use if *he* wasn't. It wasn't a bit true I had ceased to care for knowledge; little by little my curiosity not only had begun to ache again, but had become the familiar torment of my days and my nights. There are doubtless people to whom torments of such an order appear hardly more natural than the contortions of disease; but I don't after all know why I should in this connexion so much as mention them. For the few persons, at any rate, abnormal or not, with whom my anecdote is concerned, literature was a game of skill, and skill meant courage, and courage meant honour, and honour meant passion, meant life. The stake on the table was of a special substance and our roulette the revolving mind, but we sat round the green board as intently as the grim gamblers at Monte Carlo. Gwendolen Erme, for that matter, with her white face and her fixed eyes, was of the very type of the lean ladies one had met in the temples of chance. I recognised in Corvick's absence that she made this analogy vivid. It was extravagant, I admit, the way she lived for the art of the pen. Her passion visibly preyed on her, and in her presence I felt almost tepid. I got hold of "Deep Down" again: it was a desert in which she had lost herself, but in which too she had dug a wonderful hole in the sand—a cavity out of which Corvick had still more remarkably pulled her.

Early in March I had a telegram from her, in consequence of which I repaired immediately to Chelsea, where the first thing she said to me was: "He has got it, he has got it!"

She was moved, as I could see, to such depths that she must mean the great thing. "Vereker's idea?"

"His general intention. George has cabled from Bombay."

She had the missive open there; it was emphatic though concise. "Eureka. Immense." That was all—he had saved the cost of the signature. I shared her emotion, but I was disappointed. "He doesn't say what it is."

"How could he—in a telegram? He'll write it."

"But how does he know?"

"Know it's the real thing? Oh I'm sure that when you see it you do know. Vera incessu patuit dea!"

"It's you, Miss Erme, who are a 'dear' for bringing me such news!"—I went all lengths in my high spirits. "But fancy finding our goddess in the temple of Vishnu! How strange of George to have been able to go into the thing again in the midst of such different and such powerful solicitations!"

"He hasn't gone into it, I know; it's the thing itself, let severely alone for six months, that has simply sprung out at him like a tigress out of the jungle. He didn't take a book with him—on purpose; indeed he wouldn't have needed to—he knows every page, as I do, by heart. They all worked in him together, and some day somewhere, when he wasn't thinking, they fell, in all their superb intricacy, into the one right combination. The figure in the carpet came out. That's the way he knew it would come and the real reason—you didn't in the least understand, but I suppose I may tell you now—why he went and why I consented to his going. We knew the change would do it—that the difference of thought, of scene, would give the needed touch, the magic shake. We had perfectly, we had admirably calculated. The elements were all in his mind, and in the secousse of a new and intense experience they just struck light." She positively struck light herself—she was literally, facially luminous. I stammered something about unconscious cerebration, and she continued: "He'll come right home—this will bring him."

"To see Vereker, you mean?"

"To see Vereker—and to see *me*. Think what he'll have to tell me!"

I hesitated. "About India?"

"About fiddlesticks! About Vereker—about the figure in the carpet."

"But, as you say, we shall surely have that in a letter."

She thought like one inspired, and I remembered how Corvick had told me long before that her face was interesting. "Perhaps it can't be got into a letter if it's 'immense.'"

"Perhaps not if it's immense bosh. If he has hold of something that can't be got into a letter he hasn't hold of *the* thing. Vereker's own statement to me was exactly that the 'figure' *would* fit into a letter."

"Well, I cabled to George an hour ago—two words," said Gwendolen.

"Is it indiscreet of me to ask what they were?"

She hung fire, but at last brought them out. "'Angel, write.'"

"Good!" I exclaimed. "I'll make it sure—I'll send him the same."

# CHAPTER VII.

My words however were not absolutely the same—I put something instead of "angel"; and in the sequel my epithet seemed the more apt, for when eventually we heard from our traveller it was merely, it was thoroughly to be tantalised. He was magnificent in his triumph, he described his discovery as stupendous; but his ecstasy only obscured it—there were to be no particulars till he should have submitted his conception to the supreme authority. He had thrown up his commission, he had thrown up his book, he had thrown up everything but the instant need to hurry to Rapallo, on the Genoese shore, where Vereker was making a stay. I wrote him a letter which was to await him at Aden—I besought him to relieve my suspense. That he had found my letter was indicated by a telegram which, reaching me after weary days and in the absence of any answer to my laconic dispatch to him at Bombay, was evidently intended as a reply to both communications. Those few words were in familiar French, the French of the day, which Covick often made use of to show he wasn't a prig. It had for some persons the opposite effect, but his message may fairly be paraphrased. "Have patience; I want to see, as it breaks on you, the face you'll make!" "Tellement envie de voir ta tête!"—that was what I had to sit down with. I can certainly not be said to have sat down, for I seem to remember myself at this time as rattling constantly between the little house in Chelsea and my own. Our impatience, Gwendolen's and mine, was equal, but I kept hoping her light would be greater. We all spent during this episode, for people of our means, a great deal of money in telegrams and cabs, and I counted on the receipt of news from Rapallo immediately after the junction of the discoverer with the discovered. The interval seemed an age, but late one day I heard a hansom precipitated to my door with the crash engendered by a hint of liberality. I lived with my heart in my mouth and accordingly bounded to the window—a movement which gave me a view of a young lady erect on the footboard of the vehicle and eagerly looking up at my house. At sight of me she flourished a paper with a movement that brought me straight down, the movement with which, in melodramas, handkerchiefs and reprieves are flourished at the foot of the scaffold.

"Just seen Vereker—not a note wrong. Pressed me to bosom—keeps me a month." So much I read on her paper while the cabby dropped a grin from his perch. In my excitement I paid him profusely and in hers she suffered it; then as he drove away we started to walk about and talk. We had talked, heaven knows, enough before, but this was a wondrous lift. We pictured the whole scene at Rapallo, where he would have written, mentioning my name, for permission to call; that is *I* pictured it, having more material than my companion, whom I felt hang on my lips as we stopped on purpose before shop-windows we didn't look into. About one thing we were clear: if he was staying on for fuller communication we should at least have a letter from him that would help us through the dregs of delay. We understood his staying on, and yet each of us saw, I think, that the other hated it. The letter we were clear about arrived; it was for Gwendolen, and I called on her in time to save her the trouble of bringing it to me. She didn't read it out, as was natural enough; but she repeated to me what it chiefly embodied. This consisted of the remarkable statement that he'd tell her after they were married exactly what she wanted to know.

"Only *then*, when I'm his wife—not before," she explained. "It's tantamount to saying—isn't it?—that I must marry him straight off!" She smiled at me while I flushed with disappointment, a vision of fresh delay that made me at first unconscious of my surprise. It seemed more than a hint that on me as well he would impose some tiresome condition. Suddenly, while she reported several more things from his letter, I remembered what he had told me before going away. He had found Mr. Vereker deliriously interesting and his own possession of the secret a real intoxication. The buried treasure was all gold and gems. Now that it was there it seemed to grow and grow before him; it would have been, through all time and taking all tongues, one of the most wonderful flowers of literary art. Nothing, in especial, once you were face to face with it, could show for more consummately *done*. When once it came out it came out, was there with a splendour that made you ashamed; and there hadn't been, save in the bottomless vulgarity of the age, with every one tasteless and tainted, every sense stopped, the smallest reason why it should have been overlooked. It was great, yet so simple, was simple, yet so great, and the final knowledge of it was an experience quite apart. He intimated that the charm of such an experience, the desire to drain it, in its freshness, to the last drop, was what kept him there close to the source. Gwendolen, frankly radiant as she tossed me these fragments, showed the elation of a prospect more assured than my own. That brought me back to the question of her marriage, prompted me to ask if what she meant by what she had just surprised me with was that she was under an engagement.

"Of course I am!" she answered. "Didn't you know it?" She seemed astonished, but I was still more so, for Corvick had told me the exact contrary. I didn't mention this, however; I only reminded her how little I had been on that score in her confidence, or even in Corvick's, and that, moreover I wasn't in ignorance of her mother's interdict. At bottom I was troubled by the disparity of the two accounts; but after a little I felt Corvick's to be the one I least doubted. This simply reduced me to asking myself if the girl had on the spot improvised an engagement—vamped up an old one or dashed off a new—in order to arrive at the satisfaction she desired. She must have had resources of which I was destitute, but she made her case slightly more intelligible by returning presently: "What the state of things has been is that we felt of course bound to do nothing in mamma's lifetime."

"But now you think you'll just dispense with mamma's consent?"

"Ah it mayn't come to that!" I wondered what it might come to, and she went on: "Poor dear, she may swallow the dose. In fact, you know," she added with a laugh, "she really *must*!"—a proposition of which, on behalf of every one concerned, I fully acknowledged the force.

# CHAPTER VIII.

NOTHING more vexatious had ever happened to me than to become aware before Corvick's arrival in England that I shouldn't be there to put him through. I found myself abruptly called to Germany by the alarming illness of my younger brother, who, against my advice, had gone to Munich to study, at the feet indeed of a great master, the art of portraiture in oils. The near relative who made him an allowance had threatened to withdraw it if he should, under specious pretexts, turn for superior truth to Paris—Paris being somehow, for a Cheltenham aunt, the school of evil, the abyss. I deplored this prejudice at the time, and the deep injury of it was now visible—first in the fact that it hadn't saved the poor boy, who was clever, frail and foolish, from congestion of the lungs, and second in the greater break with London to which the event condemned me. I'm afraid that what was uppermost in my mind during several anxious weeks was the sense that if we had only been in Paris I might have run over to see Corvick. This was actually out of the question from every point of view: my brother, whose recovery gave us both plenty to do, was ill for three months, during which I never left him and at the end of which we had to face the absolute prohibition of a return to England. The consideration of climate imposed itself, and he was in no state to meet it alone. I took him to Meran and there spent the summer with him, trying to show him by example how to get back to work and nursing a rage of another sort that I tried *not* to show him.

The whole business proved the first of a series of phenomena so strangely interlaced that, taken together—which was how I had to take them—they form as good an illustration as I can recall of the manner in which, for the good of his soul doubtless, fate sometimes deals with a man's avidity. These incidents certainly had larger bearings than the comparatively meagre consequence we are here concerned with—though I feel that consequence also a thing to speak of with some respect. It's mainly in such a light, I confess, at any rate, that the ugly fruit of my exile is at this hour present to me. Even at first indeed the spirit in which my avidity, as I have called it, made me regard that term owed no element of ease to the fact that before coming back from Rapallo George Corvick addressed me in a way I objected to. His letter had none of the sedative action I must to-day profess myself sure he had wished to give it, and the march of occurrences was not so ordered as to make up for what it lacked. He had begun on the spot, for one of the quarterlies, a great last word on Vereker's writings, and this exhaustive study, the only one that would have counted, have existed, was to turn on the new light, to utter—oh, so quietly!—the unimagined truth. It was in other words to trace the figure in the carpet through every convolution, to reproduce it in every tint. The result, according to my friend, would be the greatest literary portrait ever painted, and what he asked of me was just to be so good as not to trouble him with questions till he should hang up his masterpiece before me. He did me the honour to declare that, putting aside the great sitter himself, all aloft in his indifference, I was individually the connoisseur he was most working for. I was therefore to be a good boy and not try to peep under the curtain before the show was ready: I should enjoy it all the more if I sat very still.

I did my best to sit very still, but I couldn't help giving a jump on seeing in *The Times*, after I had been a week or two in Munich and before, as I knew, Corvick had reached London, the announcement of the sudden death of poor Mrs. Erme. I instantly, by letter, appealed to Gwendolen for particulars, and she wrote me that her mother had yielded to long-threatened failure of the heart. She didn't say, but I took the liberty of reading into her words, that from the point of view of her marriage and also of her eagerness, which was quite a match for mine, this was a solution more prompt than could have been expected and more radical than waiting for the old lady to swallow the dose. I candidly admit indeed that at the time—for I heard from her repeatedly—I read some singular things into Gwendolen's words and some still more extraordinary ones into her silences. Pen in hand, this way, I live the time over, and it brings back the oddest sense of my having been, both for months and in spite of myself, a kind of coerced spectator. All my life had taken refuge in my eyes, which the procession of events appeared to have committed itself to keep astare. There were days when I thought of writing to Hugh Vereker and simply throwing myself on his charity. But I felt more deeply that I hadn't fallen quite so low—besides which, quite properly, he would send me about my business. Mrs. Erme's death brought Corvick straight home, and within the month he was united "very quietly"— as quietly, I seemed to make out, as he meant in his article to bring out his trouvaille—to the young lady he had loved and quitted. I use this last term, I may parenthetically say, because I subsequently grew sure that at the time he went to India, at the time of his great news from Bombay, there had been no positive pledge between them whatever. There had been none at the moment she was affirming to me the very opposite. On the other hand he had certainly become engaged the day he returned. The happy pair went down to Torquay for their honeymoon, and there, in a reckless hour, it occurred to poor Corvick to take his young bride a drive. He had no command of that business: this had been brought home to me of old in a little tour we had once made together in a dogcart. In a dogcart he perched his companion for a rattle over Devonshire hills, on one of the likeliest of which he brought his horse, who, it was true, had bolted, down with such violence that the occupants of the cart were hurled forward and that he fell horribly on his head. He was killed on the spot; Gwendolen escaped unhurt.

I pass rapidly over the question of this unmitigated tragedy, of what the loss of my best friend meant for me, and I complete my little history of my patience and my pain by the frank statement of my having, in a postscript to my very first letter to her after the receipt of the hideous news, asked Mrs. Corvick whether her husband mightn't at least have finished the great article on Vereker. Her answer was as prompt as my question: the article, which had been barely begun, was a mere heartbreaking scrap. She explained that our friend, abroad, had just settled down to it when interrupted by her mother's death, and that then, on his return, he had been kept from work by the engrossments into which that calamity was to plunge them. The opening pages were all that existed; they were striking, they were promising, but they didn't unveil the idol. That great intellectual feat was obviously to have formed his climax. She said nothing more, nothing to enlighten me as to the state of her own knowledge—the knowledge for the acquisition of which I had fancied her prodigiously acting. This was above all what I wanted to know: had *she* seen the idol unveiled? Had there been a private ceremony for a palpitating audience of one? For what else but that ceremony had the nuptials taken place? I didn't like as yet to press her, though when I thought of what had passed between us on the subject in Corvick's absence her reticence surprised me. It was therefore not till much later, from Meran, that I risked another appeal, risked it in some trepidation, for she continued to tell me nothing. "Did you hear in those few days of your blighted bliss," I wrote, "what we desired so to hear?" I said, "we," as a little hint and she showed me she could take a little hint; "I heard everything," she replied, "and I mean to keep it to myself!"

# CHAPTER IX.

IT was impossible not to be moved with the strongest sympathy for her, and on my return to England I showed her every kindness in my power. Her mother's death had made her means sufficient, and she had gone to live in a more convenient quarter. But her loss had been great and her visitation cruel; it never would have occurred to me moreover to suppose she could come to feel the possession of a technical tip, of a piece of literary experience, a counterpoise to her grief. Strange to say, none the less, I couldn't help believing after I had seen her a few times that I caught a glimpse of some such oddity. I hasten to add that there had been other things I couldn't help believing, or at least imagining; and as I never felt I was really clear about these, so, as to the point I here touch on, I give her memory the benefit of the doubt. Stricken and solitary, highly accomplished and now, in her deep mourning, her maturer grace and her uncomplaining sorrow, incontestably handsome, she presented herself as leading a life of singular dignity and beauty. I had at first found a way to persuade myself that I should soon get the better of the reserve formulated, the week after the catastrophe in her reply to an appeal as to which I was not unconscious that it might strike her as mistimed. Certainly that reserve was something of a shock to me—certainly it puzzled me the more I thought of it and even though I tried to explain it (with moments of success) by an imputation of exalted sentiments, of superstitious scruples, of a refinement of loyalty. Certainly it added at the same time hugely to the price of Vereker's secret, precious as this mystery already appeared. I may as well confess abjectly that Mrs. Corvick's unexpected attitude was the final tap on the nail that was to fix fast my luckless idea, convert it into the obsession of which I'm for ever conscious.

But this only helped me the more to be artful, to be adroit, to allow time to elapse before renewing my suit. There were plenty of speculations for the interval, and one of them was deeply absorbing. Corvick had kept his information from his young friend till after the removal of the last barrier to their intimacy—then only had he let the cat out of the bag. Was it

Gwendolen's idea, taking a hint from him, to liberate this animal only on the basis of the renewal of such a relation? Was the figure in the carpet traceable or describable only for husbands and wives—for lovers supremely united? It came back to me in a mystifying manner that in Kensington Square, when I mentioned that Corvick would have told the girl he loved, some word had dropped from Vereker that gave colour to this possibility. There might be little in it, but there was enough to make me wonder if I should have to marry Mrs. Corvick to get what I wanted. Was I prepared to offer her this price for the blessing of her knowledge? Ah that way madness lay!—so I at least said to myself in bewildered hours. I could see meanwhile the torch she refused to pass on flame away in her chamber of memory—pour through her eyes a light that shone in her lonely house. At the end of six months I was fully sure of what this warm presence made up to her for. We had talked again and again of the man who had brought us together—of his talent, his character, his personal charm, his certain career, his dreadful doom, and even of his clear purpose in that great study which was to have been a supreme literary portrait, a kind of critical Vandyke or Velasquez. She had conveyed to me in abundance that she was tongue-tied by her perversity, by her piety, that she would never break the silence it had not been given to the "right person," as she said, to break. The hour however finally arrived. One evening when I had been sitting with her longer than usual I laid my hand firmly on her arm. "Now at last what *is* it?"

She had been expecting me and was ready. She gave a long slow soundless headshake, merciful only in being inarticulate. This mercy didn't prevent its hurling at me the largest finest coldest "Never!" I had yet, in the course of a life that had known denials, had to take full in the face. I took it and was aware that with the hard blow the tears had come into my eyes. So for a while we sat and looked at each other; after which I slowly rose, I was wondering if some day she would accept me; but this was not what I brought out. I said as I smoothed down my hat: "I know what to think then. It's nothing!"

A remote disdainful pity for me gathered in her dim smile; then she spoke in a voice that I hear at this hour: "It's my *life*!" As I stood at the door she added: "You've insulted him!"

"Do you mean Vereker?"

"I mean the Dead!"

I recognised when I reached the street the justice of her charge. Yes, it was her life—I recognised that too; but her life none the less made room with the lapse of time for another interest. A year and a half after Corvick's death she published in a single volume her second novel, "Overmastered," which I pounced on in the hope of finding in it some tell-tale echo or some peeping face. All I found was a much better book than her younger performance, showing I thought the better company she had kept. As a tissue tolerably intricate it was a carpet with a figure of its own; but the figure was not the figure I was looking for. On sending a review of it to *The Middle* I was surprised to learn from the office that a notice was already in type. When the paper came out I had no hesitation in attributing this article, which I thought rather vulgarly overdone, to Drayton Deane, who in the old days had been something of a friend of Corvick's, yet had only within a few weeks made the acquaintance of his widow. I had had an early copy of the book, but Deane had evidently had an earlier. He lacked all the same the light hand with which Corvick had gilded the gingerbread—he laid on the tinsel in splotches.

# CHAPTER X.

Six months later appeared "The Right of Way," the last chance, though we didn't know it, that we were to have to redeem ourselves. Written wholly during Vereker's sojourn abroad, the book had been heralded, in a hundred paragraphs, by the usual ineptitudes. I carried it, as early a copy as any, I this time flattered myself, straightway to Mrs. Corvick. This was the only use I had for it; I left the inevitable tribute of *The Middle* to some more ingenious mind and some less irritated temper. "But I already have it," Gwendolen said. "Drayton Deane was so good as to bring it to me yesterday, and I've just finished it."

"Yesterday? How did he get it so soon?"

"He gets everything so soon! He's to review it in *The Middle*."

"He—Drayton Deane—review Vereker?" I couldn't believe my ears.

"'Why not? One fine ignorance is as good as another."

I winced but I presently said: "You ought to review him yourself!"

"I don't 'review,'" she laughed. "I'm reviewed!"

Just then the door was thrown open. "Ah yes, here's your reviewer!" Drayton Deane was there with his long legs and his tall forehead: he had come to see what she thought of "The Right of Way," and to bring news that was singularly relevant. The evening papers were just out with a telegram on the author of that work, who, in Rome, had been ill for some days with an attack of malarial fever. It had at first not been thought grave, but had taken, in consequence of complications, a turn that might give rise to anxiety. Anxiety had indeed at the latest hour begun to be felt.

I was struck in the presence of these tidings with the fundamental detachment that Mrs. Corvick's overt concern quite failed to hide: it gave me the measure of her consummate independence. That independence rested on her knowledge, the knowledge which nothing now could destroy and which nothing could make different. The figure in the carpet might take on another twist or two, but the sentence had virtually been written. The writer might go down to his grave: she was the person in the world to whom—as if she had been his favoured heir—his continued existence was least of a need. This reminded me how I had observed at a particular moment—after Corvick's death—the drop of her desire to see him face to face. She had got what she wanted without that. I had been sure that if she hadn't got it she wouldn't have been restrained from the endeavour to sound him personally by those superior reflexions, more conceivable on a man's part than on a woman's, which in my case had served an a deterrent. It wasn't however, I hasten to add, that my case, in spite of this invidious comparison, wasn't ambiguous enough. At the thought that Vereker was perhaps at that moment dying there rolled over me a wave of anguish—a poignant sense of how inconsistently I still depended on him. A delicacy that it was my one compensation to suffer to rule me had left the Alps and the Apennines between us, but the sense of the waning occasion suggested that I might in my despair at last have gone to him. Of course I should really have done nothing of the sort. I remained five minutes, while my companions talked of the new book, and when Drayton Deane appealed to me for my opinion of it I made answer, getting up, that I detested Hugh Vereker and simply couldn't read him. I departed with the moral certainty that as the door closed behind me Deane would brand me for awfully superficial. His hostess wouldn't contradict *that* at least.

I continue to trace with a briefer touch our intensely odd successions. Three weeks after this came Vereker's death, and before the year was out the death of his wife. That poor lady I had never seen, but I had had a futile theory that, should she survive him long enough to be decorously accessible, I might approach her with the feeble flicker of my plea. Did she know and if she knew would she speak? It was much to be presumed that for more reasons than one she would have nothing to say; but when she passed out of all reach I felt renannouncement indeed my appointed lot. I was shut up in my obsession for ever—my gaolers had gone off with the key. I find myself quite as vague as a captive in a dungeon about the tinge that further elapsed before Mrs. Corvick became the wife of Drayton Deane. I had foreseen, through my bars, this end of the business, though there was no indecent haste and our friendship had fallen rather off. They were both so "awfully intellectual" that it struck people as a suitable match, but I had measured better than any one the wealth of understanding the bride would contribute to the union. Never, for a marriage in literary circles—so the newspapers described the alliance—had a lady been so bravely dowered. I began with due promptness to look for the fruit of the affair—that fruit, I mean, of which the premonitory symptoms would be peculiarly visible in the husband. Taking for granted the splendour of the other party's nuptial gift, I expected to see him make a show commensurate with his increase of means. I knew what his means had been—his article on "The Right of Way" had distinctly given one the figure. As he was now exactly in the position in which still more exactly I was not I watched from month to month, in the likely periodicals, for the heavy message poor Corvick had been unable to deliver and the responsibility of which would have fallen on his successor. The widow and wife would have broken by the rekindled hearth the silence that only a widow and wife might break, and Deane would be as aflame with the knowledge as Corvick in his own hour, as Gwendolen in hers, had been. Well, he was aflame doubtless, but the fire was apparently not to become a public blaze. I scanned the periodicals in vain: Drayton Deane filled them with exuberant pages, but he withheld the page I most feverishly sought. He wrote on a thousand subjects, but never on the subject of Vereker. His special line was to tell truths that other people either "funked," as he said, or overlooked, but he never told the only truth that seemed to me in these days to signify. I met the couple in those literary circles referred to in the papers: I have sufficiently intimated that it was only in such circles we were all constructed to revolve. Gwendolen was more than ever committed to them by the publication of her third novel, and I myself definitely classed by holding the opinion that this work was inferior to its immediate predecessor. Was it worse because she had been keeping worse company? If her secret was, as she had told me, her life—a fact discernible in her increasing bloom, an air of conscious privilege that, cleverly corrected by pretty charities, gave distinction to her appearance—it had yet not a direct influence on her work. That only made one—everything only made one—yearn the more for it; only rounded it off with a mystery finer and subtler.

# CHAPTER XI.

It was therefore from her husband I could never remove my eyes: I beset him in a manner that might have made him uneasy. I went even so far as to engage him in conversation. Didn't he know, hadn't he come into it as a matter of course?—that question hummed in my brain. Of course he knew; otherwise he wouldn't return my stare so queerly. His wife had told him what I wanted and he was amiably amused at my impotence. He didn't laugh—he wasn't a laugher: his system was to present to my irritation, so that I should crudely expose myself, a conversational blank as vast as his big bare brow. It always happened that I turned away with a settled conviction from these unpeopled expanses, which seemed to complete each other geographically and to symbolise together Drayton Deane's want of voice, want of form. He simply hadn't the art to use what he knew; he literally was incompetent to take up the duty where Corvick had left it. I went still further—it was the only glimpse of happiness I had. I made up my mind that the duty didn't appeal to him. He wasn't interested, he didn't care. Yes, it quite comforted me to believe him too stupid to have joy of the thing I lacked. He was as stupid after as he had been before, and that deepened for me the golden glory in which the mystery was wrapped. I had of course none the less to recollect that his wife might have imposed her conditions and exactions. I had above all to remind myself that with Vereker's death the major incentive dropped. He was still there to be honoured by what might be done—he was no longer there to give it his sanction. Who alas but he had the authority?

Two children were born to the pair, but the second cost the mother her life. After this stroke I seemed to see another ghost of a chance. I jumped at it in thought, but I waited a certain time for manners, and at last my opportunity arrived in a remunerative way. His wife had been dead a year when I met Drayton Deane in the smoking-room of a small club of which we both were members, but where for months—perhaps because I rarely entered it—I hadn't seen him. The room was empty and the occasion propitious. I deliberately offered him, to have done with the matter for ever, that advantage for which I felt he had long been looking.

"As an older acquaintance of your late wife's than even you were," I began, "you must let me say to you something I have on my mind. I shall be glad to make any terms with you that you see fit to name for the information she must have had from George Corvick—the information you know, that had come to him, poor chap, in one of the happiest hours of his life, straight from Hugh Vereker."

He looked at me like a dim phrenological bust. "The information—?"

"Vereker's secret, my dear man—the general intention of his books: the string the pearls were strung on, the buried treasure, the figure in the carpet."

He began to flush—the numbers on his bumps to come out. "Vereker's books had a general intention?"

I stared in my turn. "You don't mean to say you don't know it?" I thought for a moment he was playing with me. "Mrs. Deane knew it; she had it, as I say, straight from Corvick, who had, after infinite search and to Vereker's own delight, found the very mouth of the cave. Where *is* the mouth? He told after their marriage—and told alone—the person who, when the circumstances were reproduced, must have told you. Have I been wrong in taking for granted that she admitted you, as one of the highest privileges of the relation in which you stood to her, to the knowledge of which she was after Corvick's death the sole depositary? All I know is that that knowledge is infinitely precious, and what I want you to understand is that if you'll in your turn admit me to it you'll do me a kindness for which I shall be lastingly grateful."

He had turned at last very red; I dare say he had begun by thinking I had lost my wits. Little by little he followed me; on my own side I stared with a livelier surprise. Then he spoke. "I don't know what you're talking about."

He wasn't acting—it was the absurd truth.

"She *didn't* tell you—?"

"Nothing about Hugh Vereker."

I was stupefied; the room went round. It had been too good even for that! "Upon your honour?"

"Upon my honour. What the devil's the matter with you?" he growled.

"I'm astounded—I'm disappointed. I wanted to get it out of you."

"It isn't in me!" he awkwardly laughed. "And even if it were—"

"If it were you'd let me have it—oh yes, in common humanity. But I believe you. I see—I see!" I went on, conscious, with the full turn of the wheel, of my great delusion, my false view of the poor man's attitude. What I saw, though I couldn't say it, was that his wife hadn't thought him worth enlightening. This struck me as strange for a woman who had thought him worth marrying. At last I explained it by the reflexion that she couldn't possibly have married him for his understanding. She had married him for something else.

He was to some extent enlightened now, but he was even more astonished, more disconcerted: he took a moment to compare my story with his quickened memories. The result of his meditation was his presently saying with a good deal of rather feeble form: "This is the first I hear of what you allude to. I think you must be mistaken as to Mrs. Drayton Deane's having had any unmentioned, and still less any unmentionable, knowledge of Hugh Vereker. She'd certainly have wished it—should it have borne on his literary character—to be used."

"It was used. She used it herself. She told me with her own lips that she 'lived' on it."

I had no sooner spoken than I repented of my words; he grew so pale that I felt as if I had struck him. "Ah, 'lived'—!" he murmured, turning short away from me.

My compunction was real; I laid my hand on his shoulder. "I beg you to forgive me—I've made a mistake. You don't know what I thought you knew. You could, if I had been right, have rendered me a service; and I had my reasons for assuming that you'd be in a position to meet me."

"Your reasons?" he asked. "What were your reasons?"

I looked at him well; I hesitated; I considered. "Come and sit down with me here, and I'll tell you." I drew him to a sofa, I lighted another cigar and, beginning with the anecdote of Vereker's one descent from the clouds, I recited to him the extraordinary chain of accidents that had, in spite of the original gleam, kept me till that hour in the dark. I told him in a word just what I've written out here. He listened with deepening attention, and I became aware, to my surprise, by his ejaculations, by his questions, that he would have been after all not unworthy to be trusted by his wife. So abrupt an experience of her want of trust had now a disturbing effect on him; but I saw the immediate shock throb away little by little and then gather again into waves of wonder and curiosity—waves that promised, I could perfectly judge, to break in the end with the fury of my own highest tides. I may say that to-day as victims of unappeased desire there isn't a pin to choose between us. The poor man's state is almost my consolation; there are really moments when I feel it to be quite my revenge.

# About Author

**Henry James** OM (15 April 1843 – 28 February 1916) was an American-British author regarded as a key transitional figure between literary realism and literary modernism, and is considered by many to be among the greatest novelists in the English language. He was the son of Henry James Sr. and the brother of renowned philosopher and psychologist William James and diarist Alice James.

He is best known for a number of novels dealing with the social and marital interplay between émigré Americans, English people, and continental Europeans. Examples of such novels include The Portrait of a Lady, The Ambassadors, and The Wings of the Dove. His later works were increasingly experimental. In describing the internal states of mind and social dynamics of his characters, James often made use of a style in which ambiguous or contradictory motives and impressions were overlaid or juxtaposed in the discussion of a character's psyche. For their unique ambiguity, as well as for other aspects of their composition, his late works have been compared to impressionist painting.

His novella The Turn of the Screw has garnered a reputation as the most analysed and ambiguous ghost story in the English language and remains his most widely adapted work in other media. He also wrote a number of other highly regarded ghost stories and is considered one of the greatest masters of the field.

James published articles and books of criticism, travel, biography, autobiography, and plays. Born in the United States, James largely relocated to Europe as a young man and eventually settled in England, becoming a British subject in 1915, one year before his death. James was nominated for the Nobel Prize in Literature in 1911, 1912 and 1916.

## Life

### Early years, 1843–1883

James was born at 2 Washington Place in New York City on 15 April 1843. His parents were Mary Walsh and Henry James Sr. His father was intelligent and steadfastly congenial. He was a lecturer and philosopher who had inherited independent means from his father, an Albany banker and investor. Mary came from a wealthy family long settled in New York City. Her sister Katherine lived with her adult family for an extended period of time. Henry Jr. had three brothers, William, who was one year his senior, and younger brothers Wilkinson (Wilkie) and Robertson. His younger sister was Alice. Both of his parents were of Irish and Scottish descent.

The family first lived in Albany, at 70 N. Pearl St., and then moved to Fourteenth Street in New York City when James was still a young boy. His education was calculated by his father to expose him to many influences, primarily scientific and philosophical; it was described by Percy Lubbock, the editor of his selected letters, as "extraordinarily haphazard and promiscuous." James did not share the usual education in Latin and Greek classics. Between 1855 and 1860, the James' household traveled to London, Paris, Geneva, Boulogne-sur-Mer and Newport, Rhode Island, according to the father's current interests and publishing ventures, retreating to the United States when funds were low. Henry studied primarily with tutors and briefly attended schools while the family traveled in Europe. Their longest stays were in France, where Henry began to feel at home and became fluent in French. He was afflicted with a stutter, which seems to have manifested itself only when he spoke English; in French, he did not stutter.

In 1860 the family returned to Newport. There Henry became a friend of the painter John La Farge, who introduced him to French literature, and in particular, to Balzac. James later called Balzac his "greatest master," and said that he had learned more about the craft of fiction from him than from anyone else.

In the autumn of 1861 Henry received an injury, probably to his back, while fighting a fire. This injury, which resurfaced at times throughout his life, made him unfit for military service in the American Civil War.

In 1864 the James family moved to Boston, Massachusetts to be near William, who had enrolled first in the Lawrence Scientific School at Harvard and then in the medical school. In 1862 Henry attended Harvard Law School, but realised that he was not interested in studying law. He pursued his interest in literature and associated with authors and critics William Dean Howells and Charles Eliot Norton in Boston and Cambridge, formed lifelong friendships with Oliver Wendell Holmes Jr., the future Supreme Court Justice, and with James and Annie Fields, his first professional mentors.

His first published work was a review of a stage performance, "Miss Maggie Mitchell in Fanchon the Cricket," published in 1863. About a year later, A Tragedy of Error, his first short story, was published anonymously. James's first payment was for an appreciation of Sir Walter Scott's novels, written for the North American Review. He wrote fiction and non-fiction pieces for The Nation and Atlantic Monthly, where Fields was editor. In 1871 he published his first novel, Watch and Ward, in serial form in the Atlantic Monthly. The novel was later published in book form in 1878.

During a 14-month trip through Europe in 1869–70 he met Ruskin, Dickens, Matthew Arnold, William Morris, and George Eliot. Rome impressed him profoundly. "Here I am then in the Eternal City," he wrote to his brother William. "At last—for the first time—I live!" He attempted to support himself as a freelance writer in Rome, then secured a position as Paris correspondent for the New York Tribune, through the influence of its editor John Hay. When these efforts failed he returned to New York City. During 1874 and 1875 he published Transatlantic Sketches, A Passionate Pilgrim, and Roderick Hudson. During this early period in his career he was influenced by Nathaniel Hawthorne.

In 1869 he settled in London. There he established relationships with Macmillan and other publishers, who paid for serial installments that they would later publish in book form. The audience for these serialized novels was largely made up of middle-class women, and James struggled to fashion serious literary work within the strictures imposed by editors' and publishers' notions of what was suitable for young women to read. He lived in rented rooms but was able to join gentlemen's clubs that had libraries and where he could entertain male friends. He was introduced to English society by Henry Adams and Charles Milnes Gaskell, the latter introducing him to the Travellers' and the Reform Clubs.

In the fall of 1875 he moved to the Latin Quarter of Paris. Aside from two trips to America, he spent the next three decades—the rest of his life—in Europe. In Paris he met Zola, Alphonse Daudet, Maupassant, Turgenev, and others. He stayed in Paris only a year before moving to London.

In England he met the leading figures of politics and culture. He continued to be a prolific writer, producing The American (1877), The Europeans (1878), a revision of Watch and Ward (1878), French Poets and Novelists (1878), Hawthorne (1879), and several shorter works of fiction. In 1878 Daisy Miller established his fame on both sides of the Atlantic. It drew notice perhaps mostly because it depicted a woman whose behavior is outside the social norms of Europe. He also began his first masterpiece, The Portrait of a Lady, which would appear in 1881.

In 1877 he first visited Wenlock Abbey in Shropshire, home of his friend Charles Milnes Gaskell whom he had met through Henry Adams. He was much inspired by the darkly romantic Abbey and the surrounding countryside, which features in his essay Abbeys and Castles. In particular the gloomy monastic fishponds behind the Abbey are said to have inspired the lake in The Turn of the Screw.

While living in London, James continued to follow the careers of the "French realists", Émile Zola in particular. Their stylistic methods influenced his own work in the years to come. Hawthorne's influence on him faded during this period, replaced by George Eliot and Ivan Turgenev. 1879–1882 saw the publication of The Europeans, Washington Square, Confidence, and The Portrait of a Lady. He visited America in 1882–1883, then returned to London.

The period from 1881 to 1883 was marked by several losses. His mother died in 1881, followed by his father a few months later, and then by his brother Wilkie. Emerson, an old family friend, died in 1882. His friend Turgenev died in 1883.

## Middle years, 1884–1897

In 1884 James made another visit to Paris. There he met again with Zola, Daudet, and Goncourt. He had been following the careers of the French "realist" or "naturalist" writers, and was increasingly influenced by them. In 1886, he published The Bostonians and The Princess Casamassima, both influenced by the French writers he'd studied assiduously. Critical reaction and sales were poor. He wrote to Howells that the books had hurt his career rather than helped because they had "reduced the desire, and demand, for my productions to zero". During this time he became friends with Robert Louis Stevenson, John Singer Sargent, Edmund Gosse, George du Maurier, Paul Bourget, and Constance Fenimore Woolson. His third novel from the 1880s was The Tragic Muse. Although he was following the precepts of Zola in his novels of the '80s, their tone and attitude are closer to the fiction of Alphonse Daudet. The lack of critical and financial success for his novels during this period led him to try writing for the theatre. (His dramatic works and his experiences with theatre are discussed below.)

In the last quarter of 1889, he started translating "for pure and copious lucre" Port Tarascon, the third volume of Alphonse Daudet adventures of Tartarin de Tarascon. Serialized in Harper's Monthly Magazine from June 1890, this translation praised as "clever" by The Spectator was published in January 1891 by Sampson Low, Marston, Searle & Rivington.

After the stage failure of Guy Domville in 1895, James was near despair and thoughts of death plagued him. The years spent on dramatic works were not entirely a loss. As he moved into the last phase of his career he found ways to adapt dramatic techniques into the novel form.

In the late 1880s and throughout the 1890s James made several trips through Europe. He spent a long stay in Italy in 1887. In that year the short novel The Aspern Papers and The Reverberator were published.

## Late years, 1898–1916

In 1897–1898 he moved to Rye, Sussex, and wrote The Turn of the Screw. 1899–1900 saw the publication of The Awkward Age and The Sacred

Fount. During 1902–1904 he wrote The Ambassadors, The Wings of the Dove, and The Golden Bowl.

In 1904 he revisited America and lectured on Balzac. In 1906–1910 he published The American Scene and edited the "New York Edition", a 24-volume collection of his works. In 1910 his brother William died; Henry had just joined William from an unsuccessful search for relief in Europe on what then turned out to be his (Henry's) last visit to the United States (from summer 1910 to July 1911), and was near him, according to a letter he wrote, when he died.

In 1913 he wrote his autobiographies, A Small Boy and Others, and Notes of a Son and Brother. After the outbreak of the First World War in 1914 he did war work. In 1915 he became a British subject and was awarded the Order of Merit the following year. He died on 28 February 1916, in Chelsea, London. As he requested, his ashes were buried in Cambridge Cemetery in Massachusetts.

### Biographers

James regularly rejected suggestions that he should marry, and after settling in London proclaimed himself "a bachelor". F. W. Dupee, in several volumes on the James family, originated the theory that he had been in love with his cousin Mary ("Minnie") Temple, but that a neurotic fear of sex kept him from admitting such affections: "James's invalidism ... was itself the symptom of some fear of or scruple against sexual love on his part." Dupee used an episode from James's memoir A Small Boy and Others, recounting a dream of a Napoleonic image in the Louvre, to exemplify James's romanticism about Europe, a Napoleonic fantasy into which he fled.

Dupee had not had access to the James family papers and worked principally from James's published memoir of his older brother, William, and the limited collection of letters edited by Percy Lubbock, heavily weighted toward James's last years. His account therefore moved directly from James's childhood, when he trailed after his older brother, to elderly invalidism. As more material became available to scholars, including the diaries of contemporaries and hundreds of affectionate and sometimes erotic letters written by James to younger men, the picture of neurotic celibacy gave way to a portrait of a closeted homosexual.

Between 1953 and 1972, Leon Edel authored a major five-volume biography of James, which accessed unpublished letters and documents after Edel gained the permission of James's family. Edel's portrayal of James included the suggestion he was celibate. It was a view first propounded by critic Saul Rosenzweig in 1943. In 1996 Sheldon M. Novick published Henry James: The Young Master, followed by Henry James: The Mature Master (2007). The first book "caused something of an uproar in Jamesian circles" as it challenged the previous received notion of celibacy, a once-familiar paradigm in biographies of homosexuals when direct evidence was non-existent. Novick also criticised Edel for following the discounted Freudian interpretation of homosexuality "as a kind of failure." The difference of opinion erupted in a series of exchanges between Edel and Novick which were published by the online magazine Slate, with the latter arguing that even the suggestion of celibacy went against James's own injunction "live!"—not "fantasize!"

A letter James wrote in old age to Hugh Walpole has been cited as an explicit statement of this. Walpole confessed to him of indulging in "high jinks", and James wrote a reply endorsing it: "We must know, as much as possible, in our beautiful art, yours & mine, what we are talking about — & the only way to know it is to have lived & loved & cursed & floundered & enjoyed & suffered — I don't think I regret a single 'excess' of my responsive youth".

The interpretation of James as living a less austere emotional life has been subsequently explored by other scholars. The often intense politics of Jamesian scholarship has also been the subject of studies. Author Colm Tóibín has said that Eve Kosofsky Sedgwick's Epistemology of the Closet made a landmark difference to Jamesian scholarship by arguing that he be read as a homosexual writer whose desire to keep his sexuality a secret shaped his layered style and dramatic artistry. According to Tóibín such a reading "removed James from the realm of dead white males who wrote about posh people. He became our contemporary."

James's letters to expatriate American sculptor Hendrik Christian Andersen have attracted particular attention. James met the 27-year-old Andersen in Rome in 1899, when James was 56, and wrote letters to Andersen that are intensely emotional: "I hold you, dearest boy, in my innermost love, & count on your feeling me—in every throb of your soul". In a letter of 6 May 1904, to his brother William, James referred to himself as "always your hopelessly celibate even though sexagenarian Henry". How accurate that description might have been is the subject of contention among James's biographers, but the letters to Andersen were occasionally quasi-erotic: "I put, my dear boy, my arm around you, & feel the pulsation, thereby, as it were, of our excellent future & your admirable endowment." To his homosexual friend Howard Sturgis, James could write: "I repeat, almost to indiscretion, that I could live with you. Meanwhile I can only try to live without you."

His numerous letters to the many young gay men among his close male friends are more forthcoming. In a letter to Howard Sturgis, following a long visit, James refers jocularly to their "happy little congress of two" and in letters to Hugh Walpole he pursues convoluted jokes and puns about their relationship, referring to himself as an elephant who "paws you oh so benevolently" and winds about Walpole his "well meaning old trunk". His letters to Walter Berry printed by the Black Sun Press have long been celebrated for their lightly veiled eroticism.

He corresponded in almost equally extravagant language with his many female friends, writing, for example, to fellow novelist Lucy Clifford: "Dearest Lucy! What shall I say? when I love you so very, very much, and see you nine times for once that I see Others! Therefore I think that—if you want it made clear to the meanest intelligence—I love you more than I love Others." To his New York friend Mary Cadwalader Jones: "Dearest Mary Cadwalader. I yearn over you, but I yearn in vain; & your long silence really breaks my heart, mystifies, depresses, almost alarms me, to the point even of making me wonder if poor unconscious & doting old Célimare [Jones's pet name for James] has 'done' anything, in some dark somnambulism of the spirit, which has ... given you a bad moment, or a wrong impression, or a 'colourable pretext' ... However these things may be, he loves you as tenderly as ever;

nothing, to the end of time, will ever detach him from you, & he remembers those Eleventh St. matutinal intimes hours, those telephonic matinées, as the most romantic of his life ..." His long friendship with American novelist Constance Fenimore Woolson, in whose house he lived for a number of weeks in Italy in 1887, and his shock and grief over her suicide in 1894, are discussed in detail in Edel's biography and play a central role in a study by Lyndall Gordon. (Edel conjectured that Woolson was in love with James and killed herself in part because of his coldness, but Woolson's biographers have objected to Edel's account.)

## Works

### Style and themes

James is one of the major figures of trans-Atlantic literature. His works frequently juxtapose characters from the Old World (Europe), embodying a feudal civilisation that is beautiful, often corrupt, and alluring, and from the New World (United States), where people are often brash, open, and assertive and embody the virtues—freedom and a more highly evolved moral character—of the new American society. James explores this clash of personalities and cultures, in stories of personal relationships in which power is exercised well or badly. His protagonists were often young American women facing oppression or abuse, and as his secretary Theodora Bosanquet remarked in her monograph Henry James at Work:

> When he walked out of the refuge of his study and into the world and looked around him, he saw a place of torment, where creatures of prey perpetually thrust their claws into the quivering flesh of doomed, defenseless children of light ... His novels are a repeated exposure of this wickedness, a reiterated and passionate plea for the fullest freedom of development, unimperiled by reckless and barbarous stupidity.

Critics have jokingly described three phases in the development of James's prose: "James I, James II, and The Old Pretender." He wrote short stories and plays. Finally, in his third and last period he returned to the long, serialised novel. Beginning in the second period, but most noticeably in the third, he increasingly abandoned direct statement in favour of frequent double negatives, and complex descriptive imagery. Single paragraphs began to run for page after page, in which an initial noun would be succeeded by pronouns surrounded by clouds of adjectives and prepositional clauses, far from their original referents, and verbs would be deferred and then preceded by a series of adverbs. The overall effect could be a vivid evocation of a scene as perceived by a sensitive observer. It has been debated whether this change of style was engendered by James's shifting from writing to dictating to a typist, a change made during the composition of What Maisie Knew.

In its intense focus on the consciousness of his major characters, James's later work foreshadows extensive developments in 20th century fiction. Indeed, he might have influenced stream-of-consciousness writers such as Virginia Woolf, who not only read some of his novels but also wrote essays about them. Both contemporary and modern readers have found the late style difficult and unnecessary; his friend Edith Wharton, who admired him greatly, said that there were passages in his work that were all but incomprehensible. James was harshly portrayed by H. G. Wells as a hippopotamus laboriously attempting to pick up a pea that had got into a corner of its cage. The "late James" style was ably parodied by Max Beerbohm in "The Mote in the Middle Distance".

More important for his work overall may have been his position as an expatriate, and in other ways an outsider, living in Europe. While he came from middle-class and provincial beginnings (seen from the perspective of European polite society) he worked very hard to gain access to all levels of society, and the settings of his fiction range from working class to aristocratic, and often describe the efforts of middle-class Americans to make their way in European capitals. He confessed he got some of his best story ideas from gossip at the dinner table or at country house weekends. He worked for a living, however, and lacked the experiences of select schools, university, and army service, the common bonds of masculine society. He was furthermore a man whose tastes and interests were, according to the prevailing standards of Victorian era Anglo-American culture, rather feminine, and who was shadowed by the cloud of prejudice that then and later accompanied suspicions of his homosexuality. Edmund Wilson famously compared James's objectivity to Shakespeare's:

One would be in a position to appreciate James better if one compared him with the dramatists of the seventeenth century—Racine and Molière, whom he resembles in form as well as in point of view, and even Shakespeare, when allowances are made for the most extreme differences in subject and form. These poets are not, like Dickens and Hardy, writers of melodrama—either humorous or pessimistic, nor secretaries of society like Balzac, nor prophets like Tolstoy: they are occupied simply with the presentation of conflicts of moral character, which they do not concern themselves about softening or averting. They do not indict society for these situations: they regard them as universal and inevitable. They do not even blame God for allowing them: they accept them as the conditions of life.

It is also possible to see many of James's stories as psychological thought-experiments. In his preface to the New York edition of The American he describes the development of the story in his mind as exactly such: the "situation" of an American, "some robust but insidiously beguiled and betrayed, some cruelly wronged, compatriot..." with the focus of the story being on the response of this wronged man. The Portrait of a Lady may be an experiment to see what happens when an idealistic young woman suddenly becomes very rich. In many of his tales, characters seem to exemplify alternative futures and possibilities, as most markedly in "The Jolly Corner", in which the protagonist and a ghost-doppelganger live alternative American and European lives; and in others, like The Ambassadors, an older James seems fondly to regard his own younger self facing a crucial moment.

## Major novels

The first period of James's fiction, usually considered to have culminated in The Portrait of a Lady, concentrated on the contrast between Europe and America. The style of these novels is generally straightforward and, though personally characteristic, well within the norms of 19th-century fiction. Roderick Hudson (1875) is a Künstlerroman that traces the development of the title character, an extremely talented sculptor. Although the book shows some signs of immaturity—this was James's first serious attempt at a full-length novel—it has attracted favourable comment due to the vivid realisation of the three major characters: Roderick Hudson, superbly gifted but unstable and unreliable; Rowland Mallet, Roderick's limited but much more mature friend and patron; and Christina Light, one of James's most enchanting and maddening femmes fatales. The pair of Hudson and Mallet has been seen as representing the two sides of James's own nature: the wildly imaginative artist and the brooding conscientious mentor.

In The Portrait of a Lady (1881) James concluded the first phase of his career with a novel that remains his most popular piece of long fiction. The story is of a spirited young American woman, Isabel Archer, who "affronts her destiny" and finds it overwhelming. She inherits a large amount of money and subsequently becomes the victim of Machiavellian scheming by two American expatriates. The narrative is set mainly in Europe, especially in England and Italy. Generally regarded as the masterpiece of his early phase, The Portrait of a Lady is described as a psychological novel, exploring the minds of his characters, and almost a work of social science, exploring the differences between Europeans and Americans, the old and the new worlds.

The second period of James's career, which extends from the publication of The Portrait of a Lady through the end of the nineteenth century, features less popular novels including The Princess Casamassima, published serially in The Atlantic Monthly in 1885–1886, and The Bostonians, published serially in The Century Magazine during the same period. This period also featured James's celebrated Gothic novella, The Turn of the Screw.

The third period of James's career reached its most significant achievement in three novels published just around the start of the 20th century: The Wings of the Dove (1902), The Ambassadors (1903), and The Golden Bowl (1904). Critic F. O. Matthiessen called this "trilogy" James's major phase, and these novels have certainly received intense critical study. It was the second-written of the books, The Wings of the Dove (1902) that was the first published because it attracted no serialization. This novel tells the story of Milly Theale, an American heiress stricken with a serious disease, and her impact on the people around her. Some of these people befriend Milly with honourable motives, while others are more self-interested. James stated in his autobiographical books that Milly was based on Minny Temple, his beloved cousin who died at an early age of tuberculosis. He said that he attempted in the novel to wrap her memory in the "beauty and dignity of art".

**Shorter narratives**

James was particularly interested in what he called the "beautiful and blest nouvelle", or the longer form of short narrative. Still, he produced a number of very short stories in which he achieved notable compression of sometimes complex subjects. The following narratives are representative of James's achievement in the shorter forms of fiction.

- "A Tragedy of Error" (1864), short story

- "The Story of a Year" (1865), short story

- A Passionate Pilgrim (1871), novella

- Madame de Mauves (1874), novella

- Daisy Miller (1878), novella

- The Aspern Papers (1888), novella

- The Lesson of the Master (1888), novella

- The Pupil (1891), short story

- "The Figure in the Carpet" (1896), short story

- The Beast in the Jungle (1903), novella

- An International Episode (1878)

- Picture and Text

- Four Meetings (1885)

- A London Life, and Other Tales (1889)

- The Spoils of Poynton (1896)

- Embarrassments (1896)

- The Two Magics: The Turn of the Screw, Covering End (1898)

- A Little Tour of France (1900)

- The Sacred Fount (1901)

- Views and Reviews (1908)

- The Wings of the Dove, Volume I (1902)

- The Wings of the Dove, Volume II (1909)

- The Finer Grain (1910)

- The Outcry (1911)

- Lady Barbarina: The Siege of London, An International Episode and Other Tales (1922)

- The Birthplace (1922)

**Plays**

At several points in his career James wrote plays, beginning with one-act plays written for periodicals in 1869 and 1871 and a dramatisation of his popular novella Daisy Miller in 1882. From 1890 to 1892, having received a bequest that freed him from magazine publication, he made a strenuous effort to succeed on the London stage, writing a half-dozen plays of which only one, a dramatisation of his novel The American, was produced. This play was performed for several years by a touring repertory company and had a respectable run in London, but did not earn very much money for James. His other plays written at this time were not produced.

In 1893, however, he responded to a request from actor-manager George Alexander for a serious play for the opening of his renovated St. James's Theatre, and wrote a long drama, Guy Domville, which Alexander produced. There was a noisy uproar on the opening night, 5 January 1895, with hissing from the gallery when James took his bow after the final curtain, and the author was upset. The play received moderately good reviews and had a modest run of four weeks before being taken off to make way for Oscar Wilde's The Importance of Being Earnest, which Alexander thought would have better prospects for the coming season.

After the stresses and disappointment of these efforts James insisted that he would write no more for the theatre, but within weeks had agreed to write a curtain-raiser for Ellen Terry. This became the one-act "Summersoft", which he later rewrote into a short story, "Covering End", and then expanded into a full-length play, The High Bid, which had a brief run in London in 1907, when James made another concerted effort to write for the stage. He wrote three new plays, two of which were in production when the death of Edward VII on 6 May 1910 plunged London into mourning and theatres closed. Discouraged by failing health and the stresses of theatrical work, James did not renew his efforts in the theatre, but recycled his plays as successful novels. The Outcry was a best-seller in the United States when it was published in 1911. During the years 1890–1893 when he was most engaged with the theatre, James wrote a good deal of theatrical criticism and assisted Elizabeth Robins and others in translating and producing Henrik Ibsen for the first time in London.

Leon Edel argued in his psychoanalytic biography that James was traumatised by the opening night uproar that greeted Guy Domville, and that it plunged him into a prolonged depression. The successful later novels, in Edel's view, were the result of a kind of self-analysis, expressed in fiction, which partly freed him from his fears. Other biographers and scholars have not accepted this account, however; the more common view being that of F.O. Matthiessen, who wrote: "Instead of being crushed by the collapse of his hopes [for the theatre]... he felt a resurgence of new energy."

### Non-fiction

Beyond his fiction, James was one of the more important literary critics in the history of the novel. In his classic essay The Art of Fiction (1884), he argued against rigid prescriptions on the novelist's choice of subject and method of treatment. He maintained that the widest possible freedom in content and approach would help ensure narrative fiction's continued vitality.

James wrote many valuable critical articles on other novelists; typical is his book-length study of Nathaniel Hawthorne, which has been the subject of critical debate. Richard Brodhead has suggested that the study was emblematic of James's struggle with Hawthorne's influence, and constituted an effort to place the elder writer "at a disadvantage." Gordon Fraser, meanwhile, has suggested that the study was part of a more commercial effort by James to introduce himself to British readers as Hawthorne's natural successor.

When James assembled the New York Edition of his fiction in his final years, he wrote a series of prefaces that subjected his own work to searching, occasionally harsh criticism.

At 22 James wrote The Noble School of Fiction for The Nation's first issue in 1865. He would write, in all, over 200 essays and book, art, and theatre reviews for the magazine.

For most of his life James harboured ambitions for success as a playwright. He converted his novel The American into a play that enjoyed modest returns in the early 1890s. In all he wrote about a dozen plays, most of which went unproduced. His costume drama Guy Domville failed disastrously on its opening night in 1895. James then largely abandoned his efforts to conquer the stage and returned to his fiction. In his Notebooks he maintained that his theatrical experiment benefited his novels and tales by helping him dramatise his characters' thoughts and emotions. James produced a small but valuable amount of theatrical criticism, including perceptive appreciations of Henrik Ibsen.

With his wide-ranging artistic interests, James occasionally wrote on the visual arts. Perhaps his most valuable contribution was his favourable assessment of fellow expatriate John Singer Sargent, a painter whose critical status has improved markedly in recent decades. James also wrote sometimes charming, sometimes brooding articles about various places he visited and lived in. His most famous books of travel writing include Italian Hours (an example of the charming approach) and The American Scene (most definitely on the brooding side).

James was one of the great letter-writers of any era. More than ten thousand of his personal letters are extant, and over three thousand have been published in a large number of collections. A complete edition of James's letters began publication in 2006, edited by Pierre Walker and Greg Zacharias. As of 2014, eight volumes have been published, covering the period from 1855 to 1880. James's correspondents included celebrated contemporaries like Robert Louis Stevenson, Edith Wharton and Joseph Conrad, along with many others in his wide circle of friends and acquaintances. The letters range from the "mere twaddle of graciousness" to serious discussions of artistic, social and personal issues.

Very late in life James began a series of autobiographical works: A Small Boy and Others, Notes of a Son and Brother, and the unfinished The Middle Years. These books portray the development of a classic observer who was passionately interested in artistic creation but was somewhat reticent about participating fully in the life around him.

## Reception

### Criticism, biographies and fictional treatments

James's work has remained steadily popular with the limited audience of educated readers to whom he spoke during his lifetime, and has remained firmly in the canon, but, after his death, some American critics, such as Van Wyck Brooks, expressed hostility towards James for his long expatriation and eventual naturalisation as a British subject. Other critics such as E. M. Forster complained about what they saw as James's squeamishness in the treatment of sex and other possibly controversial material, or dismissed his late style as difficult and obscure, relying heavily on extremely long sentences and excessively latinate language. Similarly Oscar Wilde criticised him for writing "fiction as if it were a painful duty". Vernon Parrington, composing a canon of American literature, condemned James for having cut himself off from America. Jorge Luis Borges wrote about him, "Despite the scruples and delicate complexities of James, his work suffers from a major defect: the absence of life." And Virginia Woolf, writing to Lytton Strachey, asked, "Please tell me what you find in Henry James. ... we have his works here, and

I read, and I can't find anything but faintly tinged rose water, urbane and sleek, but vulgar and pale as Walter Lamb. Is there really any sense in it?" The novelist W. Somerset Maugham wrote, "He did not know the English as an Englishman instinctively knows them and so his English characters never to my mind quite ring true," and argued "The great novelists, even in seclusion, have lived life passionately. Henry James was content to observe it from a window." Maugham nevertheless wrote, "The fact remains that those last novels of his, notwithstanding their unreality, make all other novels, except the very best, unreadable." Colm Tóibín observed that James "never really wrote about the English very well. His English characters don't work for me."

Despite these criticisms, James is now valued for his psychological and moral realism, his masterful creation of character, his low-key but playful humour, and his assured command of the language. In his 1983 book, The Novels of Henry James, Edward Wagenknecht offers an assessment that echoes Theodora Bosanquet's:

> "To be completely great," Henry James wrote in an early review, "a work of art must lift up the heart," and his own novels do this to an outstanding degree ... More than sixty years after his death, the great novelist who sometimes professed to have no opinions stands foursquare in the great Christian humanistic and democratic tradition. The men and women who, at the height of World War II, raided the secondhand shops for his out-of-print books knew what they were about. For no writer ever raised a braver banner to which all who love freedom might adhere.

William Dean Howells saw James as a representative of a new realist school of literary art which broke with the English romantic tradition epitomised by the works of Charles Dickens and William Makepeace Thackeray. Howells wrote that realism found "its chief exemplar in Mr. James... A novelist he is not, after the old fashion, or after any fashion but his own." F.R. Leavis championed Henry James as a novelist of "established pre-eminence" in The Great Tradition (1948), asserting that The Portrait of a Lady and The Bostonians were "the two most brilliant novels in the language." James is now prized as a master of point of view who moved literary fiction forward by insisting in showing, not telling, his stories to the reader. (Source: Wikipedia)

# NOTABLE WORKS

## NOVELS

Watch and Ward (1871)

Roderick Hudson (1875)

The American (1877)

The Europeans (1878)

Confidence (1879)

Washington Square (1880)

The Portrait of a Lady (1881)

The Bostonians (1886)

The Princess Casamassima (1886)

The Reverberator (1888)

The Tragic Muse (1890)

The Other House (1896)

The Spoils of Poynton (1897)

What Maisie Knew (1897)

The Awkward Age (1899)

The Sacred Fount (1901)

The Wings of the Dove (1902)

The Ambassadors (1903)

The Golden Bowl (1904)

The Whole Family (collaborative novel with eleven other authors, 1908)

The Outcry (1911)

The Ivory Tower (unfinished, published posthumously 1917)

The Sense of the Past (unfinished, published posthumously 1917)

## SHORT STORIES AND NOVELLAS

A Tragedy of Error (1864)

The Story of a Year (1865)

A Landscape Painter (1866)

A Day of Days (1866)

My Friend Bingham (1867)

Poor Richard (1867)

The Story of a Masterpiece (1868)

A Most Extraordinary Case (1868)

A Problem (1868)

De Grey: A Romance (1868)

Osborne's Revenge (1868)

The Romance of Certain Old Clothes (1868)

A Light Man (1869)

Gabrielle de Bergerac (1869)

Travelling Companions (1870)

A Passionate Pilgrim (1871)

At Isella (1871)

Master Eustace (1871)

Guest's Confession (1872)

The Madonna of the Future (1873)

The Sweetheart of M. Briseux (1873)

The Last of the Valerii (1874)

Madame de Mauves (1874)

Adina (1874)

Professor Fargo (1874)

Eugene Pickering (1874)

Benvolio (1875)

Crawford's Consistency (1876)

The Ghostly Rental (1876)

Four Meetings (1877)

Rose-Agathe (1878, as Théodolinde)

Daisy Miller (1878)

Longstaff's Marriage (1878)

An International Episode (1878)

The Pension Beaurepas (1879)

A Diary of a Man of Fifty (1879)

A Bundle of Letters (1879)

The Point of View (1882)

The Siege of London (1883)

Impressions of a Cousin (1883)

Lady Barberina (1884)

Pandora (1884)

The Author of Beltraffio (1884)

Georgina's Reasons (1884)

A New England Winter (1884)

The Path of Duty (1884)

Mrs. Temperly (1887)

Louisa Pallant (1888)

The Aspern Papers (1888)

The Liar (1888)

The Modern Warning (1888, originally published as The Two Countries)

A London Life (1888)

The Patagonia (1888)

The Lesson of the Master (1888)

The Solution (1888)

The Pupil (1891)

Brooksmith (1891)

The Marriages (1891)

The Chaperon (1891)

Sir Edmund Orme (1891)

Nona Vincent (1892)

The Real Thing (1892)

The Private Life (1892)

Lord Beaupré (1892)

The Visits (1892)

Sir Dominick Ferrand (1892)

Greville Fane (1892)

Collaboration (1892)

Owen Wingrave (1892)

The Wheel of Time (1892)

The Middle Years (1893)

The Death of the Lion (1894)

The Coxon Fund (1894)

The Next Time (1895)

Glasses (1896)

The Altar of the Dead (1895)

The Figure in the Carpet (1896)

The Way It Came (1896, also published as The Friends of the Friends)

The Turn of the Screw (1898)

Covering End (1898)

In the Cage (1898)

John Delavoy (1898)

The Given Case (1898)

Europe (1899)

The Great Condition (1899)

The Real Right Thing (1899)

Paste (1899)

The Great Good Place (1900)

Maud-Evelyn (1900)

Miss Gunton of Poughkeepsie (1900)

The Tree of Knowledge (1900)

The Abasement of the Northmores (1900)

The Third Person (1900)

The Special Type (1900)

The Tone of Time (1900)

Broken Wings (1900)

The Two Faces (1900)

Mrs. Medwin (1901)

The Beldonald Holbein (1901)

The Story in It (1902)

Flickerbridge (1902)

The Birthplace (1903)

The Beast in the Jungle (1903)

The Papers (1903)

Fordham Castle (1904)

Julia Bride (1908)

The Jolly Corner (1908)

The Velvet Glove (1909)

Mora Montravers (1909)

Crapy Cornelia (1909)

The Bench of Desolation (1909)

A Round of Visits (1910)

## OTHER

Transatlantic Sketches (1875)

French Poets and Novelists (1878)

Hawthorne (1879)

Portraits of Places (1883)

A Little Tour in France (1884)

Partial Portraits (1888)

Essays in London and Elsewhere (1893)

Picture and Text (1893)

Terminations (1893)

Theatricals (1894)

Theatricals: Second Series (1895)

Guy Domville (1895)

The Soft Side (1900)

William Wetmore Story and His Friends (1903)

The Better Sort (1903)

English Hours (1905)

The Question of our Speech; The Lesson of Balzac. Two Lectures (1905)

The American Scene (1907)

Views and Reviews (1908)

Italian Hours (1909)

A Small Boy and Others (1913)

Notes on Novelists (1914)

Notes of a Son and Brother (1914)

Within the Rim (1918)

Travelling Companions (1919)

Notebooks (various, published posthumously)

The Middle Years (unfinished, published posthumously 1917)

A Most Unholy Trade (1925, published posthumously)

The Art of the Novel : Critical Prefaces (1934)